The fireplace was glowing red, as though a real fire was burning there.

"Glad we had this chat. Shame about the job but what the hell. One door closes, right? Be seeing you." He stepped into the fireplace. It vanished, and Mr Dawson's office wall reasserted itself. He stared at it for about twenty seconds, then shook himself like a wet dog and hit the toggle on his desk. "Next," he said.

The next interviewee manifested Himself as an earthquake, a mighty roaring wind, a firestorm and a small squeaky whisper, but Mr Dawson found it hard to concentrate.

His mind was on other things.

As Tom Holt

Expecting Someone Taller

Who's Afraid of Beowulf?

Flying Dutch

Ye Gods!

Overtime

Here Comes the Sun

Grailblazers

Faust Among Equals

Odds and Gods

Djinn Rummy

My Hero

Paint Your Dragon

Open Sesame

Wish You Were Here

Only Human

Snow White and the Seven Samurai

Valhalla

Nothing But Blue Skies

Falling Sideways

Little People

The Portable Door

In Your Dreams

Earth, Air, Fire and Custard

You Don't Have to Be Evil to Work Here, But It Helps

Someone Like Me

Barking

The Better Mousetrap

May Contain Traces of Magic

Blonde Bombshell

Life, Liberty, and the Pursuit of Sausages

Doughnut

When It's A Jar

The Outsorcerer's Apprentice

The Good, the Bad and the Smug

The Management Style of the Supreme Beings

An Orc on the Wild Side

Dead Funny: Omnibus 1

Mightier Than the Sword: Omnibus 2

The Divine Comedies: Omnibus 3

For Two Nights Only: Omnibus 4

Tall Stories: Omnibus 5

Saints and Sinners: Omnibus 6

Fishy Wishes: Omnibus 7

The Walled Orchard

Alexander at the World's End

Olympiad

A Song for Nero

Meadowland

I, Margaret

Lucia in Wartime

Lucia Triumphant

As K. J. Parker

THE FENCER TRILOGY

Colours in the Steel

The Belly of the Bow

The Proof House

THE SCAVENGER TRILOGY

Shadow

Pattern

Memory

THE ENGINEER TRILOGY

Devices and Desires

Evil for Evil

The Escapement

The Company

The Folding Knife

The Hammer

Sharps

The Two of Swords: Volume One

The Two of Swords: Volume Two

The Two of Swords: Volume Three

Sixteen Ways to Defend a Walled City

How to Rule an Empire and Get Away with It

A Practical Guide to Conquering the World

THE CORAX TRILOGY

Saevus Corax Deals With the Dead

Saevus Corax Captures the Castle

Saevus Corax Gets Away With Murder

THE EIGHT REINDEER OF THE APOCALYPSE

Tom Holt

orbit

orbitbooks.net

Orbit
Hachette Book Group
1290 Avenue of the Americas
New York, NY 10104
orbitbooks.net

First Edition: October 2023
Simultaneously published in Great Britain by Orbit

Orbit is an imprint of Hachette Book Group.
The Orbit name and logo are trademarks of Little, Brown Book Group Limited.

The publisher is not responsible for websites (or their content) that are not owned by the publisher.

The Hachette Speakers Bureau provides a wide range of authors for speaking events. To find out more, go to hachettespeakersbureau.com or email HachetteSpeakers@hbgusa.com.

Orbit books may be purchased in bulk for business, educational, or promotional use. For information, please contact your local bookseller or the Hachette Book Group Special Markets Department at special.markets@hbgusa.com.

Library of Congress Control Number: 2023942350

ISBNs: 9780316566964 (trade paperback), 9780316566971 (ebook)

Printed in the United States of America

LSC-C

Printing 1, 2023

For George Smith
From his fellow magicians at JWW

DASHER

A dark and stormy night, a deserted country road, a solitary female motorist driving an elderly, unreliable Toyota. What could possibly go wrong?

Total failure of the car's electrical systems, for one thing. The engine died, all the lights went out, the radio lapsed into silence, the car coasted to a halt and just sat there. Bother, thought Alice, or words to that effect. She reached in her pocket for her phone. Nothing, dead as a stone. She could only tell that it was there because she could feel it in her hand.

The scenario, she couldn't help thinking, was not entirely unfamiliar; except, of course, that stuff like that didn't actually happen, and there's absolutely no such thing as—

She cried out and closed her eyes, a fraction of a second too late. The brilliant white light all around her was painful, unendurable. "Oh come on," she screeched at it. She could feel its warmth on her skin.

The car was floating, as if on water. She risked opening one eye, just a bit, but all she could see was dazzle. A scooped-out feeling in her tummy suggested that the car was rising, none too steadily, as though a magnet had clamped to the roof and a winch was reeling her in. Terror flooded her, as if she'd left the window open in a car wash, together with the soft, scornful whisper of a tiny voice in the back of her head; this can't be happening; this is silly.

A gentle shudder coming up through the floor via the shock absorbers. Not moving any more. A firm but not deafening metallic clunk. I'm dreaming all this, she told herself. Gentle forward motion, causing the seat belt to press lightly on her collarbone, contradicted her. Not a dream.

A tapping noise; close, insistent. Something banging against the driver's side window. She ignored it. It grew louder. It was similar to the sound of a knuckle, but that bit clearer and sharper. It wasn't going to go away. She opened her right eye, looked and screamed.

The reason, she later realised, why the knocking didn't sound quite right was that human knuckles are covered in skin, whereas the tapper at her window had scales: small ones, about thumbnail size, a sort of iridescent greeny-gold. It wasn't the scales she had a problem with, or the head being a third bigger than the body. It was the eyes: clusters and clusters and clusters of them, on long stalks.

She had no cogent reason to believe that if she shrieked loud enough, the monster would back off, she'd be put back where she'd been taken from and none of this would ever have happened. It was, she'd have cheerfully conceded, a long shot, at best. But she couldn't think of anything else to do, so she gave it a go.

It didn't work. The monster kept on tapping.

Somewhere inside her head, a voice said: anyone or anything capable of this level of technology isn't going to be defeated by a car door. She stopped screaming and pressed the window wind-down button. It didn't work, of course. Then it did.

The monster lowered its head, though it took care not to let any part of its anatomy actually enter the car. It was, she realised, respecting her personal space. Earth?

The voice was inside her head, but she knew beyond a shadow of a doubt that it hadn't come from her. Telepathy, it said. This is Earth, right?

She discovered that you can't lie to a telepathic species. Yes, said her mind, a moment before her lips could shape the word No. Oh well.

Parcel for you.

Excuse me?

Parcel for you. Delivery.

Understanding gradually seeped through her, like melting ice dripping off a roof. Oh, she thought, right. Do you need me to sign for it?

A sea-blue laser beam hit her between the eyes. No need, we scan. Have a nice 9.16030534351145-times-the-half-life-of-Silicon-31.

You what?

Something scrabbled in her mind for the right word. Day. Have a nice day.

The monster's hand – nine-fingered and absolutely not something she wanted to think about, though she had a nasty feeling she would, every day for the rest of her life – came through the window, holding something about the size of a small cushion, wrapped in a shiny grey polymer. Somehow she forced herself to take it. The hand let go and withdrew. Her window wound up, all by itself.

The monster took a step back, and she couldn't see it any more, because of the dazzle.

The car was moving again, sinking this time. She heard the same soft clang she'd heard before, and felt a faint jar as the car stopped. Two seconds later, the terrible light went out. Five seconds after that, her car engine purred smoothly into life and the headlights and radio came on. You are my sunshine, it sang at her. She switched it off.

In her lap was the parcel. She turned on the interior light and stared at it. Just a parcel; and on it was a label. The label had signs on it, squiggles. She'd never seen anything remotely like them in her life, not even late at night after eating Limburger cheese. She discovered she could read them, quite easily. Telepathic reading, for crying out loud.

Q'xxw^etrqegr-3885/8a8!83/Z'ggwerq!tgr, Esq.

Unit 17, Sfhyoynxxxxx!xxyx Plaza,

ZZZxZ,

Alpha Centauri

– and underneath, a series of boxes, one of which was ticked:

Not at home; left with neighbour.

"I see," said Mr Sunshine, pursing his lips. "Did you bring it with you?"

Alice nodded. "I haven't opened it."

"Of course not," said Mr Sunshine. "It wasn't addressed to you."

"I hadn't thought about it in quite those terms," Alice said. "But, no, you're right, it wasn't. Look—"

Something nudged her kneecap. She was about to open her mouth and let fly when she realised it was one of the drawers of Mr Sunshine's desk. It was trying to open. Mr Sunshine saw the look on her face and smiled. "That's just

Harmondsworth," he said. "Stop it, Harmondsworth." The drawer stopped nudging. "It means he likes you," Mr Sunshine said. "You were saying."

She looked at him. She saw a big man, somewhere around seventy, with a bald head rising up through a fringe of snow-white hair like a volcano surrounded by jungle. The sleeves of his shirt – white with a pale red and green check, the sort of thing you still see occasionally being worn by old-fashioned chartered surveyors in market towns – were rolled up, revealing powerful forearms with a few faint scars and liver splodges. His thick spectacles magnified pale blue eyes, topped by dense hedges of white eyebrow. "Sorry," she said, without really knowing why.

"That's perfectly all right. You were going to ask me something."

Far below, traffic swirled, but she couldn't hear it. "What am I supposed to do with it?" she asked.

"The parcel."

"Yes."

Mr Sunshine leaned back in his chair and rubbed his upper lip with the ball of his thumb. "You know," he said, "I'm not sure I'm quite the right person to help you with this. It sounds more like a science thing."

"It's weird shit," Alice said. "My friend told me, weird shit is what you do."

"Not that kind of weird shit," Mr Sunshine said gently. He picked a business card off his desktop and handed it to her. "Read that," he said.

DAWSON, AHRIMAN & DAWSON
Commercial and Industrial Sorcerors,
Thaumaturgical & Metaphysical Engineers
Edwin Sunshine – Consultant

"Some of our practice does overlap with science," he went on, "a bit, the trailing edges of the Venn diagrams barely touching. But flying saucers and space aliens—" He shrugged, very slightly. "You might be better off talking to NASA," he said. "Or the Air Force."

She felt as though the roof had just caved in on her. "You don't believe me," she said. "You think I'm—"

"Entirely truthful and as sane as I am," Mr Sunshine said. "In fact, I don't just think that, I know."

Something about the way he said it made her shudder. "Thank you," she said, in a tiny voice.

"But that doesn't alter the fact that this isn't really my field of expertise. Basically, anything where E equals mc^2 isn't our bag. We're more sort of—"

A tiny starburst of golden flowers appeared from nowhere in front of her eyes. They hung in the air twinkling, then vanished, leaving behind a faint scent of lavender mixed with burnt gunpowder.

"Ah," she said. "Right. But I don't know any scientists, and if I did they'd laugh like a drain or have me locked up, and my friend Carol said—"

The name seemed to carry weight with Mr Sunshine. "I suppose I could have a word with one of my partn—" He stopped short and flushed. "One of the partners," he said. "She's had a certain amount of experience in spatio-temporal dynamics. If she can't help, she probably knows someone who can." He frowned, as though listening to someone raising an objection. "It can't hurt," he said. "Of course, there's the question of money. I'm afraid we're rather expensive."

"Money?"

"Well, yes."

"I've got money," Alice remembered. "What sort of figure are we talking about?"

Mr Sunshine took back the card, turned it over and wrote something on the back with a pencil. He showed it to her. It was as though there was a part for a zero in a Harry Potter movie, and all the noughts in the world were queuing up to audition. "Oh," she said.

Mr Sunshine looked at her. "Quite," he said. "Of course, if you'd gone to JWW or Zauberwerke or one of the big City firms, you'd be looking at twice that, and they don't do free initial interviews like we do. Even so—" He opened a drawer, reached in and took something out. "Not exactly cheap. Still, anything worth having very rarely is."

The thing he'd taken from the drawer was a tatty old purse. Alice looked at it. Her grandmother had had one just like it, many years ago. "How long did you say you'd known Carol?"

"We were in the same class at junior school."

"Ah." Mr Sunshine nodded. Then he made a show of looking for something – shuffling papers on the desk, moving his chair a few inches, glancing round at the floor. "Stupid of me," he said. "I seem to have lost a bottomless purse. I had it a moment ago."

"A—?"

Mr Sunshine rolled his eyes. She picked up the purse and opened it. Out of it tumbled a heap of cut diamonds, more or less enough to fill a soup bowl. She put down the purse and scooped the diamonds into her lap, then picked up the purse again. "Is this it?"

"Yes, that's the one." Mr Sunshine smiled, took it from her and put it back in his desk. "Silly me, I'm always losing things," he said. "About the money."

She piled the diamonds back onto the desk. "Would these do?"

"You dropped one."

He was right, she had. She retrieved it and added it to the pile. "That'll do nicely," Mr Sunshine said. "It's always nice when people give you the exact money. It saves having to fiddle about with small change."

She tried to remember exactly what Carol had said about Mr Sunshine. He's nice, she'd said. A bit weird, but nice. She shivered. "So you'll—"

He nodded. "No promises," he said, "but I'll do my best. And like I said, Gina will probably know someone who knows about this sort of thing. Let's see it, then."

"Oh, the parcel." She picked up the carrier bag from the floor. "It's in here."

Mr Sunshine had suddenly gone very still and very quiet. "In there. No, don't take it out," he said. "Just leave it in the bag, would you?" He dipped his fingers into his shirt pocket and produced a magnifying glass. It was jet-black. He peered at the bag through it, then put it away. The look on his face was the most disconcerting thing she'd seen all morning. "Now that's not something you come across every day," he said, and his voice was ever so slightly shaky. "You know, I think we might be able to help you after all. You wouldn't mind leaving that with us for a day or so? I'll give you a receipt."

"Sure," said Alice. She tried to hand it to him, but he gestured to her to put it on the desk. "Keep it. Please."

"No," Mr Sunshine said, "I don't think I will, thanks all the same. Just a temporary loan, while we run some tests, that sort of thing." He wiped his forehead with the back of his wrist. "Just routine stuff."

After she'd gone, Mr Sunshine went to a cupboard in the corner of the room and took out a pair of iron tongs, with which he lifted the carrier bag and put it in the dustbin. Then he looked round for something to put the tongs in.

"Mistake," said a voice from his desk.

"Don't you start."

"Really bad mistake. All end in tears."

Mr Sunshine sighed. "You didn't happen to notice where I put the hazmat bucket?"

"Top left-hand drawer."

Mr Sunshine found it and deposited the tongs. There was a faint sizzle. "She's Carol's friend," he said. "I couldn't very well send her away."

"Factual error."

"No, I couldn't," Mr Sunshine said firmly. "Not to worry, I'll pass it on to Gina. She'll know what to do."

"Factual—"

"Oh shut up," said Mr Sunshine.

In his office on the second floor, the big one that used to belong to Mr Sunshine before the office civil war, Mr Dawson was conducting an interview. Mr Dawson (207 last birthday and didn't look a day over thirty-six, and there was a reason for that) handled the firm's substantial executive recruitment portfolio. He smiled reassuringly and steepled his fingers. Usually at this point he'd look the candidate full in the eye, to gauge his self-confidence and sincerity, but in this instance, for obvious reasons, he couldn't do that.

"Tell me," he said, "about yourself."

The interviewee billowed slightly, as his bush crackled but was not consumed. "Let's see, now," he said. "Eight hundred and seventy-five million years as Supreme Being on Delta Orionis Four. Of course when I started there it was all without form and void, the contractors had made a real pig's ear of it, but I had it all up together and ship-shape in eight days flat. Then seven hundred and forty million years as the All-Highest on Baynard's Planet, to be honest with you I felt like I was really just marking time there, I mean, I ran a tight ship, don't get me wrong, but when I look back and ask myself, did I really achieve anything, did I make a difference, the answer would have to be yes but I could possibly have done even more. Omnipotencewise," he added, by way of clarification. "Then three billion years on New Kampala, but I can't talk about that because strictly speaking that's in the future in this continuum, and you know the rules as well as I do. Suffice to say it was a challenge, but that's what it's all about in this game, isn't it?"

Mr Dawson was smiling, an ominous sign to all who knew him. "Quite," he said. "What would you say are your greatest strengths?"

The interviewee flared up for a moment, filling the office with unearthly red light. "Everything," he said.

"Right," said Mr Dawson. "So, for example, you'd be hard put to it to create a rock, say, that you couldn't lift."

The interviewee was silent for a moment. "Why would I want to do a thing like that?" he asked.

Downhill all the way from there, in both senses of the expression. Mr Dawson asked the rest of the questions on his checklist, for form's sake and just in case the interviewee might say something to strike a tiny spark of interest; he didn't, and that was that. He thanked the interviewee for his time, mentioned in passing that he had a few more people to see, and said he'd let him know. Then there was a roar, like the rushing of a mighty wind, and Mr Dawson was alone. He sighed, tore his notes into seven thin strips and put them in the wastepaper basket.

Then he leaned forward and prodded a toggle on his desk. "Next," he said.

He leaned back in his chair and looked at the mantelpiece, which hadn't been there a moment ago. Nor, Mr Dawson couldn't help noticing, had the fireplace directly beneath it. He frowned. Impressing the interviewer with a startlingly original approach was all very well, but he drew the line at structural alterations.

A loud bump and a cloud of soot. Out of the fireplace stepped a fat man in a red dressing gown. He had a white beard and a sack. "Not late, am I?" he asked.

"Exactly on time," Mr Dawson said. "Please, take a seat."

The fat man looked at the chair, still smouldering gently. "I'll use my own, if that's all right with you," he said, and from the sack he produced a three-legged stool carved with entwined tendrils of holly and ivy. "Right, then," he said. "Fire away."

Mr Dawson peered at him over the top of his spectacles. "Excuse me saying this," he said, "but you do know what this interview is for?"

The fat man nodded. "Planet in an alternative universe is looking for a supreme being," he said. "That's what it said in the ad, anyhow."

Mr Dawson nodded slowly. "No offence," he said. "But are you sure you're—?"

"Qualified?" The fat man laughed. "I should think so. I was laying the foundations of the Earth when old Smiler there was still in nappies." He nodded towards the smouldering chair. "He's after the job as well, is he? Might have guessed. He's got a nerve, I'll give him that."

Mr Dawson was interested in spite of himself. "Has he?"

The fat man laughed again. It didn't sound one little

bit like ho-ho-ho. "After what happened at his last place? I take it you heard about that."

"Actually, no. I gather it hasn't happened yet."

"Not in this continuum, I guess not." The fat man nodded sagely. "Well, all I can say is, don't book any holidays on New Kampala any time in the next three billion years. Not unless you're into really extreme sports. Right, let's get on with it. You got my CV?"

Mr Dawson discovered that he had, neatly wrapped in green paper, like a cracker. "That's impressive," he said, after a quick glance. "I didn't know you used to be a thunder god."

The fat man nodded. "Mostly thunder," he said. "Bit of rain and general fertility thrown in, some smiting here and there, not that I ever really took to smiting. I always say, you can do more with a snarky word and a sarcastic comment than you can do with a thunderbolt any day of the week. Still, if what people want is smiting, I can smite." He grinned. "You bet."

A slight shiver ran down Mr Dawson's spine. "Moving on," he said. "I don't think it's exactly a secret that you've already got a job. So why do you want this one?"

The fat man stifled a yawn. "You really want to know?"

"Yes."

"Fair enough. Bit of a cock-up, if you must know."

"Ah."

"Really, I was only trying to help," the fat man said, with a hint of anger. "That's all I ever do, try and help."

"I see."

"I said to myself, I said, they'd better watch out, because if they don't they're going to find themselves in the candy floss right up to here, the way they're going on. I tried to drop a few hints, you know, casually, but—"

He spread his hands. "If they're too thick to get it, what can you do?"

"Um."

"So I laid it on the line for them," the fat man said. "I told them, if you're good and sensible and you listen to what your scientists tell you and don't insist on screwing it all up for yourselves, I'll give you a clean, cheap source of renewable energy to meet all your industrial and domestic needs. But if you're bad, you'll get coal. And what happened?"

"Quite," Mr Dawson said.

"Anyhow," the fat man said, "that's enough about me. Tell me about this gig. What are they after, exactly?"

Mr Dawson's eyes opened a little bit wider. "They want a god," he said.

"Fair enough," the fat man said. "What happened to their old one?"

Mr Dawson looked down at the papers on his desk. "He died."

"Ah," the fat man said. "So I'm probably looking at a culture of self-destructive post-enlightenment nihilism. Bummer. What's the dominant species like on this planet of yours, then?"

"Um," said Mr Dawson, looking at the brief. "Mortal bipedal humanoid, omnivore, average lifespan eighty years, early post-industrial society. That sort of thing."

The fat man frowned. "Nitrogen/oxygen atmosphere?"

"Afraid so."

The fat man rolled his eyes. "Gravity?"

"Earth standard, give or take a smidge."

"Magic?"

Mr Dawson nodded. "Within certain closely defined parameters, yes."

The fat man relaxed slightly. "If there's one thing I can't be doing with, it's orthodox Newtonian physics. Like wearing shoes a size too small, if you know what I mean. All right, you'd better fill me in on the details. I'm not saying I'll do it, mind. But I guess it won't hurt to listen."

Mr Dawson realised that somehow he'd become the interviewee. His respect for the fat man went up a notch or two. Now he came to think of it, his clients could do worse. He told the fat man about the planet, its history, geography, cultural mores and underlying values. When he'd finished, the fat man was quiet for a while, thinking. Eventually he said, "Fair enough. Now for the big question. What's in it for me?"

"Excuse me?"

"Don't play games, it doesn't suit you. What's the deal? How much do I get?"

"Um." Mr Dawson looked at the brief, which was silent on that point. "I'm not sure my client was thinking of approaching it from that angle," he said. "Remuneration per se—"

"In other words, what I can get out of the punters." The fat man pursed his lips. "You know what," he said, "that's not really how I like to do business. What I like is so much in the bank at the end of the month, no deductions, no productivity bonuses or performance-related stock options, no mucking about. The other way may give you an incentive and a keener edge and all that malarkey, but it buggers up how you look at things when you're doing the job. You've always got that percentage ticking away at the back of your mind when you're making the big decisions. Whereas if you know that come hell, high water or Richard bloody Dawkins you're still going to get your wedge come payday, you can afford to have whatsisname, begins in an in, integrity. I think that's important when you're a god, don't you?"

"Um."

"Not that I'm telling your clients how to run their planet. Not yet, at any rate. In fact, before I start doing that I want a properly detailed package, pension, health plan, the whole nine yards. That's part and parcel of being a professional, don't you think?"

"Um," Mr Dawson repeated. "No offence, but what does God want with a health plan?"

The fat man gave him a look that should have frozen his blood but didn't, then grinned. "Nice one," he said. "All right, it's a fair cop. So maybe I'm not exactly a god god."

"I never really thought of it as a grey area."

"More a sort of demiurge or genius loci. Still, a jerk-water alternative reality up the armpit of Nowhere can't afford to be choosy, now can it?"

"Unfortunately," said Mr Dawson, "yes, it can. It's a great shame, but there we go. If you haven't got that all-important bit of paper—"

The fat man clicked his tongue. "Never had the chance to go to college, me. By the time I was forty-five seconds old I was out on the street, earning a wage to support my widowed mother and seventy-four younger sisters." He paused. "You don't believe me, do you?"

"No."

"Shucks. Ah well, never mind." He stood up. The carved stool flew up in the air and vanished into the neck of the sack. "If you do hear of anything that might suit, let me know, there's a pal. Be honest with you, I'm not sure I can stick this job much longer."

Mr Dawson felt a pang of sympathy, much to his surprise. "Really?"

The fat man nodded. "It's all the faster-than-light travel," he said, "it's taking years off me. If I carry on at this rate, this time next year I'll be twelve years old. Ah well, thanks for your time."

"Just a moment." The words were out of Mr Dawson's mouth before he realised it.

The fat man was standing next to the fireplace. "What?"

"I was just wondering," Mr Dawson said. "What would you say to the occasional bit of freelancing?"

A moment later, Mr Dawson was wondering what he'd just gone and done. All the traffic in the street below had stopped. Not a single airliner passed overhead. Even the specks of dust invisible in the air stopped drifting floorward and hovered like buzzards, waiting for something. "I might," the fat man said. "Depends. What sort of freelancing?"

"Oh, I don't know," said Mr Dawson, who honestly didn't. "It just occurred to me, that's all. Someone with your rather unusual skillset. You know, getting in and out of places. Making a lot of deliveries in a short space of time. Keeping scrupulously accurate records." His mouth had gone dry, for some reason. "If you're not interested I quite understand."

"Oh, I'm interested," the fat man said, and for some reason Mr Dawson was intensely aware of the follicles on the back of his neck. The hairs weren't rising or anything like that. He just knew exactly where all of them were. He was reminded of the first time he ever met his future business partner, Mr Ahriman. Not a particularly happy memory. "Always up for good honest paying work, me," the fat man said. "No job too big or too small. Provided I can fit it in, of course."

"Of course." Mr Dawson had the oddest feeling that

the last sentence was letting him off a very big, sharp hook and relief started to well up inside him, like sweat on a forehead. "You're a busy man, I appreciate that."

"Yeah. When I'm busy, I'm busy. The other three hundred and sixty four days, I'm generally available."

"Ah." Mr Dawson swallowed. "Splendid. I'll, um, bear that in mind."

"You do that," the fat man said, and handed him a business card. It had jolly robins on it, and Mr Dawson put it away in his desk. The fireplace was glowing red, as though a real fire was burning there. "Glad we had this chat. Shame about the job but what the hell. One door closes, right? Be seeing you." He stepped into the fireplace. It vanished, and Mr Dawson's office wall reasserted itself. He stared at it for about twenty seconds, then shook himself like a wet dog and hit the toggle on his desk. "Next," he said.

The next interviewee manifested Himself as an earthquake, a mighty roaring wind, a firestorm and a small squeaky whisper, but Mr Dawson found it hard to concentrate. His mind was on other things.

Across the landing in a slightly smaller office overlooking the fire escape, Mr Teasdale, the youngest of the partners, sipped his coffee with a thoughtful expression on his face. "Not there," he said.

"I just said so, didn't I?" The young woman he was talking to glared at him. "Honestly, I don't think there's much point me being here and paying you all that money if all you're going to do is repeat every bloody thing I say."

Quite. "Sorry," said Mr Teasdale mildly. "Just wanted to make sure I'd got my facts straight." He leaned back in his chair and steepled his fingers. "Let me see those pictures again."

"You've already looked at them three times."

"Yes, well, I need to be thorough."

"I don't think you should charge me for the third time."

He held out his hand and she passed him the tablet. Scrolling through, he was struck by two things. First, she really was a very good wedding photographer, if you liked your matrimonial reportage in the style of *Time* magazine covering the Vietnam War. Second, there was nothing to see – apart, of course, from a bunch of people in clothes they'd never wear again, holding wine glasses in a large tent. "This one here," he said.

"Yes."

"She's in every picture."

"Yes. That's the point. You have been listening, haven't you? You haven't just sat there thinking about something else, at God only knows how much per second?"

It was Mr Teasdale's policy in life to like everybody as much as he could for as long as possible, and then stop. He still had a bit of a way to go, but the light was definitely there at the end of the tunnel. "Let me just clarify," he said, "to make sure I've got it straight in my mind."

That got him a sigh. He forgave it.

"Every picture you've taken," he said, "at every wedding you've covered over the last six months—"

"Seven."

"The last seven months, thank you. Every picture you've taken at every wedding, she's in it."

"Correct."

"Looking exactly the same."

"No," she said, with exaggerated patience. "Sometimes it's a different hat."

"I stand corrected. Identical except for the hat. Same

dress, handbag, shoes, same cheerful smile facing directly into the camera."

"Yes."

"And nobody's ever seen her before or knows who she is?"

"Correct. Yes."

"And you don't remember ever having—"

"Of course bloody not. Otherwise I'd have had her thrown out on her stupid ear. She wasn't there."

Mr Teasdale nodded slowly. "Got you," he said. "Appears in all the photographs but not actually there. I'll just make a note of that," he added, and did so.

"Look, are you sure you're a properly qualified whatever-you-call-it? I mean, you've passed all your exams and everything? Only you don't seem to know—"

Mr Teasdale cleared his throat gently. "It looks to me," he said, as mildly as possible, "like a textbook example of a transdimensional affinity, or Reichenstafel's syndrome."

She looked at him. "Right. You what?"

"Reichenstafel's syndrome," he repeated. "Not common, in fact something of a collector's item, but pretty well documented nonetheless. I suppose I've handled about a dozen cases in the last three years."

He had her attention. "Is it bad?"

"Can be, yes."

"Dangerous?"

"Sometimes."

"How fucking dangerous?"

He took off his glasses, wiped the lenses with the special cloth and put them back on. "That depends," he said. "Reichenstafel's is hard to quantify, in the early stages. Death, though by no means inevitable—"

"Jesus fucking Christ."

"It's just as well," he said, with tastefully subdued relish, "that you came to see me. Seven months, you said?"

She'd gone a funny colour. "About that. Look, I can take it. How long have I got?"

He smiled at her. "It's not an illness," he said. "Reichenstafel's is an affinity. It means that you and someone else have formed a special sort of connection, one that transcends time and space."

She gave him a does-not-compute look. "You mean, like true love?"

He indulged himself in a small professional laugh. "That's one sort of connection that can form a Reichenstafel event, certainly. But not the only one, by any means. It's quite rare, actually. More usually, the connection is—" He paused, choosing the right word. "Rather more parasitic than romantic."

She shuddered. "You mean, this stupid fat old woman is trying to lay her eggs in me or something?"

"Not necessarily eggs," said Mr Teasdale. "But I would say, at a guess, she wants something from you, yes."

"That's gross."

"The interesting thing, from a technical viewpoint," said Mr Teasdale, "is the hat. Not the same hat every time. Usually the image is constant."

"Fuck the fucking hat, get that horrible woman off me. Now."

Mr Teasdale took another sip of his coffee. It was still exactly the right temperature, even though it had been sitting on his desk for the last fifteen minutes. Mr Teasdale had his morning coffee sent in from a little caterer's in Plato's ideal reality, where everything is always just so. It was expensive, but he could afford it. "First," he said, "we have to find out exactly what she wants from you. Then, if at all possible, we give it to her."

"How the hell can you do that?"

"We could always try asking."

She rolled her eyes. "But she's not there."

"Almost right," said Mr Teasdale. "What you should have said is, she's not here. But she's got to be somewhere, or she couldn't be stalking you like this. All we've got to do is find out where she is, then ask her what she wants."

Hope peered out at him from her eyes, like some timid forest animal. "You can do that?"

"I think so."

"You think—"

"I have a 99.99998 per cent success rate in making contact in Reichenstafel cases," Mr Teasdale said mildly. "The thing people fail to grasp is, the affinitor isn't necessarily malevolent, just someone who wants something. And doesn't give a stuff about what he does to get it, but never mind about that. It's not evil you're up against, just extremely highly motivated self-interest."

"Lucky fucking me."

"Yes, actually," Mr Teasdale said. "Sometimes, evil can be a bitch. Self-interest, on the other hand, is at least something you can understand. Once you understand something, you can set about fixing it."

He paused. She looked at him. "Well?" she said.

"Expensive," said Mr Teasdale.

Expensive was, in Mr Teasdale's opinion, one of those magical words. It was essentially a touchstone for the human soul, stripping away the layers of pretence and self-delusion and leaving the true self exposed to view, naked and defenceless as Adam and Eve in the Garden. "How much?"

"Of course," he went on, "you could decide to do nothing, ignore it, pretend it isn't happening, carry on with your life as though nothing's wrong. Presumably you can Photoshop her out of the pictures—"

"How much?"

He said a number. For that much, you could buy a decent second-hand aircraft carrier. She made a noise like a chipmunk.

"Payable," he added, "in advance." Pause. "If it'd help, we can arrange credit."

Tears were running down her cheeks. "What?"

"With a realistically sustainable repayment schedule," Mr Teasdale went on, "spread over, say, fifteen generations. We'd need a certain level of security, of course. A mortgage on your firstborn child, that sort of thing."

"I haven't got a—"

"Not yet," Mr Teasdale said. "We tend to favour the long-term view in this business."

She scowled at him through her tears. "That's horrible," she said. "That's—"

"Yes," Mr Teasdale said, "it is. But you've got a problem, and we can probably make it go away. Or you can decide to keep the problem and deal with it yourself. And like I said, Reichenstafel's isn't invariably fatal. It's possible that this woman may be content just to carry on haunting your photographic work, as opposed to your dreams or your every waking moment. It's too early to tell for sure. Of course, if you wait till you start getting the dreams it makes it that bit less likely that we'd be able to do anything about it, but that's your choice."

She glared at him, as though through the bars of an invisible cage. "What if," she said, "I signed your nasty little mortgage and then didn't have any kids?"

That got her a sad smile. "Doesn't work like that," he said. "In any case, we don't arrange the finance ourselves, we refer you to an associated concern that handles all that side of things for us. That's if you decide to proceed. Like I said, it's up to you entirely."

"But if I don't, I start seeing this woman in my dreams."

"Quite possibly yes. Of course, you may find you like her. She looks quite nice, in the pictures. Maybe you'll get on like a house on fire."

"Fifteen generations."

"Something like that," said Mr Teasdale. "Of course, if you'd taken out supernatural insurance, the whole cost would be covered and you wouldn't have to pay a penny, but it's too late for that now. People can be so short-sighted." He stood up. "Anyway, I expect you'll want to think about it, so we'll call it a day for now, shall we? Lovely to have met you."

"No, please." Ah, thought Mr Teasdale, the magic word. "I'll do it. I'll sign anything you want. Just don't let that woman get me."

Mr Teasdale sat down again. "Just kidding," he said.

"What?"

"Not about the Reichenstafel thing," he said. "But you don't have to sign anything or give us your firstborn. I was just teasing you, because you were so rude and horrible."

"You ars—" She stopped herself. It was like seeing someone walking into a plate-glass window. "Got you," she said. "I'm sorry."

"That's quite all right."

"Nothing to pay?"

"Oh, lots," said Mr Teasdale. "But we've been in the private client business for a long time and the truth of the matter is, there just aren't enough rich people in the world with problems to make it worth our while. So we've learned to be inventive. Sign that."

He gave her a bit of paper and a pen. "What is it?"

"Trust me."

She hesitated, then signed. "What—?"

"You've just assigned me all the rights in a revolutionary new technology that'll cut carbon emissions by ninety per cent and save the planet. And, incidentally, make an absolute fortune."

"But—"

"You haven't invented it yet," Mr Teasdale explained. "But you will."

"Will I?"

"It's not the policy of this firm to reveal the future." He took the paper from her, folded it neatly, walked to the wall, took down a framed watercolour of the Manchester Ship Canal painted by his grandmother, opened the door of the safe behind it, put the paper into the safe, closed it, spun the dial four times, replaced the picture. "That would be unethical." He sat down again. "Right, then," he said, "let the dog see the rabbit. The first thing we need to do is—"

"How much did I just—?"

He gave her a look. "You do want to save the planet, don't you?"

"Yes, of course. I guess so. When you say an absolute fortune—"

"Well," said Mr Teasdale, "you won't be up to inventing or discovering anything if you've got that annoying woman whispering in your ear twenty-four-seven, you'll be too busy climbing the walls. Shall we get on?"

"Yes, but—"

"Think," Mr Teasdale said, "of all the baby seals in

Alaska. You wouldn't want anything bad to happen to them, would you?"

She gave him a look. It wasn't the friendliest look in the history of the world, but it was sufficient cause for him to believe that they understood each other. "Fine," she said. "What do we do now?"

Mr Teasdale was scrolling through the pictures again. "She reminds me," he said, "of my Aunt Veronica. Nice woman, you'd like her. I think the simplest approach would be to conjure her."

"What's that mean?"

"Technical term," explained Mr Teasdale. "It's no big deal. All it involves is, we force her to come here, confine her so she can't jump out and bite us, and ask her questions."

"Bite us?"

"Metaphorically speaking." He reached for his diary and turned a few pages. "Takes a day or so to set up. How's Tuesday?"

"How can you do that if you don't know where—?"

"Oh, we don't do the actual summoning and coercing," Mr Teasdale said with a smile, "that's what the demons are for. If you can't do Tuesday, how about Wednesday afternoon? I've got the dentist at two, so any time after three-thirty—"

After she'd gone, Mr Teasdale wrote a note for the file, looked up a few things on Wikipedia and sent an email to Robertsons to book twelve demons for 3.45 on Wednesday. Then (almost forgot) he reopened the safe, took out his pirate copy of Destiny and fiddled with it a bit so the annoying girl would be the one to invent carbon resequencing. The other partners, he knew, didn't really think much of tuppenny-ha'penny private client work, preferring to concentrate on the big corporate accounts, but Mr Teasdale begged to differ. Quite apart from the money side of things, there was a lot of satisfaction to be gained from helping ordinary people with everyday problems, not to mention the good publicity for the firm and the Brownie points it earned with the regulators. One of many things Mr Sunshine had taught him, when he first started at Dawsons; money isn't everything. Ninety-nine per cent of everything, true, but the remaining 1 per cent matters.

He called up the wedding pictures, which he'd saved to his computer, for one last look. Those hats. Apparently, the woman had three of them. Something snagged in his mind like a hangnail, but he couldn't quite figure out what it was.

Unless –

Surely not.

Only one way to be sure. He finished his coffee, recycled the mug into a fountain of gold and silver sparks and set off across the landing and up the spiral staircase to the closed file store.

When Mr Teasdale was a young junior trainee at JWW, one of the first jobs he'd been given was tidying up the firm's main archive and storage area, generally referred to by the partners as the Abyss and the junior staff as the Caves of Khazad-Dum. Not only had he survived the assignment (many hadn't), he'd enjoyed it. Mostly, he said afterwards, it was because it was his first real chance to do a job on his own, his way, without some well-meaning clown peering over his shoulder criticising his every move. A young man starting off in the business, he maintained, needs a bit of space to make his first few mistakes in. The Abyss certainly provided him with that, but he survived, his left arm grew back eventually and he learned several valuable lessons about self-reliance, ingenuity and never turning your back on a thermal binder. It was, in fact, an experience he looked back on with a certain degree of nostalgia. It would be an exaggeration to say that he'd left his heart in the basement of 70 St Mary Axe – some toes and a certain amount of liver, no more than that – but it had been a formative experience and made him the courageous and resourceful, if slightly deckle-edged, man he was today.

When he moved to Dawsons as a young assistant sorcerer, therefore, one of the first things he did was give the firm's closed file store a thorough makeover. It needed it. The last time it had seen a dustpan or a tin of paint, the firm was still Sunshine, Noctis & Gregg, the American colonists were chasing the French out of Quebec and a fashionable painter by the name of Tom Gainsborough had come to see the firm about an awkward problem he was having at work.

You wouldn't recognise the old place now. Although he'd probably be reluctant to admit it, Mr Teasdale had a certain flair for interior design. Thanks to his efforts, the closed file store was now a light, clean, airy place where people tended to linger rather than escape from by the skin of their teeth. Mr Dawson, for example, often used it to unwind after a difficult morning, and he was there now, sitting in a big leather armchair beside the pool watching the flamingos.

"Morning, Brian," he said without looking round. "How's it going?"

"Oh, the usual," said Mr Teasdale. "Saw a client with a suspected Reichenstafel, no big deal. How about you?"

Mr Dawson yawned. "I've been tied up all morning

with that piss-arse job we got passed on from Cannings," he said. "I can see why they didn't want it."

"Ah, yes," said Mr Teasdale. "So, have you found God yet?"

Mr Dawson was used to Mr Teasdale's jokes. "Bunch of deadheads," he said. "Wouldn't trust any of them to part a bowl of soup, personally. Never mind, it pays the bills. Talking of which."

Mr Teasdale sighed. "Yes, it's covered," he said.

"Glad to hear it," Mr Dawson replied. "Look, if you want to fritter away your time on private client stuff that's your business, just so long as you remember, we're not a bloody charity."

"I told you, it's covered." Mr Teasdale made an effort to stay nice. "In twenty years, we'll be so rich we won't know what to do with it all. Guaranteed."

"Oh," said Mr Dawson, frowning. "One of those."

"Wealth beyond the dreams of—"

"Yes, fine, that's wonderful," Mr Dawson interrupted, "but I'm the one who's got to bother his pretty head with cash flow. It's not much use the money being there in twenty years—"

"Yes it is."

"Up to a point," Mr Dawson said irritably. "But every time I have to go into the future to get a few quid for the electric and the business rates, it's costing us nineteen pence in the pound in commission and charges. That's just chucking money away, Brian, it's stupid. Look, I haven't got a problem with you doing your own thing so long as you drop a few pennies in the cocoa tin occasionally, you know that. And a bit of pro bono, within reason—"

"Thanks," said Mr Teasdale. "I'll remember that, if ever I decide to do any."

"Look." Mr Dawson stopped himself with an effort. "There's no point you and me falling out about this. Well, is there? It's not me you want to be worried about. It's—"

"Of course," Mr Teasdale said quickly. "I'm sorry."

"You know what he's like," Mr Dawson said. "Where money's concerned."

Mr Teasdale bit his lip. "Message received and understood." He hesitated. "Heard from him lately?"

"No."

Mr Teasdale felt a surge of relief. "He's definitely away, or you just haven't heard from him?"

A wild look flashed across Mr Dawson's eyes. "It's not like that," he hissed, "and you know it. He's everywhere."

Something in the way he said it made Mr Teasdale's skin crawl. "Theoretically," he said mildly. "Anyway, let's not talk about him, you know it always depresses you. I'm looking for something."

Mr Dawson sighed and leaned back in his chair, as though he was some form of liquid soaking into the fabric. "What?"

"Those paintings we used to have tucked away behind those crates of old computer stuff. You haven't seen them lately, have you?"

Mr Dawson thought for a moment. "I know the ones you mean," he said. "Gina had them in her office at one point, I'm sure of it."

"I'll ask her." Far away in the distance, a column of weary elephants came down to the lake to drink, scattering the flocks of brightly coloured birds. Somewhere, a lion roared. "You don't know where they came from, do you?"

"I think Ted Sunshine took them to settle a bill. He was always doing stuff like that."

A sore point with Mr Dawson, so Mr Teasdale skated over it. "Been here a while, then."

"They were here when I joined. What's so special about them, anyhow?"

"Hats," Mr Teasdale said. "Long story."

"Story with a happy ending involving us getting paid? Sorry," Mr Dawson added quickly, "didn't mean to start all that again. Look, I'm off to talk to Gina in a minute, I'll ask her about them, all right?"

"Thanks."

"No problem. Out of interest, what sort of hats?"

"Different ones."

"Ah. That clears that up, then."

After Mr Dawson had gone, Mr Teasdale had a good look round and came across a number of quite interesting things, but no paintings. That in itself was curious, and quite possibly relevant. He fished a small scientific instrument out of his pocket and took a few readings.

As he'd thought. At some point, someone or something had distorted the fabric of time inside the closed file store. Not a deliberate temporal incursion, and not a space/time incident or anything like that, nothing that needed to be reported to the insurers; the trace residues were cumulative rather than explosive, and there was no telltale yellow-green glow or slight smell of frying bacon. Instead, it was as though somebody had stored a rather large quantity of time here, and where it had rested against the walls and the floor it had bent them slightly. Well, he thought, it's a store room, nothing unusual or sinister about that. Occasionally they stored things for old and valued clients, as a favour, at a price, and several of Ted's and Gina's pet punters had been known to dabble in the bulk time business. He glanced up at the ceiling and figured out that directly above his head was the boardroom, where they held the partnership meetings. That might also account for it. Nothing to see here, or to worry unduly about. And almost certainly nothing with a direct bearing on the question of hats, or a hat, or just possibly three different hats that might, in some almost mystical sense that he was only just starting to grope towards, conceivably all be the same hat—

He glanced at his watch, a Flexichron ZX3. Seven a.m. in Tokyo, he noted, and on Delta Coriolis Six it was a Wednesday. More to the point, he had ten minutes to comb his hair, grab a bunch of flowers from somewhere and get his sorry carcass to Covent Garden to meet Consuela for lunch. That's me, he thought, always running out of time. Now there's irony.

"Oh, I know the ones you mean," said Gina Noctis, looking up from her paperwork. "Women in frocks. Gainsboroughs or something like that."

Mr Dawson nodded. "Seen them lately?"

"Not for ages. Didn't we sell them to pay for the new roof?"

"You're thinking of the Raphael cartoon. I have an idea I saw one of them a few weeks ago, but I'm buggered if I can remember where. Anyway, if anything comes to mind, tell young Brian. He's got some bee in his bonnet about them because of some charity case he's working on."

Gina didn't say anything, but her inner tongue clicked. Whenever Tom Dawson started moaning about Brian doing private client work, it meant he was under pressure from – Well. She understood, therefore she forgave. With something like that hanging over him, no wonder he got tetchy about money. "What does he want a bunch of old paintings for?"

"Something about hats."

"Ah."

Mr Dawson was perching on the corner of her desk, a curiously informal, almost boyish thing for a man of his age and dignity to do. And he hadn't come here to talk about missing paintings. "What?" she said.

Mr Dawson looked at her. "He's got one," he said. "I know he has."

"Oh not that again." Gina made a show of rolling her eyes. "We've been into all that a million billion times. He hasn't got one."

"Yes he has."

"No he hasn't." She made an effort and got a grip. "He hasn't got one because they're impossible. Therefore they don't exist. Therefore he hasn't bloody well got one."

"Yes he has."

Gina sighed, tapped a few keys on her keyboard and turned her laptop round so Mr Dawson could see the screen. "Read," she said.

"Read it. Makes no odds. He's got one."

She dismissed the document, a scientific paper by Professor van Spee of the Chicago Institute for Supernatural Studies irrefutably proving for all time that bottomless purses can't and don't exist. "Even if he's got one," she said, "which he hasn't—"

"Yes he bloody well has. Why else do all his trailer-trash clients always pay in diamonds?"

"Oh for crying out loud. Does it matter, so long as they pay?"

Mr Dawson was getting angry. "Yes, when they're

paying me with my money. That purse is partnership property. He should've handed it in when—"

"When you forced him out."

A long sigh. In spite of everything, Gina realised, she was still sorry for him. "You know how I'm fixed," he said.

"Yes, I know."

"If I only had that stupid purse, all my troubles would be over. I could snap my fingers in his face and tell him to go to—" He stopped, closed his eyes for a moment, opened them again. "Go home," he said. "As it is—"

"Did it occur to you," Gina said quietly, "that if the purse is partnership property, it's not yours. Or mine or Brian's or Jerry's or anybody's. It's his. Dawson, Ahriman and Dawson, remember?"

"He doesn't know about it."

Gina gave him a grim smile. "You reckon? I don't think there's much that goes on around here that he doesn't know about."

"You're not helping, you know that?" Mr Dawson stood up, balled his fists and stuffed them in his jacket pockets. "Look, if we had that stupid purse, none of it would matter. There'd be so much money—"

"I'm not sure he sees it like that," Gina said softly.

"He must do. Otherwise it makes no sense. For God's sake, Gina, what more could anybody want? It's a bottomless frigging purse. A fifth share of infinity is infinity. And then I'd be off the hook."

Gina said nothing. If he wanted to believe that, let him. When someone's addicted to hope, it's sheer cruelty to cure him.

"That's why it's so stupid," he went on. "Infinity means plenty for everyone. Which means Ted could carry on funding his stupid charity cases, exactly the same as he's doing now, and we – Fuck it, we could all retire. The nightmare would be over. But, no, bloody Ted Sunshine's got to keep it for himself, just so he can play fairy godmother to half the losers on Benefits Street."

Gina looked at him. He wasn't a bad person really, just very, very stressed. "You could try asking him," she said.

That got her the wolf-in-a-trap look. "Oh sure," Mr Dawson said. "Ted Sunshine's going to help me out because I ask him nicely. Danger, low-flying pigs." The wolf in his eyes looked at her hungrily. "It'd be different coming from you," he said. "He'd listen to you."

Yes, she thought, because I didn't force him out of the partnership and steal his life's work. "No," she said.

"For pity's sake, Gina." He stopped, and all the energy seemed to drain out of him, like oil from the crankcase of a Land Rover. "Fine," he said. "You aren't going to help me. Great. Who needs you?"

"Tom—"

"I'm sorry." He was, too. She remembered him as he'd been when she first met him: young, ambitious, not a care in the world, revelling in the glorious power and sheer fun of his newly discovered profession like a leaping dolphin enjoying the sea. A lot had changed since then, of course; Tom included. The new partnership, the deal with Mr Ahriman, the office civil war, the terrible realisation of what they'd all got themselves into. But there were times when she looked at him and caught a flash of sunlight reflected on the dolphin's shining flipper, and so she could still forgive him, no matter what.

"I'll talk to him." She hadn't intended to say that.

"Will you? Oh thank God. It'd be such a weight off my mind."

Now look what she'd gone and done. "It won't do any

good," she said. "Because he hasn't got one. Because they don't exist."

"Just talk to him. He'll listen to you." Mr Dawson sat down again, this time in a chair. "How long have you known him? Of course he'll listen to you."

"There's listening and there's agreeing, Tom. You treated him very badly."

"I had no—" Mr Dawson bit off the last word, like someone in a restaurant eating octopus. "Yes," he said, "I did, didn't I? You can tell him that from me, if you think it'll do any good."

"You know what he'll say to that."

"Yeah. Fine words and parsnips. Why parsnips, for crying out loud?"

When she walked into Mr Sunshine's room, the air was full of smoke. "What's going on?" she said, reaching for her handkerchief.

Mr Sunshine nodded at the steel wastepaper bin, which had melted all over the floor. Liquid metal lay on the carpet tiles in a shimmering pool. "The metal's not hot," Mr Sunshine said. "That's what's so odd."

"Interesting," Gina said. "Would you mind opening a window? I can't actually breathe."

"Oh, right." Mr Sunshine sometimes forgot that other people needed oxygen. "Harmondsworth. Extractor fan."

A drawer of his desk slid open, and all the smoke was drawn into it. Then the drawer snapped shut. "Sorry about that," Mr Sunshine said. "You'd better be careful not to tread in it, by the way. I have no idea what it does."

She glanced at the pool, which was slowly spreading. "Bet you anything you like it invalidates our insurance. Tom'd have a fit."

"He's health-and-safety obsessed, if you ask me," said Mr Sunshine. "Talking of Tom, the answer's no."

"Ah."

"No I haven't got one, and no he can't have it."

Oh well. It didn't occur to Gina to ask how he knew what she'd come to ask. He just knew things like that. "You don't think you could stretch a point, just this once."

"Could. Don't want to."

"Fine," she said. "And there was me, thinking you were better than that."

"Who, me? Not likely."

Subject closed, for now. "What is that, anyhow?"

"Ah." Mr Sunshine's eyes twinkled behind his glasses. "That's what I was about to ask you. Take a look. Don't get too close."

She went across the room and peered at the ruins of the wastepaper basket. "A parcel wrapped in grey plastic."

"That's what I thought."

"Which melted your bin. Without heat."

"Apparently the client was carrying it round for days in a shopping bag, and she didn't look any the worse for wear. It's from space."

"We're all from space, Ted. Space is just a word for—"

"It's an extra-terrestrial parcel," Mr Sunshine amended. "Left with a neighbour."

"Oh, one of those." She frowned. "No big deal. If nobody claims it within thirty days, she can keep it."

"I don't think she wants it."

"Very sensible, if it melts things."

"I was wondering," Mr Sunshine said. "Would you mind having a look at it?"

"Have I got to?"

"I sort of promised we would."

Gina sighed. "Fine," she said. "You can make it up to me by helping me out with my rotten time sheets." She closed her eyes, breathed in deeply and tried to remember—

Remember what it was like once, long ago, before she was Gina; when she was Regina Noctis, Queen of the Night; oldest, first and foremost. It wasn't a comfortable memory. It made her mind itch, like wearing canvas next to the skin. She remembered darkness and the bite of cold air, long before the first time two flints collided. No warmth, no light, just her. Gradually she began to shed her corporeal form, molecule by molecule, atom by atom. She felt like a snail out of its shell, for a little while. Then she started to feel something else: a roaring, gushing joy, out of the box, free ... Like gunpowder ignited, turning from solid into gas, unstoppable expansion, unrestrainable energy, absolute force—

"I hate this," she said. "Can't Harmondsworth do it?"

"He's sensitive."

"So am I fucking sensitive."

"Gina. Go fetch."

She snarled and let go, and suddenly she knew who she was. Amazing: why did she put up with it, why had she ever consented to be contained, restrained, belittled like that, cooped up in a skin bag with a lot of old rubbish like civilised behaviour and consideration for others and respect for human life? The hell with all that. She was out, she was back, she was herself again—

She had a job to do. For Edwin. Sod it, never mind. Pull yourself together, girl, and attend to the matter in hand.

She was blind, of course, and had no fingers to feel with, but she had so much more. She let herself seep through the gaps in the lattice of molecules that comprised the flexible grey polymer. It wasn't a variety she was familiar with, not from around here, different; better. She allowed herself to linger for a moment, revelling in the first unfamiliar texture she'd come across in a very long time, then slid through. Would you mind having a look at it, he'd said, as though it was nothing. He had no idea. But then, how could he possibly understand? How could anyone?

Hello, she thought. You're odd.

The thing inside the grey polymer wrapping was – Let's stop and think about this one, shall we? Alive? Deceptive concept. You think you know what it means, but you don't really. A more useful word would probably be active, as opposed to passive; something capable of initiating action on its own initiative. Intelligent? A common human misconception, that things have to be alive to be intelligent; just ask the screwdriver you can't find or the slice of toast that intuitively seeks the floor jam side down. Purposeful: that was more like it. She still wasn't absolutely sure what the thing was, but it was as full of purpose as an orange is full of juice. Definitely not something you'd want to leave lying about. In fact, if you had more brains than a clam, you wouldn't want to be in the same galaxy.

"How are you getting on?" said a voice, long ago, far away, familiar.

"Nearly done," she called back, then realised she had nothing to make a sound with. Better get a move on, or Edwin would start to get concerned about her. He worried, bless him. She reached out and smeared herself onto the surface of the thing, searching for an opening.

There wasn't one. It was sealed, solid, all one piece. Not made of atoms. It was one great big atom. She crawled across it, barely able to find anything she could adhere to. Hello, she said. Are you friendly?

Not a pore, fissure or crack anywhere. No. Go away.

It was frightened. She knew that particular brand of fear. The last time she'd felt it this intensely she'd been clinging to the casing of a bomb, just before it exploded. Poor thing, it had had plenty to be afraid about, and all its worst fears had suddenly come true.

Will it hurt?

Ah, she thought, we're getting somewhere. I don't know, she said. What are you going to do?

What I must.

Right, got you. You don't have to do it yet, do you? she thought soothingly, and waited for a reply.

I suppose not.

Better. Then I wouldn't, if I were you. No rush. Take your time. You might want to think about it.

What's there to think about?

Oh dear. Relax, she commanded. Deep breaths. Go to sleep.

Much to her surprise, it worked. She felt the consciousness ebb and fade and go dark, no doubt instinctively recognising something about its new companion. She waited for a little while, then carefully she reached out with her metaphorical nails and teeth and began to gnaw a little hole in the impenetrable casing—

DANCER

"You were a long time," Mr Sunshine said.

"Was I?"

The weight of her body was unendurable; no, it was simply irksome, then a mild annoyance, then perfectly normal. She flexed her fingers and her toes, reminding herself how they worked. "Forty-seven seconds," Mr Sunshine said. "I was starting to get worried."

She smiled at him. "I'm a big girl," she said, "I can take care of myself."

"Well?"

She realised she was exhausted, as though she'd just run a mile up a steep hill. "Definitely something in there," she said.

"I'd sort of gathered that. From the fact that the bag wasn't all floppy."

"Something strong," she said. "And very, very malevolent. And scared stiff."

"Fair enough," Mr Sunshine said. "Mind you, that

could mean anything. I bought some South African brandy once that fits that description precisely."

"I don't think it's brandy," Gina said.

"Probably not. Did you find out anything else?"

"Sort of." She told him about the flawless mono-atomic shell, and explained what monoatomic means. He nodded thoughtfully. "Built to last, then," he said. "Like a Magimix."

"I don't think it was built," she told him. "I think it grew. Or was grown, I don't know. It doesn't know either. I asked."

He raised an eyebrow. "Did you now," he said. "Not sure I'd have had the nerve to do that myself. Have a Brownie point."

"Thank you. Not sure I've earned it, though. I couldn't get it to tell me anything much."

"Probably just shy."

"Definitely that. And, like I said, very frightened. I really don't know what to make of it, to be honest. There was one thing."

"What?"

"There was something written on it. But I can't figure out what it means."

Mr Sunshine looked at her over the rims of his spectacles. "I doubt that," he said.

"Oh, I can read the letters and understand the language. But it doesn't make any sense."

"Like James Joyce."

She sighed. She'd known him a long time. "I put it to sleep," she said, "so we should be all right for a bit, until it wakes up. After that, though, I really wouldn't like to be answerable for the consequences. I think we should get rid of it, while we have the chance."

"Can't do that," Mr Sunshine said firmly. "It doesn't belong to us. Client's property. You know the rules."

"Fine. Get your client's permission and then get rid of it. You said she doesn't want it."

Mr Sunshine frowned. "But it's not hers," he said. "It wasn't addressed to her. Therefore she can't give permission, therefore we can't get rid of it. It's a nuisance, but there it is."

"I know. Pity, though. I have a nasty feeling it's going to make trouble."

"I think you're probably right," Mr Sunshine said sadly. "So what exactly did the writing on it say?"

Gina frowned. "Not sure I want to say it out loud," she said. "I mean, you never know. It could be a coded trigger command or an incantation or something like that. To be honest with you, it could be anything."

Mr Sunshine nodded. "Write it down," he said.

So she did. When she'd finished, Mr Sunshine picked up the envelope on the back of which she'd scrawled the words, in her elegant handwriting—

Not to be opened before Christmas.

Consuela Teasdale (she'd kept the name after the divorce) had been working at JWW for seventeen years or a month, depending on how you looked at it. On her first day, she'd had the misfortune to blunder into an inadequately labelled causality loop, carelessly mislaid by her predecessor, who'd been fired for gross negligence. A causality loop is one of those things where you get trapped in time, the same day or hour or ten minutes repeated endlessly, over and over again. It was sheer rotten luck that Consuela's predecessor had left one lying about in the ladies' toilet. When they finally figured out how to get her out of there she hadn't aged a day or even (remarkably, considering) lost weight, and the firm immediately paid her seventeen years back pay without a quibble, together with a substantial bonus and a gold clock for long service to the firm. Even so.

"I'm not bitter," she said through a mouth full of salad leaves, "and it's a really good job with great prospects, miles better that what they had me doing at Bettinsons, which is why I stayed on and haven't sued their arses into the middle of next week. It's just—"

"Yes," Mr Teasdale said. "Quite."

"And don't tell me stuff like that hasn't ever happened at your place, because I know for a fact it has."

Mr Teasdale frowned. "Really?"

"Oh come on," Consuela said, carefully selecting a breadstick from the glass. "What about Jerry Dawson?"

"Oh, that." Mr Teasdale shook out his napkin. "Jerry doesn't count."

"He's a partner."

"Theoretically."

"He's on the letterhead."

"He's in a steel box in the strongroom," Mr Teasdale pointed out, "and he only comes out for partnership meetings. The rest of the time—"

"Still a partner, though."

A sore point, which a more tactful person would have hesitated to rub in with such vigour. Tom Dawson's evil twin – hence Dawson, Ahriman and Dawson – hadn't had a separate existence until an unfortunate mishap during what should have been a perfectly routine transmigration-of-souls job had split Tom Dawson into the two component halves of his own psyche. It had come as a bit of a blow to his (now their) partners, especially since Jerry Dawson proved to be so antisocial and vicious that it was necessary to keep him disembodied and confined in a strong electro-magnetic field while still being entitled, under the terms of the partnership agreement, to an equal share of the net profits.

"What everybody says," Consuela went on, "is, if Tom Dawson's what's left after the nasty side of him got filtered out, what the hell must he have been like to start with? Because let's face it—"

Her point was largely valid, but a certain residual loyalty to the firm prompted Mr Teasdale to change the subject. "I got a new Reichenstafel case today."

"Wow." Consuela was impressed. "I've never had one of those."

He couldn't help feeling pleased that she was pleased. "You always did like the transdimensional stuff," he said.

She smiled at him, and his heart fluttered like a songbird caught in fruit netting. The first time he'd spoken to her had been at a transdimensional theory lecture, in second year. He'd asked her if she could make head or tail of all that dopplerised wave form stuff, and she'd explained by answering him from all four compass points simultaneously. You couldn't help liking someone who could do that. "Tell me about it," she said.

So he did, and as he told the tale it occurred to him that all through their long and difficult association, they'd always got on best when talking about work. If magic was involved, they were one soul shared between two bodies. The rest of the time, more like a fight between two cats on top of a high wall. "The only bit that bothers me," he concluded, "is the hats."

"Hats?"

He nodded. "Three of them. All different."

She pursed her lips. "I see what you mean."

Trust her to get the point straight away. It had taken him over an hour to appreciate the significance of the hats; the fact that a Reichenstafel projection is always a constant unified image – always the same, in every particular. Including, it goes without saying, the same hat. But the woman in the photographs had three of the bloody things. "It's probably nothing," he said. "Glitch in the transmission matrix, corruption in the body of the signal, wet leaves on the line outside Maidstone. No big deal."

She shook her head. "Not with a CUI."

"'Scuse me?"

"Constant unified image. Not possible. If there's three hats, there must be three images. And if there's three images—"

"It can't be a Reichenstafel. Yes, but it patently obviously is. Everything else about it is completely textbook."

In her eyes he could see a glint of foxlike envy; he'd done loads of Reichenstafels over the years and she'd never done one, even though she knew loads more about the theory than he did. "Sounds like it, agreed," she said.

"But with three slightly different images."

She froze with her fork a centimetre from her lips. "No," she said, in a quiet, ecstatic voice. "Not three images. A triple image."

Oink? "Sorry," he said, "I don't follow."

"Oh for crying out – Think about it, why don't you? It's a Reichenstafel, so it's got to be a CUI—"

"Constant unified image."

"Yup. Don't you get it? Constant unified means one subject, one image. So three images must mean—"

"Three subjects?"

She snapped her fingers and pointed to him, the way she used to when they were revising together and he'd got all the questions right. "Three subjects. That's logic, that is."

"Yes, but what does it mean? The woman in the pictures is always the same."

This time she did the impatient sigh. "One woman," she said, "three images. A triple image. Oh come on, Brian. Have I got to draw you a diagram?"

He felt like he'd bitten into a peppermint cream that had turned out to be toffee. "Just a second," he said. "Are you seriously suggesting—?"

"A trinity." She beamed at him. "You bet I am. Only you've got to promise me. When we write the paper, my name goes first."

"No way, Con," he said. "No such thing as a trinity, you know that. All the books—"

"Screw the books. Three hats. What else could it possibly be?" Her eyes were shining; irresistible, even if he'd wanted to, which he didn't. "This could be it, Brian. This could be my chair."

Ah, he thought. The sabre-toothed tiger out of the bag. Ever since he'd known her, what Consuela had always wanted, most in the world, hadn't been money or power or even happiness. No; what she'd set her heart on was a tenured professorship at Cambridge, Princeton or KIC Mombasa. It was the kudos, or the respect, or the research opportunities, or the free parking, he could never figure out which, but that was what she truly wanted, more than anything. And, yes; if she could prove the existence of a genuine triune entity, vice-chancellors would be fighting over her like sharks. But if she tried to and failed, the nearest she'd ever get to a job in further education would be as a lollipop lady. And the thought of Consuela dragging out a miserable existence among the ruins of her dreams was more than he could bear. Consuela triumphant, on the other hand; Consuela with her buttocks irremoveably wedged into a chair which he'd helped her to attain – Gosh, he thought.

"If we really could prove it," he said.

She leaned across the table towards him. This meant that a lock of her shiny black hair went trailing through her guacamole dip, but he decided not to mention it. "We can do it," she said. "Together."

Together – That's so not fair, he thought. That's exploiting someone else's deepest, most intimate feelings for personal gain. On the other hand, why the hell not? "OK," he said. "She's my client, mind. I'd have to square it with Tom Dawson first, and presumably you'd have to talk to Humph Wells and get permission—"

Her eyes glowed with scorn. "After seventeen years in a toilet? I don't see a problem, somehow. They're terrified of me."

Mr Teasdale leaned back in his chair. All the intensity was making his head hurt. "If only I could find those stupid paintings," he said.

"What paintings?"

"Didn't I mention the paintings? Oh, right. Somewhere at our place there's these paintings. I think they're eighteenth century, something like that. And I think the face is familiar."

"From the photographs?"

He nodded. "In which case," he said, "it's a double Reichenstafel, which is rare but not unheard of. And that might make it a bit of a bitch to fix."

"Don't you dare." Suddenly her eyes were steel pins. "Promise me. You don't fix it till I've had a chance to check it all out thoroughly. If you screw up my chance of a lifetime just for the sake of making a few bucks, I'll never speak to you again."

He remembered that he had twelve industrial-strength demons booked for Wednesday. "Fine," he said. "But I can't keep the client hanging about indefinitely, it wouldn't be fair."

"Screw the client."

He pretended he hadn't heard that. "Shouldn't be a problem," he said firmly. "You talk to Humph Wells, I'll talk to Tom, and keep your diary clear for Wednesday afternoon. It'll be fine. Just like old times."

The last bit had slipped out before he realised it, but she smiled. "Yeah," she said. "We could have some fun. We made a good team, I always thought."

Something was sticking in his throat, and he had an idea it wasn't the Thai fishcakes. Time to change the subject. "How's Hanuman?"

"Oh, he's fine. I think he misses you."

When they split up, she'd got custody of the familiar. Its corporeal form was a coal-black stump-tailed macaque, though right now it dangled from a chain round her neck in the shape of a little gold monkey with tiny sapphire eyes. He'd never actually liked it much, mostly because of its habit of stealing the dreams out of his brain while he was sleeping. She didn't know that, of course, and she doted on the little pest. "Give him my love."

He walked back to the office and stopped in the gents for a pee. He'd unzipped his fly and was squaring up to the porcelain when it cleared its throat, in a manner of speaking, shimmered and turned into Tony Bateman.

"Sorry," Tony said, "did I startle you?"

Mr Teasdale had just done up his zip in reckless haste. "A bit."

"I meant to put a sign on the door."

Mr Teasdale decided not to make an issue of it. After all, they'd hired Tony as an assistant sorceror mainly because of his shapeshifting abilities. A firm like Dawsons needed someone who could do that kind of stuff, they'd all agreed, if they wanted to offer potential clients a fully-rounded service in today's marketplace environment. True, Gina could make herself invisible, which was something, and both Tom Dawson and Mr Teasdale had bits of paper which said they could do it; but neither of them had had occasion to try since their final exams, and there's a difference between theoretical ability and actually charging the public money for it. Mr Sunshine could do it, of course, but that wasn't really any use, the way things stood. So they'd hired Tony and he'd turned out pretty well. He took a bit of getting used to, but (thought Mr Teasdale) don't we all?

"Next time, not a bad idea," Mr Teasdale said. "Out of interest, why a—?"

Tony grinned. He did that a lot. "Practising," he said. "I've got an undercover job coming up next week, and there's a couple of bits of plumbing I want to iron out before then."

Don't ask. "That's fine," he said. "You carry on. Just, in future, a sign, OK?"

"Sure thing, boss. Or I could practise in the ladies if you'd rather."

"No, don't do that."

"It isn't used nearly as much as the gents."

"Even so. Better not."

"Fair enough. I'll let you get on, then."

Tony shimmered, turned into a clothes moth and disappeared into the ventilator. Mr Teasdale stood for a moment, rapt in thought – he was speculating as to what the outcome might have been if the toilet Consuela had been stuck in for seventeen years had turned out to be someone like Tony Bateman – then remembered what he'd gone in there for and got on with it.

When he got back to his office, Gina was there waiting for him. "Found them," she said.

"Sorry?"

"The paintings. You know, the ones you were looking for. Ladies in frocks."

"Frocks? "You mean hats."

"Hats, too."

"Zowee," said Mr Teasdale happily. "Where are they?"

"You'll never guess."

He wouldn't have done, not in a million years. "What the hell are they doing in here?" he said, when they'd got there and she'd shown him.

"Search me."

"They weren't here – hang on, when was the last partnership meeting?"

"Second Tuesday of the month," Gina said, "so that makes it last week. No, you're right, they weren't. I'd have noticed."

Too bloody right she'd have noticed, and so would he, given what usually hung on the walls of the large downstairs meeting room. "That's a bit odd, in itself," Gina said, echoing his thoughts precisely. "I know I didn't put them here, or you, and I can't see Tom doing it."

"Or Tony or Ted or Jenny Swordfish."

"I don't know about Ted," Gina said thoughtfully. "Or at least not him, that bloody Harmondsworth. I wouldn't put anything past Harmondsworth."

They thought about that, both of them. "Assuming it wasn't him, though," Mr Teasdale said.

"It's odd, yes. Well?"

"Well what?"

"You wanted to see the pictures. Here they are."

He'd forgotten all about the pictures. "Women," he said. "Eighteenth century."

"Who's a clever boy, then?"

"You know me," Mr Teasdale said. "Can be trained to perform simple tasks." He peered at the three paintings, trying to make sense of what he saw. Three paintings: each one depicting two women, women in frocks; women in frocks and hats. In all three paintings, one of the women was different and unfamiliar, the other was the same and instantly recognisable; a cheerful, smiling woman, stout, dimpled, wearing a hat. Three different hats.

A trinity, thought Mr Teasdale, except everybody knows, they don't exist. He could picture the diagram in his textbook, *First Steps in Metaphysics*: a triangle with broken lines and the caption, three into one won't go. Consuela, he knew from bitter experience, didn't give a damn about presents. You could buy her diamonds or Lamborghinis or genuine Watteaus or Warhols and she'd just look at you and dump them in the next charity bag that came through the door. But if he could contrive to give her irrefutable proof of the existence of a real live triune entity, something that'd stand up to peer review in the *Journal of Transdimensional Studies*; that, he felt, would be different. That would be—

"Oh," Gina said, her voice intruding on his reverie like

a brick through a window, "and I looked out the file."

"File?"

"Wake up, Brian. Yes, the file. I got it out of storage. Found it in two shakes, thanks to your super-duper indexing system."

"There's a file."

"Of course there's a file, you halfwit, there's always a file." She had something in her hand; an old-fashioned padded envelope, the sort filled with fluffy grey stuff instead of plastic bubbles. "I had a quick flick through. Want to know what happened?"

He nodded, still staring at the paintings. Hats. Three hats.

"Well," Gina said, "it all started in seventeen fifty-something, when a fashionable London portrait painter came to see old George Loveridge about a problem he'd been having – You don't remember George, do you?"

"Before my time."

"Of course, he would be. Anyway, this painter—"

"Thomas Gainsborough."

"That's right. Isn't Wikipedia a wonderful thing? In my day we had to make do with disembodied talking heads and magic mirrors. Anyhow, Tom Gainsborough, nice man but seriously bad breath, made his living painting rich women in frocks. Good money, and he had a waiting list as long as your arm. Problem was, he'd finish a piccy and leave it to dry, and when he came back the next morning, she'd be there."

"In the painting."

"Precisely. And, no, nobody had a clue who she was, just like your punter with her wedding snaps. Anyway, as you can imagine this was a bit of a nuisance, because aristocratic ladies who'd spent a fortune having themselves done by Gainsborough didn't really want to share a frame with some stranger they'd never clapped eyes on before, and it was no use trying to pretend she was some kind of allegory, like Wisdom or Virtue or anything like that, because just look at her, she patently isn't. More like someone's aunt, you know, the sort you've got to invite to things but would really rather not."

"I don't know," Mr Teasdale said. "She looks rather jolly."

"Jolly," Gina said, "isn't a recognised allegorical trope. Anyhow, Tom tried painting her out, but that was no good, it screwed up the composition of the picture, and anyhow, she'd only come back a week later. Very embarrassing if he'd already delivered it to the customer."

"That's interesting," Mr Teasdale said. "When my client Photoshops her out, she stays Photoshopped."

"That's modern science for you," Gina said. "And people say there's no such thing as progress. Anyhow, you can see why Gainsborough came banging on the door. It was driving him nuts, poor bugger."

"Right," Mr Teasdale said. "So what did this George whatsisname do about it?"

"Loveridge," Gina said. "And he didn't do anything. He was still figuring out how to go about it when Gainsborough died."

"Died."

Gina nodded. "Suddenly."

"Ah."

"Without paying his bill," Gina added, "which is why we kept the piccies in lieu. We felt it'd be embarrassing sending his widow an invoice, since we hadn't actually done anything useful. Anyhow, that's how we left it, and the wretched things have been here ever since."

"I quite like them," Mr Teasdale said. "The light palette and easy, economical brushwork is strongly reminiscent of late Van Dyck, if you ask me."

"Bullshit," Gina said, not unkindly. "So what's the big deal with the hats?"

He hesitated. On the one hand, if Consuela found out he'd shared her hypothesis with someone else, she'd kill him. On the other hand, Gina was the smartest person he'd ever met, with the possible exception of Ted Sunshine. And he could trust her, couldn't he? He thought about that.

"I don't know," he said. "It's just, they're different."

"Most hats are." Gina looked at him, then at the artwork. "Of course," she went on, "it's a bit unusual to have substantial differences in appearance in the recurring pictorial manifestations in a Reichenstafel affinity."

"Constant unified image."

"That's the baby. Clever old you for knowing that. Usually they're exactly the same."

"Usually."

Gina frowned. "Invariably. You know what, Brian, this might be one for the journals."

"Oh, I don't think so," Mr Teasdale said quickly. "I think it's more likely that Gainsborough got bored painting the same hat over and over again, so he changed it."

Mistake. Thou Shalt Not try any funny business with Gina Noctis. The fact that she didn't comment said it all. Time to divert the attention stream, if possible.

"Someone needs to have a word with Tony Bateman," he said. "I was in the loo a while ago and just as I was about to—"

"Let me guess," Gina said. "Your bloody ex."

"What's she got to do with anything?"

"You've brought her in on this, haven't you?"

"No. Well, yes. I just happened to mention it, over lunch."

"You halfwit." Gina sighed. "You just won't learn, will you?"

Mr Teasdale resisted the urge to whimper. "There's no reason we can't still be friends."

"Balls," said Gina. "How many times have I got to tell you, stay away from that woman? She's no good for you, trust me."

"I think you're a bit hard on her, frankly."

"Oh for crying out loud. Who was it who had to talk you down off that ledge the last time? No, sorry, I tell a lie, the time before last. Last time it was the noose hanging from the hot-water pipes in the boiler room, and the heating's never been right since."

"Can we not talk about her, please?"

"You ought to get out more, Brian," Gina said patiently. "Meet someone nice. Get on with your life. There's plenty more fish in the sea and guess what? Only relatively few of them are barracudas."

"I'll try and bear that in mind," Mr Teasdale said stonily. "Thank you ever so much for your concern."

"Screw you, too," Gina said. "Only, think about it. Please. Believe it or not, I do actually have other things to do with my time apart from following round after you collecting up the shrapnel."

Ask Jenny Swordfish what was the most wonderful thing that had ever happened in the history of the universe, and she'd have replied without a moment's hesitation: online banking.

Jenny had been the cashier at Dawsons for three years;

not long enough to remember the dark old days before the internet, when doing the banking meant stuffing all the cheques and wire-transfer forms and treasury notes of different currencies and denominations into an old plastic shopping bag and taking them to the nearest branch. Since Dawsons, like nearly all the reputable firms in the trade, had its business accounts with the Bank of the Dead, it's not difficult to understand why the change to online meant so much to her. All she had to do was tap a few keys on a keyboard; no winding torchlit passages, no trips through the pitch dark on a creaking, leaky old boat, no sacrificing goats, no more walking in under an archway inscribed ABANDON HOPE, ALL YE WHO ENTER HERE, all the scary stuff she'd heard about from Mr Bevan, who'd retired the year she joined. True, the BotD's password and security protocols were a tad more stringent and imaginative than those of its mainstream high-street competitors, but since they tended not to involve feeding honeycakes to three-headed dogs, she wasn't complaining.

She took a sip of her coffee and typed in a password. Nothing. Frozen screen. Nuts.

She counted to thirty, then tried again. The screen went black for a second or so, and then, in the exact centre, the Eye appeared. It was lidless and red and seemed to stare directly into her soul.

"Oh, fuck a beetle," Jenny said wearily. "You again."

There appears, said a voice deep inside her head, to have been an attempt to obtain unauthorised access to your account information, originating from this device. Verification is required before you can be permitted to proceed.

Sometimes at this point, if you switched everything

off and turned it back on again – She leaned back in her chair, groping for the electric socket in the wall. A hand grasped her wrist. It was as cold as a corpse and slightly sticky. She looked down but there was nothing to see. She sighed.

Verification.

"Fine," Jenny said, "let's do it. I'll just finish my coffee, all right?"

The invisible hand let go. She leaned forward again, picked up her mug and drained the last two mouthfuls. Then she put the mug down on the desk. It shimmered and turned into Tony Bateman.

"Sorry," he said, helping her back into the chair she'd just fallen out of. "Didn't mean to startle you."

"Don't do that," Jenny said. "You know it grosses me out."

Tony had smears of lipstick on both cheeks and a grin on his face. "Sorry."

"I could report you for doing that." He was still grinning. "It's inappropriate."

"Yes, all right, don't go on about it. Can I have a few of those yellow forms for sending money back into the past? I used to have a stack of them but I ran out."

She opened a drawer, took out a pad of yellow forms and thrust it at him. "Remember," she said, "three copies. One for me, one for the file and one for Compliance. Got that?"

"Why is there a big red eye in the middle of your screen?"

"Oh, that. Stupid thing's locked me out and I've got to do all that verification rubbish."

"Ah, right. I thought it felt a bit chilly in here."

She glanced at him. The glance said, I would never

dream of asking anybody, especially you, to hang around and keep me company through the verification process, which is purely routine and which I'm perfectly capable of handling with no trouble at all. On the other hand, if you will insist on staying, that wouldn't be entirely objectionable. Tony caught the glance and nodded. For a jerk, he was surprisingly fluent in Unspoken.

"So what happens now?" he asked, in a low, talking-in-church voice.

"Well, usually, they—"

Out through the screen, like an actor appearing through closed curtains, came a creature. It started out small, but quickly grew until it was the size of a large ten-year-old. Its skin was the pale, matte grey of unmixed Portland cement, its eyes were huge and green and when it opened its mouth you could plainly see its three yellow teeth. It had skinny arms and very big hands.

"Oh," Tony said, in a voice very slightly higher than usual. "One of those."

"Well, it's since they introduced this new level four security," Jenny said. "It'll be all right so long as you don't do anything it thinks is a threat."

The creature squatted on the desktop in front of her, its bony wrists on its knees. "We asks it questions," it hissed, in a voice like oily condensation just inside your ears.

"Yes, all right," Jenny said. "Fire away."

"It doesn't like us, my love," the creature said. "The nassty fat one doesn't like us one bit. But we don't care. We asks it three questions, and if it gets them wrong, we eats it, yes, my love, we gobbles it all up." The eyes glowed traffic-light green, so bright you could've read by them.

Tony was gazing at the creature with horrified fascination. "Is it always like this?" he whispered.

"This is the level-six protocol," Jenny whispered back. "You should see the level eight."

A hiss from the creature, like steam. "No helping," it said. "The ugly skinny one mustn't help the nassty fat one, no, my love, otherwise we eats them both. We asks the fat one questions, and if she answers wrong—" The green glow was fierce enough to microwave a frozen pizza. "We asks the first question now, my love. Ready or not, here we comes."

It rocked back on its heels, tilted its head back, closed its eyes and began chanting in a high, shrill voice –

> *"Where pot steams and knife gleams,*
> *Fire glows and dreamer dreams,*
> *First he fusses,*
> *Then he cusses,*
> *Then he stamps and screams."*

"Oh, that's easy," Tony said. "Gordon Ramsay."

"Mustn't help." The creature's hands shot out, the fingers hooked like talons, stopping just short of Tony's throat. "Ugly skinny one mustn't help," it screamed, "or we eats them both. No helping, my love, that's the rules. Not fair otherwise."

"Gordon Ramsay," Jenny said.

"Not fair. Cheating."

"It's the right answer, though. Well, isn't it?"

A long, low hiss, and the eyes glowed a sort of dark ivy. "Nexxt question:

> *Seven seers with seven stones,*
> *What did they see?*
> *Orange eye in brown face*
> *All in a yellow sea."*

Jenny thought for a moment. "Poached egg on a muffin with Béarnaise sauce. Isn't that eggs Benedict?"

The creature growled dangerously. "The nassty fat one can't know, the nassty fat one is cheating, but we can't prove it, no, my love, we can't. But we asks the third question and then we eats them—

> *The other day upon the stair*
> *I found ten bucks that wasn't there.*
> *Ten trillion bucks weren't there today,*
> *Enough my many debts to pay."*

"Ooh, I know that one," Jenny said, clapping her hands together. "Quantitative easing."

The creature shot her a look so savage that she instinctively recoiled. "Swordfish, Swordfish, we hates it for ever," it squealed, "however, access to your accounts in now permitted. Have a nice day." Then it tore out its own throat with its fingernails and vanished.

The lights, which had dimmed, came back up. Her screen cleared and she found that she was looking at the BotD home page, albeit in an alphabet she'd never seen before—

"Ancient Sumerian cuneiform," Tony said, reaching past her for the mouse. "Hang on, that ought to do it." He opened a window and clicked. The screen was now in Martian Linear C. "Nuts," he said, clicking again. "All right, try that."

The screen went shiny gold and started laughing hysterically. Jenny took the mouse away from him and clicked a few times. The home page reappeared, this time in English. "It's fine," she said, "so long as you don't play with it."

"Sorry," Tony said. "Only trying to help."

"Please don't," Jenny said. "And you do realise, you nearly got us both eaten, showing off like that. And if you do that coffee cup thing one more time, I'll tell Gina Noctis. Got that?"

Tony muttered something about only a bit of fun, then nodded. "Right," Jenny said, "glad we got that cleared up. Now I've got a lot of work to do, so why don't you run along and play?"

She hadn't meant to slap him down quite so hard, though he'd deserved it. "Sorry," he said. "I was just kidding around, I didn't mean – Sorry."

Apologies, Jenny thought, are a bit like money: in theory, acceptable everywhere, supposed to be equal in value to the thing they're traded for; flash around a walletful of freshly printed apologies and everybody thinks you're the man ... Doesn't work like that, she decided. Still, he probably hadn't realised that, so in his terms he was doing his best. So she decided to accept his apology the way a grown-up accepts a child's home-made Christmas present: useless and vaguely insulting that anyone believes you could be palmed off with something like that, but it's the thought that counts.

"Forget it," she therefore said. "But unless there's something else you want, I am quite busy."

He edged away, a study of a puppy who's burnt his nose on the hot-water pipes. Jenny reached for the stack of cheque requisitions and the staple remover, which wasn't there—

"Can you see my staple remover anywhere?" she said, more to the room than anyone in particular.

Tony was just about the leave. "No," he said, having looked. "What the hell's a staple remover?"

"You know," she said, looking in all the drawers of the

desk, one by one. "Dinky little thing, looks like a Chinese dragon with really long teeth, and you bite staples out of things with it. Otherwise you've got to pry them apart with your fingernails and I hate that."

"I know what you mean. No, sorry, can't see it."

"Hell." In front of her were the cheque requisitions; a pink form stapled to a green sheet and a yellow memo. Dozens of the loathsome things, all needing to be done in time to catch the post. "Oh well, the hell with it. Why can nothing ever stay put in this place?"

Tony glanced at his watch. "How would it be if—?"

"What?"

He shimmered and turned into a staple remover. Jenny looked at it, sitting there on her desk looking pleased as Punch, and burst out laughing. "Oh, come on," she said. "You're an associate sorcerer, you've got work you should be doing."

He shimmered and turned back. "No bother," he said. "I'll stay late and do it. Staying late gets you Brownie points."

She looked at him. "Sure you don't mind?"

"Nah."

"In that case," she said, "if you could make the teeth a tad more curved, and I like the ones with the little plastic pad, so you don't chafe your fingers."

He frowned. "You wouldn't happen to have a picture, would you?"

She didn't, but Google did. "Like that," she said. "Maybe the teeth a little bit more pointy."

"Does it have to be chrome-plated? Only, plating gives me a rash."

"Ordinary stainless will do fine, if you can manage that."

"Piece of cake." He shimmered, and there on the desk was the best staple remover he could possibly be. She reached out and picked it up. It was faintly warm.

The windows of Mr Dawson's office rattled. All the lights had gone out, but that hardly signified, since the glare emanating from the other side of his desk was painfully bright, even through sunglasses. Forked lightning crackled out of the smoke detector and earthed itself in Mr Dawson's coffee cup.

"WHERE WERE YOU," said a Voice from the centre of the glare, "WHEN I LAID THE FOUNDATIONS OF THE EARTH?"

Mr Dawson sighed. "Yes, thank you, we'll let you know," he said. The glow went out, the windows stopped rattling, a card with a fancy logo and an email address floated flowly down and landed on Mr Dawson's desk as he crossed a name off a list with a heavy stroke of his pen. He paused, sniffed and switched on the extractor fan. Too much ozone gave him a headache.

He took another look at the list. He checked it twice. He sighed. Fifteen billion sentient beings were going to have to make do with one of those deadheads as their supreme being, unless he could come up with a viable alternative. Why, he asked himself, does everything always have to be my fault?

"Hello, Tom."

His head jerked up as though he'd been hanged. Sitting in the chair recently occupied by the thunder-and-lightning guy was someone he hadn't seen for a while, and whose absence had caused him very little distress, if any at all. "Hi," he said feebly. "I didn't know you were back in the UK."

"Oh, you know me, Tom," said Mr Ahriman, his partner. "I'm everywhere."

Which was, strictly speaking, true. But Mr Dawson tried very hard not to think about that. "Great to see you," he said. "You're looking good."

"Liar," said Mr Ahriman pleasantly, "and, no, by any meaningful criteria, I'm not. How's yourself?"

"Oh, so-so."

"Yes," Mr Ahriman said, and Mr Dawson felt like there was a terrier inside his chest, shaking and worrying his heart. "Right, that's the small talk out of the way. Where's my money?"

"Um," said Mr Dawson. "What money?"

Mr Ahriman favoured him with a thin smile, and it occurred to the very small part of Mr Dawson's brain that wasn't immediately occupied with registering terror that it was a great pity that Mr Ahriman wasn't eligible to be on the list. After all, he had all the effortless presence and power that the other candidates so singularly lacked. Also, if he could be persuaded to take the job, he'd be off in a completely different continuum, for ever and ever—

"Sorry," said Mr Ahriman. "Not my bag. Can you honestly say you see me as the compassionate and the merciful? No, thought not. The money, Tom. Where is it?"

"I wish you wouldn't read my mind," Mr Dawson mumbled. "It's not a very friendly thing to do, is it?"

"Ah, but I'm not your friend," Mr Ahriman said, "I'm your business partner, there's a difference."

"Fine," Mr Dawson said. "Look, if you know what I'm thinking, why do you bother asking me at all?"

"Because I like to see you squirm," said Mr Ahriman, with a gentle smile. "But we can do this non-verbally, if that's what you'd prefer."

A number of images appeared in Mr Dawson's mind. He screamed.

"Now that we're both singing from the same hymn sheet," Mr Ahriman said, "I'll just say this. Try harder. Work faster. Get stuck in. Don't be such a girl. Got that?"

"Got it."

"Outstanding," Mr Ahriman said, giving Mr Dawson a friendly pat on the shoulder. "Oops," he added. "That wasn't a new suit, was it?"

"No."

"That's the great thing about navy, doesn't show the scorch marks. Be seeing you, Tom. Look after yourself."

Mr Dawson looked up. The chair was empty. He stood up, tottered as far as the wastepaper basket and threw up. He'd just finished wiping bits off his chin when the door opened.

"Sorry," Gina said. "Bad time?"

He got up. All his joints ached and his head was swimming. "A bit," he said. "He was here. You just missed him."

"Lucky me. What's that smell?"

Mr Dawson made it back to his chair, just about. "We had a little chat about money," he said.

"Ah."

Talking was hard, because the stomach acid had stripped all the surfaces off the inside of his throat. "Bottom line," he said, "we need to make a lot more money quickly. Otherwise—" He looked at her.

"When you say a lot more money—"

Mr Dawson let his head sink into his hands. It was still spinning like crazy, but it took some of the weight off his neck. "He was a bit vague about actual figures," he said. "I got the impression it was along the lines of, think of a number, double it, double it again—"

"I don't think he cares about money," Gina said, "not per se. What he's into is the pain it causes."

"He's good at that," said Mr Dawson. "Actually, I don't give a stuff about his motivation or what he wants out of life, I'd just quite like to get him off my back for five minutes. So, we need ideas. Got any?"

"Probably not. Not the kind you're thinking of, anyhow."

"Then get some," Mr Dawson said. "Stat. Tell Brian, partnership meeting here, Wednesday at six. All the ideas we can possibly come up with, and then some."

"Hang on." Gina felt her skin prickle. Goosebumps. Talking of which, why geese, particularly? "Full partnership meeting?"

"Full partnership meeting."

"Jeez. Are you sure?"

"Yes."

Was it her imagination, or had the temperature dropped about five degrees? "Fine," she said. "I'll tell everybody."

"Not everybody."

A second can be a very long time. It only took a second for the primordial node to blast out the universe, but if you have a really expensive radio telescope you can hear the echoes of that second to this day. A second passed; one of those. "Oh come on, Tom. We can't not tell him. He'll be livid."

"If you tell him, he'll try and come. I've got enough on my plate right now without Ted Sunshine making a scene."

"But he'll know anyway. He always knows everything."

"Fine," Mr Dawson said. "You tell him. Tell him to stay away."

*

When you spend your working life on the edge, in the shaded zone where the Venn diagrams of Real and Unreal reluctantly intersect and To Be Or Not To Be is a very good question rather than a quotation, fear is a luxury you generally can't afford. But Mr Teasdale had a penchant for luxury, and he indulged himself in the form of a profound phobia about dentists. Mind you—

"There you go," the dentist said, applying a little gentle pressure. She was Australian and very good at her job. Something gave. "You'll be better off without that little bastard, I promise you."

She dropped the extracted tooth into a basin. It made an unusually heavy clunk. "Rinse away," she instructed, and Mr Teasdale swilled his mouth out with the nice pink liquid, then spat into the basin. The pink liquid swirled away, leaving behind a few shreds of what looked remarkably like gold leaf.

"Fuck a lizard," said the dentist.

She was staring at the tooth she'd just pulled out. It was, of course, pure gold.

"Id owwite," Mr Teasdale hastened to assure her. "Peffecly nawmuw. Doan hinkaba'it."

"But—"

"Doan hinkaba'it."

He could've explained, of course. Maybe he should have done so when he first signed up as a patient. In third year, one of the options had been alchemy; in alchemy you have to do a practical, and Mr Teasdale had chosen making a philosopher's stone; unfortunate mix-up with a beaker of elixir and a glass of cherryade, which happen to look identical. Ever since, all Mr Teasdale's discarded body parts and bodily products turned to .999 pure gold fifteen seconds after leaving him. Yes, that, too. And that. And, yes, it can be awkward but he'd had plenty of time to get used to it and arrange his life accordingly. In fact, it had been a prolonged bout of diarrhoea that had provided him with the capital to buy into the partnership in the first place—

But, yes, on balance he really ought to have explained first, because it's hard to be lucid and convincing when half your face is frozen stiff. Fortunately, he had a fall-back position which never failed. He reached into his pocket, took out his wallet and selected a photo-ID card. On it, among other things, were a name that wasn't strictly speaking his and the abbreviation MI6.

"Cla'ified," he said. "No a urd to a'ybo'y. Unerstood?"

"Fuck a lizard," the dentist breathed, awestruck. "You mean, like James Bond and stuff?"

Telling outright lies wasn't in Mr Teasdale's nature, so he winked. It seemed to do the trick. He retrieved the tooth and the wisps of gold leaf, signed various bits of paper and left.

The dentist's surgery was ten minutes' walk from the office. By the time he got back, the anaesthetic had worn off and Mr Teasdale had grown a new, perfectly sound tooth to replace the old one. In his desk drawer he had a bottle of rather special painkillers that really worked. Two of those, and it was as though the whole disagreeable incident had never happened. Lot of fuss about nothing, really.

His phone buzzed. "Your demons are here from Robertsons," said a voice.

"Thanks, stick 'em in the waiting room till I get there." He hesitated. "Harmondsworth?"

"Yup."

"What are you doing on reception?"

"Helping out."

Mr Teasdale sighed. "Right," he said. "I'll be there in two shakes."

It wasn't that he didn't like Harmondsworth; he was fine, in small doses, and at times it seemed like he positively enjoyed helping out, filling in, doing small but useful jobs for people. At other times – You had to be careful, that was all. Always remember, this is Harmondsworth we're talking about, and never ever turn your back on him for an instant.

The reception desk was apparently unoccupied when he got there. Mr Teasdale opened a few drawers, then found one that appeared to be locked. He knocked on it gently with one knuckle.

The drawer slid open an inch. A blue light emanated from the opening. Mr Teasdale pulled his hand away sharply and warmed it under his armpit.

"Thanks for minding the store," Mr Teasdale said. "You can go back upstairs now."

"What if I don't want to?"

"Ted probably needs you for something."

"Oh, all right."

The drawer flew open and Mr Teasdale turned away sharply, though not quickly enough to avoid getting an eyeful of what, for some reason, he always tended to think of as Pentecostal fire; anyway, it was the sort of dazzle that stays with you for ages, whether your eyes are open or shut. "Thanks again," he called out after it, because you didn't want to get on the wrong side of Harmondsworth, if you could help it. Then he shut the drawer, which was empty and smelt strongly of frankincense.

Which left the problem of who was going to look after reception, answer the phone, all that sort of thing.

A perennial nuisance, and it was all very well for Tom Dawson to say they couldn't afford to pay someone full-time, it looked bad to clients and leaving the front office unattended was a disaster waiting to happen. He sighed, pulled a single hair from his head and breathed on it. Then he let it go. It drifted down onto the floor and transformed into an exact replica of himself.

"Hello," said the hair, in an idiotic sing-song voice which always irritated him. "What do you want me to—?"

Mr Teasdale scowled at it, though really none of it was the hair's fault. The hair turned into a fair approximation of Naomi Campbell, circa 1990. Mr Teasdale felt rather guilty about that, but he was in a hurry and it wasn't his responsibility to organise staff rosters. "Mind the desk. Answer the phone. If there's any mail, sign for it. Got that?"

"Sure," the hair said. "That all?"

"That'll do for now."

He went through into the waiting room, where the demons from Robertsons were sitting round the table with the elderly magazines on it, playing snap. They looked up as he walked in. "Hi, boss," said one of them cheerfully. He recognised about half of them from previous jobs.

"Afternoon, lads," he said. "Sorry to have kept you."

"No worries," said a demon with the head of a fish. "Nice place you've got here."

"Thanks," Mr Teasdale said. "Got everything you need?"

One of the demons held up a black plastic bin liner. "All here, chief."

That was one of the things he liked about Robertsons. They were professionals. "Great," he said. "Right, follow me. The punter'll be here soon, so you can start setting up."

He led them to the big interview room and left them to it. By the time he got to the front desk the client was already there, with her laptop under her arm, asking his hair if she fancied doing a bit of freelance modelling in her spare time. It'd have been amusing to eavesdrop, but he was paying for the demons by the minute.

"Through here," he said. "Everything's ready."

By the time he got back to the big interview room, everything was well under way. It was bitter cold and pitch dark. "You might want to keep your coat on," he advised the client. "Watch out, there's a chair just – Oh, you found it, never mind. Take a seat, we'll be ready for you in two shakes."

From all four corners of the room simultaneously came faint whisperings, and a soft but persistent scratching, as of claws on parchment. Something scuttled over his foot. He groped for a chair and sat down—

"Sorry, chief."

"That's all right," he said, as the pain of frostbite shot up his sciatic nerve like information along a fibre-optic cable. "My fault."

"No worries."

He settled himself in his chair. "Not long now," he told the client. "If you could get one of the pictures up on your screen."

The laptop glowed next to him. The light from it didn't seem able to travel very far in that environment, but he could just about make out the face of the jolly woman, under her hat.

"That her, boss?" whispered a voice in his ear.

"Yup."

"Cool. Let the dog see the rabbit."

A ball of blue fire materialised in mid-air, hovered for a moment, then swooped down onto the screen, passed through it and came out the other side. It curved gracefully through the darkness, came to a halt and gradually moulded itself, as though it was plasticine in the hands of an invisible sculptor, into the jolly woman's face.

Mr Teasdale cleared his throat. "Hi," he said. "Thanks ever so much for coming."

The face turned and looked at him. Its eyes met his and he forced himself not to cry out. You know what they say about not looking into the sun; double that and add 15 per cent for luck. But Mr Teasdale knew about this stuff, especially the vital importance of maintaining eye contact.

"What?" said the face.

"Well," Mr Teasdale said, "if it's all right with you, we'd rather like to know who you are."

The face didn't like that, one bit. Mr Teasdale felt the intensity of its displeasure the full length of his optic nerve and right back deep into his brain. "Really," said the face.

"Well, yes," said Mr Teasdale, whose jaw had started aching again. "You see, you're making it quite hard for my client to earn a living, so if we can sort of clear up what it is you want, that'd be quite nice for everybody all round, don't you think?"

"You want to know what I want."

Little bits of gold leaf were biting into Mr Teasdale's gums. "Yes, actually."

"Very well. On your head be it."

The face, it turned out, didn't do metaphorical. The ball of blue fire shot in between his eyes. A fraction of a second later, it came out of his left ear. A fraction of a second can be a very long time.

"Right," Mr Teasdale croaked, when he'd got his voice working again. "Got you. If you'd like to leave it with me, I'll see what I can do."

"Presumptuous mortal," said the ball of blue fire. "Miserable creature of a day, farewell."

The ball exploded in a blaze of sparks. Then all the lights came back on, and the demons were busy packing up, folding things and putting them in boxes and zip-up bags, hoovering under the chairs, squirting aerosols of air freshener. The client stared at them, frozen in horror, but Mr Teasdale made no effort to reassure her. He had other things on – in – his mind.

"Cheers, then, boss," said a demon. "We'll see ourselves out."

Mr Teasdale nodded. It was the best he could do, and the demons seemed to understand. They left quietly, closing the door behind them. He stood up, found that his knees weren't up to that sort of abuse and sat down again.

"What," asked the client, "were those things?"

It took him a moment to figure out what she was talking about. "Oh, them," he said. "Demons. From Robertsons. We could've got a better deal from Honest John's House of Fiends, but in this business, frankly, you get what you pay for."

"They were—" She shuddered. "Were they real?"

"Real as you and me," Mr Teasdale said, trying not to sound impatient. It was hard to remember sometimes, when he found himself faced with a new and challenging technical problem, that for the customer all this stuff was new and quite possibly a little bit intimidating. "We don't need them any more," he said reassuringly. "So you needn't—"

"They're real. They exist. Oh my God. Does that mean

there's, like, you know, a hell? And a heaven? And God and stuff?"

"Moving on," Mr Teasdale said, "I think I can say we've now got a handle on all of this, and with any luck we ought to be able to sort it out for you, though I wouldn't be happy committing myself to a hard-and-fast timescale at this moment in, um, time. We know what we're up against, though, going forward, and that's absolutely half the battle. Five-eighths, really."

She was staring at him. "Because if there's, like, you know, a God or something, I – I don't know. What should I do?"

He looked at her. It wasn't an uncommon reaction, but he never felt comfortable dealing with it. "Eat more organic vegetables," he said firmly. "I think He'd like that. And try and cut your carbon footprint down as much as you possibly can."

"That'd help?"

"Well, it can't hurt, certainly. Meanwhile, while you're doing that, I'll crack on with the next stage of getting that woman out of your pictures."

The look on her face suggested that the intrusive woman was the least of her problems, right now. Oh dear, he thought. But she'd paid in advance so that was OK, and in his experience these sudden epiphanies tended to wear off in a day or so, leaving behind nothing more than confusion and embarrassment. "Maybe," she said, "I should get a bicycle. You know, instead of a car."

He nodded approvingly. "That's the ticket," he said. "I'll show you out. This place is a bit of a maze until you're used to it."

He got rid of her. His hair was still on the front desk. He glanced over her shoulder at her computer screen and noted that while he'd been gone, she'd managed to dis-prove Einstein's theory of general relativity and was about to have a stab at the laws of thermodynamics. Chip off the old block, he thought. "Jolly good," he said, "carry on."

He went up the stairs to his office. His legs ached and his ankles hurt. He remembered that they had a part-nership meeting at six. "Bloody hell," he moaned softly to nobody in particular, closed his door and sat down in his chair.

Well now, he thought. Probably what he ought to do was get it all down on paper, in the form of an attendance note, before he forgot any of it. That was proper proce-dure, and the insurance company got very stroppy if the attendance notes weren't on the file and up to date, but he decided that the chance of him ever forgetting anything of what the intrusive woman had told him were pretty slim, in fact size zero. Even so. He woke up his screen with a sullen prod and started to type.

He hadn't got far when the door opened. Nobody ever knocked at Dawsons.

"Well?" said Gina.

He leaned back in his chair. "Oh, fine," he said. "I had to have it out, but actually it was a piece of cake and it stopped bleeding almost immediately."

She glared at him. "After that," she said.

He closed his eyes and let all his muscles sag. "You will not believe," he said, "what I've gone and got myself into this time."

She sat down. "Spit it out," she said.

He took a deep breath, eyes still shut. "I got in touch with the hats woman," he said. "Three guesses who she turns out to be."

"Brian, I'm not in the mood."

"Three guesses."

Sigh. "Someone we know, obviously."

"That's not a proper guess. Try again."

"I don't know, do I? Tell me."

"Fine," Mr Teasdale said. "Are you sitting comfortably? Then I'll begin."

PRANCER

M r Sunshine pulled open the top left-hand drawer of his desk and took out the bottomless purse.

Harmondsworth had, of course, told him about the partnership meeting, to which, of course, he hadn't been invited. Which was all wrong, needless to say, but there wasn't a great deal he could do about it without starting a full-scale war, and for some reason he had a feeling that now wasn't the right time for all that. Accordingly—

He opened another drawer, in which sat the mysterious parcel, Not To Be Opened &c. He frowned. Technical problem. "Harmondsworth," he said. "Flights of angels."

"Coming right up."

Harmondsworth's idea of a flight of angels wasn't one he entirely shared; there were only three of them and they looked more like dissipated butterflies. But they soared in, swept the mystery package out of the drawer, hovered with it balanced between their tiny, beating-so-fast-as-to-be-invisible wings, then at his direction lowered it into the bottomless purse, whose mouth expanded to take it and then contracted back to its normal size. Then the angels fizzled out like sparklers, and Mr Sunshine was left holding the purse. It was heavier than normal, and almost uncomfortably warm.

"Smart," said Harmondsworth. "There's nowhere you can hide it where he won't find it, but now he daren't touch it for fear of getting frizzled up."

"You could've hidden it," Mr Sunshine said, with mild reproach. "In with you."

"No. Sorry. I have to live there."

Mr Sunshine sighed. Fair enough, he thought. "Could you at least make it glow a bit?" he said, "so it actually looks contaminated?"

"Sure."

The purse glowed with a revolting green light. "Perfect," Mr Sunshine said, and put the purse away in its drawer, which he then locked with a small brass key. "Now then," he said. "About that parcel."

"Been investigating," Harmondsworth said. "Not good."

"You don't say."

"Ran spectrographic analysis. Performed quantum scan. Created virtual simulation in order to ascertain metaphysical density quotient in seventeen different spatio-temporal aspects."

"And?"

"It's not from around here."

"I sort of gathered that. Anything else?"

There was an unusually long pause. "You're not going to like this."

Mr Sunshine frowned. "Go on."

"Belongs to someone."

"Oddly enough, so do a lot of things. What about it?"

"Someone we know."

"Ah."

"Someone in particular."

He'd known Harmondsworth a long time, and vice versa. Between them, therefore, some things didn't need to be put into words, even assuming that appropriate words could be found. "Oh balls," said Mr Sunshine. "Not really?"

"Afraid so."

"For crying out loud." Mr Sunshine composed himself, just in time. Already, outside the window, the sky was iron-grey and the first raindrops were starting to fall. "Harmondsworth."

"Present."

"Have we got a recent address for – for—?"

"Yes."

"That's all right, then. Wrap it up in brown paper and send it on."

"Address recent but obsolete. Not there any more."

"She's not there?"

"Address not there. Blown up."

That figures, thought Mr Sunshine. You make yourself sufficiently unpopular, people start reaching for the nuclear warheads. "Hang on, though," he said. "We've got an address, haven't we? On Alpha Centauri."

"Confirmed."

Mr Sunshine hesitated. It was a lot to ask. On the other hand – "Harmondsworth."

"Present."

"You wouldn't do me a small favour, would you?"

"No."

"Oh, come on. It's not all that far. Practically down the end of the street."

"Distance to Alpha Centauri currently 4.37 light years. No scheduled public transport. Very cold in space."

For a split second, Mr Sunshine was angry. People saying no to him had that effect. He could command; issue a direct order. But did he want to do that? To Harmondsworth? No, he decided, probably not. The fact that you can do a thing often means that you can't; not if you have to live with yourself afterwards. "Fine," he said, "you don't have to if you don't want to."

"I don't want to."

"But it leaves us with a serious problem," Mr Sunshine went on. "It means there's a real danger she'll turn up here to collect it."

"Horror."

"Quite. Of course, that doesn't affect you as directly as it affects me. Even so—"

"Horror."

Mr Sunshine sighed and looked at his watch. In ten minutes they'd be starting the partnership meeting, without him. One damn thing after another. Maybe, he thought, maybe it really is time to retire; pack it all in, get away from it all, a cottage in the country somewhere, roses round the door, a nice bit of garden to look after, a kennel for Harmondsworth outside the back door, peace, tranquillity, watching the suns set on the verandah with a glass in his hand, contentment, boredom, senescence, death. Or maybe not. The alternative was taking arms against a sea of troubles and by opposing ending them, but he was used to that. "Forget it," he said. "It was just an idea."

"Noted."

"And if she comes here," Mr Sunshine said decisively, "we'll just have to try and be nice to her, that's all."

Partnership meetings – formal ones, with minutes, as opposed to casual bumpings-into-each-other in the corridors and heated discussions in the mail room – didn't happen every day at Dawsons, so there were established protocols, almost verging on rituals. Meetings always took place in the big conference room on the fifth floor (in the ordinary course of events the building only had four floors). The partners sat around a beautiful round table made of figured walnut and polished to a mirror finish; the finish was, in fact, a genuine functional imp-reflecting mirror, which means that your reflection in it shows you as you truly are. In the middle of the table there would be a small rosewood box with its lid open. Inside the box was a chip of masonry salvaged from the Palace of Truth after it was finally demolished. Inside the Palace of Truth, you don't need reminding, it was physically impossible to tell a lie. Whether or not the chip actually had the same effect nobody was entirely sure, mostly because they were too scared to put it to the test. On the conference room walls hung portraits of all the partners, placed so that they had their backs to them, understandably enough. There was a reason why none of the partners looked a day over forty, but they didn't necessarily want to be reminded of it.

The whole point of a round table is that it doesn't have a head, but traditionally the partners only used one side of it, forming a semicircle. The other side of the table was reserved for Mr Ahriman, who never turned up, though a pad of paper, pencils and a cup of tea were always laid out for him, just in case. Gina Noctis always took the minutes, because she was the only one of them with legible handwriting.

"Right," Mr Dawson said, "we're all here, let's get started. Minutes of the last meeting taken as read?"

Everybody nodded, and a faint tapping noise came from the massive iron box on the tabletop opposite the fifth, empty, chair. One tap for yes, two for no. Two taps.

"Pack it in, Jerry," said Mr Dawson irritably to his evil twin inside the box, "this is no time for larking about. Minutes of the last meeting approved as read?" One tap. "Thank you. Let's move on. Item one on the agenda, we need to generate considerably more income. Suggestions?"

Dead silence.

"Oh, come on," Mr Dawson said, "there's got to be something we can do. Brian. How's the irritable bowel syndrome?"

"I haven't got irritable bowel—"

"Yes, but you could have."

Mr Teasdale scowled at him. "We've already been into all that about a million times. What comes out of me is mine, period, end of conversation."

"Not if it's on partnership premises," Mr Dawson said wearily. "In which case, it's partnership property. Come on, Bri. Sometimes you've got to take one for the team."

"No."

"That's a rather selfish attitude, if you don't mind me saying so."

"Tough."

Frantic tapping from inside the iron box, subsiding gradually. "All right," Mr Dawson said, "if that's your last word, we'd better move on. Gina."

"I don't know why you're looking at me like that," Gina said. "I haven't got any ideas."

"Gina—"

"You can't just summon a meeting and expect Brian and me to solve all your problems. It's not fair, unloading it all on us. We didn't get you in this mess, remember, so I don't see why we should be expected to get you out again."

"Gina. Please."

"What I don't understand," Mr Teasdale said, "is why you don't just buy the bastard out. One-off capital sum and we're shot of him, for good."

An agonised look passed over Mr Dawson's face. "You think I haven't tried. He won't play ball. You know as well as I do, he isn't in it for the money."

"He can't have it both ways," Mr Teasdale said stubbornly. "Either he wants to squeeze you for every penny he can get, or he doesn't."

"You don't know him like I do," Mr Dawson said quietly.

There was no answer to that. Mr Teasdale and Gina exchanged an uncomfortable look. "All right," Mr Teasdale said, "let's explore our options. Expand the business. Get into profitable new sectors."

"Such as?"

"Um."

Mr Dawson looked at him. It was the sort of expression you might expect to find on the face of a dying sun. Mr Teasdale's brain raced, lost its traction and spun out of control. "Entertainment and media," he said.

"What?"

What indeed? "Well," he said, "you've heard of Industrial Light & Magic? We could do that."

The dying sun looked sceptical. "Last I heard, Zauberwerke had all that side of the business sewn up.

No offence, but the last thing we need right now is a pissing contest with Otto Schlimm and his boys. Besides, it'd take too long. We need to find a way of getting more money out of our existing client base. Suggestions?"

Gina frowned. "Go take a running jump?"

"That's a suggestion, certainly," said Mr Dawson. "But not a helpful one. Come on, Gina, what about hustling some of those old-money clients of yours? Find some problem they never knew they had and fix it for them."

Gina's eyes flashed, and the whole building started to shake. "Fuck you, Tom," she said. "It's taken me a thousand years to earn the loyalty and trust of my client base, and I'm damned if I'm going to throw all that away just because you've got yourself into a jam. This is all your fault anyhow. If you hadn't squeezed out Ted Sunshine—"

The iron box rocked violently to and fro and fell off the table onto the floor. Condensation was dripping down the oak-panelled walls. Mr Teasdale made an awkward coughing noise.

"Moving on," he said. "What about financial services?"

The other two turned their heads and looked at him. "Go on," said Mr Dawson.

"Well." His mind was a total blank. Then a voice from his subconscious whispered something in his inner ear. "Historically based fiscal engineering," he said.

"What the hell is that supposed to mean?"

Good question. He waited for the prompt. It came. "A whole new spatio-temporally grounded approach to tax efficiency for major corporations," he said. "All right, try this. You're a giant multinational with a virtual monopoly on e-commerce, but you find you're making ridiculous sums of money and nasty governments want you to pay tax on it. So what you do is this. You start up a small wholly owned subsidiary in, say, 1539, and another in 2520, and you hive off your excess profits into the past, generations before corporation tax was even thought of—"

"Old hat," Mr Dawson snapped. "Orinoco have been doing it for years. And Weeble."

"Oh." Mr Teasdale frowned. "Have they? I didn't know that."

"God, you're naïve. Anyway, JWW and Sympersons practically own that sector, we'd never get a look-in. Also, as I just said, it'd take too long. We need revenue now." He sighed, slumped forward and let his head drop into his hands. "All right," he said. "I vote we go through our current workload case by case and see what scope we've got for gouging the customers hollow. Brian, you first."

Mr Teasdale hesitated. "I'm not sure I've got anything particularly relevant to the—"

"Oh come on," Mr Dawson snapped. "You're working on something, aren't you? You're not just sitting with your feet up reading a book?"

"Tom," Gina said. "Lay off him, will you?"

"Of course I'm working on something," Mr Teasdale snapped back. "I'm up to here with work, if you must know. It's just, I don't think what I've got going right now is gouging-friendly."

Mr Dawson pulled a face. "Piss-arse private client stuff. If I've told you once—"

"Oh it's not that," Mr Teasdale replied dangerously. "Quite the opposite, if you must know. This is too big—" He stopped, two syllables too late. Mr Dawson was looking at him. So was Gina Noctis.

"Too big?" she echoed. "Brian, is this something we need to notify the insurers about?"

He shook his head. "It's under control, I promise you. I can handle it."

"Is there money in it?" Mr Dawson demanded.

Mr Teasdale thought about that. "Well," he said, "I guess money is a part of Everything, so I'd have to answer yes, there is."

"Everything," Gina said. "Brian, we don't do Everything. It explicitly says so in the partnership agreement. We don't do divorce, missing persons, stray pets or Everything. It's not worth the hassle."

"Shut up and let him finish," Mr Dawson said. "What have you done?"

So Mr Teasdale told them all about it, beginning with the hats and ending with what the blue ectoplasmic face had told him, deep inside his mind. When he'd finished, he leaned back in his chair and wiped his forehead with his sleeve.

"Christ almighty," Gina said.

Mr Dawson looked like an American lawyer who's just been run over by God. "There's money in that," he whispered. "Loads of money."

Mr Teasdale gave him a terrified look. "Yes, but—"

"Tom," Gina said, with a terrible urgency, "let me talk to Ted Sunshine. If I explain just how bad things are, I'm sure I can get him to help you out with that purse of his. I know he hates you, but if I asked him to do it for my sake—"

"Screw Ted Sunshine," Mr Dawson said quietly. "We don't need him. We're going to be rich."

"Tom, I'm a partner in this firm and I'm telling you here and now, we are not going to—"

"Shut your face, Gina, you're outvoted. Jerry and me against you and Brian, and I've got his—" he nodded towards the empty chair "—proxy, so it's three to two. Sorry, but there it is. I'll just get you to note that in the minutes."

Gina was furious. "Since when did Jerry get a vote?"

Mr Dawson shrugged. "He's a partner, Gina, same as you and me. It's a done deal. Live with it."

There was a terrible moment. If anyone had been foolish enough to strike a match, a lot of maps would've needed to be redrawn. Then Gina said, "Of course. We've voted on it, so that's fine. I'll write it down like you said. Just don't blame me, that's all."

Mr Dawson looked at her, and it occurred to him that just possibly she knew something about all this that he didn't. If circumstances had been different, he'd have asked. As it was, he didn't really think he could. "Great," he said. "Thank you so much for your cooperation. Now, let's talk this through and figure out how we're going to optimise it, from a revenue perspective."

By his foot, the iron box rattled violently. He ignored it.

Tony Bateman had been working late, but nobody seemed to have noticed. He scowled at his office wall, which looked back at him in the manner of Nietzsche's abyss. A whole hour; complete waste of time and virtue. If a tree falls in the forest and there's nobody there to saw it up into planks and sell it to a lumberyard, what good is it to anybody? Answer: none at all.

Actually, working was a slight overstatement. He had the KostSlasha discount warehouse file open on the desk in front of him, but he hadn't looked at it; he'd spent the hour of his irreplaceable life since theoretical going-home time reading customer reviews on whichhelicopter. com, though unless he got a decent bonus this year, the research was largely academic. Still, the Airbus looked pretty cool, but the Agusta probably had the edge over the Kawasaki in honest-to-God bang-for-buck durability, as against the sheer street legend status of the Bell—

Something scuttled. He looked up from his screen, finger hovering. Mice? In this office? Really? Anything's possible, but he didn't think so. He waited, holding his breath. There it was again, the patter of tiny paws. I'm good at this, he remembered, A* in first-year end-of-term exams. He visualised the scuttler with his mind's eye, envisioned an outcome and let fly.

As the smoke cleared and the ringing in his ears died away, he also remembered the examiner's caveat, scrawled at the foot of his assessment report: must be careful not to overdo it. Ah well.

He stood up, expecting to see tiny gobbets of mouse shrapnel sprayed across the wall. Instead, he saw a woman in a business suit lying on the floor with her head in the wastepaper basket. Fuck a stoat, he thought, I've killed someone.

That proved not to be the case; and when she groaned and lifted her head out of the bin he was able to update his assessment: an attractive brunette in a business suit, madder than a wet hen. "You idiot," she said. "You could've killed me."

Not really, since the charge was tailored to a twenty-gram mouse rather than a fifty-kilo human. He didn't point that out, however, because sometimes the truth isn't what people want to hear. "Sorry," he said. "I thought you were a mouse. Actually," he added, with a frown, "you were a mouse."

"Don't be ridiculous."

"No," Tony said, "you were. I know, because I

visualised you. You were about yay long, grey, with a tail."
He grinned. "It's OK," he said. "I'm one, too."

"A mouse."

"A shapechanger."

She wilted slightly, or maybe melted would be closer
to the mark. "Fine," she said, "I was a mouse. What are
you going to do about it, report me?"

"Well," Tony said, "you don't work here and you were
sneaking about after hours disguised as a mouse, so
maybe I should, since you mention it."

She shook her head. "I wouldn't if I were you," she said,
"not unless you enjoy being embarrassed. So happens I'm
a very close personal friend of one of the partners."

"No kidding." His mind whirred and clicked. The way
she'd said it implied – "You must be Brian Teasdale's—"

"Ex-wife, yes. Consuela Teasdale. And you are?"

"Tony Bateman."

"He hasn't mentioned you."

"Well, why would he? I'm just a wage slave."

She grinned. "A wage slave with an interest in private
helicopters."

Gosh, he thought. From the other side of the
room, transformed into a mouse? "Only entry-level,"
he mumbled.

"Sure. Now, let me give you a word of advice."

"All right."

She looked straight at him, and he couldn't help
noticing that her eyes were as deep and as brown as the
bottomless pits of you-know-what reserved for blasphem-
ers in the third circle of hell. "You don't want to bother
with the Agusta."

"No?"

"Nah. If it ain't a Sikorsky it's not worth having. So if I

were you, I'd carry on saving up my pennies until I could afford the real thing. Nobody likes a cheapskate. Is Brian in his office, do you know?"

"Haven't seen him," Tony said, in a voice that came out all funny.

"Shucks. Doesn't matter, I know the way."

She transformed back into a mouse, darted into a tiny hole in the skirting board and vanished, leaving Tony staring. It took him a surprisingly long time to pull himself together.

The mouse emerged at the bottom of a drainpipe in a back alley, shook itself and walked down Moorgate towards the Bank. Bastards, she thought. Evil, cheating, treacherous bastards.

At least her brief foray into industrial espionage had confirmed her suspicions; it had to be a trinity, it couldn't be anything else, not the way Brian had described it at the meeting. Maybe even a – She realised there wasn't an established academic term for four entities in one, and 'foursome' probably had the wrong connotations. Anyhow, maybe even one of those. So far, so good; but not once during the meeting had that rat Brian mentioned her name or the fact that he'd promised faithfully to bring her in on the case; strongly implying that either he'd forgotten all about her or that he was too scared of that jerk Dawson to make good on his solemn undertaking. For crying out loud, she thought, is he a man or a mouse? Well, quite. A rat and a mouse; suddenly, rodents everywhere. The difference was, she could stop being one any time she liked. She wasn't sure the same held true for her ex-husband.

The firm of JWW, formerly J. W. Wells & Co. before

the hedge fund bought out the few surviving partners, has been in St Mary Axe for centuries, back when that splendid highway was still just a muddy ditch. These days, you can't just walk in off the street. If you're a client, you send a text message from wherever you happen to be and a footman in full livery materialises in front of you and escorts you through a transdimensional portal into the main lobby. The staff entrance is rather less ostentatious. Senior management gain access by walking on the crack between two specific paving stones directly outside. Junior staff have to turn themselves into raindrops and aim for the guttering on an adjacent building. Theoretically, Consuela should've been a raindrop, but use of the crack had been given to her as part of her settlement package after the toilet incident, at her express insistence. She wasn't one of Nature's raindrops, as anyone who knew her well would be happy to confirm.

Once you're inside, you'd never guess that you were in a building that doesn't, strictly speaking, exist. The JWW offices are situated in Custardspace, an artificial dimension invented and patented by the late Professor van Spee (of Leiden) when he was briefly a partner in JWW. Originally, Custardspace was intended for limited applications, such as the hugely successful portable parking space (take it anywhere, unroll it, simple as that). Later on, in collaboration with the much-dreaded venture capital outfit Blue Remembered Hills Inc., JWW retroengineered the concept so as to be applicable to real estate, building huge developments of luxury homes in tiny cracks and crevices of the space/time continuum undetectable by any instrumentality known to current science, but still offering quick and easy access to shops, public transport and a wide range of leisure facilities. A knee-jerk reaction to the collapse of the Summeracres retirement resort into the existential void led to onerous planning restrictions which made Custardspace uneconomic as a source of building land, but nevertheless JWW, with a touch of defiance befitting one of the oldest and proudest firms in the profession, insisted on using it when they built their new office complex at the turn of the twenty-first century. Faceless local government bureaucrats immediately issued an enforcement order requiring that the whole lot be pulled down forthwith, but since JWW (Holdings) Ltd has its registered office on 7 Alpha Leonis somewhere around AD 6260, there's not a lot they can do about it. The Lord Mayor of London no longer sends the JWW CEO a Christmas card, but that's about it.

Thanks to a nasty outbreak of open-plan design about the time of the refit, Consuela had a workspace rather than an office. In theory, this should've resulted in ideas sharing, networking and team-structured problem-solving in conjunction with the dozen or so other unfortunates kettled up in the cattle pen. In practice, the first thing everybody did was run up the most impressive set of Chinese walls that his or her professional abilities allowed. Consuela's bit of space was protected by curtains of fire, extending from the carpet to the ceiling, through which only the pure in heart and colleagues of her pay-grade and above could pass without being utterly consumed. This meant she had to fetch her own coffee, but she reckoned that was a small price to pay for not having people breathing down her neck all the time.

She stepped through the fire, which had the added benefit of burning away all the dust and grime of the city streets, and dropped into her chair. Twenty-six messages for her on her screen, but she couldn't be bothered with them.

The bastards, she thought; all the partners in Dawsons in general, and Brian in particular, all banded together to cheat her out of the first, possibly the only authentic trinity so far discovered. She'd see about that.

When a volcano cools, its fiery effluent turns to hard, hard rock. Slowly and deliberately, Consuela dissected the situation, looking for a weak point she could burrow in through. It didn't take her long. Dawsons were only involved and authorised to act in the matter because this idiotic wedding photographer – what was her name? Lilith something, Lilith McGregor – was their client. So: easy peasy. If Lilith decided to take her business elsewhere, Dawsons would be out of the game, simple as that, and she'd have it all to herself. All she had to do was persuade this silly little girl that she'd be better off with JWW handling her business, rather than some ma-and-pa outfit with an office over a chemist's shop—

Overstating the case just a bit, maybe, but not by all that much. The problem was, JWW did tend to charge rather a lot of money for its services, and doing jobs for free was frowned on by the management. She had, she knew, a certain degree of latitude thanks to the toilet thing, but she wasn't convinced of her ability to parlay that into taking on a major project with no prospect of the firm getting paid for it. Unless—

She clicked on a few things, and up came the client database. She selected a particular client, read the brief and smiled. That, she decided, would do nicely. Of course she'd have to clear it with the boss, but that oughtn't to be an insuperable difficulty, especially if it meant robbing a client from under Tom Dawson's nose; no love lost there, open secret. Provided it was done tactfully, no problem at all.

A few keystrokes and she had a nicely phrased memo ready to send. She read it over and sent it. A minute or so later, back came the reply from her direct superior. It read:

Sure, kiddo. Go for it.

She grinned. Practically a licence to kill, and print money. Her only regret was that she wouldn't be there to see Brian's face when he realised what she'd done to him. Hey-ho.

"Get away," said Mr Sunshine.

"Straight up," said Gina. She hesitated. "Ted," she said, "you don't happen to know these people, do you?"

Mr Sunshine's face was illegible, like badly weathered hieroglyphs. "I might do," he said. "I know lots of people. But it sounds like it was all a very long time ago, so I don't suppose they'd remember me."

Gina doubted that, but he was doing the Big Stone Face, so she let it go. "Ring any bells?"

"Most things do," Mr Sunshine said evasively. "My life is a veritable feast of campanology. But nothing immediately springs to mind. Look," he added, sitting down at his desk and opening a drawer, "why don't we run through it all again, just to make sure I've got it straight in my head?"

"Ted—"

"Please," Mr Sunshine said. The inside of the drawer was glowing blue, and it occurred to Gina that maybe the recapitulation wouldn't be solely for his benefit. "I'd have thought," she said, nodding at the drawer, "he'd have heard it all already."

A hard look crossed Mr Sunshine's normally aimiable face. "No," he said. "Apparently Tom Dawson's found some new way of keeping Harmondsworth out. So he wasn't there at the meeting."

If that's true, Gina thought, Tom is considerably smarter than he looks. She resolved to bear that in mind. "All right," she said. "From the top?"

"Please."

"Here goes, then," Gina said. "It turns out to be all about that Gainsborough woman."

"The one with the hats."

"That's right. Now at least we've got a name for her."

"Tiamat the Destroyer," Mr Sunshine said. "Ancient triple-aspected Goddess of Life, Death and Rebirth in ancient Mesopotamia. With you so far."

"Well," Gina went on, "that's who's taken to cropping up uninvited in Lilith McGregor's wedding snaps. Also in Tom Gainsborough's paintings, but he died before he could do what she wanted him to. Apparently, associating with this woman is bad for you."

A muscle twitched at the side of Mr Sunshine's face. "Apparently," he said. "Tiamat the Destroyer. Haven't heard that name in a long time."

"Lucky old you," Gina said, "because by all accounts she's not a very nice person. In one of her aspects, anyhow. Presumably when she's being Life and Rebirth she's an absolute sweetie."

"Oh, I don't know," Mr Sunshine said. "Anyhow, let's get on. Tiamat—"

Gina looked at him. "You seem to be having trouble with the name."

"Not really. It's just – Well, you know how it is. You know someone for thirty years as Tom or Gus or Max, and so when people start talking about Thomas and Augustus and Maximilian it all sounds a bit odd somehow."

"I see. You know her as—"

"I wouldn't say know exactly. But back in the day, she was mostly known as Dolly."

"Dolly?"

Mr Sunshine nodded. "Short for the Abominable Idolatry of the Ishmaelites. Pal of mine used to call her that, and it sort of stuck. You know how these things do. There was a time people used to call me Smiler. Not any more, I'm delighted to say."

"Dolly."

"It'd make it easier for me, if that's all right with you."

"All right," Gina said. "Dolly the Destroyer—"

"Just Dolly will do."

"This woman," Gina said, "claims to have been trapped in an asteroid for four thousand years, thanks to a spell cast on her by an evil wizard."

"Her ex-husband."

"That's right, yes. Anyway, she's really not happy about it, and although she can't get out of the asteroid without the key, recently she's figured out how to make it do what she wants. So right now she's got it pointed at Planet Earth with the throttle set to ramming speed."

Mr Sunshine nodded. "That's Dolly all right. Sorry, I keep interrupting. Go on."

"A collision," Gina went on, "would crack open the asteroid and release her unharmed but would also destroy the planet. Omelettes and eggs, as far as she's concerned, but she thought it would be nice to give us a chance to sort things out amicably first. Look, you obviously know all this already, so why don't you tell your little pal there all about it and let me get on with something else?"

"He'd rather hear it from you," Mr Sunshine said. "He likes you."

"Does he?" Gina said, startled. The idea of Harmondsworth liking anybody except his master hadn't occurred to her before. "Good grief. All right, then. Actually, that's about it. She says that unless someone gets her out of there she's going to smash the Earth and we're all going to die, but if we could possibly release her before the moment of final impact, she'll make it worth our while."

"That, presumably," said Mr Sunshine, "is the point where Tom Dawson started paying attention."

"Well, yes," Gina said. "Apparently, when Dolly and her ex split up, she got Earth as part of the divorce settlement. But then he locked her up in the asteroid, out of pure spite, so it's never been much good to her. She says that if we can get her out, she'll give us twenty-five per cent of the Earth and all that therein is. Tom liked the sound of that a lot."

Mr Sunshine nodded slowly. "It'd get you-know-who off his back, certainly," he said. "For a while, at least. Remind me," he went on, "how this Lilith McGregor comes into it."

"Oh, her. Our client. She's Dolly's daughter."

Mr Sunshine couldn't help smiling. "Fancy Dolly having a grown-up kid," he said. "Time flies, doesn't it?"

Four thousand years. Quite. "She's not her daughter exactly," Gina said. "To be precise, she's an eternally recurring reincarnation. Mortal, human and practically normal, but when she dies her soul is reborn into a replacement body or something like that, and so on for a hundred and twenty generations. Anyway, that's why her. Mother/daughter affinity, the strongest bond known to exist anywhere in Nature."

Mr Sunshine looked at her. "You never had kids, did you?"

"No. Why?"

"No reason. Go on."

"Actually, that's about it," Gina said. "I told Tom, we don't do divorce—"

"I thought that was Everything."

"Divorce and Everything. Besides, this is Everything, too. Two very good reasons why we shouldn't touch it with a ten-foot pole. Tom wouldn't listen. Look, has your little friend heard enough yet?"

Mr Sunshine peered into the drawer, and the blue light lit up his face. "He gets the general idea," he said, and closed the drawer. "Awkward," he said.

Gina breathed out slowly through her nose. "Why didn't you tell me you know this Dolly person?"

"If I told you everybody I know, we'd be here for a very long time and we'd neither of us get any work done."

"And the wicked ex?"

"Him, too," Mr Sunshine said. "Though to be fair, there were faults on both sides. There usually are, when couples split up."

"Ted, he locked her up in an asteroid. For four thousand—"

"And now she's proposing to crash that asteroid into our planet," Mr Sunshine pointed out. "Mostly, at a guess, because she knows Hubby's got a soft spot for it. Otherwise, there's plenty of uninhabited rocks out there in space she could prang her asteroid against, but instead she chooses us. Like I said, that's Dolly all over."

"If you know her," Gina said, "maybe you could have a word with her."

Mr Sunshine made a rude noise. "The chances of

Dolly listening to me are pretty remote," he said. "No, if I stuck my oar in it'd only make things worse, trust me."

"Sounds like you two have history."

"There's a lot of history about," Mr Sunshine pointed out. "Besides, Dolly's not my client. I haven't been asked to help with this case. I wasn't even allowed to come to the meeting. Professional etiquette therefore requires me to keep my nose out of it, and that's something I'll be delighted to do. Never let it be said that Ted Sunshine ever poached a colleague's client. You simply don't do that sort of thing. You know that."

"But nobody's told Tom you know these people. If he knew that—"

"Don't you go telling him," Mr Sunshine said sternly.

"And anyway," Gina added, "this Lilith person isn't Tom's client, she's Brian's. You like Brian. You wouldn't mind helping him out, now would you?"

If Mr Sunshine's resolve wavered, it was only for a moment. "Brian didn't seem too put out that I wasn't asked to the meeting," he said. "At least, I don't seem to remember him kicking up a fuss about it. Well, then."

"Well what?"

Mr Sunshine gave her a how-dare-you-be-in-the-right-all-the-time look. "If you must know, my loyalties are just a tad divided where Dolly and her ex are concerned. Therefore, I choose to keep well clear. If you don't stick your nose in, it won't get bitten off. And that," he added cheerfully, "is your actual wisdom."

"Fine," Gina said, reining back her impatience with an effort. "But couldn't you at least give me a bit of advice, based on your deep inside knowledge of the parties involved? That wouldn't count as actually doing any-thing. And you know how much you love giving advice."

"Only when people don't want to hear it."

"Make an exception. Just this once."

Mr Sunshine sighed. "If you want my opinion," he said, "the only one who can sort this mess out is the ex. Presumably, he's got the key to the asteroid, or he knows where it is. If she gets the key, she won't need to use Earth as a sort of stationary hammer."

"And he'd listen to reason?"

"I really doubt that," said Mr Sunshine. "But you could try bribery and threats. Unless he's changed a lot since I last saw him, either of those might just do the trick."

Gina waited. Mr Sunshine smiled at her. "All right," Gina said, "what's his name?"

"You're not going to like this."

"What's his name?"

Mr Sunshine thought for a moment, opened his desk drawer, glowed blue with reflected light, shut the drawer, scratched his chin. "How would it be," he said, "if I had a word with him myself?"

Gina breathed out slowly. "You'd be all right with that?"

"To be honest, no. But I'd be even less all right with giving out his name like a free sample. So, lesser of two evils, really."

"In that case," Gina said, "go for it. Can I tell Tom?"

Deep frown, and outside a few flakes of snow fell. "I suppose you ought to," he said. "You can tell him that I aim to resolve this problem and give the firm's client full satisfaction, as is our policy. As regards a quarter of the Earth, it'd probably be better if his chickens went uncounted for the time being. He won't like that," Mr Sunshine added happily. "What a shame."

Gina left, having thanked him sincerely. He slid open a certain desk drawer. "Well?" he said.

"Here we go again."

"Not necessarily."

"Optimist. I'll get his number for you."

"Sorry," said Mr Sunshine, "whose number?"

"You know. Him."

Mr Sunshine's face hardened. "Certainly not."

"But you told the Noctis female you were going to—"

"I lied."

"Crikey."

Mr Sunshine scowled. "Oh come on," he said. "I can lie if I like, can't I?"

"You're very good at it."

"Thank you."

"But is it appropriate? All things considered?"

Mr Sunshine's face went a funny colour. "Get lost," he said. "Who made you my conscience, anyhow?"

"You did."

"Yes, all right, but I didn't mean it—" Mr Sunshine took a deep breath. "Having weighed the moral imperatives carefully and given all due consideration to the many conflicting factors, I choose not to fulfil the promise Gina wheedled out of me through blatant emotional manipulation. How's that?"

"Much better."

Lilith McGregor sat outside a café listening to her silence download. It was probably her favourite, although the ex-boyfriend who'd given it to her definitely wasn't. A hundred and eighty minutes of absolute dead silence, performed by the Boston Symphony Orchestra conducted by James Levine. Around her, the world roared like a hungry tiger but in the space between her earbuds, nothing but tranquillity.

She was supposed to be editing the pictures from her latest wedding shoot, but there didn't seem to be much point. Bride with unknown woman; bride and groom with unknown woman; bride, groom, bride's mother and father and unknown woman; bride wearing crash helmet dancing topless on table with unknown woman. She might as well give up and get a job in a call centre.

Her news feed winked at the top corner of her screen. She didn't usually bother, but right now something like a good war or tidal wave might take her mind off her troubles. She took a look.

Archaeologists, she read, digging at an undisclosed site in Jordan had just discovered the biggest ancient statue ever found, dating to around 2000 BC. At 92.1 metres tall, it was ever so slightly shorter than the Statue of Liberty; but whereas the latter was a hollow shell, the newly unearthed artefact was solid basalt. It represented a standing female figure with three heads, and an inscription on the base identified it as an ancient Mesopotamian goddess, Tiamat the Destroyer.

There were pictures of the heads. Two of them she didn't recognise. The third—

"Oh come on," she said aloud, though of course she couldn't hear herself because of the earbuds.

Not, she decided, three heads. More like two heads with unknown woman. Except she wasn't an unknown bloody woman, was she? Oh no. She was her mother—

The mood was completely ruined, so she pulled the earbuds out and pocketed them. Weirdness, she thought; why me? At school she'd been the only kid who didn't like Harry Potter – because it was silly, all those witches and wizards and magic, and everybody knew it wasn't real, so pretending was just plain stupid. Now, it seemed, weirdness had marked her for its own. The ridiculous technical anomaly ruining her work and keeping her from earning a living wasn't a faulty circuit or an aberrant algorithm, it was a Goddess of Death from the Bronze Age, who was also, in some unspeakably freaky way, her mum—

No way. True, she couldn't remember her real mother, who'd died when she was a baby, but that hadn't really mattered all that much, since Dad had remarried very soon after and her stepmother had always been fine, of adequate quality and fit for purpose. These days she was a vague, comfortable voice on a phone, who sent WhatsApp pictures of her latest patchwork projects and agreed with everything she said; exactly what Lilith wanted from a parent, which wasn't really very much. But Tiamat the Destroyer . . .

The irritating thing was, she believed it, every word. Belief is when you just know, in the angry red face of all the evidence and all the logical arguments. Now, when she looked on her screen at the face of Unknown Woman, she was all too painfully aware of the resemblance. Same nose, same mouth and chin. And all that weird shit about one hundred and twenty reincarnations; she wanted to reach inside her ear with a giant toothpick and hook the idea out of her brain, but she knew it was true. Just knew, that's all.

And now, apparently, they'd dug up a ninety-metre statue of Mummy in the desert somewhere. Coincidence? She was rather inclined to doubt it. But Mummy was on her way, driving a three-hundred-mile-circumference asteroid straight at the Earth, or so the man from Dawsons had told her.

She thought about that. She knew she ought to be

really, really scared, but for some reason she wasn't. Instead she was annoyed, embarrassed, angry – sure and certain symptoms, she couldn't help thinking, that Tiamat really was her mother after all. What the man from Dawsons hadn't been able to tell her was what anybody was proposing to do about all of this. She'd asked him, of course, but all she'd got out of him was a load of flannel about consulting with his colleagues and formulating a joined-up action plan; Latin for I haven't got a clue. The hell with him, she thought, he's useless. She really never ought to have gone to him in the first place, and as soon as she had a free five minutes, she was going to write a real stinker of a review on Facebook. Meanwhile—

"Excuse me."

Someone was standing beside her. Lilith looked at her and saw a smart, impressive woman in her early thirties, dressed in a navy blue business suit and holding the very latest model tablet. We all see our angels in a different way. The traditionally minded see flowing white draperies and wings. Lilith saw the cool, confident face and the LoganBerry XP7000, and knew she was in the presence of a superior being.

"Excuse me," repeated the superior being, "but are you Lilith McGregor?"

"Yes, that's me. Who the hell are you?"

The woman handed her a business card. "Consuela Teasdale," she said. "Mind if I sit down?"

"Teasdale," Lilith repeated.

Consuela smiled grimly. "My ex-husband. I think you know him."

"Yes."

"He's a jerk."

Lilith frowned. The card read:

Consuela Teasdale
Assistant Mage
JWW
COMMERCIAL & INDUSTRIAL SORCERY & MAGIC,
THEOLOGICAL AND PARANORMAL ENGINEERS
70 St Mary Axe, London

"This," said Consuela, "is highly unethical and I could probably get struck off just for talking to you like this, but I felt I couldn't just stand by and do nothing while my idiot ex screws up your case. That man," she added with feeling, "is a menace. I could hit him, I really could."

"He's no good?"

"Useless," Consuela said. "You deserve so much better."

Well, of course. Nevertheless, Lilith pursed her lips. "So naturally you want me to bring my business to you instead."

Consuela laughed. "Oh, I know how it sounds, but it's not like that at all. This Tiamat thing is really important. It'd be a crime against humanity to leave it in the hands of an idiot like Brian Teasdale."

"You realise I haven't got any money."

"Doesn't matter," Consuela said briskly. "My firm, JWW, has been retained by the United Nations to solve all the world's problems—"

"Really?"

"Oh yes. After all, we're the best in the business, so naturally they came to us. Here, take a look for yourself."

On the screen of the LoganBerry was a scan of a letter, on UN headed notepaper, signed by the current Secretary General. Lilith read it. Perfectly genuine, as far as she could tell. "Shit," she said reverently. "That's pretty impressive."

"Well, yes," Consuela said. "It's also a damn good reason why you should entrust your business to us, rather than a cowboy outfit like Dawsons. Anyhow, it also means you won't have to pay a penny. You'll be our client, naturally, but the UN will pick up the tab."

"You're sure about that?"

"You have my word," Consuela said. "And I'll put it in writing, of course. It just so happens I've got a client agreement already drawn up for you to sign." She swiped the screen. "You'll want to read it carefully first, naturally."

Lilith read it. It all seemed perfectly straightforward, and there it was in black and white, not a penny to pay. "Fine," she said. "What do I—?"

"All I need is a thumbprint, there and there. Great, that's all there is to it. You're now officially a client of JWW. I'll write to Brian straight away and tell him to send me his file." Her face softened into a very human grin. "He'll be livid."

"You won't get in trouble?"

"Trouble," Consuela said, "is my business." Her fingers strayed to a gold monkey pendant dangling from her ivory neck. "Right," she said, "enough precious time's been wasted as it is, thanks to your no-good previous advisers. We need to get cracking, now. I take it you're free for the rest of the morning?"

Lilith considered her laptop, crammed with spoiled images. "I guess so," she said. "Do you need me for something?"

Consuela stood up. "Ever been in a helicopter before?"

No, Lilith hadn't. Nor was she aware that it was possible, let alone legal, for one to land in the middle of a busy street in the middle of the day in central London, but apparently it was, so that was all right. "Where are we going?" she said, as the chopper soared high over the skyscrapers.

"I've scheduled us a meeting with a specialist consultant."

Wow, Lilith thought. "Great."

"Polly Basescu," Consuela said, raising her voice over the roar of the engine. "She's the Kawaguchiya Integrated Circuits Professor of the Sum of Human Knowledge at the University of Reading. Smartest person in the world."

"In the world?"

"No shit," Consuela said. "You'll like her, she's a doll. Look her up, if you like."

Lilith did just that and found that the professor had 5,764,917 positive reviews on TripAdvisor. So it was true. "She knows everything," Consuela went on, "all that was, is and shall be. So I thought that'd be a good place to start."

Eminently sensible, Lilith thought. She could feel a great load shifting off her shoulders, thanks to the superior being sitting next to her in the helicopter's cramped aft compartment. Here, she felt in her bones, was someone who knew what to do, and in two shakes of a lamb's tail the asteriod would be diverted and all her pictures would be mum-free and it would be as if none of this nonsense had ever happened—

The helicopter dropped like a stone, hovered for a moment and deposited itself into a perfectly sized space (marked 'helicopters only') in a car park. The rotors subsided and her door popped open. "This way," Consuela said.

A few minutes later, they were in the lobby of a building that looked like a rather dreary hospital, but which Consuela assured her was the Sum of Human Knowledge faculty building. They were issued with visitors' passes (for some reason, the photo on Consuela's pass didn't come out very well) and rode in a lift to the seventeenth floor. They walked along a corridor that smelt faintly of orange peel and stopped outside a door. Consuela knocked. A voice said, "Come in."

"Hi, Polly," Consuela said. "This is Lilith. I told you about her on the phone."

Professor Basescu was eating a sandwich. She looked so like Consuela they might have been sisters. "Hi," she said, through a mouthful of sandwich. "Take a seat, with you in a second."

The room, Lilith noted, was somewhat sparse. A desk, with nothing on it. Three chairs. Bare walls. One big window behind them, with a view of the car park. In the hand not holding the sandwich, the professor clutched another LoganBerry XP7000 (but the case of hers was lilac, not sky blue), inside which, presumably, nestled the Sum of Human Knowledge. Lilith felt reassured, and leaned back in the chair, which was tolerably comfortable.

"Sorry to have kept you," the professor said. "Right, how can I help you guys?"

"Just to recap," Consuela said. "We've just found out that Lilith's mother is Tiamat the Great Goddess."

"Oh, her." The professor nodded approvingly. "With you so far."

"It turns out," Consuela went on, "that four thousand years ago, Tiamat's ex-husband locked her up in an asteroid, which is now on a collision course with Earth."

The professor nodded. "I know," she said. "We've been watching it."

"Really?" Lilith felt a twinge of apprehension. "It's close enough to see with a telescope?"

The professor smiled. "No way," she said. "We established its existence by observing diametric phase flux patterns in the antipositron flow at the Ridiculously Big Hadron Collider at Rittersbach. Sort of like that trick you do at school with iron filings and a magnet. It's there all right. Sodding great big thing, coming straight at us. Sorry, you were saying."

"Tiamat," Consuela went on, "not unreasonably, wants to be released from the asteroid, but she can't get out without the key. Her ex has it stashed away somewhere. If the asteroid hits Earth it'll be disintegrated into space dust – so will we, of course – and she'll be free, but she says she'd rather not take out the planet unless it's absolutely necessary. If we can get the key and send it to her, she'll divert the asteroid and everything will be fine."

"I call that very reasonable," the professor said. "Generous, even."

"So what we want to know," Consuela went on, "is what to do next. Any suggestions?"

The professor thought about it for a moment, consulted her LoganBerry, then leaned forward on her desk and smiled. "What do you think?"

"Well," Consuela said, "I think we have two options open to us, which we ought to explore simultaneously. One, find Tiamat's ex and make him give us the key."

"Love it," said the professor. "Go on."

"The other," Consuela continued, "is for Lilith here to have a word with her mum, tell her we're on the job, and ask her to go easy on the crashing-into-the-planet side of things while we're tracing her ex and making him see reason."

"Perfect," the professor said. "Go for it."

"You think so?"

"Pure gold," the professor said, "can't miss. Exactly what I was going to suggest."

"And you'd sign a report to that effect?"

"Like a rat up a drain," the professor said. "Sketch something out for me and I'll get it back to you straight away."

"Thanks," Consuela said. "Sorry to be a pain, but we need something on the file to cover ourselves with the professional indemnity insurance."

"Absolutely," the professor said. "Anything to help out the United Nations. Talking of which, have you heard from Tony lately?"

"I spoke to him last week, as a matter of fact. He and Cherie send their regards."

"Bless," the professor said fondly. "Sweet guy."

Consuela stood up. "Well," she said, "I think that just about covers everything. I'd love to stay and chat, but I expect Lilith's got things she needs to do. Thanks again. All my best to Hugo and the kittens."

And then they were back in the helicopter, high above the rooftops. "It's always worth getting an outside opinion from a properly qualified expert," Consuela said. "I don't suppose Brian suggested anything of the sort."

"No," Lilith said, "he didn't."

Consuela clicked her tongue. "That's the old-fashioned way," she said. "Do it yourself, keep it in-house, ramp up the billable hours, we don't need no stinkin' experts. We like to think we've outgrown all that at JWW."

Lilith had been thinking. It hadn't been easy, because sweet-scented fumes of reassurance kept drifting up into her mind and clouding it over, like condensation on the inside of your windscreen. "Do we actually know where to find my mum's ex?"

"Leave that to me," Consuela said briskly. "We have the resources at JWW. That's what comes of having the foresight to invest in people on the scale we do."

"My mum's ex." She paused. "Would that make him my dad?"

Consuela looked out of the window. From that height, you could be forgiven for thinking that you could see all the kingdoms of the Earth. "That's kind of a grey area," she said, "what with all the reincarnation stuff. We can't say for sure whether the genetic matrix passes bipartially or only via the double X chromasome. Tiamat is definitely your mother, but that's as far as we can go at this stage, until we get the results of the tests."

"But you want me to talk to her."

"It's essential," Consuela said. "Basically, it's the cornerstone of our strategy. You don't object, do you?"

"I guess not."

"I'll be there with you, naturally."

Lilith felt a surge of relief, such as Pooh and Piglet would have felt on seeing Christopher Robin striding towards them. "In that case," she said, "that'll be fine. Will there have to be those things?"

"Excuse me?"

"Last time, when Brian Teasdale did it, there were things. Demons."

Consuela laughed. "Oh God, that's so like Brian. I'm amazed he doesn't write all his letters with a quill pen. We don't do demons at JWW."

"That's good. I didn't like them much."

"Who does? Don't worry, there won't be any of that crap on my watch. Demons, for crying out loud." She laughed again. "That's like making a phone call with two cocoa tins and a piece of string. Typical Dawsons.

They can't bring themselves to spend the money to buy decent tech."

The helicopter swooped. For a moment, Lilith felt uncomfortably alienated from her intestines, but she glanced at Consuela, who didn't seem in the least bothered, and drew comfort from her presence. She felt safe. Even if the cockpit were suddenly to fly open and she went tumbling headlong to the ground, she was pretty sure Consuela would bear her up so her foot wouldn't even get bruised. "I'm so glad you're doing all this for me," she said. "I feel so much better about it now."

"All part of the JWW service."

When she got home, Lilith scanned the news channels for any reports about giant asteroids. There weren't any; well, there were quite a few, but only in places where there are always giant killer asteroids, just as there are always potted palms in dentists' waiting rooms. She allowed herself a moment's smugness at the expense of all those poor second-raters out there who weren't clients of JWW and didn't have access to the real skinny. Probably best if they never learned the truth. It would only bother them, and all to no purpose, since there was nothing they could do. Meanwhile, Consuela was on the case and it'd all be sorted out with a minimum of melodrama and fuss. She paused to consider the implications. For all she knew, stuff like this was going on all the time, existential threats to the species and the planet, and Consuela and others like her were beavering away keeping everybody safe, with precious little reward and no recognition whatsoever. Still, if you were someone like that, recognition or even abject adoration from ordinary little people wouldn't matter all that much, because what stock would you as a superior being put in the opinions of creatures so far below you as to be, for all intents and purposes, plankton? You'd know what you'd done, and that would be enough.

What if the horrible abusive ex did turn out to be her father? She didn't like that thought at all. You can't choose your parents; other people do that for you, and as often as not they make a hash of it. Nobody can say it's your fault. Even so. What kind of a man would lock someone up in an asteroid for four thousand years, out of (she assumed) sheer spite? A jerk, obviously. A creep. Query: would someone like that be prepared to listen to reason, even when the fate of an entire planetful of sentient beings hung in the balance? Probably not. But presumably Consuela had a handle on that. She'd fix him. She'd make him squirm, and then she'd get the key off him and everything would be fine. She was, after all, a professional. All in a day's work for someone like her.

She opened her laptop and spent a few minutes studying the obtrusive face in all her photographs. That poor woman, she thought, it can't have been fun for her. True, she was apparently some sort of Goddess of Death – Or was she? That's what Brian Teasdale had told her, but she knew all about Brian Teasdale now, so it was entirely possible that Mum was nothing of the sort. Consuela, she remembered, had called her the Great Goddess. Well, of course. Her mother, after all.

VIXEN

Mr Teasdale got the file request later that day. No explanations: simply, Lilith McGregor is now our client, please forward all relevant materials in your possession. Where in God's name had that come from?

As if he needed to ask. He felt as though someone had stuck a spigot in his toe, and all the energy in his body was slowly draining down and gurgling out, a dribble at a time. I try, he thought. I do my best. And then she comes along and—

He went to see Mr Dawson, who was on the phone. "It's not that we can't make your goldfish immortal, Mrs Enderby," he was saying, "technically speaking it's actually quite a simple process. But I feel duty bound to point out that it's extremely expensive and there could be significant side effects – Well, increased size, for one thing, you could be looking at something the size of a medium to large killer whale, and talking of which, the process has been known to affect the animal's – Yes, sorry, the fish's temperament, and then you're getting yourself into the field of compliance with all the dangerous animals legislation – Yes, occasionally people have been eaten, though of course, it does depend – Well, yes, we could design you a suitable security package, but that's just going to add to the cost, and at the end of the day one goldfish is pretty much like another, and – At the very least think it over and get back to me, and if you decide that's what you really want to do, then of course we'll be happy to – Yes, thank you, Mrs Enderby, a pleasure talking to you, goodbye." He put the phone down, closed his eyes and counted to ten. "Brian."

Mr Teasdale grinned. "On the other hand," he said, "her husband is CEO of Consolidated Landrape."

"Quite. Mr Dawson sighed. "What can you do? We commit to a job we're bound to lose money on, or we risk losing a major corporate client. There are days when this business makes my teeth ache."

"Talking of losing clients."

Mr Dawson looked at him. "Oh God," he said. "What've you done now?"

"Not me," Mr Teasdale said. "JWW. They've poached the McGregor woman."

"Oh for crying out loud." For a very brief moment, Mr Dawson seemed to flicker, and in his place Mr Teasdale thought he could see a hideous desiccated thing, its skin adhering to its bones like shrinkwrap, wispy hair reaching to the floor, grotesquely curled fingernails like lions' claws – the man, if you could call him that, in the portrait that hung on the wall behind him during partnership meetings. Then the regular Mr Dawson was back, and he wasn't happy. "You idiot," he roared. "How could you let that happen?"

"It wasn't my—"

"Don't give me that. Have you got any idea how much that job means to this firm? Did you even think for a second about the rest of us? Your partners? No, thought not. You halfwit."

"Tom."

He could feel Mr Dawson's eyes on him. It was an intrusive procedure. "Oh come on," he said, "you didn't. You can't have."

"I don't know what you're—"

"You told that poisonous ex of yours all about it. Well?"

"I may have mentioned—"

Mr Dawson breathed out. Hard to believe that much air could be safely contained in a human body at any one time. "It's not your fault," he said. "You can't help having been born stupid, raised a moron and given the finest education in idiocy that money can buy. Presumably when you were young your parents sold your brain to a research lab, and that can't have helped either. I don't blame you. It's my fault, for ever letting you come within a million miles of my business."

"Tom."

"Sorry," said Mr Dawson. "May have got a bit carried away there, brooding on the wrongs done to me by a total fuckwit. So, what are you going to do about it?"

"I don't see there's a lot we can do."

"Bullshit." Mr Dawson glared at him. "You can talk to your client, make her see the error of her ways, and get her back. Sharpish."

"Tom, that's unethical, you know that."

"So's pinching the stupid tart in the first place. Didn't stop your ex, did it? Fine. She wants to play that game, let's give her a masterclass in it."

"Tom," Mr Teasdale said, "if we start doing stuff like that, doesn't that just lower us to their level?"

"You say that like it's a bad thing. You're not a bad kid, Brian, though you're incurably stupid. But unless you come down from the arid uplands of the moral high ground into the rich lowland pastures of cheating and duplicity, you're no fucking use to man nor beast. Got that?"

"Yes, Tom."

"So you'll deal with it."

"Yes, Tom."

"Good boy. Now piss off and let me pull myself together in peace. If one more thing goes wrong today, I might very well turn into something nasty and start eating the cleaners."

No idle threat. Brian backed out of the room and closed the door. In doing so he met Gina, coming out of the ladies' toilet.

Brian pointed to the door he'd just come through. "Don't go in there," he said.

"Wasn't planning to. Problem?"

"You could say that."

Gina sighed. "I remember when we were just a bunch of professionals, doing our work and doing it cheerfully and well. Mind you, back then if you wanted a knife you had to knap it out of a chunk of flint. What've you done now?"

"Why does everybody always assume—?"

"Because it's always you," Gina explained sweetly. "Let's grab a coffee and you can tell me all about it."

Mist, the consistency of taramasalata but a sort of pale grey colour. There was no light, of course; in this environment light can't exist. Over the years people have come here with torches, halogen beacons and arclights, all in perfect working order but nothing comes out of them. Mr Sunshine, however, was different. But even he wasn't at his brightest and best down here. He glowed, just enough to see his hand in front of his face, but that was about it.

He was tapping his way with a long stick. A curious thing to do, since there was nothing to tap it against, apart from the mist, which needless to say wasn't actually there. The mist is how the human brain and optical nerve processes what it sees in this place, which is nothing at all; in this place, you don't so much see as jump to wildly erroneous conclusions, because if you don't jump you fall, and if you fall here you can't get up. It's that sort of place.

The tip of the stick prodded nothing at all, and Mr Sunshine heard a soft splash. He stopped dead in his tracks and waited. For a long time, nothing. Then he heard – quite possibly erroneously – a faint creaking, as of a ship's ropes and timbers. Maybe the mist concentrated and grew darker, maybe it didn't. Maybe it concentrated into a vague shape, squarish, of indeterminate size, maybe not.

"Turned out nice again," said a voice.

"Hi, George." Mr Sunshine held out his other hand. In it were two gold coins. They vanished from between his palm and fingertips. A wooden gangplank appeared out of nowhere, and Mr Sunshine walked up it. He heard a sound like oars in water, although there were no oars and no water.

"That Lewis Hamilton," said the ferryman. "Think he'll do it again this year?"

"It all depends on Monaco," replied Mr Sunshine. "If he can win there, I reckon he's in with a chance."

"Vettel can still catch him if he does all right at Melbourne."

"Nah," said Mr Sunshine. "He'd still need to win Bahrain, and the Ferrari's all wrong for those corners."

"You could be right," said the voice. "Staying long?"

"Hope not, George."

"Now then, Mr S," the voice said warningly. "Not the H word, OK?"

"Sorry, George."

The trip took no time at all, because there is no time at all in this place. "Mind the step," said the voice, and Mr Sunshine minded it, though of course it wasn't there. But he didn't want to hurt the voice's feelings.

"See you in half an hour," Mr Sunshine said.

"Maybe," said the voice. "Maybe not."

Mr Sunshine didn't look round, because that's something you just don't do in this place. If he had, he'd have seen nothing at all, and quite definitely not a ship. He sighed. He was cheerful by nature, always looking on the bright side of life, but here there's nothing to look on the bright side of. He took a packet of caster sugar from his jacket pocket, ripped it open and filled the palm of his hand. Then he started broadcasting, like a farmer sowing corn.

Most of the sugar simply disappeared, but a few specks didn't. They glittered in the pale glow of Mr Sunshine, and he scattered a few more handfuls in their general direction. Then he took a long stride forward, the sole of his shoe crunching on the granules. The sugar path was narrow, about nine inches across, so Mr Sunshine went slowly and carefully. No hurry, after all. Not here.

There's safe as houses, but houses burn down or get repossessed. There's safe as the Bank of England, and see where that got us. And then there's as safe as the Bank of the Dead, which offers, among other competitively priced services, the most secure, most discreet safe deposit boxes in the Multiverse. Provided you've got your key, you can pop in and pop out again at will, any time of the day or night, no names, no pack drill. What's not to like?

Then there was no sugar left, so he stopped where he was. Nothing happened. He tried whistling a tune to cheer himself up, but no sound came out. He upended the bag over his hand, but there was nothing in it, not so much as a single crystal. Bother, he thought.

"Hi, Ted. Sorry to have kept you."

Mr Sunshine looked up. A small man in a dark grey suit was standing in front of him. He was flat, as in two dimensions only. Nobody's perfect.

"Not to worry," Mr Sunshine said. "I was enjoying the view."

The flat man smiled. "You're a scream, Ted, you know that?"

Mr Sunshine, who never felt the cold, shivered. "Anyway," he said. "So, how's things with you, Charlie? Business OK?"

"Never better. You?"

Mr Sunshine frowned. "So-so," he replied. "Grandkids doing all right?"

He'd said the right thing. The flat man beamed. "Going great guns," he said. "Tina's a lawyer with a big corporate firm in Hong Kong. Eric, he's specialising in leveraged takeovers with Schliemann Brothers in Frankfurt. Celine hasn't quite made her mind up yet, so she's taking a year out to study contemporary dance. Irving—" He hesitated, pulled a small, wry face. "I don't know," he said. "You do your best for them. It's just—"

"Kids nowadays," Mr Sunshine said. "He needs to find his groove, that's all." He paused for a moment, then said, "We can always use a good intern at our place. I could talk to Tom Dawson."

The flat man looked at him. "That's really sweet," he said, "but you know how it is. All that stuff, lying about. Better not."

Mr Sunshine, who'd been counting on that reaction, nodded stoically. "You're probably right," he said. "Don't worry about it, it'll all come right in the end."

"Everything does," the flat man said firmly. "We should know. Anyhow, that's enough about that. What can I do for you this bright spring morning?"

Mr Sunshine shivered again. "The box," he said.

"Ah. This way." A path, an extension of the sugar line, glowed a faint green in front of them. "Got your key?"

Mr Sunshine patted his pocket. "Damn," he said, "it must be in my other coat. Just kidding," he added, pulling out a small, flat brass key. "Lead on."

The flat man turned – For a moment he was invisible, then very narrow indeed, then a perfectly flat back walking in front. Mr Sunshine followed, taking extreme care where he put his feet. On either side of the path nothing changed; it might as well have been one of those rolling-road things you get in gyms and airports. Occasionally the flat man waved and greeted people Mr Sunshine couldn't see. Maybe they waved back, maybe not.

The mist, which wasn't there, thickened, and you might have been forgiven for getting a vague impression of a wall. The flat man stopped, took a plastic card from his pocket and presented it to a patch of nothing, which scanned it and went bleep. "How's Gina?" the flat man said, as the wall faded away. "Still up to her old tricks?"

"You know Gina," Mr Sunshine replied, his fingers crossed behind his back.

"She's a laugh a minute," the flat man said. "Tell her to drop by any time she's in the neighbourhood. We're always glad to see Gina."

Nothing had changed, because nothing can come of nothing (Shakespeare), but directly ahead was a bank of safety deposit boxes, reaching from a long way down to a long way up, and the same in the x axis. The flat man pulled over a set of old-fashioned wooden steps, climbed to the top rung, reached high over his head and stuck a small key in a small keyhole. Then he came down again. Mr Sunshine climbed up, inserted his key in the other lock and turned it. A door swung open. Mr Sunshine pulled on a glove, reached inside the box, which was empty apart from some crystals, a chunky bitumen-covered statue of a bird, a notebook and a sheaf of Get-Out-Of-Death-Free cards, bundled together with a rubber band. He put something in it, then closed the door and pocketed his key. "All done," he said, and retreated down the ladder, which vanished.

"Just sign here," said the flat man. "And here and here and here and here and here. Oh yes, and here. Great stuff, thanks. You got time for a coffee?"

"Not really," Mr Sunshine said, a degree too casually. "Thanks all the same."

"You sure? We've got bagels."

"Really," Mr Sunshine said.

The flat man shrugged his two-dimensional shoulders. "Maybe next time," he said. "Well, it was great seeing you again, Ted. Don't be a stranger, you hear?"

"Count on it," said Mr Sunshine. "I'll see myself out."

He turned and walked away, taking exquisite care to

go in a precisely straight line, since the green glow had died away. After a while he heard sugar crunch underfoot. A while later, no sugar. The ship loomed up out of the mist. He sucked a whole lot of nothing into his lungs and breathed out slowly.

"Hey, Ted. You forgot your key."

It almost worked. He very nearly turned round. "So long, Charlie," he called out, facing resolutely forward. He couldn't blame him for trying, but he really wished he wouldn't.

"Done what you came for?" the ferryman asked, as the oars creaked and the ship began to move.

Mr Sunshine nodded. "Yup."

"Pity you weren't here Tuesday for the fête. They had craft stalls and a flower show and a live band and everything."

"Sorry I missed it," Mr Sunshine said.

"Next year, maybe."

"Maybe," Mr Sunshine said, and the gangplank swung out, and he walked down it. His knees were a bit wobbly, probably from sitting still. "Look after yourself, George."

"You, too."

Some time later, back in his office with all the lights on and the heating turned right up, Mr Sunshine took the copy of the receipt Charlie had given him out of his top pocket and tried to unfold it. Bad move. You know how, when you put a piece of paper on the fire, it turns grey but it still looks just like a piece of paper, until you touch it and immediately it collapses into dust? Like that. Oh well, never mind. Besides, if you can't trust the Bank of the Dead, who can you trust?

Life, Consuela Teasdale will tell you if you're ill-advised enough to let her, is best lived in freefall. You climb as high as possible, you launch yourself out into the wide blue yonder, and you wait till the very last moment before pulling the ripcord. Anything less than that is mere compromise, which is just another word for giving in.

Her ex-husband had an unfortunate habit of extending the metaphor, with an emphasis on how important it is to make sure your parachute is in tip-top working order and that you've actually remembered to put it on before you jump; one of the many reasons why he wasn't her husband any more. Even so, he'd had a point. When you're as feisty and kick-ass and attitude-crammed as Consuela Teasdale, it's all too easy to neglect the tiresomely basic stuff, such as putting the dustbins out or booking the car in for its MOT or renewing your library books or having a plan of action before promising the client that everything's going to be fine.

But that was all right, now that she had Erica. "Hi," she said to the phone. "Something I'd like you to do for me, when you've got five minutes."

Erica was the intern. Four feet nine, thin as a rake, wispy mouse hair scraped back in a bun, glasses, did as she was told. Nominally she was assigned to Toby Porteous in Pest Control, but since he was usually out of the office culling werewolves and hammering stakes into vampires, there wasn't much she could usefully do. Consuela had come across her one day sitting all alone in the library, working out alternative solutions to Fermat's last theorem just to help pass the time. At heart, Consuela was just an old softie. She'd taken pity on the kid and found her various things to do, for which the poor waif was pathetically grateful. And since she had a knack of doing them particularly well ...

"Hi," Consuela said, as Erica drifted into the room and stood looking down at her shoes. "Busy?"

"No."

"Fine. In that case, there's a little job I need doing. Up for it?"

"Yes."

"Great, it's like this." Quickly and succinctly she ran through the facts of the case, neglecting to mention the trinity aspect but otherwise admirably thorough. "You see the problem," she added.

"Yes."

Consuela frowned. Some of her best friends were monosyllables, but just for once it'd be nice to have something a bit more fulsome: gosh, maybe, or wow. "We need to find a way of getting in touch with this Tiamat's ex."

"Yes."

"It would help," she ground on, "if we knew who he is."

"Yes."

"But right now, we have no idea."

"No."

"Right. Fine. Do you think you could possibly find out?"

Pause for thought, lasting three seconds. "Yes."

When Erica said yes, she meant it. A wave of relief washed over Consuela, of which she gave no sign. "Great," she said. "You do that, then. Let me know when you've finished."

"Yes."

"Cool. Off you go. Thank you," she added, as the door closed. She drew in a long, deep breath and let it out slowly. Then she reached for her Things To Do list, and drew a tick in the margin.

The door opened again. Erica was back. "That was quick."

Erica shook her head. "There's a letter for you," she said. "I was passing, so I brought it. I'm sorry," she added, and left.

A letter: how quaint. She glanced at it and saw the Dawsons monogram embossed on the envelope. That made her grin. Probably Tom Dawson threatening her with the wrath of God for stealing their client; should be good for a laugh. She flipped the envelope open, but there was no letter inside. In fact it was empty, apart from something that looked suspiciously like a single human hair.

She was almost quick enough, but not quite. She was out of her chair and had her hand on the fire extinguisher when the hair rose up out of the envelope and morphed into Brian Teasdale, who smiled at her and turned the fire extinguisher into a rat. Consuela had a thing about rats. She dropped it, and it scuttled under her desk.

"I'd forgotten you can do that," she said.

"Hi," said Brian's hair. "You never could get the hang of it."

"I always thought it was so brave of you," Consuela said. "I mean, considering how few hairs you have left."

Brian Teasdale was sensitive about the small bald patch on the crown of his head. His magically induced simulacrum, on the other hand, couldn't care less. "Nice try," he said. "This other thing, though. Not so nice."

"Drop dead, Brian."

The hair sighed. "Oh come on," it said. "Stealing other people's clients. That's unprofessional."

"So's promising me a trinity and then cutting me out stone dead."

The hair had the grace to look uncomfortable. "That wasn't me," he said, "that was Tom Dawson. And I never said I wouldn't share. Just, not openly. I'd have let you see the file, you know I would."

"Maybe you would and maybe you wouldn't," Consuela said. "It's all academic now. She's our client, and there's nothing you can do about it."

The hair shrugged. "That's not strictly true," he said. "Hanuman."

"Now just a—" was as far as she got. Then the gold chain around her neck, from which dangled the little monkey pendant, started to tighten. You'd have thought a thin, delicate thing like that would've snapped under the strain long before it got tight enough to block off her windpipe, but apparently not. She turned a fetching shade of puce and sank to her knees.

"Oops," said the hair, "almost forgot. If you can't breathe, you can't promise to give me my client back. Ease off a bit, Hanuman, there's a good boy."

Forty-five seconds of long, hard, rasping breaths later, Consuela turned her head and looked at the hair. "You arsehole," she said.

"Me? I'm only a hair." It smiled. "Brian would never lay a finger on you, you know that. He reckons that any man who hits a girl isn't fit to live. But I'm just a thin tube of keratin under the influence of non-Newtonian physics, and I couldn't give a stuff."

"That," Consuela said, "was aggravated assault. You do realise you can go to prison for that."

"Fine," said the hair. "No skin off my nose and there's plenty more where I came from. Well, maybe not plenty, but enough. Oh, I wouldn't do that if I were you," the hair continued, as Consuela tried to lift the chain off over her head. "Hanuman might not like it."

She dropped the chain as though it was red hot.

"Nasty little beast," she said. "I never liked that monkey, not one bit."

"Then you should've let me have him after the divorce, shouldn't you?" the hair said. "Now then, about that file."

"Bastard. I should've known if you didn't get your own way, you'd turn violent."

The hair smiled ominously. "You forget," it said. "I was there that time you poured hot soup in his lap because he'd borrowed your nail scissors without asking. Of course, I was little more than a follicle at the time," it went on, "on account of you having half scalped the poor devil for squeezing the toothpaste from the middle of the tube two weeks earlier."

"I didn't say I wasn't violent. I just said—"

"You know what," said the hair. "You two deserve each other. You belong together, really you do."

"Drop dead."

"Preferably in a secure facility surrounded with barbed wire and patrolled by dogs. Still, none of my beeswax, if that's how you two want to carry on, please yourselves. In the meantime, I want that file. And your signature on a release letter. Now."

"I'll get you for this."

"Quite probably. And I expect you'll do something really vindictive and horrible, which is why I'm glad I'm just an inanimate object temporarily invested with sentience. It means I don't have to put up with any of your shit. The file or asphyxiation. Your choice."

"Brian would never—"

"I know. That's why you got me. The file."

Consuela got up, opened the filing cabinet and took out a blue folder. "Thank you," said the hair. "Now I'll just trouble you to dash off a quick email to your client to let her know you can't act for her any more, and then I think we're all done."

None of which took very long. The hair glanced at the screen, then reached over her shoulder and hit the send button. "There now," he said. "That wasn't so bad, was it?"

"Yes, actually."

"Really? I'm sorry. Still," said the hair, "console yourself with the thought that this time tomorrow you'll still be alive and conscious and capable of feeling the warmth of sunlight. I, on the other hand, will be just another dumb organic wire under a hat. The incredible richness of human experience—"

"Piss off," Consuela said. "Hope your end splits."

The hair sighed. "Fine," he said. "In that case, I won't trouble you with the rest of the message."

"What message?"

"Sorry," the hair said. "I seem to have forgotten. All this negativity and spite seems to have driven it clean out of my head. Something to do with how Brian hopes you can still work together on this in spite of everything and he'd really like to keep you in the loop, provided that—"

"What?"

The hair closed its eyes, scratched its head, bit the knuckle of its forefinger. "No, sorry, it's gone," it said. "It was something you needed to do to show him there's no hard feelings, you're still interested in working together and you want to see anything he finds out about trini-something-or-others. On the tip of my tongue. No, it's gone. Ah well, never mind."

Consuela sprang like a tiger and grabbed the lapels of his jacket. "If you don't tell me, so help me, I'll—"

"Really," said the hair. Then it turned into a

pterodactyl, caught the file in its beak and flew out of the window. It wasn't the sort of window that opens, but it didn't seem to matter terribly much.

Mr Dawson poured himself a drink.

As a rule, he rarely touched the stuff. What's the point, he used to say, of swilling a liquid that tastes like petrol and makes you even more stupid than you already are? As a mood enhancer, it's primitive, like starting a fire with two flints, and if you want to make your world an easier place to live in, usually it's more efficient to track down the source of your problems and kill it, instead of merely forgetting about it for a while and waking up with heartburn and a headache.

Some problems, however, can't be solved, only endured or not thought about, in which case a tumblerful of 110 per cent proof can be helpful, even if only as a counter-irritant. He gulped it down, winced, dropped the glass in the trash, folded his arms and said, "Come in."

The door didn't open, but Mr Ahriman was sitting in the chair on the other side of the desk. He hadn't come in because he was already there. Everywhere, remember?

"This is unusual," said Mr Ahriman. "You wanting to see me."

"Thanks for dropping by."

"Not a problem."

"There's something—" Mr Dawson's mouth had gone dry, and every last trace of alcohol had vanished from his system. "I need your help."

"Help," Mr Ahriman repeated. "Heavens above." He smiled. There are some people whose smiles make the world a better place. Mr Ahriman wasn't one of them. "I'm touched," he said. "That's so sweet."

"I need some information. And I thought—"

"Absolutely," Mr Ahriman said. "Well, you've come to the right place. It'll cost you, mind, but I imagine you considered that before you asked me. Right, where do I start? The capital city of Venezuela is—"

"That's not what I—"

"I've started," said Mr Ahriman firmly, "so I'll finish. The capital city of Venezuela is Caracas. Population, five million. Principal industries, financial services and retail, with some manufacturing in the northern suburbs. Average yearly rainfall—" He stopped and grinned. "You're not writing any of this down."

"That's not what I wanted to ask."

"Really? Shucks. It'll still cost you. One year."

Mr Dawson tried not to whimper. He didn't make a very good job of it. "What I wanted to ask you," he said.

"Yes?"

"I had a client," Mr Dawson said, "only that bitch from JWW—"

"Excuse me," Mr Ahriman interrupted. "*We* had a client. Partners, remember? And, yes, you lost her, but now you've got her back."

"I have?"

"Yes, about fifteen seconds ago. No thanks to you," Mr Ahriman added. "That was young Mr Teasdale, showing more initiative than I'd have given him credit for. That boy is smarter than he looks. Information," he added. "Three months."

"But I didn't ask—"

"No, but it's something you really ought to know, believe me. Now then, where were we? Ah yes. Your client."

"Do I really have to go through all this? You know it all already."

"So I do," Mr Ahriman said pleasantly. "Clever old me. You need to know the identity of Dolly's – sorry, Tiamat the Destroyer's ex-husband. Am I right?"

"Yes."

"Six months. Now, I'm going to tell you, but you're not going to believe me."

"If I don't believe you, will it cost me extra?"

"Yes."

"I believe you."

Mr Ahriman grinned. "That's what I like to see," he said, "unquestioning faith. Moves mountains, so I'm given to understand, but dynamite's quicker. Shall I write it down for you? Only you never know who's listening."

"All right."

Mr Ahriman nodded, then his left hand lashed out. His nails caught Mr Dawson just below the knuckles, which immediately gushed blood. Mr Ahriman produced a quill pen from nowhere; he dipped it in the blood and scribbled two words on the back of an envelope. Mr Dawson craned his neck to read them. "You're kidding," he said.

"Am I?"

"No, absolutely not," Mr Dawson said quickly. "You're sure about that?"

"Question or statement?"

"Statement."

"Of course it is," said Mr Ahriman. "I always tell the truth, you know that. Anyway, if that's everything, I really ought to be making tracks. You haven't forgotten what I told you about the money, have you?"

"No," Mr Dawson said. "I hadn't forgotten."

"That's my boy. Let's say five years for the information. But only because I like you."

Mr Dawson took out his handkerchief and wrapped it

tight round his gashed knuckles. "That's good to hear," he said. "Thanks for dropping by."

"Any time," said Mr Ahriman, and he vanished. The chair he'd been sitting on was smouldering and there was a sort of yellowish incrustation on the fabric where his head had rested. Five years.

Mr Dawson looked at the two words on the envelope back, scrawled in his own blood. Five years, he decided, well spent. Actually, a bargain.

Mr Ahriman was incapable of lying. Therefore what he'd written down must be true. In which case, all his troubles were – Well, not over exactly, or at least not yet, but better than nothing.

Nothing – He'd been to the Bank, of course, at various times, so to him nothing wasn't the vague and nebulous concept that it is for most people. He'd seen nothing in the raw. The last time he'd been there, to sign the specimen signatures to open the partnership accounts, it had nearly broken his heart. Envy, jealousy, longing – Everyone else had this to look forward to, but not Tom Dawson. He should be so lucky. For Mr Dawson, better than nothing was an oxymoron: how could anything possibly be better than that? Than escape? Freedom – ?

But the two words scribbled on the envelope: they were something else. Better than nothing. Even better than nothing. If only he could play his cards right—

Cards; that reminded him. He opened his desk drawer and rummaged about. Rubber bands, pencils, pencil sharpener, batteries for a calculator he'd thrown away in 1998, a tangled bundle of treasury tags – when was the last time we used those? – nine rounds of ammunition with sterling silver bullet heads, a small screwdriver, a golden apple inscribed *For the fairest*, a manual for a laser printer with instructions in Tibetan and Elvish, two blocks of staples, a Vernier caliper, a clerical collar, toenail clippers, an empty matchbox, a jeweller's loupe, a bottle of fin gloss (for mermaids: happy days), a slightly creased business card with a jolly robin on it—

Joy to the world. He picked up the card and looked at it. I got plenty of nothing, he hummed to himself, and nothing's plenty for me. It was turning into rather a pleasant day.

"The thing of it is," said Tony Bateman, "I'd have got away with it if only I hadn't sneezed."

Mr Teasdale scowled at him. "That doesn't make it better," he said. "Actually, it makes it a whole lot worse."

"Really?"

"Really," Mr Teasdale said. "It demonstrates a deplorable lack of remorse, for one thing. Instead of admitting you did a truly bad thing and trying to learn from it, all you can say is, I'd have got away with it, if only. That's not good, Can't you see that?"

Tony had the grace to look suitably ashamed. Of course, he could equally easily have looked like a toaster, so Mr Teasdale wasn't entirely prepared to take him at face value. "Also," he added, "you can't be a particularly good shapeshifter if you sneeze when you're on the job." He frowned. "I didn't even know a bra could sneeze."

"This one could," Tony replied.

"Fine," Mr Teasdale said. "So, not only are you guilty of flagrantly unethical conduct, you're also useless at your job. Luckily for you, I happen to know the clients personally and I was able to calm them down, so we won't be facing a lawsuit and you won't be going to jail. Not this time, anyhow. The fact remains—"

"Oh come on," Tony said. "How could she ever have proved it? There's no way—"

"Oh for crying out loud." You could always yell when Mr Teasdale was genuinely angry, by the pale green glow emanating from his ears. "Have you been listening to a single word I've said? We don't do that stuff. Not because we might get caught or sued. Because it's wrong."

"Sorry."

"No," Mr Teasdale said, "you're not, that's the whole point. You're just standing there waiting patiently till I run out of anger and you can go and have your morning coffee. That's just not good enough. I've had it with you. You're fired."

Tony went white as a sheet. "You can't do that."

"Yes I bloody well can."

"I know my rights," Tony said, unwisely. "You've got to give me a written warning, and—"

Mr Teasdale snapped his fingers. Out of nowhere appeared a bubble, floating in mid-air and really rather beautiful. Inside it, a sad-looking Tony was being handed a piece of paper by a grim-faced Mr Teasdale. On the wall behind him there was a calendar, with all the days crossed off up to the fourteenth, which was last Wednesday. "Don't mess with me," said Mr Teasdale, "and I won't mess with you. Find yourself a cardboard box and start putting your stuff in it. I've had about as much of you as I can take."

Mr Teasdale heard the door close, but didn't look round. He sat down and tried deep breathing, but it didn't really help. He opened the Dartington Extruded Plastics file and tried to read the last few letters, but his eyes skidded off the words like tyres on black ice; no traction.

"Got a moment?"

Tom Dawson never knocked. Mr Teasdale closed the file and pushed it aside. "Sure," he said.

"I've just been talking to young Bateman."

"Don't start on me," Mr Teasdale said. "He goes."

Mr Dawson sat down. "No," he said. "We need a shapeshifter and he's all we could get. I've told him, one more step over the line and we'll be down on him like a—"

Mr Teasdale gave him a look that should've peeled all the skin off his face. But Mr Dawson was in the habit of talking to Mr Ahriman, so no dice. "You gave him his job back. After I fired him. He went to you behind my back and you—"

"We need a shapeshifter," Mr Dawson repeated. "He won't do it again. He's not such a bad kid really, just a bit undisciplined."

"He's a creep," Mr Teasdale shouted. "He thinks it's funny sneaking into changing rooms and turning into women's underwear. He ought to be struck off for that."

Mr Dawson sighed. "Yes, well, it's an imperfect world, oh dear, never mind. Well done for sorting it out with the punters, by the way. You always did have a knack for flannel."

"That's another thing. Anybody who can turn a blind eye to that sort of thing isn't the kind of client we should be doing business with. It's wrong, Tom. Can't you see that?"

"Lots of things are wrong," Mr Dawson said firmly. "Is that a sorry state of affairs? Yes, it is. Do I lose sleep over it? No, I don't. Look, the kid played a stupid prank and got caught, but you sorted it all out, so no harm done. Meanwhile, we've got more important things to think about. I know who Tiamat's ex is."

The many delinquencies of Tony Bateman vanished from Mr Teasdale's mind like panic-bought toilet rolls. "You're kidding me."

"Straight up."

"How did you—?"

"You don't want to know," Mr Dawson said convincingly. "But it was worth it." He grinned. It was an alarming sight. "Tell you what. Give you three guesses."

"Tom, I'm not in the mood. Who is it? Someone we know?"

"Three guesses."

"Oh for pity's sake. I don't know, Father bloody Christmas. Tom, who—?"

"Oh. Somebody must've told you."

In every good cartoon there's always the moment where the cat chases the mouse off the edge of a cliff without realising and is caught for about a second running like mad in thin mid-air, until he notices the absence of solid ground and drops like a stone. Starring Mr Teasdale's mind as the cat. "You what?"

"Tiamat the Destroyer's ex-husband is Santa Claus."

"There is no—" Mr Teasdale froze, as thirty years of sincere trusting disbelief crashed round his ears like a Philistine temple. "There really is a Santa Claus?"

"Yup. As a matter of fact, he was in my office only the other day. Nice chap, but a bit scary."

"Are you sure?"

The look on Mr Teasdale's face. Half an hour ago, Mr Dawson was pretty sure he'd never laugh again. It was nice to find out he'd been wrong. "Sure I'm sure," he said. "The man himself. Even came down the chimney."

"We haven't got a chimney."

"I know. More to the point, I asked him if he'd be

prepared to do a bit of freelancing for us now and again, and he gave me his card." Mr Dawson produced it and handed it to Mr Teasdale, who stared at it. "That's what I like about life," Mr Dawson went on. "Most of the time it shits in your ear, but just occasionally it gives you a beautiful smile and a big wet kiss and you can see why you bother with it. Not only is there a solution to this problem, it's practically in-house. You do realise what this means, don't you?"

"There really is a Santa—"

"I'm off the hook," Mr Dawson said, "and we're going to be obscenely rich. Because when I ring up the United Nations and say, I can divert this asteroid that's about to wipe us all out but it'll cost you, and they say, all right, how much—"

Mr Teasdale seemed to wake up out of a strange dream. "This is true, right? You're not kidding me?"

"Scout's honour, Brian. No shit, this is not a drill. If we play our cards right, we're going to have to have all the stationery reprinted. Dawson and Dawson. All right, Dawson, Teasdale and Dawson. You realise what this means? I'll be rid of him—"

He stopped himself short, as though his parents were in the next room and he was worried they might have heard something. "Just a second," Mr Teasdale said. "All right, we know who the ex is. It doesn't necessarily follow that he'll do what we want him to."

"Are you kidding? He was in here interviewing for a job. A job which is mine to bestow as I see fit. And, right now, the way I see him getting the job is fitter than a Russian gymnast, provided he does us a little favour. You know what, Brian, if I didn't know better I'd swear it was Destiny."

Brian took a long, deep breath and let it out slowly. "You're sure you haven't got your wires crossed," he said. "You're sure it's – Well, him?"

Mr Dawson nodded. "Actually, it was staring me in the face all along. In fact, it's so obvious, if I wasn't so monumentally thick I'd have figured it out for myself. Obviously they know each other, from the old country."

"You've lost me."

"What? Oh, right, you don't know your basic mythology, fair enough. Presumably where you went to school you could either do Western civilisation and culture or pottery. Bet you throw a mean pot to this day. Santa's a thunder god."

"Excuse me?"

"Thunder god," Mr Dawson repeated. "First worshipped in early Bronze Age Mesopotamia around 3000 BC. There's statues and wall carvings and seal impressions of him all over the shop, driving a flying chariot drawn by stags and raining down thunderbolts on the unbelievers. His chariots of wrath the deep thunder-clouds form, and dark is his path on the wings of the storm, that kind of thing. He was all the rage in Ur and Nimrud and all those sort of places, back when your ancestors and mine were huddled in caves knapping flints and gnawing leftover elk. And guess who his trouble-and-strife was, in the good old days? Tiamat the truffing Destroyer. It's all on Wikipedia, but I was too idle to bother looking it up."

Mr Teasdale's eyes were perfect circles. "Santa?"

"Not in so many words under that exact particular name, but what the heck, we don't know what to call him and we're civilised. You know: Santa, Father Christmas, Papa Noel, Kris Kringle. Back then it was Ba'al and Hadad and Teshub and Marduk. Presumably in those days gods had names like we have Gmail accounts, people started blocking you as Enlil so you started over from scratch as Melkor. Definitely the same bloke, though. Winged chariot, inexhaustible horn of plenty, main festival at midwinter, travels round the world in no time flat, compiles the Great Scroll, knows who's naughty and who's nice, the whole nine yards. Staring me in the face the whole time, it was. It's astounding how somebody as clever as me can be so breathtakingly stupid, but there it is."

"Tom," Mr Teasdale said, "stop talking. Thank you," he added, as Mr Dawson glared at him. "I just want to get the facts straight in my mind before it explodes. You know Santa?"

"Yup."

"And he wants something from you."

"Oh good, you were listening after all. That's right."

"A job? But he's got a—"

Mr Dawson smiled. "By the sound of it, not for much longer. But the gig I've got lined up for him would suit him down to the ground. Sorry, was I talking too much? I do that when I'm happy, which probably explains why I do it so rarely. Look, there's probably a cloud in there somewhere if you take the whole thing to bits and grind it up in a pestle and mortar, but for the time being let's focus on the silver lining, because that would be cheerful and happy instead of bloody depressing. We've cracked it, Brian, my boy. Just for once, we're so far ahead of the game we can barely make it out against the distant horizon. Isn't that nice?"

"I guess so." Mr Teasdale said. "And it means the Earth won't be destroyed and the human race won't be wiped out. That's got to be a good thing, I guess."

"Absolutely," Mr Dawson said. "Like I always say, it's nice when you can help other people at the same time as making a very large amount of money. It's what being in the business is all about. Right, then. It's your file, strictly speaking, but I'm the one with the personal contact, so how'd it be if I made the call to Santa and got the ball rolling? I'll keep you copied in, naturally. Well? How about it?"

"Sure," Mr Teasdale said. "Um, what are you going to say to him?"

Mr Dawson hesitated. He hadn't actually got as far as that. "Oh, the obvious," he said. "If you want the God job, let's be having that key. Keep it simple. A nice friendly, breezy chat between two men of the world, is how I see it. We both know the score, sort of thing, you scratch my back, et cetera. He's not a bullshit kind of guy. It'll be a breeze, you'll see."

"God job?"

"Don't ask. Client confidentiality and all that jazz. I had to sign a bit of paper when I got the gig, don't apotheosise and tell. It's no big deal, but you know what a stickler I am for protocol. Talking of which, I've got a good mind to file a complaint with Professional Standards about that bloody ex-wife of yours pinching our client, but I won't if you're still sweet on her. Your call. Well?"

"It's not as simple as—"

"Nothing ever is," Mr Dawson said, "but I need a decision from you, now. You want me to crucify her or not? Entirely up to you, I couldn't give a monkey's."

"In that case, no," Mr Teasdale said, a trifle too casually. "I mean, it's water under the bridge and I don't suppose she'll do it again. Why make trouble unnecessarily?"

Mr Dawson gave him a wide, warm smile. "You clown," he said.

"Excuse me?"

"Clown," Mr Dawson repeated. "As in halfwit, imbecile or loser. She makes your life hell, then she dumps you, and still you can't bear to let go. Still, it's up to you."

"Yes," Mr Teasdale said. "As a matter of fact, it is."

"Cool. Go for it. Whatever turns you on. Of course, if you had half the common sense of a whelk, you'd forget all about her. Find yourself a nice, good-natured, sympathetic girl who'll take the trouble to understand you. Better still, do as I do and hire one by the hour. Ah well, it wouldn't do if we were all alike. I'll forget about writing that letter. One less thing for me to do, so that's all right. I think I'll go and make that call. You wouldn't happen to know, is Greenland an hour ahead of GMT or an hour behind?"

When he'd gone, Mr Teasdale spent the next two minutes just breathing. There was something about conversations with his senior partner that left Mr Teasdale feeling like he'd just spent the night in a tumble drier, except that if you did that, at least you'd come out feeling clean. Interviews with Mr Dawson, however, seemed to have the opposite effect.

He took his phone from his pocket and looked at it. He had, after all, promised. In the back of his mind he could hear Mr Dawson's voice: she makes your life hell, then she dumps you, and still you can't bear to let go. Somehow, that made the decision easier. If Tom knew what he was about to do, would he approve? Would he hell as like. In which case, Mr Teasdale decided, it's probably the right course of action. He prodded the screen. "Hi," he said.

"You arsehole. You total shit. You complete and utter fucking—"

Which reassured him that at least it wasn't a wrong number. "Listen," he said. "I found out something about the case."

"Darling. What?"

He told her. There was a long silence. "Hello? You still there?"

"You're joking, right?"

"Absolutely not. Tom Dawson just told me. He seemed really happy about it, so it must be true."

More silence. Then: "I guess so. Well, this is great. And Tom actually knows—"

"So he says, and I believe him. Look," said Mr Teasdale, "what do you actually need in order to prove she's a trinity?"

Pause. "Scans," Consuela said. "A biometric matrix analysis. A DNA sample wouldn't hurt, either. All you have to do is set up a meeting and I can handle all of that."

"I'll see what I can do," Mr Teasdale said. He paused. "Look, I'm sorry about all the trouble."

"Forget it."

"I hope the hair wasn't rude or nasty or anything. I told it, don't do anything I wouldn't do, but I've been using a new conditioner lately, and sometimes it makes my hair, well, a bit full of bounce and body—"

"Not a problem, really. Oh, and by the way, I changed my mind about Hanuman. I was wrong, he belongs with you. Keeping him was just me being spiteful."

"Really?"

"Absolutely."

Mr Teasdale's heart was like a singing bird. "Thanks, Consuela, that's really sweet. I miss the little chap."

"I'll hand him over next time I see you. Talking of which, when are you free for lunch? There's this new

143

Tajik place just opened in Shepherd Market I'm dying to try, if you fancy it. Apparently they do an amazing anchovy qurutob."

In the back of his mind, a virtual Tom Dawson was stuffing a sock in his mouth to keep himself from laughing. But never mind about that; Mr Teasdale was scanning his diary. "I can do Thursday."

"Brilliant. See you then."

Consuela Teasdale ended the call and put her phone down on the desk. Calm, she told herself, control; there'll be plenty of time for ripping his lungs out later, but right now she needed to be at the top of her game, magnificently serene. She sent for Erica, who came straight away.

"Job for you."

"All right," Erica said. "Oh, while I think of it, you wanted to know about Tiamat's ex-husband. I found out. It's Santa Claus."

"Yes, I know that. In fact, if you'd told me a bit earlier you could've saved me a really boring lunch."

"Sorry."

Consuela shook her head. "Can't be helped now, I suppose. I just wish, when I ask you to do something for me, you'd do it while it's still actually relevant. Still, you can only do your best. My fault for expecting too much. Now, then. How do you perform a biometric matrix analysis on someone without them realising you're doing it?"

Erica bit her lip. "I don't know."

"Then go away and find out. And when you've done that, get hold of the necessary equipment and set it up in the small interview room."

"All right."

"And nip down to Robertsons and borrow their

semiotic phase inducer, the Kawaguchiya, not the Hewlett Packard, and a couple of spare energy cells."

"All right."

"And reschedule my lunch with the archbishop on Thursday, find out everything you can about transmigration of souls, and get me a double butterscotch latte and a slice of angel food cake. OK?"

"I'm on it," Erica said, and left. Useful kid, Consuela thought to herself as she opened a new file. Wonder how she found out about Santa. Still, that didn't matter any more. Clarity of purpose; a straight line between desire and fulfilment. Anything else would be a waste of time; it'd be silly.

Her hand strayed to the chain round her neck. She hadn't dared to try taking it off. It was typical of Brian that he had more gumption in a single hair than in all the rest of him put together, and he didn't even suspect it. She'd been fond of him once, unbelievable but true. Since then – During her long, lonely vigil in the ladies' lavatory at JWW, the thought of how she was finally going to get even with Brian Teasdale had been the only thing that had kept her going. But never mind about all that. He'd keep.

Erica came in with her butterscotch latte. The stupid girl had forgotten the sprinkles, but she couldn't be bothered to make an issue out of it.

"No thanks," said Santa.

Mr Dawson stared at him. "You what?"

Santa nibbled the crust of his mince pie. Getting hold of mince pies in the middle of summer hadn't been easy, but Mr Dawson had contacts. "You heard. Thanks but no thanks. I've decided I don't want the job after all."

"You're kidding me," Mr Dawson said. "You don't want to be God?"

Santa shook his head. "Thought I did," he said with his mouth full, "at one point, but then I said to myself, Kris, you've been there and done that and what did it get you? Nothing but grief and heartache, not to mention antisocial hours and everybody going on at me all the time like everything was my fault. Didn't help that it was all my fault, come to that, so you can add a stinking rotten guilty conscience to all of the above. So, on mature reflection, stuff it. I'd rather work for a living."

Just when you think you've heard it all. "Can we just go back a bit and clarify?" Mr Dawson said. "You're turning down a chance to be the supreme being—"

"In some jerkwater trailer-park reality nobody's ever heard of? You bet. And don't give me any of that flannel about all realities being equal, because they aren't."

"Yes they are," Mr Dawson said. "Multiverse theory plainly states that every bifurcation from the original stem is of equal validity. That's science."

"Really. Well, you know where you can stick it. Oh, I know what it says in theory, but let's face it, stuff doesn't work like that. There's cool-gang realities, and then there's the other side of the tracks, and this dump you're offering me is definitely the latter category. Well, you wouldn't want to live there, would you?"

Mr Dawson hesitated. Every bifurcation in the space/time continuum arises from what you might call an issue. Is rain wet or isn't it? Which socks will Norman choose to put on today, the beige or the teal? If I drop this carrot, is it written in stone that it's got to fall to the ground or can't we all sit round a table like rational adults and search for a compromise? The bifurcation that brought into being the reality for which Mr Dawson was currently acting owed its existence to a referendum in which the majority of sentient life in the universe had decided to opt out of Newtonian physics. The answer to Santa's question was, therefore, probably not. Even so.

"You're missing the point, surely," Mr Dawson rallied gamely. "Even if the place is currently a bit of a dump, which is by no means admitted, once you're in there and you've got your feet under the table you can fix it up exactly how you want it, because you'll be Him. You know, the Man. Can't be doing with Mondays? The hell with them. Blue skies make you want to throw up? Paint 'em green. The thought of having to spend one more day in sequential linear time driving you nuts? Just click your fingers and, hey presto, time is now a recursive helix. You can do that sort of thing when you're the Big Guy, you know that. All right, at the moment it may not be the hottest blip on the spectrum, but I bet you, in six thousand years you could make this reality trend like there's no tomorrow. Of which there wouldn't have to be one," he added, "if you happened not to feel like it."

Santa grinned at him. "Nice try," he said. "And, yes, there's aspects of being my own boss that do have a certain appeal, I grant you that. Like, for example, I could have a zonking great big flood, and then repopulate the cosmos with a dominant species that wasn't unbelievably, suicidally stupid. Nobody's ever tried that before, and I think it could be a winner."

"There you go, then," Mr Dawson said, though he wasn't convinced it was possible. "Take the job, give it a go. What have you got to lose?"

"Ah," Santa said. "That's the point, isn't it? You're not offering me this job because you think I represent the best possible ethical system money can buy. You want me to do something for you. Right?"

Mr Dawson breathed out slowly through his nose. "Just supposing that was the case," he said. "That wouldn't be so terrible, would it? I mean, surely that's the essence of the God business."

"Really?"

"Granting prayers? You bet. Give me what I want and you can be my strength and my redeemer any day. That's what it's all about, surely."

Santa gave him an odd look. "That's how most people think it works, I grant you. But you've got it a bit arse-about-face, haven't you? Shouldn't it be, you're God, I want this, thank you, how do you like your burnt offerings? What you're suggesting is, I want this, you can be God provided you give it to me. That's a bit – I don't know, maybe just a tad cold-blooded."

Mr Dawson frowned. "I don't think so," he said.

"Yeah, well, each to his own, I guess. Makes no odds, as far as I'm concerned. I'm not stupid, you know, even if I do wear a red dressing gown in the daytime. I know what you're after, and the answer is no."

Nuts, Mr Dawson thought. "Bet you you don't."

"Idiot," said Santa, not unkindly. "I know what everybody wants, remember? And what you're dying to see poking out of your stocking on Christmas morning is me making nice with that bloody woman. And I'm telling you, it ain't going to happen."

Mr Dawson was a man of many talents. He could turn water into Chablis and policemen into terrapins. He could wind back the clock, transmute base metal into government bonds, summon spirits from the vasty deep, pull a rabbit out of a hat, conjure up tempests, raise the dead, restore lost youth and adjust the fabric of reality so that his Rolls-Royce Silver Ghost counted as an agricultural vehicle for tax purposes. What he was best at, however, was negotiation. "That's just silly," he said.

"You what?"

"Silly," Mr Dawson repeated, feeling immensely grateful that forty generations of English speakers had worked so long and so hard to craft the perfect word for him to use at that precise moment. "Well, isn't it?"

"Get stuffed."

Mr Dawson didn't smile, though he felt like doing so. "That's it, is it? That's your carefully thought out and meticulously reasoned response. Question: why shouldn't you do this trivial little thing to save the planet from destruction and get rewarded with apotheosis? Answer: get stuffed. You must lend me your edition of Plato one of these days. I suspect it might not be the same as mine."

"Get stuffed," said Santa, "with knobs on."

"Mphm." Mr Dawson nodded. "Is it possible I'm sensing residual traces of anger here?"

"You bet you are."

"That would explain it. I was trying to account for why a universally respected demigod like yourself would be prepared to stand idly by and allow his planet to be smashed into rubble while passing up on the chance of absolute power over an entire tangent of space/time, and then I realised. He's still pissed off at his old lady. Well, that's all right, then. Makes perfect sense when you put it like that."

"You don't know her," Santa growled. "If you did, it would."

"Yes, well, I haven't met her. But I'm going to be meeting her real soon, and she'll be arriving on an asteroid, and two seconds later I'll be dead. I don't know, maybe I'm allowing this total-annihilation-of-the-planet thing to cloud my judgement. If so, I apologise. But on the other hand, while we're on the subject of clouded judgement—"

Santa sighed. "Fine," he said. "Ten out of ten for effort, nine out of ten for deductive reasoning, but the answer's still no. What makes you think I'd have any influence over her anyway? If I get involved, it'll just make her more bloody-minded. If I go down on my bended knees and beg her not to smash the planet, you can practically guarantee she'll do it, just to be annoying."

"You could let her out of the asteroid."

"No I couldn't."

"You've got the key."

Santa looked at him with deep compassion. "No," he said, "I haven't."

Imagine you were freewheeling down a long, straight downhill road and someone had thought how hilarious it would be to stretch a length of thin wire across the road at roughly throat height. As far as Mr Dawson was concerned, a bit like that only more so. "Excuse me?"

"I haven't got it."

Mr Dawson rolled his eyes. "Let me guess," he said. "You put it in a safe place, and now you can't remember where."

"I put it in a safe place all right," said Santa. "I put it in a safety deposit box in the vaults of the Second Interstellar Bank on Beta Orionis Four. But it's not there any more. It's gone."

"Gone."

Santa nodded. "Someone wrote to them with my access codes and my signature, asking them to forward it to some address on Alpha Centauri Prime I'd never heard of. Everything was exactly right, according to the bank guys, but it wasn't me."

"Hang on a—"

"Because naturally, the moment I heard what Dolly was up to, I was on to the Second Interstellar like a rat up a drain, telling them to send me the key, stat."

"But—"

"On account of, I didn't really want to see the planet smashed to rubble if I could help it. Call me an old softie if you like, but there you are, sometimes I think all that ho-ho-hoing is starting to rot my brain. But they hadn't got the key, because they sent it – they thought – to me, only of course they didn't. So, no, I haven't got the key, and, no, I don't know where it is. So, no, I can't unlock Dolly's asteroid and let her out, which means the only way I have of stopping her from trashing the Earth is asking her nicely. Which, for various reasons I won't go into right now, is unlikely to succeed, even if I was prepared to do it, which I'm not." He paused and ate another mince pie. "Trust me," he said, "my heart bleeds for the human race, of course it does, it bleeds like mad. But there's not a great deal I can do about it, so what the heck."

Mr Dawson stared at him. "Oh," he said.

"You never said a truer word," Santa replied, wiping crumbs from his moustache. "Anyway, that's enough about that. About this job. Without the strings attached, I wouldn't mind having a stab at it. What about it?"

That got him a scowl. "In your dreams," Mr Dawson said.

"Fine. In that case I'll just pack up my bits and bobs, load up the sleigh and set off into the wide blue yonder. I'm not a hundred per cent sure that reindeer can breathe in the vacuum of space, but since they can't talk or fly faster than the speed of light either, I don't suppose they'll be all that worried. I'd just like to add that it was a pleasure knowing you, albeit briefly."

"Thank you."

"But I can't, because it wouldn't be true. So long, creature of a day. You failed miserably, but don't beat yourself up about it."

"That's sweet of you."

"I'm like that." A fireplace appeared in the wall, underneath a mantelpiece decked with boughs of holly. Santa got up and hefted his sack. "Oh, there's just one thing."

"What?"

"There is another."

"Come again?"

Santa grinned. "That was a quotation," he pointed out. "I haven't got a hope in hell of sweet-talking Dolly into not smashing your planet, but I know someone she might listen to."

There's that experiment they show you at school, where they connect electrodes to a dead frog and make it spasm. Mr Dawson spasmed. "Really?"

"Maybe, maybe not," he said. "But since you have absolutely no alternative, you might consider giving it a try. Her brother."

"She's got a brother?"

"Several, actually. You should know that, being a scholar."

"Remind me."

"Seriously? Oh, all right. In the beginning was the Word—"

"Skip that bit."

"From which," Santa went on regardless, "we gods

were formed, at least we were in Mesopotamia, I really wouldn't care to be dogmatic about anywhere else. Anyhow, there was this word, and we were all bits of it. If memory serves, I was a B."

"I bet you were."

"Dolly was a D, naturally, and her brother was an S. I always thought he'd have been better off as a comma, but nobody asked me. We didn't exactly get on, to be honest with you. I was basically thunder, rainfall and divine retribution, Dolly looked after the death side of things and her brother was light, vegetation and general administrative support. And, yes, inevitably from time to time we ended up treading on each other's toes, you know how it is in a small business. Anyway, there we all were, back in the old country. Happy days."

"Her brother."

"What? Oh yes. He's still around here somewhere, last I heard. They were never exactly close, mind, even back then. I remember when we were married she moaned about him all the time."

"He's still around," Mr Dawson repeated. "You mean, on Earth?"

A broad grin spread across Santa's face. "That's what I like about you mortals," he said. "You don't know everything. You think you do, but you don't. So from time to time you find out stuff that really blows your socks off, and when that happens the look on your faces—"

"Who is he? Please. Tell me his bloody name."

"That's what you want Santa to give you, is it?"

"Yes."

"Have you been good?"

"All right, you can have the stupid job."

"Thank you, though you didn't actually answer my

question. The man you're looking for is – Oh, you're going to wet yourself when I tell you."

"Please?"

So Santa told him.

"I'm confused," Lilith said. "I thought you weren't working for me any more."

Consuela forgave her the words working for, which didn't quite chime with her view of the practitioner/client relationship. "Strictly speaking, no, I'm not," she said. "But, then, I never was. I act for the United Nations, remember?"

"What? Oh, yes, so you do, I'd forgotten that."

"And in my professional opinion, my client's interests can best be served by getting you to persuade your mother not to turn the Earth into a cloud of fine grit. Try one of these cannoli, they're really quite good."

Which indeed they were, and there was a fifteen-second pause mostly occupied with munching. "Have I got to?" Lilith eventually said.

"Depends," Consuela replied, sipping her coffee. "Obviously nobody can make you if you don't want to, but if you don't and your mother obliterates the Earth, I imagine you'll feel quite bad about it, though not," she added, "for very long. It's entirely up to you and your conscience, naturally, but if you ask me, if you're serious about saving the planet, doing this one small thing for it is even more important than energy-saving light bulbs."

Put like that— "Oh, all right, then. But what makes you think she'll listen to me?"

Consuela smiled. "Nature," she said. "The bond between mother and daughter. Quite possibly the most powerful force in the Multiverse." As she spoke the words, she couldn't help thinking about her own mother, who lived on a narrowboat with fourteen cats, an unwholesome amount of marijuana and the collected works of Allen Ginsberg, and was in the habit of covering her ears with her hands and humming loudly until Consuela went away. "Of course she'll listen to you," she said. "Especially if I tell you what to say."

Putty, in other words, in her hands. She left Lilith in the coffee shop guzzling cheesecake and walked slowly back to St Mary Axe. Properly speaking, of course, she ought to tell Brian she was in touch with his client, but that could probably wait until the fait was safely accompli; if he didn't know about it, he couldn't stick his oar in, and that way everybody would be happy. If she was honest with herself, she couldn't really imagine Lilith persuading the top off a bottle, let alone the Queen of Death to spare an entire world. That was beside the point. All that mattered was manoeuvring herself into the same room as a real-life genuine trinity and taking the necessary scans and readings to prove she was right. If doing so also saved the planet, fine. If not, she'd just have to leave all that side of things to Brian and Tom Dawson. It was what they were being paid for, after all. Someone was bound to save the planet, because someone always did, otherwise it wouldn't still be here, would it? Meanwhile, she had this truly unique opportunity to get what she wanted and thoroughly deserved, and what could be more important than that?

Erica was waiting for her when she got back to her office. "I borrowed Robertsons' semiotic phase inducer like you told me to," she said. "The mass inversion condensator was sixteen degrees out of alignment, so I fixed it."

Consuela nodded absently. "I need to talk to a goddess," she said. "How would I go about it?"

"Prayer?"

That got the scowl it merited. "Or," Erica went on, "you could summon her through demonic intercession, using Ordovan metempsychotic protocols to—"

"No demons," Consuela said firmly. "The punter did demons already, so that's no good. Come on, think. You're supposed to be smart, aren't you?"

Erica thought. "How about a challenge?"

"You what?"

"A challenge," Erica repeated. "The Kuniyoshi-Friedman process, but modified to take account of real-time distortions in the carrier wave."

Consuela would never have thought of that in a thousand years. "Yeah, right," she said. "I challenge the Goddess of Death to one-on-one mortal combat. Why do I think there's a problem with that?"

"You concede, naturally," Erica said, "the moment she appears. You can do that, there's loads of precedents. And then, at least you've got her there, so you can talk to her. Isn't that what you wanted?"

Genius. She'd forgotten about the precedents. "Well, if that's the best you can come up with, I guess it'll have to do. Get it set up, will you? Any time today will be fine."

"All right. I'll need the key to the stationery cupboard."

Consuela handed it over. "Mind you bring it straight back," she said. "Oh, and there's a button come off my coat. See to it, there's a doll."

"You might have told me."

Mr Sunshine stood up and walked to the window. Properly speaking, Mr Sunshine's office overlooked the small courtyard where they corralled the wheelie bins, but Mr Sunshine didn't like looking at stuff like that. So instead he had a view out over Waterloo Bridge, except on Fridays, when it was the Promenade des Anglais. Occasionally, when nobody was looking, it was Atlantis. "Really," he said. "Why?"

Mr Dawson made an effort and didn't yell. "Oh, I don't know," he said. "The survival of the human race, maybe. That sort of thing."

Mr Sunshine sighed and turned away from the window. "Sit down," he said. Immediately, the armchair reserved for visitors on the other side of Mr Sunshine's desk turned into a low three-legged stool. Mr Dawson glared at him and sat on it.

"Look," Mr Dawson said, "we don't exactly get along, and that's fine. Nobody says we have to, so long as it doesn't get in the way of running the business. We can hate each other like poison and still work together. Most people do, after all. That and the spinning jenny are what made British industry great. But mutual loathing's one thing. Not telling me something like that is quite another."

Mr Sunshine sighed. "It's private," he said. "Personal."

"Not when it directly affects the business of this firm," Mr Dawson shouted. "Sorry," he added quickly, as Mr Sunshine looked at him. "Got a bit emotional there, on account of my life being on the line and silly things like that. Maybe I ought to write out five hundred times, I must not let fear of death get in the way of good manners."

Mr Sunshine gave him a crooked grin. "It's not death you're afraid of, is it, Tom? But fair enough, you've made your point. Maybe I should've mentioned it, at that. To Gina, anyhow. Or Brian."

"Yes," said Mr Dawson. "You should."

"I'd stay clear of the moral high ground if I were you," said Mr Sunshine. "You may find the air's a bit thin up there if you're not used to it. All right, so now you know. What about it?"

"For crying out—" Mr Dawson took a deep breath. "Perhaps," he said, "if it wouldn't be too much trouble, you might just possibly see your way to talking to her. Maybe even asking her nicely if she wouldn't mind crashing her asteroid somewhere else. As a personal favour to you."

Mr Sunshine made a soft growling noise that had very little to do with language. "Don't start all that," Mr Dawson said. "And if you're planning on zapping me with a thunderbolt, why don't you just go ahead and do it, instead of pulling silly faces? Though I've got to tell you, if you think that sort of thing impresses people, you're sadly behind the times. Nobody loves a smiter any more, Ted. It's time you accepted that and moved on."

"We're not on speaking terms."

"Well," Mr Dawson said, "now's your chance to put it all right. Now wouldn't that be nice? Come on, Ted. Just because it's me saying it doesn't mean it isn't true."

That was the trouble wth fighting with Tom Dawson. "You have no idea what you're asking," Mr Sunshine said, as the sky outside darkened and black clouds blotted out the sun. "You don't know her. She's—"

"Family," Mr Dawson said. "Your kid sister."

It's a truism that the ace of trumps only takes one trick. It's knowing when to use it that makes you dangerous. "Yes, all right," Mr Sunshine said bitterly, "and thank you ever so much for reminding me, after I've spent the last two thousand years trying to forget it. He told you, presumably."

"Your brother-in-law. Well, ex."

"How nice of him. What else did he tell you?"

"This and that. Stuff about the old country. You know what, Ted," Mr Dawson went on, "I try not to be judgemental, but I take that a bit hard. How long have we known each other? And all that time, you never told me you're a god."

"Was a god," Mr Sunshine said. "I don't do that sort of thing any more."

"Was a – Sorry, Ted, does not compute. You can't just stop."

"Yes you can," Mr Sunshine said firmly. "And I did. Cleared my desk, handed in my thunderbolt and my badge, walked out, never once looked back. It's no life for a person of conscience, believe me."

"Of course I believe you, Ted, you're the fucking Almighty, I have no choice. No, don't pull faces, I'm talking to you. You can't just turn out to be the Maker of Heaven and Earth and not expect there to be consequences."

"Was, for crying out loud. Don't you understand tenses? I told you, that's all in the past."

"Oh sure. And an infinite being is so pinned down by linear sequential time. Well, it explains a great deal, anyhow. The superior attitude, the peering-down-your-nose, holier-than-thou—"

"But I am holier than thou, Tom. Come to that, so are most rattlesnakes."

"That's beside the point. You know what? People like you make me sick."

"Former gods?"

"Toffs," Mr Dawson said, with what might just have been genuine feeling. "The idle talented. The privileged few. People like you who've always had it easy never even had to try. You want water? Just smack a rock, no need to sully your lily-white fingers turning a tap. You want to work miracles? A click of the fingers. You didn't spend years working a lousy McJob to pay your way through night school to be a miracle-worker, it was just handed to you on a plate. You know what? To me, this – being a partner in a high class magic firm – is the pinnacle of achievement. This is what I've slaved and starved and sold my soul and fought tooth and nail my whole life for. To you, this is slumming. You're just playing at it, aren't you, like Marie bloody Antoinette playing at shepherd-esses. Whereas I had to—"

He stopped dead. Mr Sunshine looked at him. Utter contempt and heartfelt compassion don't usually go well together, but Mr Sunshine had the knack. "Fine," he said. "But you had no call to go forcing me out of the partnership. That was low."

"You were ruining the business. Running it into the ground."

Mr Sunshine raised an eyebrow. "Two hundred and seventeen per cent annual return on capital isn't running a business into the ground," he said.

"It is when he's—" Mr Dawson stopped again, his chest heaving, as though he'd just run a mile uphill carrying heavy suitcases. "Whatever," he said. "So, you're a god, big deal. I don't care. I'm every bit as good as you are, or better. And I'm the senior partner of this firm and you're just a consultant, so either you do as you're told or you can clear your desk and be out of here by this time tomorrow. Do I make myself clear?"

For a moment, Mr Dawson wondered if this time he'd finally crossed the line. But Mr Sunshine just looked at him, as though he was a piece left over from a totally different jigsaw puzzle, and then he laughed. "Nice try, Tom," he said. "You almost had me going there for a moment. Luckily for you, you hadn't, which is why you're still breathing." He shrugged. "You want me to go, I'll go. I imagine Gina'll go with me, and Brian, too, probably. In fact, this firm will probably go down in nautical history as the only sinking ship where everyone else left and the rats stayed. Now then, is that what you want?"

Mr Dawson deflated like a punctured tyre. "No, of course not," he said. "What I want is for you to talk to your sister. Ask her not to destroy the planet. If you do that small thing for me, then maybe we can take another look at how things are structured around here. Partnershipwise."

Mr Sunshine had been around the block a few times. Time was, in fact, when he went round the block precisely once every twenty-four hours, shining into every crack and crevice where anything unknown or secret might be hiding. Just occasionally, however, he ran into something he hadn't seen coming a mile off, such as Mr Dawson's skill as a negotiator. He paused for a second, and his hesitation was the kind of endorsement of Mr Dawson's technique that money simply can't buy. Then he took a deep breath. "OK," he said. "You got me."

Mr Dawson grinned. "Really?"

Mr Sunshine nodded. "I think that's what's known in the business as an offer I can't refuse. Were you planning on making it all along?"

Mr Dawson shook his head. "Not unless I had to."

"I believe you," Mr Sunshine said, "thousands wouldn't. All right, I'll talk to her."

"Jolly good."

"But first—" Mr Sunshine pointed through the window. Waterloo Bridge wasn't there any more. Instead, Mr Sunshine's office overlooked a vast primeval forest, stretching as far as the eye could see. "Familiar?"

"No."

Mr Sunshine opened the window. A blast of hot air filled the room, and the scent of pollen and rotten leaves was overpowering. "I grew up here," Mr Sunshine said. "The best days of my life would be overstating the case, but there's been worse places, over the years. That over there—" He pointed at something Mr Dawson couldn't distinguish from the surrounding ocean of treetops— "is the Rumaila oil field in southern Iraq. Or it will be, one day." The sky grew dark. "Now then," Mr Sunshine went on, "see that tiny point of light just peeping through the clouds? That's me, as a teenager."

"How sweet," Mr Dawson said. "Has this got anything to do with anything?"

"And that," Mr Sunshine added, as a meteor streaked across the sky and crashed into the forest, which immediately burst into flames, "is Santa."

Mr Dawson sighed. "Get on with it," he said.

So Mr Sunshine got on with it.

Once upon a time, he insisted on beginning, there was a huge forest and in the forest lived a lot of trees and some ferns, but that was about it, because this was a long time ago, before there were even beetles. It was only when the giant meteorite struck and did something or other to the planet's orbit and therefore the climate that things started getting complicated, a fact which wasn't wasted on the local vegetation spirits.

"You stupid, careless, clumsy idiot," said their

spokeswoman to the pilot of the meteorite as he scrambled out of the giant crater his impact had caused. "Why the hell can't you look where you're going?"

"Sorry," the pilot said. "I got caught in an ion storm just coming out of the Trimaris nebula, then I guess I must've skidded on a patch of dark matter, because—"

"You were going too fast," the spokeswoman interpreted. "Showing off. Probably texting. And now look what you've done."

The spokeswoman had a high, shrill voice and plenty of it, but the pilot couldn't help noticing she was kinda cute, if you like 'em green and frondy. "Jump-started evolution on your world, by the looks of it," he said. "Hey, get a load of that. Woodlice." And the morning and the evening, incidentally, were the fifth day.

"Yuk," said the spokeswoman firmly. "Creepy-crawlies."

"True," conceded the pilot. "Although give 'em a day or so and they'll be yay high, walking on their hind legs and discovering the Higgs boson. Still, you're probably right. I can do you a quick flood and everything'll be jake."

The spokeswoman considered the woodlice and saw that they were good, or at least not as bad as all that. "Nah," she said. "Screw it. What harm can they do?"

And that, as they say, was the start of a beautiful friendship, much to the disgust of the spokeswoman's brothers and sisters, who didn't approve of pets, romance or their sister having more fun than they did. But the stranger knew how to shape ambient static electricity into thunderbolts, so after a while they decided to keep their ethical and ecological concerns to themselves and find things to do in other parts of the forest. Meanwhile, the pilot and the spokeswoman wandered happily through the steamy glades, when they weren't doing other things, and the pilot happened to mention that it wouldn't be a bad idea to get rid of some of the trees, because otherwise all their fallen leaves would eventually get buried under billions of tons of rock and compressed into a thick black sludge which might well cause problems further along the line; and the spokeswoman said, yes, what a good idea, we'll do that, but what with one thing and another they never got around to it—

"Is this going anywhere?" Mr Dawson interrupted. "Because it's a very pretty story but my attention span's a bit finite, and—"

"You're the one who got so uptight about not being told things," Mr Sunshine pointed out. "So I'm telling you things, and you're moaning at me."

"There's things and things," Mr Dawson pointed out. "On balance, I prefer my things with a side of relevance."

"Fusspot," Mr Sunshine said. Outside, the jungle vanished and Waterloo Bridge reappeared, shining in the freshly fallen rain. "All right, you want the bottom line, here it is. Dolly and Santa were blissfully happy together for millions of years, when they weren't scratching each others' eyes out, but eventually all good things must come to an end and they split up. Lawyers got involved—"

"Ah."

"Quite. Dolly got the sea, the sky, the dry land, all that therein is, the sun, moon and stars, the past, the present, the future, ten-to-the-power-of-infinity dollars a month alimony and custody of the humans. Santa ended up living in a one-room igloo working as a delivery driver."

"The old, old story."

"Indeed. But it didn't end there."

"Didn't it?"

Mr Sunshine shook his head. "My sister is many

things," he went on. "A businesswoman isn't one of them. Unfortunately she couldn't accept that. We tried to tell her, of course, but the more we tried the less she was prepared to listen. Two thousand years after the divorce, she'd lost the lot."

Mr Dawson was impressed. "The Earth and all that therein is? Really?"

Mr Sunshine nodded. "She had a bit of bad luck, of course."

"Obviously."

"Mostly it was the bad luck to have been born stupid. Anyway, she ended up practically giving the business to the El-Jay Consortium, and the rest is theology."

Mr Dawson's eyes narrowed. "So she doesn't actually own—"

"Not so much as a blade of grass, no, not any more. So if she promises you Asia in return for helping her, bear in mind it's not hers to give."

Mr Dawson had a SatNav's happy ability to recalculate the route when Life insists on taking a wrong turn. Loads of money had just evaporated in the harsh glare of Mr Sunshine's revelation. On the other hand, not getting splashed by an asteroid had to be worth something to the boys who held the purse strings at the UN – to pluck a figure out of the air, say, loads of money. Enough to get Mr Ahriman off his back? Maybe, for a little while. It'd have to do. "So the Earth isn't even hers to trash?"

"Decidedly not. Unfortunately, she had a bit of trouble accepting that. She's not what you'd call a good loser."

"One of those."

"Indeed," said Mr Sunshine. "She went around holding rallies and stirring up the faithful, saying that the sale was all a fix and a put-up job and really she'd bought out the El-Jays, not the other way round. It was all starting to get a big ugly at one point. She'd got hold of this asteroid, and she was threatening to crash it into the planet unless the El-Jays agreed to some sort of power-sharing deal, but you know what they're like about having no other god but them. I tried to reason with her, naturally, but all she could do was rant on at me about draining the swamp and building some wall or other, so I decided to save my breath."

"Sensible."

"No, not really," sighed Mr Sunshine. "I should've done something, and I didn't. Instead, it was Santa who dealt with it. He sneaked into Dolly's asteroid down the chimney—"

"An asteroid with a chimney."

"Apparently it had one," Mr Sunshine said, "though I imagine only briefly. Anyway, he locked her out of the navigation system and set it adrift in intergalactic space. Give her a chance to cool down and get a grip, he said."

Mr Dawson nodded slowly. "I'm thinking that was maybe not such a good idea."

"You could say that," Mr Sunshine said. "What he in fact did was give her a chance to work up a really good head of resentment. That was around three thousand years ago and, if I know her, she's probably madder than ever. Which is why, to be honest with you, the thought of talking to her doesn't appeal much. She's my sister and I love her dearly, but you know what they say about absence making the heart grow fonder. I haven't seen her for three thousand years and I'd just reached the point where I could think about her and not feel the urge to hide under the bed."

Mr Dawson looked at him gravely. "You did promise," he said.

"Did I? I suppose I did. It's a bit of an ask, though. Maybe I could send Harmondsworth instead."

The drawer of Mr Sunshine's desk, which had been open an inch or so, slammed shut. Mr Dawson looked at it, and saw the key turn in the lock.

"Or maybe not," said Mr Sunshine. "No, I guess it's something I have to do myself, otherwise it won't stand any chance at all of working. Tell you what, though. By the time I've finished I'll have earned that partnership."

Mr Dawson didn't say anything. Mr Sunshine looked at him. "About that," Mr Dawson said.

"Don't start."

"No, really, that's fine. It's just, I can't help wondering. I mean, you used to be a god, for crying out loud—"

"Used to be. The tense is important."

"Yes, all right, granted. Even so, I've got to ask. Since you've been all that and done all that and got all the T-shirts, why the hell should it matter to you so much about being a partner in a small niche sorcerors' office in northern Europe? Me, yes, it's all I care about, I admit that. But I'm a mortal human. You're—" He shrugged. "Whatever. Why should you care?"

Mr Sunshine looked at him for three seconds.

"Fine," Mr Dawson said. "I'll mind my own beeswax. Even so, it's a mystery, isn't it?"

"Go away," Mr Sunshine said quietly. And Mr Dawson went.

COMET

"Oh," said Gina to the staffroom kettle. "You're still here, then."

The kettle turned into Tony Bateman. "'Fraid so," he said.

"I thought Brian fired you."

"Mr Dawson decided to give me another chance."

"Did he now." Gina wrinkled her nose. "Well, we all make catastrophic errors of judgement every so often, and why should Tom Dawson be any different? Just one, thing, though. If I ever catch you doing something like that again, inside the office or out of it, I'll make you wish you really were a kettle. Got that?"

Tony shuddered. "Loud and clear."

"Splendid. And from now on, unless explicitly required to be otherwise in the line of duty, just be yourself." Her frown deepened, just a smidge. "I know. I wouldn't want to be you, God knows, it must be absolutely ghastly, but somebody's got to do it, I suppose, and it's always been standard operating practice in this firm to give the truly rotten jobs to the least valuable members of staff. Now get out of my sight, before I say something hurtful."

Tony hurried to the door, hesitated, took his life in his hands and turned back. "You knew it was me?"

"What, the kettle? Yes, of course."

"How?"

Gina sighed. "The power of the inner eye," she said. "The ability to see past the surface, right down to the sub-atomic level. Also, you were wearing a European plug."

"Ah."

"You haven't gone yet."

"Sorry," Tony said, and went. Alone at last, Gina looked round for the real kettle but couldn't find it. Why could nobody ever leave things where they ought to be?

She knew why. "Harmondsworth," she said.

At first, nothing happened. Then a drawer in the kitchen unit slid open, and there was the kettle. She took it out and put it on the worktop. "Are you in there?" she said.

"Yes."

"Well, come out. I want to make a cup of tea."

"No."

Interesting. "You're hiding, aren't you?"

"Yes."

Gina instinctively retreated a long pace. Say what you like about Harmondsworth, and she frequently did, but he was a supremely rational creature. If he could usefully serve his master he did so, regardless of inconvenience, loss of dignity or physical harm. But if he perceived danger and there was nothing he could contribute, he hid. "Harmondsworth," Gina said, "what's going on?"

No reply. Frustrating; but when Harmondsworth made his mind up to withdraw, there was very little anybody could do to make him change it. Plugging in the kettle and turning it on wouldn't help. He'd probably like that. "Is it Ted?" she asked. "Is he in trouble?"

"Yes."

"Bad trouble?"

"Very, very, very, very bad."

And instead of rushing to defend his master with tooth, claw and whatever else he happened to have (a field of intense but fruitless speculation among the partners over the years), he was hiding in a kettle. "What sort of bad?"

"Awful."

"I see. Thank you. Sorry to have disturbed you."

On the worktop a cup of tea materialised. It was almost certainly single-source Darjeeling, with just the right amount of milk and one no-calories sweetener. She materialised a yellow sticky, wrote on it OUT OF ORDER, stuck it on the kettle and put it away in the drawer. Nuts, she thought. Now what?

She took her tea back to her office, and found Brian Teasdale waiting for her. "You look pleased with yourself," she said. "What've you done?"

"Me? Nothing. Look, guess what. Tiamat the Destroyer's ex-husband is Santa Claus."

Gina put her tea down on the desk. "That's what I like about this business," she said. "Any day of the week, people can breeze into your room and say something like that to you, and you can be pretty sure they're not raving mad or working for the *National Enquirer*. It certainly beats working in road haulage. You what?"

"Tiamat the Destroyer," Brian said. "The woman with the hats in the Gainsborough paintings."

"Yes, I know all that. Santa?"

"Yup."

"Santa Claus? Fat man with a beard? Chimneys? Reindeer?"

"The very same. And Tom Dawson knows him and he's going to talk to him, and everything's going to be fine."

Oh dear. "Brian," she said gently, "don't get your hopes up. I just found Harmondsworth in the staff room, hiding in a kettle."

Mr Teasdale frowned. "Oh."

"Quite. From which I deduce that Tom had his chat with Santa and it didn't go well. Or something like that. Anyhow, things have probably moved on since you got cheerful. Sorry."

Mr Teasdale sagged. "I don't understand. What could possibly have gone wrong?"

"I suggest you ask Tom."

"I suppose so."

Over the years, pity had got Gina into more trouble than she cared to remember. On the other hand, he looked so miserable – "Or I could ask him for you," she heard herself say, before she had a chance to bite her tongue off at the root.

"Could you? Thanks. You can talk to him much better than I can."

Which was a statement of fact, after all. "All right then, if I've got to. Not that I've got anything better to do, after all. It's amazing we ever get any work done around here."

So she went to Mr Dawson's room. Sitting in his chair was an angel. "Hi," said the angel, smiling beatifically, "I'm sorry I'm not here to deal with your concerns right now, but I'll be back again before you know it, and everything will be fine." Then she vanished in a cloud of sparkles. Nuts, Gina thought, and went to see Mr Sunshine.

Who, needless to say, wasn't in his office, and the view from the window was a narrow courtyard filled with overflowing dustbins. Gina said a rude word, looked in the drawer for Harmondsworth, who wasn't there, then decided to think instead of just doing stuff. Knowing Mr Sunshine as she did, where should she look for him? Ah, yes.

It's a rule of office life that the smallest rooms attract the most people. The cashier's room was the smallest regularly used space in the building. It therefore contained, when she opened the door: Jenny Swordfish, behind the desk stapling yellow slips to pink carbons; Tony Bateman, sitting on the edge of the desk drinking coffee; and Mr Sunshine, rummaging about in a box file beside the window. At the sight of Gina, Tony flickered a little, as if his first instinct was to turn into something small and very fast; then he solidified and gave her a sheepish grin. She ignored him. "Ted."

Mr Sunshine didn't look up. "With you in a minute. Talk to Jenny or something."

Tony Bateman slid off the desk, eased past Gina and left the room. "What about?"

"I don't know, do I?"

Gina breathed out through her nose. "Lovely weather we've been having," she said.

"Have we?" said Jenny.

"Depends on what you like, I suppose. Look, Ted, there's something I need to ask you about. Are you going to be long?"

"Probably no more than six feet one inch."

Jenny shot her a he's-in-one-of-his-moods look. "It's

the partnership accounts," she whispered, dipping her head in the general direction of the box file. "I told him, he's not supposed to look at them, but—"

"He can look at them," Gina said firmly. "But does he have to look at them right now?"

"Yes," Mr Sunshine said, not looking up. Gina sighed, then sat down on the desk. "So," she said, as Jenny reached for another stack of pink carbons, "what changes in Venezuelan foreign policy do you foresee as a result of the restructuring of the Chicago commodities exchange?"

"Well—" Jenny began to say, and then Mr Sunshine closed the file with a loud click and put it back on the shelf. "Seen all I need to see," he announced briskly, "thanks ever so much. Sorry, Gina, what can I do for you?"

"Not now, Ted, can't you see I'm having a conversation? Now then, presumably you feel as I do that further deregulation could only serve to overstimulate an already—"

"Sorry," Ted said, in a tone that suggested he wasn't in the least. "Gina, can I talk to you? Outside?"

Gina gave Jenny a dazzling smile. "Later," she said, and stood up. She waited till the door had closed behind them, then said, "Ted, sometimes you can be so—"

"He's letting me back in the partnership," Mr Sunshine said.

Gina stopped dead in her tracks. "Seriously?"

Mr Sunshine nodded. "If I can get Dolly to forget about wrecking the Earth. So I was looking at the last few years' accounts, and you wouldn't believe the way he's been ripping you all off, it's an absolute—"

"What makes him think she'll listen to you?"

"She's my sister. For a start, he's been siphoning money off into offshore accounts—"

"Your what?"

"Didn't I mention it? Oh, right. Yes, she's my sister, has been for yonks. Anyway, the first thing I'm going to do when my name's back on the letterhead is to insist on a thorough external audit, because I'm pretty damn certain we can get the little creep on false accounting—"

"Ted." She hadn't meant to shriek, but on reflection she didn't regret it. "Stop drivelling and explain. Tiamat the Destroyer is your—"

"Yup. And Santa Claus is her ex-husband, but there's not a lot he can do, so it's down to me, apparently. There's not a lot I can do either, come to that, but that's beside the point. The deal I made with Tom was, I'll get my partnership back if I try to persuade her. So I'll try. I'll probably fail, but I'll have tried. And then—"

"And then the planet will be bits of floating shrapnel, and there won't be any more partnership." She paused to drawn breath. "Really? Your sister? I didn't know you had a—"

"There's lots of things you don't know." Ted paused, then went on. "By the same token, there's a hell of a lot of stuff you do know, and a lot of the stuff you do know I don't, even though I know a lot of stuff. But there's also a lot of stuff you don't know but I do. That's just the way it is." He stopped talking for a moment and frowned. "Good point," he said. "If the world really is destroyed, it sort of takes the shine off me being a partner again. On the other hand—"

"Ted, I'm not sure there is another hand. I think what we're looking at is a classic help-me-Obi-Wan-you're-my-only-hope situation. It's you or nothing."

"Fuck," said Mr Sunshine succinctly. "Oh well. Nothing like a really strong incentive to reduce you to a quivering mass of nervous insecurity. I'll just have to do my best, that's all."

Gina nodded encouragingly. "After all," she said, "she's your sister. Deep down, that's got to mean something, surely."

"Let me guess," Mr Sunshine said, "you're an only child. Not to worry. We'll get all this Dolly nonsense sorted out in two shakes of a lamb's tail, and then everything will be fine. You'll see."

Gina looked at him. "It's good news about the partnership," she said. "Just one thing, though."

"What?"

"Well," Gina said. "If Dolly's your sister and she's a goddess, what does that make you?"

Mr Sunshine chewed his bottom lip for a moment. "Worried," he replied. "Come on. Let's go and think about what I'm going to say to her."

The Kuniyoshi-Friedman process, though reliable and reasonably cheap, isn't as popular among practitioners as you'd expect it to be. To a certain extent, this is because it involves a lot of technology – banks of gleaming white boxes that bleep, and miles and miles of red, green and blue electrodes – which doesn't really jive with the mystique which so many members of the profession seek to cultivate. It's a bit like pulling your rabbit out of your hat with a tractor beam, or removing the lady from the box a split second before you push in the long knives using a teleportation device. It works and it's efficient, but somehow it doesn't really seem like proper magic, somehow, and magic is what the punter is paying for, or at least he thinks he is.

Sometimes, though, it's precisely the impression you

want to create, especially with the younger generation of clients who don't really believe in magic but who think that technology can do anything – pull rabbits from hats, saw women in half or even store a megabyte of data for more than five minutes without corrupting it beyond hope of recovery. Lilith McGregor, Consuela decided, fell squarely into the latter category. Blinking lights and bits of wire screwed into her head would reassure her and give her a comfortable sense of things being under control. Besides, the alternative was demons and Consuela felt about demons the way she felt about rats, only slightly more so.

Erica had seen to the setup. She knew where all the bits of wire were supposed to go, and how to calibrate the scanners and make the interface compatible with Portals 9.1 and all that nonsense, which suggested that she was a competent electrician, if nothing else, and Consuela was happy to leave her to it. She spent a contented quarter of an hour catching up with her billing until reception called to let her know Lilith had arrived.

"This isn't like the other place," Lilith said, as Consuela escorted her across the atrium to the glass-box elevator.

Consuela smiled. "No," she said, "it isn't. Mind the step as you get out."

It wasn't just the elevator that was made of glass. So were all the walls and all the floors, giving the visitor an impression of walking on air through a floating world uninhibited by gravity. To those in the trade it was especially impressive, because it was all real (at eye-watering expense) rather than conjured up by magic (costing no more than two minutes of a practitioner's time to mumble the appropriate spells). Rival firms tended to dismiss it all as a vulgar display of conspicuous expenditure, which of course it was, but they struggled to keep the hint of envy out of their voices as they did so. A real forty-foot-high fountain in the main reception area, for crying out loud, with real parakeets, however much did that cost? In which case, they must be doing very well indeed ...

Erica had set up all the gubbins in the small interview room on the ninth floor. Consuela pressed a button – genuine circuitry, incantation-free technology – and the walls went dark. There was also an electric light, which Consuela switched on. The current that fed it was generated by a hundred thousand captive goblins running round a treadmill in the basement, but nobody ever mentioned that. As far as the management was concerned it was real electricity, and that was all that mattered. "Have a seat," Consuela said, "I'll be with you in a moment." She hit the intercom. "Erica? Are we ready to go?"

"Yes."

She lowered her voice. "What do I do?"

"Well, first you recalibrate the induction ram feeder matrix to the subject's neuroelectrical impulse ratio—"

"Get in here."

"Coming."

"Now then," Consuela said, putting on her big smile, "We've got a couple of minutes before my assistant arrives, so I'll just run through what we're going to do. I link you up to the big machine over there—"

"Gosh," said Lilith, looking at it. "Isn't that a Hewlett Packard XP9000 solid-state verteron resynthesiser with a Kawaguchiya N7701 expansion chamber slaved to the reverse-parallel cyclotron?"

"Yes," said Consuela helplessly. "Naturally. Anyway, you put on these headphones, and—"

"But how did you overcome the problem of parataxic feedback through the correlative interstatic jumpers?"

"Ah." Consuela beamed at her. "That would be telling. Anyhow, you put the earphones on, we plug in all the little bits of spaghetti and, hey presto, there you are in interdimensional paraspace. Then all I have to do is issue the challenge—"

"The what?"

"Oh, just a technicality. Then your mum shows up, and you two can have a nice chat. That's all there is to it, really. Then, when we're done, we can go to lunch."

Lilith took a deep breath. "All right, then. Shouldn't you be pre-charging the antipositron resonators?"

"Not with this model," Consuela said firmly, "it does it all for you."

"But surely—"

At which moment the door opened and Erica came in. Consuela rounded on her. "You did remember to pre-charge the positron—?"

"Antipositron resonators. Yes," Erica said, pointing to a glowing red light. "It's all ready when you are."

"Right, let's get cracking." Erica flipped some switches and pressed some buttons, and the whole room glowed blue. A ball of green fire burst out of the top of one of the white boxes and hovered in mid-air about six inches from the tip of Consuela's nose, hissing like a snake. Consuela edged away slowly, trying to look as though this sort of thing happened every day. Erica didn't seem to have noticed it. "Contact established," she said, sounding bored. "Challenge issued. Standing by."

The ball of fire trebled in size, wobbled and began to drip, like burning plastic. The flaming drips pooled on the floor and quickly built up into a column, like a stalactite speeded up; not just a column, a woman, taking shape from the feet up. "Challenge accepted," Erica sang out as the shoulders formed, then the head. "Challenger requires you to select your weapon of choice for combat to the death. Available options include swords, thunderbolts, nuclear warheads, comets, dark matter and derogatory epithets. Choose your weapon or concede the fight—" She paused. "—now."

"Concede," Consuela said, very quickly. "I give in. Very sorry to have bothered you."

The fiery woman, who now had a head and a face not entirely unfamiliar from the photographs, wasn't listening to her. She was gazing at Lilith. "You again," she said. "Now what?"

Behind her, various pieces of equipment whirred into life but she didn't seem aware of them. Consuela nodded to Erica, who moved quickly and quietly to a console and started pressing buttons.

"Hi, Mum," Lilith said.

The fiery woman stopped flickering and cooled into a more or less conventional human shape; she still glowed and you could probably have toasted bread on her, but now she was recognisably the woman in the pictures. "So that's it, is it?" she said. "You want me to spare the Earth and not incinerate your little friends. Well, tough."

"But Mum—"

The woman sighed. "Sorry," she said, "but it's a matter of principle. I was going to spare this horrible little planet if someone unlocked me and let me out, but then I got to thinking about how nasty everyone's always been to me and how nobody lifted a finger to release me for all that time, so I decided to fry the lot of you and serve you bloody well right. " She paused and scowled. "Of course, I might have known you'd side with him."

"But Mum," Lilith said, "if you blow up the Earth, I'll get blown up, too. That's so unfair."

The woman sighed. "That's so typical," she said, "always putting yourself first, not stopping to think about other people, even your own mother. No, it's just me, me, me all the time. I suppose I should be used to it by now, but it still hurts."

"Mum." All trace of pleading had vanished from Lilith's voice. "You can't possibly do this. It sucks. You're being totally unreasonable."

"Me," the woman snarled, "unreasonable. Oh, I like that. I'm not the one who goes around locking people up in asteroids and casting them adrift in intergalactic space. I'm not the one—"

"No, but you don't seem fussed about blowing up whole planets. Mum, that's horrible. How could you be so thoughtless? Think of all the baby elephants in Africa. And the people, too," she added. "Billions of people. What harm did they ever do you?"

The woman breathed fire through her nose, melting the vinyl on the arm of Consuela's chair. "What good did they ever do me, come to that? Answer, none. Besides, they're trespassing on my property."

"It's not your—"

"They've got no right to be there. I didn't say they could come and breed all over my planet. Besides, if they don't want to fry they can leave. I'm not stopping them."

"Mum, they can't. They haven't got spaceships."

The woman shrugged. "It's not my fault if they can't be bothered to help themselves. If they choose to spend trillions of dollars on stupid wars instead of space exploration, that's their lookout, not mine. I can't be held responsible for other people's irresponsibility."

"Mum."

"Don't pull faces, you'll stick like it. Look," the woman went on, "you think you're fond of them, they're your pets, but you aren't really."

"Yes I am. I love them."

"Your fellow humans? Really?"

"Yes."

The woman giggled. "That's so sweet. All right, we'll try a little thought experiment. When was the last time they elected someone to public office who actually made things better for anybody?"

"Um."

"Quite. Let's try another one. Name three multinational corporations who put the common good above making money?"

"Um."

"Too difficult? All right, then. Give me a human political philosophy that hasn't been responsible for the deaths of at least a million people."

"Um."

"Fine. Let's try a really easy one. Name me ten of your fellow human beings you actually genuinely like."

Pause. "That still doesn't make it right, Mum."

"Oh for crying out loud." The woman made a show of counting to ten under her breath. "Tell you what," she said. "I'll make you a new heaven and a new Earth, just as soon as the first heaven and the first Earth have passed away, and there will be no more sea—" She hesitated, frowned, then went on, "Unless you want some sea, of course. Personally I can't stand the stuff, but you're welcome to have some if you like. Not to mention," she added coaxingly, "new people. Genuinely nice, kind, generous, well-meaning people with none of that free will nonsense, who'll do what they're told without arguing the toss all the damn time."

"Mum—"

"Here's the deal," the woman went on. "I've got a planet out back of the Antares cluster, haven't been there for yonks but I assume it's still there. I'll give it a makeover and you can have it." She smiled warmly, a disconcerting sight. "And I'll make you some humans to play with, all your very own, you can be a queen or a goddess or whatever you like, it'll be fun. It's got to be better than living here, with these—" She stopped and drew a deep breath. "People."

Lilith's eyes had gone very wide. "My own planet?"

"Absolutely." The woman's eyes glowed with cunning. "Yours to do what you like with. Green skies, grey seas, unspoilt taupe beaches. No pollution. A completely unfucked-up environment."

"I don't know."

"Or," the woman went on irresistibly, "I could make it post-industrial with dangerously high CO_2 levels, and you could save it. You'd enjoy that."

"But Mum—"

"You'd be its redeemer," the woman said. "You could ban all the cars and close down all the coal mines and have all the electric kettles lined up against a wall and shot. You could take it right back to the Stone Age if you wanted to, and everybody would be so grateful. Just say the word and I'll see to it. Anything you want."

"It sounds nice," Lilith said doubtfully. "But if you make all the problems on purpose just so I can fix them—"

"Much better than having problems that just arise

randomly, I always say. But think of all the good you could do. I could make you a whole bunch of criminally unethical international corporations to regulate, or thousands and thousands of nasty rich people to tax, and millions and millions of starving, desperate peasants to give all the money to. Or if you're very good, I could let you have a shitload of endangered species to save from extinction. Cuddly ones, not spiders or any of that crap. Now what could be nicer than that?"

"But it wouldn't be real," Lilith said. "It'd be—"

"Bullshit," the woman said abruptly. "It'd be as real as anything. All right, how's this? I'll make over the planet whether you like it or not, and then give you the chance to save it. So, if you don't, all those starving children and fluffy panda cubs will die, and it'll all be your fault." She beamed sweetly. "How do you like them apples?" she said.

"But that's silly," Lilith said. "In order to save the pandas on that planet, I'd have to abandon the ones on this one. And the people," she added. "And the pandas on the other planet wouldn't have needed saving if you hadn't made them to be saved in the first place. So really it'd just be making things worse." She paused and frowned. "I think."

"Oh for crying out loud," the woman said. "Look, here I am bending over backwards to be nice and you're just being totally unreasonable. If you want the stupid planet you can have it. If not, you can stay here and get blatted like everybody else and I'll reincarnate you into something marginally more sensible, like a pebble. I don't want to sound insensitive but I really do have other things on my mind apart from your ridiculous—"

"Mum."

"That does it," the woman said. "I'm a goddess and

this is my planet, and I'll do with it what I choose and I
didn't come here to be lectured by a stupid little child.
I've offered you everything you could possibly want, all
the kingdoms of the new Earth, and you're just being
ungrateful and stubborn and I've got no patience with
that sort of thing, it's just being wilful and showing off.
It's worse than the old days. If you're the sort of human
who's living here now, it's high time you all got blown to
smithereens because you really, really deserve it." She was
glowing an ominous red now, and several of the machines
were bleeping frantically. "I'll give you one last chance.
Are you coming with me or would you rather stay here
and frizzle into a crisp? It's entirely up to you. Never let it
be said I ever tried to bully anybody into doing something
they don't want to."

"No," Lilith said.

"Fine," the woman said. "Screw you, then."

Lilith burst into tears, jumped up and ran out of the
room. The woman turned her head and gave Consuela
the benefit of three full seconds of her undiluted personality. Then she smiled. "Somehow," she said, "you
seem to have got the impression that you're cleverer than
me. Trust me, this is not the case." She waved her hand
towards the bank of bleeping white boxes, which all went
deadly quiet. "In case you were wondering, yes, you were
right." She blurred for a moment and then there were
three of her, as though Consuela had been drinking,
and then there was just one again. "And you can prove
it, too. All right, then, here's your reward. You'll write
that paper for the technical journals, and it'll make you
so famous they'll give you the O-So-E-Z-Chop'N'Blend
chair of quantum metaphysics at Berkeley, twenty-four
hours before I smash the planet into gravel. Have fun,"

she added. "And don't say I never give you anything."
Then she vanished as well, and all the lights came on full.

There was a long silence. Then Erica stood up and
switched off all the equipment. "Readings complete," she
said, "and you need to get all this stuff back to Robertsons
by half past four. Oh, and you know what? You can stuff
your stupid job. I quit."

Consuela barely registered what she'd said. It was all,
she thought, so bitterly unfair. All she'd done was arrange
things so that a mother and her daughter could get
together and reconcile their differences, and in return she
was going to get what she wanted most of all in the whole
wide world one day before the whole wide world ceased
to exist – So much worse than not getting it at all, and
with death thrown in as a sort of buy-one-get-one-free—

Death. Eek.

Consuela had always prided herself on knowing exactly
where she was going, and the Hereafter most definitely
wasn't on her itinerary. She didn't actually know a great
deal about death – where it was, what happened when you
got there, how long it went on for, did it hurt, was it bad
for you, that sort of thing – but that was a field of scholarly
enquiry she had no interest in pursuing, not even if there
were loads of research grants and rock-solid tenure. Her
attitude was rather more along the lines of get-that-thing-
the-hell-away-from me, and most of the time she simply
didn't think about it at all. But that crazy woman was
going to kill her, which would ruin everything, unless—

She went back to her office. Her coffee was stone-cold.
She was about to call down to Erica for another cup when
she remembered that Erica wasn't there any more. God
damn it. Why were people so horribly inconsiderate?

Unless someone did something about it. She stopped

and thought about that. Naturally, all along she'd been assuming that someone else would deal with the Earth-getting-wasted problem while she got on with the serious business of securing her own future. That was what other people were there for, after all, to handle the day-to-day stuff while the superior beings pursued happiness and achieved achievements. But now she'd met Tiamat the Destroyer and seen her in action; did it seem reasonable to believe that a bunch of deadheads like Tom Dawson and – saints and ministers of grace defend us – her very own darling Brian were going to be able to stop her doing whatever she damn well pleased? Answers on the back of a flying pig to the address in the *Radio Times*. In which case, unless she could hitch a lift off the planet with some passing life form who just happened to breathe oxygen, she was going to die. Quite soon.

Her stomach churned and her knees felt like soggy pasta. Unless someone did something about it, the someone in question being me. For there is none other that fighteth for us, but only me. Oh God . . .

Pull yourself together, girl. It's all right. You can do this.

No, said a little voice in the back of her head, you can't. She knew that voice quite well. She didn't like it much, mostly because it told her the truth, a commodity whose supply had a tendency to exceed demand. For a genuine free spirit, the very best the truth can ever be is a starting point, a fixer-upper in need of a great deal of tender loving imagination. At its worst – like now, for example – it's a brick wall across the highway, with barbed wire, search-lights and dogs. No, you can't. That lady, Tiamat or whatever her name is, names are, is one tough cookie, three tough cookies, and more than a match for little Consuela. She'd have you for breakfast. Actually, she already has.

In which case, Consuela decided, she needed to tell someone. The police? NATO? Starfleet? Get real. Mortals, two-legged mayflies, hedgehogs beneath Her chariot wheels. All right then, what about superior mortals? It so happened that she was sitting in a building crammed with them. There was Toby Porteous, head of pest control, who slew dragons and slaughtered were-wolves; Becky Chang, director of perceptual and effective magic, who summoned up vast armies of mail-clad spectral warriors for the movies because it was cheaper than CGI; Emily Pendleton, who headed up the JWW necromancy team and who could raise countless hosts of the undead just as soon as the client's cheque cleared the bank; better still, Dennis Tanner, i/c mining and minerals and hereditary King of the Goblins. She considered them all, and in her mind's eye saw each of them in turn going squish under Tiamat's two-inch Cuban heel. Human, all too human, the lot of them. No more use than a chocolate fireguard.

In which case, there was only one thing for it. If she got caught, it went without saying she'd lose her job and never work in this business again. At any other time, that thought would've sent her courage scuttling down the nearest rabbit hole. But death made even that seem unimportant, and if she succeeded – She paused and thought about that. The woman who saved Planet Earth; not a bad thing to have on her CV. She took a deep breath. This wasn't going to be easy.

Deep in the vaults of 70 St Mary Axe is a strongroom. Not the main strongroom, in daily use, but another one, whose very existence is one of the firm's most closely guarded secrets; Consuela only knew about it because of her uncanny ability to read memos upside down.

Naturally the door was locked and naturally the only key was on the CEO's keyring and naturally the CEO wasn't likely to be in any hurry to part with it, probably because he was relying on what was inside the hidden strongroom for making his own getaway from the planet shortly before zero hour. And naturally it wasn't just any ordinary lock, vulnerable to skill, knowledge and a hairpin. And of course it went without saying that even if she did manage to get the door open, there'd be an alarm system the likes of which the world had never seen, and so on and so forth—

She yawned, turned herself into a gnat and flew off to find the keyhole.

The hell with it, Mr Sunshine thought, and jerked open his desk drawer. "Harmondsworth," he said, "my chariot."

"Seriously?"

"Seriously."

"Oh boy." The blue light inside the drawer flickered and ebbed. "You haven't really thought this through, have you?"

"The chariot. Now."

"It'll all end in—"

"Now."

The drawer slammed shut, nearly catching his finger. Outside the window (Leninsky Prospekt with a view over the park, just for a change) the sky darkened and thunder growled ominously. Suddenly a twin fork of lightning slashed the sky like a razor—

"Harmondsworth," said Mr Sunshine. "Pack it in."

No more lightning; but it was dark as a bag out there, and the rain was hammering on the windowpane. Mr

Sunshine sighed. Dark is his path on the wings of the storm sounds great in theory, but Mr Sunshine had reached the point in his life where he no longer relished getting soaked to the skin. From another drawer he took a foldaway plastic mac, unfolded it and put it on, drawing the hood over his head. The window blew open from the inside. Just beyond it, floating in the air, was the chariot.

Mr Sunshine regarded it with mixed emotions. Strictly speaking it wasn't much to look at, because back in the early Bronze Age, if you wanted a wheeled vehicle of any description you started with a tree and a not particularly sharp bronze axe and you kept going until you had something that'd get the job done, more or less. It looked more like a hay cart than a chariot: plank floor and sides, four small solid wheels, a pole sticking out of the front to which were harnessed six bored-looking donkeys. Viewed from the perspective of where he'd reached rather than where he'd come from, it looked like the sort of thing children go for rides in at the seaside. Once it had been the Chariot of the Sun. It hadn't changed, but times had.

"What's that appalling smell?" Mr Sunshine asked.

"I gave it a lick of creosote," Harmondsworth informed him. "Look, do you want it or not?"

It hasn't changed, times have; what about me? Mr Sunshine frowned. "I'm getting too old for this, Harmondsworth," he said. "I thought I told you to put in seat belts."

"There aren't any seats."

True. He was going to have to stand all the way, like travelling on the Underground. "All right, fit one."

"Can't. Any significant structural alteration will upset the balance of the power-to-weight ratio, making it impossible to create a stable verteron field, which would screw up the relativity dampers. You'd get there, but you wouldn't get then. You could end up anywhen, and then it'd all be my fault, as usual."

Good point. For various reasons, most of them valid, Mr Sunshine had no great wish to revisit the past. As for the future – The classic definition of an immortal is someone who hasn't died yet. That was something Mr Sunshine preferred not to think about. "Fine," he said, "I'll just have to rough it, then, won't I? But it'd be nice if just once—" He stopped. This was Harmondsworth he was talking to. "Sorry."

"That's perfectly all right."

"I didn't mean to hurt your feelings."

"Doesn't matter. It's only me."

"If you really want to do some lightning—"

"Can I?"

"Go on. Just a little bit."

A flash, bright as arc welding, and a roll of thunder that made the floor shake. "All done?"

"Affirmative."

"Jolly good." Hugging his plastic mac tight round his neck, Mr Sunshine stepped through the window into the cart. The donkeys took no notice of him. "Giddy up," he yelled. One of them turned its head and looked at him. "Giddy up right now, you stupid animals, or you're sausages," he amended. The donkeys considered for a long moment, then arched their necks and plodded out into the wind and the rain, the cart following them, its wheels rumbling over nothing at all. "Engage quantum slipstream drive," Mr Sunshine ordered. Nothing happened. "Mush!" he tried, and for a split second the cart was nine miles long, infinitely wide and half a micron thick, and then—

There are some people who enjoy faster-than-light travel. Mr Sunshine was no longer one of them. Possibly it was something to do with the fact that, in the run-up to achieving escape velocity, his body was extended to infinite size before being stuffed into an infinitely small hole; no big deal when you're young, flexible and up for pretty much anything, but tiresome verging on annoying for those of more mature years. Oh for pity's sake, he muttered to himself as he was threaded through the eye of the galactic needle; and then it was all over for the time being and he was outside.

Outside of what? Very good question. All around him, stars zipped past like hailstones, and he crimped the collar of his plastic mac tight around his neck, as though there was a real danger that a stray star might get inside, like a wasp. Maybe that wasn't as silly as it sounded. Very few practitioners of FTL travel actually know what's going on or understand how it all works, and Mr Sunshine wasn't one of them.

At least the cart seemed to be holding together, more or less. The sides were attached to the floor by copper nails, driven in at an angle and clented over; if you put your weight on them they wobbled a bit, but the indescribable stresses of quantum dislocation didn't seem to be bothering them unduly. The six donkeys, meanwhile, were ambling along at (relativistically speaking) a slow walking pace, occasionally lowering their heads to see if there was anything edible growing on the floor of hyperspace, which there wasn't, but at heart they were optimists. It occurred to Mr Sunshine to wonder if they actually served any useful purpose, or whether they were only there for show. It was all, he decided, about faith. If there were donkeys, you believed that there was something pulling the cart, therefore it was capable of moving. No donkeys, no faith, no motion. Bronze Age science.

A loud, sustained whimpering caught his attention, partly because there shouldn't be any sounds in the interstellar void. Harmondsworth? Unlikely. Harmondsworth was an Olympic-class whimperer when occasion demanded, but Mr Sunshine knew his own familiar well enough to know when he was present; by the pricking of his thumbs, as often as not. If not Harmondsworth, then who the hell was it? Mr Sunshine sighed and reached inside his mac for his wallet, from which he drew a small mirror. Properly speaking, he didn't need an Imp-Reflecting glass to see the true forms of concealed or enchanted objects, but using his inner eye in hyperspace tended to bring on one of his migraines.

"Oh," he said, "it's you. Serves you right."

A patch of creosote sucked itself up out of the grain of one of the planks that made up the floor of the cart, and turned back into Tony Bateman. "F-fuck a stoat," he mumbled. "What's happening to me?"

"We're in hyperspace," Mr Sunshine said, with a certain grim joy. "Travelling at three hundred and seven times the speed of light in a wooden cart pulled by donkeys. Can I drop you off somewhere or shall I just throw you out into the slipstream?"

"Don't be like that," Tony whined, his eyes tight shut. "I didn't mean anything by it."

"Really."

"Really," Tony assured him. "I was just looking for somewhere quiet where I could practise seeping. There's this job lined up where I've got to be a coat of plastic emulsion, so when that creepy sidekick of yours took a can of creosote from the stores I followed him and thought, why not?"

Mr Sunshine indicated the starscape with a broad

gesture. "This is why not," he said. "I thought Mr Teasdale told you, no more shapeshifting unless you're actually on an assignment."

"Practising counts as active service, surely." Tony gave him a spaniel look, then ducked as a star screamed by, apparently an inch from the top of his head. "Look, you won't tell Dawson about this, will you? Only I need this job, and—"

"Yes, but does the job need you?" Mr Sunshine looked at him, then clicked his tongue. "Creosote, for crying out loud," he said. "Actually, that's pretty impressive."

"I'm good at liquids," Tony said. "I make a great margarita."

Mr Sunshine started to think why someone would want to turn himself into a cocktail, then made a conscious decision not to. "What the hell," he said. "Throwing you off the cart would disrupt the hyperspatial displacement field and dump me back into real space, which would mean having to go through all that getting-back-up-to-speed nonsense again, and I really can't be bothered. I suggest you soak away back where you came from and keep your mouth shut till this is all over."

"Sure," Tony said, then pulled a sad face. "Balls," he said. "Can't."

"What?"

"It's this hyperspace stuff," Tony said sadly. "I can't seem to, you know. It's not working."

Mr Sunshine rolled his eyes. "You mean I'm stuck with you as you for the rest of the trip?"

"Looking that way."

"Joy unbounded," Mr Sunshine sighed. "Just what I need, excess baggage. Fine. At least try and make yourself useful."

"Of course," Tony said, eager to please. "What can I do?"

Mr Sunshine thought for a moment. "I suppose I could use a charioteer," he said. "I had one in the old days, on special occasions. Can you drive one of these things?"

"No."

Mr Sunshine shrugged. "Neither can I, but it never stopped me in the past. All right, grab hold of the reins—"

"The what?"

"These bits of leather tape," Mr Sunshine explained, "and don't make any sudden movements. Try and bear in mind that you're strictly symbolic, all right? Splendid. Make it so."

Silence for a while, as Tony concentrated hard on not moving suddenly. Then he said, "Where are we going, exactly?"

"To see my sister," Mr Sunshine said. "She's horrible. You won't like her one bit."

"Oh come on, she's your sister. She can't be that bad."

Mr Sunshine scowled. "Why is it that whenever I tell people how loathsome my relatives are, they won't believe me? I'm telling you, she's ghastly. She's got the idea from somewhere that destroying inhabited planets is acceptable behaviour. That's why I'm going to see her, to try and talk her out of it. Not," he added, "that it'll do any good. She has many skills, but listening isn't one of them."

"Destroying planets?"

"Yup." Mr Sunshine pulled a sad face. "When she was a kid, it was pulling the wings off flies. Then when she was a bit older she graduated from flies to angels, and since then she's got a lot worse. To be honest with you, I'm not looking forward to this." He glanced up, studying the patterns of dopplering stars. "Nearly there," he said.

"Now remember, don't say a word or move or breathe or anything. Just leave everything to me."

Tony had gone a funny colour. "Seriously," he said. "Angels?"

Mr Sunshine nodded. "And ministers of grace," he said, "and pretty much anything else that didn't get out of the way quick enough. Right, if that's Cassiopeia we need to hang a left."

The cart lurched, and one of the donkeys flicked its ears as they shot downwards through ninety degrees. Then all that dreary infinitely-big-and-infinitely-small stuff, then a loud popping noise as they burst out of nowhere into real space—

"Now then," said Mr Sunshine in a rather shaky voice, "if I did my sums right and everything's gone exactly to plan, this should be the edge of the asteroid belt surrounding the third moon of Delta Leonis Six. If not, I have absolutely no idea where we are and we'll probably end up having to walk home. Fingers crossed."

Tony Bateman had never been on the edge of an asteroid belt before. "Is that it?"

"You sound disappointed."

"Well, it's just that – I mean, I was expecting ... " He shrugged. "It looks different on TV," he said.

"Different?"

"Better composition. This is just a big black thing with a few speckles." He frowned. "It doesn't seem, well, meant, if you get my drift. I thought it'd be—"

"Tidier?"

Tony shrugged. "Different. Ah well."

"That's the thing about reality," Mr Sunshine said gravely. "No class. Now, it would help matters enormously if I actually knew what we're looking for, but unfortunately I don't. No, I tell a lie, we're looking for an asteroid." He paused while he counted. "I make it seventy-six thousand, four hundred and fifty-seven asteroids," he said. "How about you?"

"Sorry, I—"

Mr Sunshine nodded. "Of course," he said, "you ran out of fingers. Mind you, there's no guarantee that Dolly's asteroid is one of this lot. I only chose this asteroid belt because she was rather fond of it when we were kids. Hang on, though. What's that?"

Tony Bateman followed the line of Mr Sunshine's extended finger. A very large hovering rock, he didn't say.

"Take us in," Mr Sunshine said. "I want a closer look."

"Sure. How do I do that, exactly?"

Mr Sunshine grabbed the reins and gave them a little flick, which the donkeys completely ignored. "Please," he added. The donkeys ambled forward, swishing their tails. "Like that," he said. "Now then, let the dog see the rabbit."

"Rabbit?" queried Tony Bateman, but Mr Sunshine wasn't listening. All his attention was fixed on the nearest asteroid, and as the donkeys lumbered closer, Tony could see why. It was different, somehow. It was smoother than the others, and rather more symmetrical. Its surface gleamed slightly, whereas the others were dull matte. And it was pink.

"That's not a rabbit," Tony observed.

"No."

"Why's it that funny colour?"

Mr Sunshine didn't answer. Pink could suggest the presence of a higher-than-average percentage of sinderotanium in the asteroid's core matrix, presumably the result of quantum reflux in the final nanoseconds of the

Big Bang. But Mr Sunshine didn't think so. "Activate the long-range sensors," he said quietly.

"Excuse me?"

Mr Sunshine sighed and reached for a pair of binoculars hanging from a copper nail driven into the side of the cart. "That's Dolly's asteroid all right," he said. "Look."

He passed the binoculars to Tony, who peered through them. "What am I looking for?" he said.

"About eight o'clock on the outer edge."

"Ah."

"Precisely."

Tony handed the binoculars back to Mr Sunshine. "Why don't they just drift away into space?" he asked.

"Probably trapped there by the asteroid's gravitational field."

"That's a lot of empty prosecco bottles."

"That's Dolly for you."

"Right," Tony said, "so we've found the right asteroid. What next?"

"Good question." Mr Sunshine frowned. "To be honest with you, I haven't really thought this through. I mean, we can land. Probably we can land," he added. "But I'm not sure how much good that'll do us."

"Really?"

Mr Sunshine nodded. "For a start," he said, "the chariot's life support system only operates inside the vehicle's spatio-dynamic footprint, which means that if we get off it, you won't be able to breathe, not that that matters because you'd freeze to death pretty well instantaneously anyway. I'd be all right, but I'd still have the problem of getting inside that thing. If there's a door, I can't see it. Besides, it's locked, and I don't have the key."

"Ah."

"I'm guessing," Mr Sunshine went on, "that there's a window or a garbage chute or something like that, or else how can Dolly throw out all her empty wine bottles? So presumably I could yell to her down the chute and she could yell back, if she's talking to me, which I seriously doubt. Of course she hasn't seen me for something in the order of three thousand years, so maybe she'll be prepared to talk, if only to tell me things about myself. Or maybe not, I just don't know. In which case, we've wasted our time coming here. In a strictly non-relativistic sense, of course."

"Fine." Tony paused for a moment. "Maybe we should just give up and go home."

"Not a bad idea," Mr Sunshine said. "Would that it were possible. Unfortunately, I don't think we've got enough fuel for that."

"Fuel?"

"Carrots," Mr Sunshine said. "Oats, hay, that sort of thing. I think my original idea was to sponge some donkey fodder off Dolly after we'd had our little chat and made friends again, always assuming she's got something like that in there. Mind you, the donkeys aren't fussy, they'll eat practically anything. Shoes, straw hats, prawn mayonnaise sandwiches—"

"You mean," Tony said, "we can't get home?"

Mr Sunshine shrugged. "I could walk," he said, "but it would take me eleven million years. As for you—" He sighed. "Let's hope I can find a way of talking to Dolly and she's in one of her better moods."

"What are the chances of that?"

"Slim," Mr Sunshine said. "But what the heck. Giddy up, you stupid animals. Please."

The chariot lurched forward. Tony borrowed the

binoculars and searched for anything that might be a door, window or hatch. "Hey," he said, "I've found something."

"Jolly good," Mr Sunshine said. "What?"

"It's a sort of hatch," Tony said. "Definitely a hatch. It's sliding open."

"Right," Mr Sunshine said. "That could be a good sign."

"You bet," Tony said. "It's a quarter open. Now it's a half. It's completely open. Something's coming out."

"Ah."

"It's sort of silvery," Tony said. "Shaped a bit like a frankfurter, with fins on the end. Hard to say how big it is at this range, but probably quite big. It's come all the way out, it's turning. It's turning towards us."

"Rats," said Mr Sunshine. "Raise shields."

"Sorry?"

Mr Sunshine reached past him and grabbed a wicker screen, about three feet square, with a hand grip in the middle. Back in the day, it offered a modicum of protection against arrows, javelins and slingshots, at extreme range. Whether it'd be any good against a quantum torpedo with a matter/antimatter total annihilation warhead remained to be seen. He handed it to Tony. No point having a dog and barking yourself. "Go on, then," he said. "Raise it."

"Like this?"

"Higher and a tad more to the left. No, your left. That's the ticket. Now, we'll see if that'll make a blind bit of—"

The security division of JWW would have you believe they're the hardest, meanest bad-ass mothers on the planet, and they'll send you a glossy brochure to prove it on the slightest provocation. It says a great deal about their track record that when JWW's senior management decided to construct a really safe place in which to store their most valued possession, they hired Zauberwerke AG to design and install it. Partly it was a case of, if you want a job done properly, get someone else to do it; partly it was the thought of one of their own knowing all the flaws, wrinkles and weak spots in the system. Mostly, though, Zauberwerke were cheaper than having it done in-house.

The gnat perching on the handle of the strongroom door didn't know that, of course. All she knew was that there was no keyhole, likewise no gap under or above the door to crawl through. More to the point, there was no door, just a doorhandle sticking out of the wall.

She sighed. Magic, how quaint. Since there was no point being a gnat any more, she turned back into Consuela Teasdale and sat on the floor with her back to the opposite wall, feeling angry. Stupid, she decided. It was just plain stupid that at this extremely important point she should run up against something she had to stop and think about. Magic, for crying out loud.

Now then, she thought, I can do this.

When is a door not a door? When it's a wall. Whoever designed this thing would almost certainly have started from that obvious premise. If you want to keep people out of a specified area, the best way to go about it is to make sure there's no means of access. Musashi, the greatest swordsman who ever lived, decreed that the best way to win a fight is not to fight. By the same token, the best way to secure a door is not to have one. Instead, have a wall.

When is a wall not a wall? When it's a door. Security, they say in the business, is a perfectable science; it's the customers who ruin everything. The perfect strongroom doesn't have a door, it has a wall instead. But annoying customers want to be able to get in and out. Therefore the wall has to be, under certain highly circumscribed conditions, a door—

They'd covered all this, of course, in second year. Ninety-nine times out of a hundred, she'd been taught, the easiest and best way to deal with doors that turn out to be walls is to treat them as walls and smash holes in them. This can be done quickly and efficiently with a wide selection of demolition spells, high explosives or a steel ball on a chain. If you're reluctant to make a noise and a mess, don't be. There are plently of ways to deaden sound, repair structural damage and sweep up dust and bits of plaster without resorting to a dustpan and brush. Only in very exceptional circumstances, such as a Level Nine anti-intruder curse or when you're being paid by the hour, should you consider trying to pick the lock of a wall. It's more trouble than it's worth, honestly.

Consuela considered the wall. She got up and tapped it with her knuckle. She put her ear to it and listened. Then she opened her LoganBerry and called up the floor plans of 70 St Mary Axe. The strongroom wasn't on the plans, obviously. Magic, she said to herself, I hate magic.

In which case, screw magic. Let's approach this sci-entifically. Solid objects, such as walls, can easily be penetrated by small packets of electromagnetic energy, emanating from the electron cloud of an ordinary every-day atom. With her fingernail, she picked a molecule from her scalp and rolled it between her fingertips until it broke down into its constituent atoms, the way she'd been taught in first year. She peered at the atom until she could make out the electron cloud, a sort of greasy smudge, like olive oil on the meniscus of a washing-up bowl. She looked at the cloud until the cloud looked at her. "Hi," she said. "Feeling energetic?"

The electron cloud had probably heard that one a million times before. It gave her a what-is-it-now? look. "Thanks," she said, "that's fine. You can go now."

It's much easier to turn yourself into something if you know what you're turning yourself into. She'd never been an X-ray before, but actually it was no big deal. She considered the wall. It wasn't quite as solid as it had been a moment ago. In fact, it was nothing but a floating cloud of soft goo. Geronimo, she muttered under her breath, and charged.

X-rays don't have heads, which is probably just as well; no head, no concussion when you slam into a solid object at high speed. She opened her eyes. She was human again, lying on the floor about eighteen inches from the wall. Unlike an X-ray, she had a head. It hurt.

Like that, is it? she thought. Fine.

In third year, you could do demolition (including thunderbolts, artificially induced earthquakes and incantations of mass destruction), or you could do History of Metaphysics, which was two lectures a week and no practical. Consuela had opted for History of Metaphysics. Very little of what she'd learned had stayed with her, but she remembered how Dorokhov discovered the principle of Specific Inherent Latency. He'd done it by conjuring an intensive Somewhere Else field inside the exopentagram of a heavily localised quantum Peculiarity, blowing himself to smithereens in the process—

What exactly is a smithereen, she asked herself, as she whipped up a Somewhere Else field using her phone, a pencil sharpener and her left contact lens as a makeshift omnidirectional condenser. Not that it mattered; in two shakes of a lamb's tail, the wall would be lots of them, but that was all right because a temporal pancake flip and a high-powered stasis inverter would scoop them all up and put them back exactly where they'd been, with her on the other side, just as soon as she'd finished inducing the Peculiarity, which was a piece of cake provided you remember that effect has to precede cause in order to achieve destructive force, hence the handy jingle, E after C except before D – She slid the pencil sharpener under her phone and trained the contact lens on it, counted to four and turned herself into a diamond to withstand the impact of the blast.

Nothing happened.

Later, she figured it out. Whoever built the wall had saturated it with multiple inherent contradictions, which absorbed the violent expansion of the Peculiarity and vented the force of the explosion resulting from the mutual annihilation of the possible and the impossible into the outer metasphere, where they would ultimately reassemble and congeal as a series of marginally toxic half-truths. That would explain the dizziness, the faint smell of newly baked bread and the barely perceptible warm spot on the wall, just below the stupid doorhandle.

She stopped being a diamond, stood up and stamped her foot. Not fair, she screamed to herself, as it gradually dawned on her that whoever built the stupid strongroom might just possibly be smarter than she was. Which wasn't right, on a fundamental level . . . She gave the wall a savage kick, proving in the process that the wall was also harder than her toe.

A man came round the corner and walked towards her, reading something. He looked up as he passed her, and she vaguely recognised him. Mr something-or-other, he'd been pointed out to her at some nebulous office function. "Anything the matter?" he asked.

It occurred to her that there are more ways of killing a cat than chopping it in half with a cleaver. "Sorry," she said, "I'm new here."

The man, who was middle-aged, thin on top and thick round about, gave her an encouraging smile. "It's a bit of a maze till you get used to it," he said. "Where are you looking for?"

The thing he'd been reading, she saw, was a memo: from somebody or other, to Derek Goldman. She knew who he was; head of the Inhuman Resources team, very senior management indeed. "The strongroom," she said. "Mr Suslowicz wanted me to fetch something for him."

"Strongroom's down the stairs on your left."

"Not that strongroom. The other one."

"Ah, right." Mr Goldman grinned. "And Cas Suslowicz forgot to give you the access code."

"Do you need an access code? Sorry, I didn't know."

"Oh yes." The grin became a smirk. "That's Cas all over, don't tell him I said so. He'd forget his own head if it wasn't stuck on. Here, let me do it." He placed one hand on the wall and covered it with the other. "You're not supposed to see," he explained. "Terribly hush-hush." A door – Georgian-style panels – instantly materialised around the handle, which Mr Goldman turned. The door swung open. "There you go," he said. "Make sure you pull it shut after you leave."

It doesn't do, according to all the latest self-help books, to live in the past, and Gina Noctis agreed, more or less. True, the past was her registered domicile for tax purposes, but that's not the same as living there, just as

Orinoco-dot-com doesn't actually have its main offices on a tiny volcanic atoll in the middle of the Pacific. It had been fun being the Queen of the Night while it lasted and she didn't regret a minute of it, but times had changed and so had she, and she was perfectly happy with who she was now, and reasonably confident about who she was going to be in the future. The power, the glory, the abject terror she'd inspired in everybody across whom her shadow fell – Yes, but she'd been there and done that and moved on. Mostly, what she was doing now was so much more interesting.

It was different, though, for other people; she acknowledged that. Some people hadn't had the same advantages as she'd had. They'd never commanded shadow legions or led the Wild Hunt, they'd never known what it's like to sit enthroned in darkness, where you can be whatever you want to be because nobody can see what you truly are. Now that was true freedom. Gina had cheerfully traded it, after she'd had all the fun that she could possibly get out of it, for light and certainty and the company of other sentient beings. She'd been in a position to make an informed decision, and she'd decided it was time for a change. But other people – Tom Dawson, for example. Tom hadn't been spontaneously generated by the friction of Time; he hadn't sprung fully-armed from the universal omnimatrix while the first shockwaves of the Big Bang were still racing towards the curved walls of Infinity. He'd been born and brought up in Slough. You can forgive a man a great deal once you know something like that about him.

You've got to make allowances, was Gina's motto, and she tried her best to live by it. Even so – She knew all about Mr Ahriman, of course, and that made a big difference.

Tom Dawson wasn't a fundamentally bad person. He was a perfectly ordinary person who'd made an unfortunate business decision and was having difficulties living with the fallout. By the same token, the Black Death was just a bunch of normal, well-adjusted microbes doing what normal, well-adjusted microbes do. The circumstances aren't the fault of their victim. Society is to blame.

Some things, however, were beyond even Gina's capacity to forgive, and the memo that had appeared on her desk was one of them—

From: T Dawson
To: all partners and staff

It has come to my attention that members of staff have been using the firm's crystal skull to predict winning lottery numbers. The skull is a very expensive piece of precision equipment which the firm cannot afford to replace and use of it by untrained and unauthorised personnel invalidates our insurance. This practice will now cease, with immediate effect.

Of all the pompous, small-minded – Not that Gina had ever done anything like that herself. If she ever wanted to win a lottery, all she'd need to do would be to choose the numbers and of course they'd win, if they knew what was good for them. But treating grown-ups like naughty kids wasn't the way to run a civilised business. She screwed the memo into a ball, consumed it instantaneously with actinic fire and went to have a word with Tom Dawson.

He wasn't in his office; instead, that stupid angel was sitting at his desk, preening her wing feathers with a tiny gold comb. "Hi," she said, with the same toothpaste-ad smile as before, "I'm sorry I'm not here to deal with your concerns right now—"

"Shut it," Gina said. "Where is he?"

The angel was, of course, simply a projection, insubstantial and not actually there, but Gina wasn't in the mood to be baffled by technicalities. "Sorry," said the angel, "I don't – Oh my God, I exist, that's so amazing. I can think, so presumably I am. That's so incredibly cool. Did you do that?"

"Yes," Gina said. "Where is he?"

"You turned me from a holographic recording into a real live person just like that? That's got to be the most brilliant thing ever. How did you—?"

Gina took a long step forward, grabbed the angel's ear and twisted it. "Ow," said the angel. "That hurts."

"Yes," Gina said. "Welcome to existence. Where's Tom Dawson?"

"He had to go out," the angel whimpered. "Meanwhile, if you'd care to leave a message—"

"Where did he go?"

"Unavailable data. Please don't do that, I don't like it."

"I'll give you unavailable data," Gina said. "Replay the moment of his departure, stat."

"Can I do that?"

"If I say you can, you can."

"OK. But would you please leave off twisting my ear? Thank you." The angel sat up straight, shot Gina a hurt look and closed her eyes. "Replaying moment," she said.

Two translucent forms flickered into view. One of them was Tom Dawson, with his back to the office wall. The other was Mr Ahriman. "Play sound," Gina snapped.

"Audio not available."

Mr Ahriman was advancing slowly, with a grin on his

shimmering see-through face. Tom had backed away as far as he could go. The Queen of the Night can do many things; lip-reading, curiously enough, isn't one of them. "Extrapolate audio from all available records," Gina commanded.

The angel gave her a look. "Hey," she said, "just who do you think I am, Tennessee Williams?"

But there wasn't any need of audio. The look on Tom Dawson's face told Gina all she needed to know, and if she needed confirmation, Mr Ahriman provided it by grabbing Tom by the throat, lifting him off his feet and stuffing him in his jacket pocket. "End playback," the angel said. "That's when he left."

The image of Mr Ahriman melted away in a shower of red sparkles. Gina stood for a moment staring at where it had been, then shook herself back into life. "He took him."

"Looks like it," the angel said. "I guess him leaving triggered my program and here I am. Hey, does that mean I'm now a real person, with thoughts and feelings and fundamental human—?"

"Go away," Gina said, and the angel vanished.

Nuts, thought Gina. It had to happen, of course, sooner or later. Eventually the cat gets tired of playing with the wounded fieldmouse; the lure of its calorific content exceeds its play value, and down the hatch it goes. She could see where Mr Ahriman was coming from. The world was about to be destroyed. Tom Dawson would be destroyed with it, and if he was reduced to his component atoms he'd be no fun to torment any more. Gobble him down now, therefore, while there was still time. Heaven (or wherever it was that Mr Ahriman came from) forbid that Tom should in any sense escape the consequences of his ill-advised actions through the fortuitous intervention of a speeding asteroid.

Even so, Gina thought, that's a bit rough. Tom Dawson had borrowed stake money from Mr Ahriman to buy his way into the partnership, which he'd then taken over by guile, treachery and inhumanly brutal use of elbows; all he'd wanted was to make something of himself, to succeed. A pity he'd had to ruin everything in the process, but you couldn't blame him for aspiring, just as you can't blame a tree for growing out of a tiny seed. If the seed happens to fall into a crack in a wall, that's not its fault. Tom was simply a normal, well-adjusted human being doing what normal, well-adjusted human beings unfortunately tend to do. It wasn't fair that he should be punished for it.

Gina considered that, and various related issues, then sighed. It wasn't just Tom Dawson's presumable future as a soul in eternal torment; it was also the fact that Mr Ahriman would still be a partner in the firm. Indeed, given that he'd just foreclosed on Tom's share of the business, Mr Ahriman would be the senior partner, and therefore by implication the boss of her. Now that, Gina told herself, could easily be downright tiresome.

More nuts, she thought; bushels and bushels of the stupid things. She let her mind dwell for a moment on the concept of partnership, and the unavoidable fact that it's the people we share with who annoy us the most. Tom Dawson might be a devious, ruthless, razor-tongued arsehole with Dark Age sensibilities and about as much fun to be around as a plutonium brick, but – Well, you get used to people, and contempt isn't the only thing that familiarity breeds. Life without Tom would be like beer without hops. In which case, the only thing for it was to rescue the bastard.

She imagined the look on Ted Sunshine's face when she suggested the idea to him, then dismissed the thought from her mind before it broke anything. Pity: she needed allies, and, for all his many faults, Ted was right up at the top of her list of people she'd want with her in a fight. But she had to be realistic, which meant Ted was out of the reckoning. Which just left Brian Teasdale – A nice enough boy and pretty smart for a mortal, and if that wasn't damning with faint praise, she didn't know what was. Still, Brian could be relied on to do as he was told, so long as he was told in the right way. The only motivation he'd need was the thought of Mr Ahriman taking the chair at partnership meetings. Once that had been pointed out to him, the rest would be easy.

She found him in his office, turning water into wine by remote transmutation for a major multinational distillery. "With you in a tick," he said, not looking up from the golden bowl he was staring into. "I've just got to the tricky bit."

The tricky bit, in context, meant shearing the molecular bonds in 3.345×10^{60} molecules of water simultaneously by sheer force of will, so she decided to wait. It didn't take him long, bless him. "Sorry about that," he said, looking up from the bowl, the contents of which were now a dark burgundy. "Now, what can I do for you?"

"It's Tom," she said. "Ahriman's got him."

The bowl slipped between Mr Teasdale's knees and hit the floor. "You what?"

"Stuffed him in his pocket and vanished in a cloud of sparks," Gina said. "I'm guessing he decided to foreclose and Tom didn't have the money. Anyhow, he's gone."

"Fuck a stoat," Mr Teasdale said with feeling. "That means Ahriman—"

"Yes," Gina said. "Unless we do something."

"Such as?"

"Get Tom back."

Mr Teasdale gave her a very sad look. "Gina—"

"Yes, I know. Trouble is, life isn't all beer and skittles. Sometimes you've got to bite the bullet and do nasty things."

"Not," Mr Teasdale pointed out, "when they're physically and metaphysically impossible. That's Ahriman you're talking about. The Prince of—"

Gina frowned, warning Mr Teasdale of the fragility of the ice he was just about to plant his boot on. "I know perfectly well what he's the prince of, Brian. And that's a nuisance, but it can't be helped. We owe a duty to a colleague in distress."

"Balls," Mr Teasdale said succinctly. "It can't be done. And if you think I'm going to sit my arse on a lemon squeezer for Tom bloody Dawson, you must be—"

"Brian," Gina said. "Shut up, there's a good boy."

Mr Teasdale gazed at her as though she'd just hit him with a stick. "Oh come on, Gina," he said, and then the muscles of his neck slackened and his shoulders drooped. "Fine," he said. "How, exactly?"

Good question.

CUPID

Tony Bateman opened his eyes. Then he closed them again, and opened them again, and screamed.

At least he thought he screamed, but maybe not. He was pretty sure he'd screamed, but he couldn't have or he'd have heard himself, a long shrill wail of abject terror, a scream worthy of Fay Wray clutched in the monkey's fist. But he hadn't heard a thing.

In space, he remembered, nobody can hear you scream; valid point. But in space there are stars, several of them, and he couldn't see a single one, he couldn't see anything, although his eyes were definitely open because he prodded the corners of his eyelids with his fingers, just to be sure.

Blind, and deaf as well. He'd heard of cases like that, and even his intolerably frivolous heart had been wrung with spontaneous pity. But his sense of touch was working, because he'd just prodded his eyelids, and he could feel pain—

Quite a lot of it, actually. His head hurt, and he felt like he was bruised all over. Well, that was understandable, since the last thing he remembered was getting hit by a quantum torpedo ... Oh balls, he thought, I must be dead.

That would account for the not seeing and not hearing, but not the being able to feel, or the pain in his head, knees and ribs. But I must be dead, he rationalised, because there's no way in hell I could've survived a direct hit from a bloody great bomb.

He yearned for data, but there didn't seem to be any. I ache all over, therefore I am; fair enough, but mere existence isn't everything. He counted his limbs: two arms, two legs, head, nothing seemed to be missing, his tie was still round his neck. The souls of the dead don't wear ties, not even the souls of dead accountants. And if I'm not dead, I must be—

He closed his eyes. It made no difference, but it was what he did when he wanted to concentrate. Now then, let's start by assembling the facts. Facts, get fell in. Thank you.

I can feel my body, but I can't see or hear anything. Right, so how do seeing and hearing work? Hearing is the eardrums picking up sound waves, seeing is the retina analysing reflected photons. Touch and sensation come from nerve endings bumping into things; in this case, bits of me. But we've already established that I exist, so no surprise there. Photons and sound waves, on the other hand, come from outside.

He suddenly felt as though he'd swallowed a cannonball. I can feel, but I can't see or hear. I can feel me, because I exist. But I can't see or hear because nothing else exists. Nothing can come from outside because there's no outside for it to come from. Spiffing.

Actually, said a voice inside his head, that's not strictly true.

"Excuse me?" he said, or at least he thought he'd said it, but he couldn't hear a dicky bird.

Almost right, said the voice, but not quite. It's because you're in the Bank.

Tony could feel panic creeping in from the shadows around the edge of his mind. Bad enough to be the only existent thing in the universe; but to be the only existent thing in the universe and crazy as a jay bird – "Who are you?" he demanded at what would have been the top of his voice, if only he'd had one. "And what bank?"

The Bank of the Dead, the voice replied. That's where we are.

We, he thought. Plural. "Who are you?"

Ted Sunshine, you halfwit, who else?

Joy flooded Tony's mind like monsoon rain. "You're alive," he said. "Thank G—"

No, said the voice. And neither are you.

Joy turned off like a light. "Sorry, what did you just say?"

We're dead, replied Mr Sunshine. What did you expect, when you just passed through the epicentre of a black hole?

"The what?"

The epicentre, Mr Sunshine repeated, of a black hole. You know what a black hole is? Splendid, one of those. The torpedo hit the shield, and because it had way more mass than we did, we got knocked spinning two thousand light years, until the gravitational pull of the black hole caught us and pulled us in. At which point we died, understandable enough.

"But you said we're in a bank somewhere."

Yes, said Mr Sunshine, the Bank of the Dead.

"But you said we died."

Oh for crying out loud, said Mr Sunshine. Yes, we died. We were utterly consumed. Even I can't get sucked into the heart of a black hole and get away with it.

"But you said—"

Shut your face, said Mr Sunshine, calmly and not unkindly, while I explain. We died. We're now in the land of the dead."

"Oh."

Luckily for us, Mr Sunshine went on, the fact that I've been a customer of the Bank for a very, very long time means I get certain privileges.

"Really?"

Oh yes. I get bespoke wealth management advice, preferential credit solutions, a dedicated team working with me to realise my medium- and long-term investment objectives and a free calendar at Christmas. Oh, and eternal life. Well, eternal existence. That's not precisely the same thing.

"But you said—"

I continue to exist after death, said Mr Sunshine, which is more than most people can say. The downside is, I continue to exist here. Which, when you come to think of it, isn't such a good thing as all that.

"Where's here?"

In the Bank, Mr Sunshine replied. The Bank is a tiny bubble of existence in the middle of a total and utter void. Sort of like an embassy, I guess, or the Vatican. What it means is, in the midst of death I exist. So, apparently, do you, which implies that you somehow get to share my special status just because we happened to be together at the moment of annihilation, which strikes me as a bit rich, considering you've never done a thing to deserve it. Anyhow, we exist. So does an unimaginably vast amount of money, tucked away somewhere under the counter-existential equivalent of a loose floorboard. Apart from us and the money, however, that's it. All in all, Mr Sunshine concluded with a sigh, I think I was right all along. The only part of the package worth having was the calendar.

A surge of despair burst through the floodgates of Tony's mind, drowning everything in bleak horror. "You mean we're stuck here," he said. "Like this. For ever. We can't even—"

It's looking that way, Mr Sunshine said. Mind you, it's not so bad for me, I'm used to it. Well, I was. This is pretty much how it was back in the old days, before the Bang. Mind you, we didn't know anything different back then, so it wasn't so bad. We made our own amusements in those days.

"Really."

Yup, said Mr Sunshine. We explored unlimited possibilities through the medium of pure thought. We built vast constructs out of unfettered speculation and raised towering reverse pyramids of sequential hypotheses, starting with one theoretical assertion and working our way steadily upwards and outwards until Infinity was too small to contain us. In fact, according to some leading authorities in the field, we thought so much we overloaded the infinite and something gave, and that was how the universe started. I'm not sure I believe it, mind you, and I should know because I was there. But I may be wrong. Wouldn't be the first time.

"So that's what I'm supposed to do for the rest of eternity, is it? Just lie here and think."

Not at all, Mr Sunshine said encouragingly. You could

also twiddle your thumbs. I used to do a lot of that, back in the day.

Tony was glad he couldn't hear himself, because he'd have found the noise of his own snivelling distressing. "Thank you," he wailed, "thank you so fucking much, because if I hadn't been with you and your stupid private banking, I'd have been blown to bits or shredded into atoms and that would've been just fine, compared to being stuck here, like this, for ever and ever. It's just so not fair. What did I ever do—?"

Let's not go there, Mr Sunshine said quietly. And get a grip, for crying out loud. While there's existence there's hope.

"Is there?"

Probably, Mr Sunshine said. Maybe, maybe not. We'll just have to see, won't we?

It occurred to Tony that if Mr Sunshine still existed in the same way that he did, it ought to be possible to find him and smash his face in. He groped around for a bit, but there didn't seem to be anything out there apart from his own outlying limbs. He gave up. There didn't seem to be any point to anything any more.

Especially, Mr Sunshine continued, if we can get to my safe deposit box.

"Your what?"

My safe deposit box, Mr Sunshine repeated. It's a box I keep things in. Including, if memory serves, a couple of Get Out Of Death Free cards. I think they'd probably do the trick, if only we can lay our sticky paws on them.

The surge of hope was back. It wasn't quite as pristine and pure as it had been the last time; there were little bits of pessimism, cynicism and rage bobbing about on top, and instead of sweeping along like a tsunami it sort of ebbed cautiously, as though expecting someone to pull the plug at any moment. But it was hope nonetheless. "Get Out Of Death Free cards? You're kidding."

Absolutely not. The Bank used to hand them out at Christmas for a while, along with the calendar, though they stopped doing it some years ago. I think that was because they only gave them to people they knew would never use them – people like me, you see, practically immortal. But I started giving mine away to chums, and so did some of their other customers, so they soon put a stop to it. But I seem to remember there were a couple left.

That, Tony decided, was different. "That's amazing," he said. "You mean, we could actually get out of here? Go home, even?"

I don't see why not, said Mr Sunshine. But that's assuming we can get to my box, like I said. And of course, I'd need the other key.

"The other—"

It takes two keys to open it, that's standard procedure. The other keyholder's the assistant deputy general manager. We've always got on quite well, all things considered.

"What things considered?"

It's a funny thing about the Bank, Mr Sunshine said. They're entirely trustworthy as far as money's concerned, financial integrity's their middle name. When it comes to other things, though, they're as slippery as a fistful of eels. I guess we'll just have to play it by ear and see what happens.

Tony remembered that he'd been advised to get a grip; good advice, he decided. For choice, the grip would've been around Mr Sunshine's neck, but you can't have everything. "How do we find your safe deposit box?" he asked.

No idea, Mr Sunshine replied. What I've always done is call ahead to let them know I'm coming, and Charlie would be there to meet me.

"Charlie?"

The assistant deputy general manager of the Bank, said Mr Sunshine. A flat chap. His granddaughter's a big-shot corporate lawyer in Hong Kong.

"He's a friend of yours?"

I wouldn't go so far as to say that, Mr Sunshine replied. I don't blame him, of course, it's the way the Bank's bonus system's set up. For every human soul they manage to ensnare into staying in the Bank before their allotted time is up, they get a nanosecond of life.

"You what? A nanosecond?"

That's right. A whole nanosecond of self-aware existence. With an incentive like that, you can see how easily professional ethics can get lost down the back of the moral sofa. And the other side of the coin is, if one of the deadstock somehow contrives to get away on their watch, they get fifty thousand years suffering the torment of the damned and a formal reprimand. Letting me get to my safe deposit box would almost certainly count as aiding and abetting a fugitive.

"But it's your box. And if the Bank issued the cards in the first place—"

Things are a bit different down here, Mr Sunshine said. Like I said, where money's concerned, straight as a die. In other respects—

Tony whimpered. On the one hand, hope. On the other, bleak despair. All things considered he'd have been OK with either one, just so long as the agonising tug-of-war could be over. "But you've got a plan," he said. "Tell me you've got a plan."

I've got a plan.

"Wonderful," Tony said. "What is it?"

No idea, Mr Sunshine said. Now please stop talking just for a minute or so, and let me think.

Consuela pulled the strongroom door until it was almost closed but not quite, then groped on the wall for a light switch. There didn't seem to be one. Not to worry. She fingered the gold chain around her neck. "Hanuman, you useless ball of fur," she commanded. "Lights."

A beam of golden light shone from level with the gap between her collarbones out into the room, which was small and apparently completely empty. That didn't faze her in the least. The best way to hide something is, of course, in plain sight. Next best is hiding it in plain invisibility.

"I haven't got time for this," she told the room. "Reveal."

She'd got a distinction in revealing spells in college; not as impressive as it sounds, since Sunnyside was one of the more modern thaumaturgical academies, funded by venture capital and obliged to provide its shareholders with the best possible return on their investment. A distinction was 10 per cent extra, payable in advance of the actual coursework. That didn't mean she wasn't good at them. She opened her third eye and peered, and, sure enough, shadowy forms began to consolidate around the walls of the room. Sets of grey-painted angle-iron shelving, on which sat a modest number of brown cardboard boxes. Fine, Consuela said to herself. Let the dog see the rabbit.

A hand, hard as iron and strong as death, gripped her left shoulder and spun her round. A figure shimmered into existence an arm's length away from her, and she fought back the urge to scream.

"Daddy?" she said.

No, of course not, don't be stupid. Right now, her father was either sitting behind his desk contriving a hostile takeover or out on the golf course, spinning his gossamer threads around some client. The reason the creature crushing her shoulder blade looked like Daddy was because Daddy was the one person in the world she was scared stiff of. A security protocol, therefore. And how big a deal could that be?

"Prove," hissed the creature, "that you're not a robot."

"Oh don't be so—" she started to say, and then noticed that her shoulder wasn't hurting any more, even though the creature hadn't relaxed its grip. There was a reason for that. Her shoulder was now a titanium moulding.

The creature's voice was as quiet as rat's feet in a dark cellar. "Verify."

"I-am-not-a-robot," she protested. The words came out in a metallic monotone. Angrily she activated the plasma cannon built into her left arm and loosed off a volley, which bounced harmlessly off the creature's eyeball. "I-appear-to-be-a-robot-because-you-have-initiated-my-shape-shifting-abilities-against-my-will-and-caused-me-to-transform-into-an-artificial-life-form. If-you-would-kindly-pack-it-in-I-will-prove-to-you-that-I-am-not—"

Without letting go of her shoulder, which was once again flesh and blood, the creature raised its other hand and tilted her chin round to the left. On the wall opposite, she saw a projection of nine squares. Each of them appeared to be a pastoral landscape; rolling hillsides carpeted with verdant grass.

"Select all images containing a wizard," snarled the creature.

"None of them."

"Including wizards with invisibility cloaks."

"That's not—" She took a deep breath. She could do this. She strained her third eye until it practically squeaked. In the bottom left-hand square, she could just make out a sort of ripple effect. "Square G," she said. "Well?"

The wall went blank; then twelve different squares appeared. "Oh come on," she moaned, but the creature didn't seem to be listening. "Select," the creature rasped, "all images containing Pain."

Well, that shouldn't be too difficult. She looked, then tried desperately to turn away, but the creature's grip wouldn't let her. Herself at pre-school, standing alone in a corner. Herself at big school, the last to be chosen for a netball team. Herself, fat and spotty, hovering on the edge of the group clustered round the cool gang. Herself gazing hopelessly at Steve O'Gorman, who was smiling at somebody else. Herself at the Freshers' Fair—

"Bastard," she said. "All of them."

The wall went blank. Twelve more squares appeared. "Select all images," whispered the creature in a voice loaded with malicious glee, "containing Love."

"Get stuffed."

"Select all images—"

"All right," she snapped and faced the wall. Nine pictures of Brian Teasdale – at the beach, sitting outside a pavement café, up a stepladder painting a wall, soaked to the skin by a sudden squall of rain. "None of them," she shouted. "Not in a million years. Not if the future of sentient life depended on it."

Her shoulder creaked under the pressure of the creature's fingers. Even titanium can only stand so much pressure. "I-am-not-a-robot," she tried to yell, but it came out in Dalekspeak. "I-have-no-feelings-whatsoever-for-that-fat-headed-gutless-incredibly-boring—"

The creature nestled closer and whispered into her tin ear. "Prove you're not a robot."

"How-would-it-be-if-I-told-you-my-mother's-maiden-name-and-the-name-of-my-first-pet?"

"Verify."

"None-of-them," she blared, then looked again. "Well," she mumbled, "maybe Square D. He does look kind of cute with his hair all wet."

The creature relaxed its grip. If it hadn't, it'd have squished her shoulder into a bloody pulp. The wall went blank. Then three more squares appeared. "For crying out loud," Consuela said. "Aren't we done yet?"

"Select all squares—" The creature's voice was soft and far away, like the wind sighing through a fleshless ribcage. "—containing Absolution."

"Oh, that old thing." She considered the squares, only three this time. Absolution: what a funny thing to ask about.

In the first square she was sitting in an office. It was a big office, with a huge window, through which she looked down on the London Eye. He viewpoint changed and she saw at the edge of her vision a sheet of headed notepaper. There was a big JWW logo, and under it a list of names. The first name on the list was Consuela Teasdale, followed by CEO.

In the second square she was sitting in a very different sort of room. The ceiling was low, the wall nearest to her was panelled in centuries-old oak; the other walls were floor-to-ceiling bookshelves crammed with complete series of learned journals. She was sitting in a big, comfortable armchair, and opposite her perched a terrified looking young woman with a laptop on her knees reading out an essay. On a nearby coffee table was an offprint of a scholarly paper – "Born Three: The Case For Trinities Proven", by Professor C. Teasdale.

In the third square she was sitting at a narrow desk in a crowded room, peering at a computer screen and wearing headphones. A faint buzzing noise. "Hello," she heard herself say, "welcome to Picosoft technical support, how can I help you?" Short pause, then she heard herself say, "Well, first of all I'd like you to turn off your computer for me and then turn it on again—"

Consuela twisted round, regardless of the pain and the collateral damage. The creature was staring at her. "You've got to be kidding," she said. "Seriously."

The creature's hand twisted her head back to face the wall. The squares had gone. Instead there was one big square, in which a blue-green planet floated against a velvet starry backdrop. A brilliant flash of white light hurtled towards it at great speed and rammed into it. A cloud of steam, mushroom-shaped, rose up from the point of impact. Then gradually the planet began to come apart, like a swarm of bees dissipated by a gust of wind. One moment it was a sphere, perfect in its symmetry. The next it was just chunks and bits and a cloud of dust, with stars peeping through the gaps.

Consuela had stopped noticing the pain in her shoulder. "Seriously?" she said.

"Seriously," said the creature.

The three squares were back. "This is so unfair," Consuela said. "Why me? What did I ever do?"

"What did you ever do?" echoed the creature. "Verify. Select all squares containing Absolution."

In a very small voice, Consuela said, "Square C. But that's really mean. Why not Brian, for pity's sake? Or Ted bloody Sunshine? It's because I'm a woman, isn't it? You wouldn't be picking-on-me-like-this-if-I-was-a—" She stopped herself. "Seriously? Because none of them could've done it?"

"Continue."

The wall went blank. The creature wasn't there any more. Her shoulder was fine.

"Screw you," she shouted into the empty room. "And you can't hold me to it, I didn't sign anything."

A mirror appeared in front of her. It can't have been an ordinary mirror, because by the time it appeared she'd stopped shouting, but in the mirror she could see herself yelling into thin air. "Fine," she sighed. "But is that really the reason? Because none of them could have done it, only me?"

She saw her face in the mirror, and lip-read; none of them could have done it, only me. Oh, she thought. Oh well. "Just out of interest, why not? What's so special about me?"

The mirror vanished. A voice in her head, still and small and calm, whispered, Verification complete.

She took a deep breath and let it go slowly. First thing I'll do if I ever get out of here, she promised herself, I'll go round to Zauberwerke and punch somebody's head.

A noise startled her. She looked round and saw a pin lying on the floor. It had fallen from one of the shelves of a grey-painted angle-iron shelving unit, on which rested a single cardboard box. She realised she wasn't using her third eye. "Oh I see," she said aloud. "So quiet you could hear a pin—"

There was only one shelving unit. Before there'd been

half a dozen, and many boxes. Taped to one of the shelves was a brown envelope, on which someone had written in black marker pen: Silence.

Fine. She'd heard about that sort of thing. There are materials so delicate that being repeatedly battered by sound waves damages them; likewise photons, which was why there was no light switch next to the door. The glow from the little gold monkey round her neck diminished into a dull gleam.

No point, she decided, in hanging about. She advanced to the shelving unit, lifted the flaps of the cardboard box and looked inside.

"Oh, come on," she was about to say, but then she caught sight of the notice out of the corner of her eye and didn't.

Inside the box was a brass Zippo lighter, a cinema ticket, a packet of Oreos, a rubber band and a tuning fork.

He'd never admit it out loud, but Tom Dawson had a thing about heights. He didn't approve of them on a fundamental level. Come the revolution, in his view, all heights would be lined up against a wall and shot. Down, in other words, with up.

"Are you all right?" Mr Ahriman asked him.

Mr Ahriman was standing on the peak of a very high mountain, one of the very few in existence that actually comes to a point. Anyone who didn't know him might have mistaken him for an angel dancing on the pointy end of a pin. Mr Dawson, peering out from under the pocket flap of Mr Ahriman's jacket, made a sort of gurgling noise.

"We're here," Mr Ahriman said. "You can come out now."

His hand surged around the sides of Mr Dawson's

head, thumb pressing against the right temple, fingers clamped to the left. His grip tightened and he pulled Mr Dawson out, like a rabbit from a conjuror's hat. Mr Dawson felt the full weight of gravity in his feet as he dangled from the intolerable grip; agony if Mr Ahriman didn't let go, certain death if he did. A long way below he could see clouds.

"It's all right," Mr Ahriman said, "you're perfectly safe."

Mr Ahriman may have been the Father of Lies but he didn't tend to tell them very often, mostly because, coming from him, the truth was vastly more painful. If he told you you were safe, then for the time being, you probably were ...

The grip slackened. Mr Dawson felt the skin of his temples drawn into moraines by the tips of Mr Ahriman's fingers as he slid from his grasp. Before he could even yell, the pressure eased completely. He was falling—

Mr Ahriman caught him easily with his other hand. "Oops," he said. "Butterfingers." He put Mr Dawson down gently between his feet on the very apex of the mountain.

That wasn't really an improvement. Terra firma was Mr Dawson's favourite thing, but not when it had a point on it like a needle. He managed to jam the point between the sideways-curled soles of his feet, which gave him just enough stability.

"I could, of course," Mr Ahriman was saying, "just go away and leave you here. Knowing your silly phobia about high places, that might be a giggle. What do you think?"

Mr Dawson knew that if he closed his eyes he'd lose the tiny scintilla of balance that was keeping him from a very long fall. That meant he had to have them open, and see where he was. "Not bad," he forced himself to say. "But you can do better."

Mr Ahriman laughed. "You're right," he said, "I can. What we're here for is just basic orientation, like a sort of preliminary interview where we get to know each other better and figure out what each of us is looking for in our future working relationship." He sighed, and the faint breeze of his breath was enough to make Mr Dawson stagger for a moment. "Actually quite pointless, since we know each other very well indeed, don't we? But procedure is procedure and I've got to fill out the forms and tick the boxes, you know how it is. Right then, shall we get on with it?"

Up till then, Mr Dawson had been too preoccupied to notice the cold. It began to assert itself. He couldn't feel his nose, or his fingers. More to the point, he could barely feel his feet, the clamping pressure of which was the only thing keeping him from falling. "Might as well," he muttered. "Then, could we possibly go somewhere else?"

Mr Ahriman chuckled. "Was that a request?"

Rule one: don't ask Mr Ahriman for anything, anything at all, because of the price tag inevitably attached thereto. "More like a suggestion," Mr Dawson said. "A rhetorical one."

Mr Ahriman patted him on the head, very gently. "You still think you're going to negotiate your way out of this, don't you? Bless you, that's so sweet. I'm very sorry, but it's too late for that now. You defaulted on our agreement and I've foreclosed. You're mine, body and soul. Therefore," he added happily, "everything that's yours is also mine, so you have absolutely nothing left to negotiate with." He paused, then added, "You can despair now, if you like."

"Thanks," Mr Dawson said. "That'll be a great weight off my mind."

Mr Ahriman was silent for a moment. "Come again?"

"It's not the despair," Mr Dawson quoted, "it's the hope."

"Excuse me?"

Mr Dawson forced a poor excuse for a laugh. "Really," he said. "You think you know people, but obviously you don't. Despair doesn't hurt, or at least not much. When you know there's no chance it'll get better, you can just sort of hunker down and suffer enduringly. No, it's hope that really fucks you up, even just the tiniest glimmer of it. If you really wanted to torture someone, you'd give him hope. But I guess you'd need to be human to understand that."

"Mr Dawson," Mr Ahriman said delightedly. "Are you trying to play me for a sucker?"

"Just pointing out a fundamental aspect of human nature," Mr Dawson said. "I expect it's in a textbook somewhere if you want to look it up."

"What an extraordinary creature you are," Mr Ahriman said. "Anyway, let's get on, shall we? All right, here goes. Are you hungry?"

"You what?"

"Hungry," Mr Ahriman said. "Peckish, deficient in nutrition, just about ready to eat a mule. Are you or aren't you?"

Mr Dawson had to think about that one. "It's not exactly at the top of my agenda, but I suppose so, yes."

"Fine," Mr Ahriman said. "Turn those stones into bread."

"What stones?"

"Sorry, with you in a tick." A flash of light. "Those stones."

Mr Dawson could, of course, turn stones into bread just like that. In the early days of the firm, he'd had a contract with a leading supermarket chain, but it proved to be more trouble than it was worth. "Hang on," he said, "it's on the tip of my tongue. Right, then, man does not live by bread alone. Besides, I have a gluten allergy."

There was a printed form in Mr Ahriman's right hand and a biro in his left. He ticked a box. "Very good," he said. "Now then, you'll like this one. Cast yourself off the mountaintop and flights of angels will catch you and bear you safely to the ground."

Mr Dawson gave him a look. "You know what," he said, "I'd rather not."

"Go on. It'll be fine, I promise you. Scout's honour."

Mr Dawson shuddered. "You," he said, "were never a scout."

"I so was," Mr Ahriman replied, "though where I come from we preferred to call them insurgents. So that's your last word, is it? Think about it. All you have to do is jump, and in two shakes of a lamb's tail you'll be down there, safe and sound. You'd like that, you know you would."

He had a point. Even so. "I think I'll just stay here for now, if that's all right."

"You're the doctor," Mr Ahriman said. "Well, if you passed that one, this one ought to be a stroll in the park. If you'd care to look around you."

Mr Dawson did so. He saw all the kingdoms of the Earth. Also, a long way away but not as far away as all that, he saw a tiny speck in the sky that could easily be an approaching asteroid. "Done that," he said. "Well?"

"All this can be yours," Mr Ahriman said, "if you'll just fall down and worship me."

Mr Dawson looked at him. "Seriously?"

"Seriously."

"Are you absolutely sure?"

"Yes."

Mr Dawson hesitated just for a moment. "About the falling down part," he said.

"Oh, I see what you mean. In the circumstances, you can skip all that. Feel free to worship standing, if you'd rather."

"Thanks," said Mr Dawson. "In that case, praise be and hallelujah. Jubilate in excelsis. That's a particularly nice jacket you're wearing, by the way. Where did you get it?"

Mr Ahriman ticked another box. "Splendid," he said. "Right then, here's your title deeds to all the kingdoms of the Earth, if you'd just sign there, and there, and there, oh yes and there – Thank you. Your Majesty," he added. He handed Mr Dawson a piece of paper. "Well," he said, "I have to admit, I'm disappointed. I really thought you were smarter than that."

Mr Dawson looked up from the document. "Excuse me?"

"Oh come on. All this belongs to you, but you belong to me. And now, just to put the icing on the proverbial cake, you do so willingly. It's childish of me but I love it when that happens." Mr Ahriman looked up. He was observing the approaching asteroid. "Not," he added, "that it happens very often. In fact, this is the first time that old chestnut's actually worked, because everybody else I've tried it on over the past hundred thousand years had more sense. Do you realise," he went on, "that in all of human history you're my very first worshipper?"

Mr Dawson had gone a funny colour. "Get away," he said.

"No kidding. And that was a nuisance, because until I managed to get a worshipper, I couldn't be a real god. Particularly awkward under the current circumstances, because only gods are going to be able to get off-world before the big smash and escape. Thank you ever so much. I can honestly say you've been worth every penny I paid for you."

Mr Dawson gazed at him.

"Really," Mr Ahriman went on, "it's the ultimate win-win situation. I get to carry on living. You get what you always wanted – You know, the money and the power and the real estate. True, you won't have it for very long and I don't suppose it'll be much use to you, teetering up here, but that's really not for me to say, is it? You always wanted to make the big score, hit the jackpot, improve yourself. Well, didn't you?"

"Yes," Mr Dawson said, with just a hint of residual defiance. "Yes, I did."

"Quite understandable. You're from Slough, aren't you?"

"That's right."

"Mphm. Well, you've come a long way from there, no doubt about it. I don't suppose you can even see Slough from here. No, I tell a lie, there it is, that thing like a soup stain. And nobody ever helped you or gave you a leg-up. You did it all yourself, by your own unyielding effort. No silver spoon in your mouth, that's for sure. And look at you now. All the kingdoms of the Earth." Mr Ahriman clicked his tongue. "Things may not have turned out exactly the way you planned, but nobody can deny you got stuck in, pulled yourself up by your bootstraps and really showed 'em back in the old neighbourhood."

Mr Dawson scowled at him. "Thank you," he said.

"No worries. Now your last thought can be, I did it my way."

"Yes," said Mr Dawson. "I did."

"Oh yes," Mr Ahriman said, "you made something of yourself all right. To be precise, a fool. Adios, amigo."

Mr Ahriman vanished. "Just a minute," Mr Dawson said.

Mr Ahriman reappeared. "Was there something?"

"Just to clarify," Mr Dawson said. "All this lot is now mine, right?"

"Yup."

"All of it? As far as the eye can see?"

Mr Ahriman smiled. "Don't sell yourself short," he said. "You're not allowing for the curvature of the Earth. A heck of a lot further than the eye can see, as a matter of fact."

"Thank you." Mr Dawson took a deep breath: awkward, since his throat and lungs seemed to be filled with something. It felt like cream cheese, but that seemed improbable. More likely it was fear. "And you're saying you've got me because—?"

"Excuse me?"

"You claim," Mr Dawson said, "that I'm yours, body and soul. I'd be grateful if you could just clarify your grounds for saying that."

Mr Ahriman glared at him. "Don't give me that," he said. "We both know why. I served you with a notice to repay what you owe me. There was a deadline. The deadline passed. I foreclosed."

"Mphm. When, exactly?"

Mr Ahriman glanced at his watch. "Three hours ago."

"Right," said Mr Dawson. "Three hours ago where, exactly?"

"Sorry, I don't think I—"

"Time," Mr Dawson said, trying very hard not to let his voice break up, "is relative. As in, when it's 9 a.m. in New York, it's 11 p.m. in Sydney. And so on and so forth. By the way, where are we precisely? I'm guessing the Himalayas because of the altitude, but maybe not that far east?"

Mr Ahriman's face went blank. "I can see where you're going with this," he said. "It won't wash."

"Actually," Mr Dawson said, "I think it will. Our agreement was made in London, UK. Over there," he added, pointing. "Now let's see, if that's Slough, and that's Paris, so that must be Athens, and that over there is presumably Jeddah – What was the deadline in that foreclosure notice of yours? Twelve noon on the sixteenth?" He squeezed his numb face into a smile. "It isn't twelve noon yet. Not where we are now."

Mr Ahriman licked his lips. "It was when I served it."

"That's as may be," Mr Dawson said. "But it isn't now. Or, rather, here. Here, I've still got time to pay you what I owe you. And, by an extraordinary coincidence, I've just come into some money. Thanks for that, by the way. Oh, and praise be and hallelujah. I'm quite sincere about the worship, by the way. I ought to be, you've just answered all my prayers."

Mr Ahriman was doing mental arithmetic. "You think you're so clever," he said.

Mr Dawson nodded. "So clever, yes. Clever, no. Actually, I'm incredibly stupid, or I'd never have got mixed up with you in the first place. But so clever, yes. I take it," he added, "that so clever means thick as a brick but nonetheless cleverer than you."

Mr Ahriman gave him a look you could've stored

mammoths in. "By my calculations," he said, "all the kingdoms of the Earth, at current market valuation and bearing in mind the fact that they're about to get splatted by an asteroid, are worth precisely nothing. Think again."

"Fair enough," Mr Dawson replied. "But that includes all the cash money in all the banks in all the kingdoms of the Earth, which is lawful tender and therefore not susceptible to fluctuations in market value, and it's mine and I'm giving it to you. Not enough to pay off the principal of the loan, but I think you'll find it covers the interest. And according to our agreement—"

Mr Ahriman was perfectly still and silent for maybe three seconds. Then he grinned. "You know what?" he said. "I think I'll let you have that one. I mean to say, there's bound to be a fallacy in your argument somewhere, because you're an idiot and always have been. But all things considered, I'm reluctant to let you off so lightly. I thought I'd finished with you, but maybe I haven't after all."

Mr Dawson shook his head. It wasn't easy, because the cold had reached the tendons of his neck, but he made the effort. "You bet your life you haven't," he said. "You said it yourself, just now. In order to get off this planet before it's destroyed, you need a worshipper. You need me." He allowed himself a grin, as a special treat. "I hadn't realised that until you told me just now. And you were saying I had nothing left to negotiate with."

Mr Ahriman glanced up at the asteroid. It was too far away for any device made by human hands to observe, but he could see it clear as anything. "Sorry," he said, "but I think I've lost track. Am I the one manipulating you, or is it the other way round?"

"Six of one and half a dozen of the other," Mr Dawson

said generously. "Which is, after all, what negotiation is all about. Rule number one of free collective bargaining: if you aim to bring the other guy to his knees and scalp him, first give him what he really wants. The art of the deal lies in the instant of perfect symmetry when you're screwing and being screwed at precisely the same moment."

Mr Ahriman looked up again and sighed. "In that case," he said, "it's a deal. In payment of accrued arrears of interest, I accept all the kingdoms of the Earth. Except," he added, "Slough. Slough you can keep. You deserve it."

"Thank you. Got a pen?"

Mr Ahriman lent him one, and Mr Dawson quickly endorsed the title deeds back to Mr Ahriman and handed them over. "Thanks," Mr Dawson said. "It's a pleasure doing business with you."

"For a moment, you made me believe you really mean that."

"I do," Mr Dawson said. "It's making the deal that does it for me, always has been."

They looked at each other with something approaching respect (approaching, in the same sense that the asteroid was approaching the planet). "Well," Mr Ahriman said, "so long. The next interest payment's due in a month. Don't be late."

Mr Dawson shot a quick glance at his feet, still clenched to the apex of the mountain. "Just a moment," he said. "What about—?"

"Oh, that." Mr Ahriman nodded. "I'll leave you to find your own way down, if you can. Do take care of yourself, I'd hate anything to happen to you."

"No, please—"

"Sorry," Mr Ahriman said, "but there doesn't seem to be

anything in the small print about rescuing you from mountaintops. Tell you what I'll do, to show there's no ill feeling. I'll make it so you don't freeze to death. There," he added, and Mr Dawson's feet suddenly exploded in a nightmare of pins and needles. "Now, either you can try and climb down the mountain without slipping and falling, or you can stay there for as long as you can possibly cling on and see what happens. Entirely up to you. None of my business. Ciao for now," he added, with a smile. "It's been a blast."

He vanished into thin air, which was the only sort there was at that altitude.

Mr Dawson looked around, then down at his feet. The upper of his left shoe had just started to rip away from the sole – Vexing, because he'd paid a great deal of money for those shoes not so long ago. Vexing for other reasons, too.

How long, he wondered, would it take Mr Ahriman to get off the planet? About as long, he decided, as it would take the sole of his shoe to pull away from the upper – At which point his precarious grip on the pointy mountaintop would give way, and he'd plummet to his, let's not think about that, shall we, not until we absolutely have to. Approximately that long, he decided. Clearly, the moment his head hit the distant rocks, the faith in the divinity of Mr Ahriman that it contained would be dissipated and lost – He reviewed his options. He could jump right now, thereby thwarting his tormentor before he had a chance to do his flit. Very noble, very righteous, but he wasn't sure he wanted to do that, thanks all the same. Freezing to death was out, because Mr Ahriman had generously granted him internal central heating, because it'd spoil everything if he froze solid and died too soon. He could stay where he was, hoping that someone or something would swoop in and rescue him in the nick of time, and let the bastard get away. Or he could simply stop believing—

No, he couldn't do that. Blessed are those who have seen and yet have not believed; but Mr Dawson had seen, and he lacked the mental flexibility to deny an incontrovertible fact, except where the Inland Revenue were concerned. He loathed Mr Ahriman with every fibre of his being – always had, if truth be told – but that didn't mean he didn't believe in him.

An unpleasant thought struck him. When he'd first met him, Mr Ahriman had been a shadowy sort of figure, more a whisper coming from the shadows in the corner of the room than a physical presence. It was only after the money had changed hands and the agreement had been signed and Mr Dawson had condemned himself to the path that had led him, inevitably in hindsight, to this inconveniently pointy spot that he'd gradually become a recognisable person, with a face and a nose and hair growing out of his ears. Only, it slowly dawned on Mr Dawson, once I decided he could deliver on what he was promising; only once I started to believe. So, if I hadn't allowed him to convince me, all those years ago, it looks rather as if he'd never have become what he is now, an all-powerful entity, to all intents and purposes a god. So, if you cared to look at it from that perspective, I did it to myself—

There's nothing like realising how colossally stupid you've been to dissolve the soul, like a slug in a pot of salt. For crying out loud, he thought. Talk about your halfwits.

A tiny light flicked on inside Mr Dawson's mind. Halfwit. Half as in 50 per cent. Dawson, Ahriman and Dawson.

He allowed himself the tiniest grin imaginable.

DONNER

Tony Bateman counted 999,999, then stopped. "Have
you thought of anything yet?" he said.

"Yes, actually."

Tony realised he'd heard that last remark, rather than
feeling it in his bones. "How did you do that?" he asked.

"You clown," said Mr Sunshine. "Open your eyes."

"They're open." Tony checked, just to make sure. "I
tell a lie," he said, as the faintest possible gleam of grey
light scorched his retina. "It's because I was counting. I
always close my eyes when I concentrate." He stopped.
"Who's that?"

"Forgive him," said the flat grey outline of Mr
Sunshine, "he's an idiot. Charlie, this is Tony Bateman.
Tony, this is Charlie."

"Pleased to meet you," said an impossibly thin
line, which then turned sideways and became a sort
of approximation at a human being – Rather as if one
of those weird blind fish at the very bottom of the sea

had heard a vague description of a man and had tried to draw one.

"Charlie's pleased to meet everybody," Mr Sunshine said. "That's not necessarily an endearing trait, in context."

Charlie laughed. It wasn't a cheerful sound. But at least it was a sound, and the grey light he diffused was still light. "Charlie exists," Mr Sunshine explained. "Well, sort of. At least, he exists when the Bank has customers."

"What does he do the rest of the—?"

"Paperwork, mostly," Charlie said. "Routine admin, monthly returns, compliance, staff assessment reports, that sort of thing. I find it's the opposite of existing, in a way that merely not being there could never be."

Tony decided that you probably couldn't offend Charlie, in the same way you'd be hard put to it to set light to the sun. Even so, best not to push his luck. "Well, we're here," he said. "Gives you a chance to—"

"Shine," Charlie said. "Believe me, it's appreciated." He turned to face Mr Sunshine, turning back into the shortest distance between two points as far as Tony was concerned. "You sent for me," he said.

"That's right," said Mr Sunshine. "I want financial advice." He paused, letting the implications sink in. "As a private banking customer I'm entitled to one-to-one investment counselling twenty-four-seven. Which is why," he added, "you were obliged to turn up."

"Perfectly true," Charlie said. "And no skin off my nose, obviously. Quite the reverse, in fact. Well then," he went on, "I have to say that in your current circumstances the most helpful advice I can give you is, you can't take it with you. Other than that, I'm not sure what I can offer. If you were interested in minimising your estate's exposure to inheritance tax, I'm sorry to say you've left it a bit late."

"Not strictly true," Mr Sunshine said.

"Excuse me?"

"About taking it with me," Mr Sunshine said. "Well, actually it's sort of true and not true. You can't take it with you, but you can put it there beforehand so it'll already be where you need it when you arrive."

Charlie smiled. "Ah, I see," he said. "Your safe deposit box."

"Precisely."

"No problem," Charlie said. "If you'll just let me have a copy of the grant of probate and a letter of authorisation from your executors, I'll get on it straight away."

Tony decided that Mr Sunshine hadn't been expecting that. But he took it well. "Really?" he said, with an admirably casual smile. "How'd it be if I signed for it myself?"

Charlie shook his head, rather an alarming sight from where Tony was standing. "Sorry," he said. "Rules is rules. The property of a deceased client can only be released to his duly accredited legal representatives."

Mr Sunshine looked at him. "Are you saying I'm dead?"

"Not to put too fine a point on it," Charlie said, "yes."

"Meaning that at some point in time I died."

"Yup."

"Time," he said pleasantly, "has no meaning here. I may have died back up there somewhere, but not down here, otherwise we couldn't be having this conversation. Jurisdictional issue," he added, "you may want to ask your legal department about it. But obviously I'm not dead here, or at any rate I'm not as dead as all that, because when I sent out my request for financial counselling, you felt obliged to turn up." He grinned. "Sorry, Charlie, but you can't have it both ways."

The thin straight line chuckled. "Well spotted," he

said. "It was worth a try, but you always were a sharp one. No hard feelings, right?"

"No hard feelings, Charlie. Now then, let's have that key."

"Sure," Charlie said. "Hang on there a moment while I fetch it."

He vanished, and the light went with him. His own silly fault, Tony heard inside his head. He was so anxious to grab a few minutes of existence he conveniently forgot about the rules, and now of course he can't contradict himself.

"Oh I see," Tony said. "That's why the first thing you asked him for was financial advice."

Too right, said Mr Sunshine. I wouldn't want his advice under any other circumstances whatsoever, he'd just try and sell me one of their in-house ISAs. Look out, he's coming back. Do me a favour and don't speak unless I tell you to, all right?

Sure, Tony remembered just in time not to say.

The thin vertical line was back, only now it had a key dangling from one side and a tin box held just above knee height on the other. "If you'll just sign the register," Charlie said. "Splendid, thank you. Yes, and there, thank you, all done." A table materialised out of nowhere and Charlie put the box down on it. "Here we are," he said, fitting his key in the lock and turning it. "You have got your key, haven't you?"

"I never go anywhere without it," Mr Sunshine said firmly.

"Only," Charlie went on, and the edge in his voice was like a razor blade nestling in a bouquet of roses, "I was a bit concerned it might come under the heading of, you know, stuff you can't take with you. I'd hate for you to have to go all the way back Topside and fetch it – Oh, wait, you can't do that, can you? That's a pity."

"Not a problem," Mr Sunshine said. He extended his forefinger and turned it sideways. It grew wards, just like a key. He thrust it into the lock and twisted it through ninety degrees, and Tony heard a soft click.

"I'd just like to point out," Charlie said, after a moment of intense silence, "that that's not an officially approved key. Only officially approved keys—"

Mr Sunshine looked at him. "Not now, Charlie, all right? Fun's fun, but there are limits. Anyhow, the box is open now, so what are you going to do about it?"

"I was just saying, that's all." Charlie took a long step back, and Mr Sunshine lifted the lid of the box. For a few moments, almost infinitely prolonged as far as Tony was concerned, he scuffled about inside the box, the way you do, pushing things aside and looking under things. Then he made a sort of soft snorting noise, indicative of supreme joy. "Here we go," he said. "Just look what I've found. Two Get Out Of Death Free cards."

"Fancy that," said Charlie.

"Well, quite."

Mr Sunshine held up two small pieces of card. They were edged in black and carried a pressed black seal. "One for me," he said, "one for the waste of space over there. Just confirm they're in order for me, Charlie, there's a pal, and then I think we'll be going."

When he took out the cards he'd dislodged something else, which fell out of the box, landed on the table, bounced and dropped to the floor. Charlie stooped and picked it up. "Thanks," Mr Sunshine said. It was an old fabric purse, very tatty, with a tarnished clasp. "Wouldn't want to lose that, I have a feeling it might come in handy one of these days."

The clasp sprang open. Something dropped out of the purse onto the table. It was one of those days. "Hey," Charlie said. He reached out to pick it up, then drew his hand away sharply. "Hey, Ted," he said. "You know better than that."

"Excuse me?"

"You know the rules," Charlie said reproachfully. "No objects of offworld origin to be kept in safe deposit boxes if they exceed $10^{9,000,000}$ terajoules in shearing force."

"No kidding."

"That's the rule," Charlie said. "Anything over that invalidates our insurance. Sorry, but I'm going to have to ask you to take it away with you when you leave."

"Ah." Mr Sunshine smiled. "So I'm leaving, am I? Jolly good."

There was a moment of dead silence. "It's looking that way," Charlie said, in a voice as cold as the Tuesday after the heat death of the universe. Nice one, Ted," he added. "You sure played me for a sucker that time."

"Actually," Mr Sunshine said, "I didn't. I'd forgotten all about this little tinker." He picked it up gingerly. It didn't burn his hands, presumably because he wasn't really alive yet, only existing. "Sorry," he said. "I only brought it down here because I didn't fancy leaving it lying around upstairs. I don't even know what it is, to be honest with you."

"Oh, that's easy," Charlie said. "It's the key to an asteroid."

A soft thump, as the object slipped through Mr Sunshine's fingers and hit the table. He retrieved it quickly. "You sure about that?"

"Sure I'm sure," Charlie said. "It's a Zg[ip{u-p'ggggg'n Technologies NPX9000 Super Plus Extra, best locking device money can buy. We looked into fitting them here at the Bank, but the thaumaton radiation they give off has a nasty habit of burning holes in space/time unless you've got the right insulation, so we went with Yales instead. Yup, I'd know one of those babies anywhere. And I'm sorry, but you can't keep it here. Rules is—"

"Yes," Mr Sunshine said. "Quite. Well now, fancy that. Of course I'll take it with me. Sorry to have bothered you with it in the first place."

"No harm done," Charlie said. "Well, nice seeing you, Ted. Drop by any time, you're always welcome."

Mr Sunshine wrapped the object in his handkerchief – a special handkerchief, don't ask – and dropped it in his pocket. "Thanks, Charlie. All my best to the grandkids. How's young Irving doing, by the way?"

"Not bad, according to his probation officer. His mother thinks this time he may have turned the corner."

"That's good to hear," Mr Sunshine said. "Right then we'd better be going. Come on, Tony."

"No," Charlie said. "I'm afraid not."

Mr Sunshine froze. "Excuse me?"

"Sorry," Charlie said, "but he's staying here." He held up the two cards. "The thing of it is," he said, "this one here's in date, but this one's expired. Ran out yesterday, as a matter of fact. Just think, one day earlier and you'd have been absolutely fine."

"Yes, but time has no meaning—"

Charlie shook his head. "Sorry," he said. "Rules is rules. You can go, but not your friend. He stays."

Tony opened his mouth to scream, but Mr Sunshine held up his hand. "Let's get this straight," he said. "Only one card is valid, right?"

"Afraid so."

"So one of us can go home, but the other one's got to stay here."

"Yes."

Mr Sunshine took a deep breath, though what of it's hard to imagine. "Fine," he said. He put his hand in his pocket and took something out. "Here," he said. "Catch."

Tony dropped it, needless to say. He stooped and picked it up. The handkerchief it was wrapped in was brown with singe marks.

"Take that," he said, "to Gina Noctis, tell her it's the key to Dolly's asteroid. She'll know what to do. Well, maybe. You'd better hope she does, because otherwise you'll be back here pretty damn quick, and then I'll have wasted my card for nothing. Go on, scoot."

Tony stared at him. Once again he opened his mouth, but Mr Sunshine gave him a ferocious glare. Instead, he pointed to himself. What, me? Seriously?

Mr Sunshine nodded. "Hop it," he said, "before I change my mind. And no more turning yourself into women's underwear, got it? That's definitely a condition of your parole."

Tony nodded so hard he nearly strained a tendon.

"Good lad," Mr Sunshine said. "Well, lad, anyway. Now get out of my sight."

Tony was about to ask how he was supposed to do that exactly, but then he remembered he wasn't allowed to talk – And then he was falling, and falling further, and then he hit something very hard.

He opened his eyes. The something was the desk in Jenny Swordfish's office. He was sitting, he realised, in her out tray.

*

A brass Zippo lighter, a cinema ticket, a packet of Oreos, a rubber band and a tuning fork.

Consuela stared at them for about thirty seconds. Come on, she ordered herself, you can do this. But should I have to? Why me? Why only me? And why does everything have to be difficult?

The key to achievement (and from achievement comes success, and from success comes happiness) is, of course, engineering for oneself a position in life where you have people to do all the work for you, while keeping the rewards for yourself. Consuela reckoned she'd cracked that one when she acquired Erica, an entirely competent little person with absolutely no personality, but the ungrateful bitch had thrown a hissy fit and stomped off, which was so unfair. Erica, she felt sure, would've taken one look at this chaotic assembly of junk and said, in that flat, quiet little voice of hers, Oh, that's the whatsisname for a whatchamacallit, you fit A into B and recalibrate it to resonate transmorphically with C and there you go, and would you like me to do it for you?

I need Erica, she decided, right now. She reached for her phone and had almost finished composing her come-back-all-is-forgiven text when she noticed she had no signal. Figures, she thought; this is, after all, a Zauberwerke magically shielded vault, so inevitably there's going to be one of those field suppression thingies. Erica would know the technical term; also the detailed specifications and how to get round it. But bloody Erica wasn't bloody there, was she? People can be so selfish.

Think again, she thought. But all she could think of was—

"Hanuman?"

A slight pressure on the back of her neck told her that

the little gold monkey was bouncing up and down on his chain. She grabbed it. She felt it pulse once or twice in her palm, then stop moving.

"Hanuman," she said. "Front and centre, stat."

The little gold pendant disappeared from her hand and a heavy weight descended on her shoulder. Something flicked horribly across her face. A tail.

"Hanuman—"

The monkey hopped down off her shoulder and squatted in front of her, his head cocked quizzically to one side, a surly look in his round, red eyes. "Well?"

It was the first time Hanuman had ever deigned to talk to her. Hitherto, he'd addressed his remarks exclusively to Brian. But Brian wasn't here, was he? Another selfish bastard. "Hanuman," she said. "What are those things in that box on the shelf?"

The monkey didn't move. "A Zippo lighter, a cinema ticket, a packet of Oreos, a rubber band and a tuning fork," he said. "What of it?"

"What," Consuela said patiently, "are they for?"

"The lighter," Hanuman said, "is for setting fire to things. The cinema ticket gains admission to a cinema, though these days people tend to use QR codes on their phones. The Oreo biscuits are nominally a nutritional supplement, though leading medical opinion—"

"Taken together," Consuela said, "what are they for?"

The monkey scratched itself, lashed its tail, got up, hopped up onto the shelf and peered into the box. "Good question," it said.

When this is all over, Consuela promised the universe, Brian can have him back, whether he likes it or not. "In case you hadn't figured it out for yourself," Consuela said, "we're in the most heavily guarded vault in the JWW building, and the only stuff being stored here is the junk in that box. That suggests—"

"A purpose," Hanuman said, "well, obviously. These items taken together comprise something either unspeakably valuable or extraordinarily dangerous, or both. It's probably fair to assume," he went on, "that these are not an ordinary Zippo lighter, cinema ticket, rubber band, packet of Oreos and tuning fork, since if they were it ought to be possible to purchase identical components in any everyday retail environment and duplicate the effect, in which case the valuable item would be not these articles here but the formula or recipe. I would take the view, therefore, that these articles are not what they seem to be."

"I can see why Brian likes you."

"Thank you," said the monkey. "I shall now proceed to scan each item with an imp-reflecting mirror, to ascertain its true nature. Hold on a tick, I'll be right back."

The monkey vanished, then reappeared almost instantaneously holding a pink powder compact. He opened it, and held each of the bits of junk up to it in turn. "In passing," he said.

"What?"

"In passing," Hanuman repeated, "I'd just like to point out that I'm doing all the work and you're just kibitzing, but that's perfectly all right because I'm staff and you're management. There's a principle here, about corporate responsibility and the greater including the lesser, which is probably lost on you but nevertheless has a certain degree of validity, which is why I'm doing all this for you."

"You never used to give Brian all this grief."

"Indeed. You might ask yourself why. But I don't suppose you will. What I was about to say before you interrupted is, this state of affairs is normal and usual and entirely consistent with the trope of the Hero, or Heroine, throughout human cultural history. Personally I think it sucks, but since I'm staff I would think that, wouldn't I? After all, the Hero or Heroine is always young and sexy and well-connected, so nobody gives a stuff about the gnome, good fairy or talking animal who actually knows the knowledge and does the hard graft. I just wanted to say that."

"Finished?"

"Yes," said the monkey. "Now, then. The lighter is fuelled with 0.28764 millilitres of the Spirit—"

"What spirit? Gin?"

"The Spirit," said the monkey, "don't show your ignorance. If lit using the primitive convection system and archaic flint ignition built into the lighter, it will generate the True Flame, which burns without consuming and can do pretty much anything you care to name. There's enough gas in the lighter to run it for three-eighths of a second, so effectively you only get one shot. With me so far?"

"Go on," Consuela said.

The monkey curled its tail round its haunches. "The cinema ticket," he said, "is for the only seat in the Multiverse Multiplex, which has only shown one film since the moment of All-Creation."

"Got you," Consuela said. "What film?"

"It's a real-time live-action interactive documentary," said the monkey. "It's everything that happens in every single variant and bifurcation of reality in every single alternate universe, screened simultaneously. The film is called *What's Really Going On*."

"Cool," Consuela muttered. "All right, what about the rubber—?"

"Band," said the monkey. "The rubber band is made

out of the essential fabric of space/time. That means it's absolutely strong and infinitely flexible. It binds the universe together."

"I thought that was gaffer tape."

"Gaffer tape will do," said the monkey, "but this stuff is better. With this rubber band, you could keep a shattered planet from falling apart, or power an Infinity Generator, or tie up God. You could also extend a moment indefinitely, always assuming you had a moment that was that good. In your case, I would tend to doubt it."

"Yes, thank you," Consuela said. "What about the biscuits?"

"The tuning fork," said the monkey, "when struck against a solid object, emits the Primal Note, on which is based the ruling harmony of the music of the Spheres. In effect—"

"I like the Spheres," Consuela said. "Though their last couple of albums have been a bit, well, you know—"

"The Primal Note," said the monkey, "produces order out of chaos. It imposes a fundamental harmonic where otherwise there would only be random fractal collisions. You could really do with one of these," he added pleasantly, "for your underwear drawer. Not to mention your personal life, though it's not really my place—"

"Right," Consuela said grimly, "noted. The biscuits."

"Ah," said Hanuman, "the biscuits. As far as I can tell—"

"Yes?"

"They're biscuits. According to the packaging, they contain flour, sugar, palm oil, corn syrup, baking soda, salt, riboflavin, soya and chocolate. The last named," he added, "would seem to me to be highly significant, if not conclusive."

"You what?"

"Sugar," said the monkey. "Various kinds of spice. And chocolate, which is— ? Come on, do I really have to spoon-feed you with every little thing?"

"Chocolate?"

"Yes, chocolate. What is chocolate?"

"Well," Consuela said, after a moment's thought, "there's theobromine, and xanthoids, a certain amount of caffeine, seratonin, a spot of phenylethylamine, naturally—"

"Not what's in chocolate," said the monkey. "What is chocolate?"

"Um," said Consuela. "Well, it's nice."

The monkey clicked his fingers and pointed at her. "Correct," he said, then waited, then sighed. "Fine," he said, "I'll spell it out for you. Sugar. Spice. Something nice. Actually, it should be all things nice, but let's not split hairs. Is the penny starting to fall, or it is still languishing in mid-air?"

"What little girls are made of – Hang on," Consuela said. "That's just silly."

The monkey shrugged. "That's magic for you," he said. "Nobody ever said it was one of the sensible, grown-up sciences. My guess is, if you replaced the Oreos with slugs, snails and the tail of some unfortunate dog, you'd get something pretty much the same but fundamentally different." He paused, waited for a reaction that didn't come, and went on: "I don't know if there's a particular significance to Oreos or whether a Snickers bar would do just as well, but, then again, this isn't really my area of expertise. Of course a Snickers bar would contain nuts, to which some people are violently—"

"Shut up," Consuela said, "and let me think." She thought. "Well?"

"Can I stop shutting up now?"

"Yes. Well? What does it all mean?"

Hanuman sighed. "Right then," he said. "You've got your True Flame, you've got your insight into what's really going on, you've got your fabric of space/time, and the Primal Note. Suggest anything?"

"A lot of useful kit."

"Precisely. Add to that the matrix for a girl. What do you get?"

"I don't know, do I? Wonderwoman?"

"Close enough," Hanuman said. "Right, I don't think you need me any more, so I'll just turn back into bling and let you get on with it. I really don't know what Brian ever saw in you, to be honest."

The monkey vanished, and Consuela felt a sharp tug on the back of her neck. She took a deep breath. So that was what it all meant. But what did it all mean?

Wonderwoman? Close enough. A nasty thought crossed Consuela's mind, particulary distasteful since she had a horrible feeling it was the truth. "Oh come on," she said aloud. "You're kidding, surely."

A voice in her head, unpleasantly simian, whispered, Say the magic word. "What magic word, for crying out—? I'm sorry. What's the magic word? Please?"

The packet of Oreos split violently up its seam. The tuning fork lifted up into the air and fell back, sounding a piercing note that made Consuela's teeth hurt. The rubber band twanged, causing a breeze that fluttered the cinema ticket. The lighter's little wheel spun a full revolution. There was a blinding flash of pink light, which made Consuela instinctively shut her eyes.

She opened them again. Through the pink burn across her retina, she saw someone standing where the shelf and the box used to be. Oh God, she thought, I was right.

"Erica?" she said.

"Oh for God's sake," said Jenny Swordfish. "Look, you've already been warned about that."

Tony tried to stand up, but his foot was wedged between the wires of a horribly distorted in-tray. "Sorry," he said. "But it's not like that, really. Look, I've got to see somebody, right now."

"It's high time you saw someone, if you ask me. Trouble is, nobody here's qualified."

"One of the partners," Tony said. "Gina Noctis, or Brian Teasdale. It's important. It's about Mr Sunshine."

Jenny gave him a look. "What've you done?"

"It's not me, honest. Well," he amended, "I guess it's a teeny bit my fault, because of stowing away on the chariot, though I didn't mean to do that. And if I hadn't been there, Mr Sunshine would be alive instead of me. I mean as well as me. It's complicated."

Jenny had gone white. "Mr Sunshine would be alive?"

"Yes, and he isn't. At least he's existing, but he's not alive. Look, I really need to talk to Gina Noctis."

Jenny already had the phone in her hand. "She doesn't seem to be in her office. Look, if you've done anything to Ted Sunshine, so help me I'll rip out your liver and feed it to my goldfish."

"It wasn't me. The second card was out of date, that's all it was."

Before Jenny could hit him with the stapler, the door opened and Gina came in. "What's going on?" she said. "I could hear you two yelling right down the corridor."

Tony explained. When he'd finished, Gina looked at him. "You moron," she said.

"It wasn't me, really," Tony said. "I didn't do anything."

For a split second, she fixed him with the full power of the Queen of the Night. "Not on my carpet," Jenny wailed, and Gina let him go. "Bugger," she said, with feeling. "On top of everything else, that's just what we need."

"What everything else?"

"Quiet, you." Gina took a deep breath and let it go slowly. "Well," she said, "at least now we've got the key to that stupid asteroid. Oh there you are," she added, as the door opened.

"What's going on?" Brian asked. "I could hear you lot right down in Reception."

Gina rolled her eyes and gave him a quick résumé. Brian sat down on the desk. "Oh boy," he said.

"At least," Gina repeated, "we've got the key. Come on, you, let's be having it." Tony took it from his pocket and laid it on the desk. The handkerchief was now charred black. Brian zapped it with a containment field before it burnt a hole in the chipboard. "Actually," Gina went on, "that's not bad. We can let Dolly out and save the planet."

Brian gave her a stern look. "How do we get there?" he asked. "Taxi? Bus?"

"That's not an insurmountable problem," Gina said. "Ted Sunshine being dead, on the other hand, is."

Brian massaged his forehead, where a headache was rapidly forming. "I'd got the impression he's some kind of—"

"Yes," Gina said, "he is. But he got kicked into the eye of a black hole. That, I'm afraid, will do it every time."

"Really? I didn't know that."

"Well, now you do," Gina said irritably. "And thanks to this object here, he's got no way of getting out again.

That's really—" She made a noise that might just have been mistaken for a kind of sob. "Anyway," she went on briskly, "I can't see there's anything we can do about that right now. Saving the planet, on the other hand—"

She stopped. A horrible rattling noise was coming from under Jenny's desk. Gina closed her eyes. "Not now," she said. "I'm really not in the mood."

The rattling was coming from a steel box. It was getting louder and more frantic. "Is that Jerry in there?" Gina asked.

Jenny nodded. "He used to be in the stationery cupboard but he turned all the paper clips rusty, so Mr Dawson said—"

"We ought to see what he wants," Mr Teasdale said doubtfully.

"Screw him," Gina said. "He's nuts."

"He's nominally a partner in this firm," Mr Teasdale pointed out. "Name on the letterhead, all that."

Gina sighed and hauled the box up onto the desk. "It'd be different if he ever did a stroke of work," she said. "Well? What do you want? Only we're a bit busy right now."

The rattling made the desk shake. "Do you think we ought to let him out so we can ask what—?"

"No," Gina said, very firmly indeed. "Absolutely not. Jerry? Can you hear me, Jerry?"

The rattling stopped, and was followed by four clear bell-like notes, the sound of something solid being bashed against a steel plate. "I think he can hear you," Mr Teasdale said. "Ask him what he—"

"You bloody well ask him," Gina snapped. "He gives me the creeps, and you know what? These days that takes some doing."

"Fine," Brian sighed. "All right, here goes. Jerry? Are you there?"

A boom rather than a chime. "He's there all right," Gina said. "Go on, then, get on with it."

Pause; then a furious high-speed tapping. "Now what's he playing at?" Gina said. "I knew we shouldn't have taken any notice, it only encourages him."

"I think that's Morse code," said Jenny Swordfish.

"Don't be silly, Jerry doesn't know Morse – No, I beg your pardon, you're right. Sorry, Jerry, can you give us that again from the top? We didn't realise—"

Tapping of passionate intensity, like a million monkeys with a million typewriters trying to see which of them could write the entire works of Shakespeare first. "Is anyone getting this?" Mr Teasdale asked.

Jenny nodded. She was writing very fast, in shorthand, on the backs of a stack of yellow petty cash reconciliations. "He's probably just moaning about the air conditioning again," Gina said. "Why is it that everybody in this office complains about the air conditioning, but nobody ever does anything about it?"

The tapping stopped. Jenny looked up. "Shall I read it to you or just tell you the gist of it?"

Mr Teasdale had some experience of Jerry's particular brand of oratory, which reminded him of some of the livelier bits of the Old Testament. "The gist, please."

Jenny nodded. "Mr Dawson – the other Mr Dawson – is stuck on top of a mountain and wants you to rescue him."

Gina blinked. "Come again?"

"Mr Ahriman stranded him there," Jenny said. "He reckons he can hang on for about three more minutes and then he'll slip and fall to his death, and, if that happens, Mr Ahriman will take over his share in the partnership, which you probably wouldn't like, Mr Dawson says. So if you wouldn't mind pulling your fingers out—"

Gina and Mr Teasdale looked at each other. "Telepathic connection," Gina said. "Something else we didn't know about. I'll have to have words with Tom when I see him. Honestly, that man. All right," she added, "that's for later. I take it we really don't want Ahriman as senior partner?"

Mr Teasdale was too moved to speak, so he nodded.

"Me, too," Gina said. "All right, how on earth are we supposed to snatch Tom Dawson off a mountaintop in the Himalayas in just under three minutes? Options?"

One of the drawers of Jenny's desk shot out like the cork from a champagne bottle. It flew across the room and hit the wall. A window shattered.

"Harmondsworth," Gina said. "I was wondering where he'd got to."

Mr Teasdale gazed at the shattered window for a moment, then shrugged and muttered something under his breath. The glass shards flew back into place, all except one which was trapped under Jenny's shoe. It wriggled a couple of times, then gave up. Mr Teasdale had seen that in the movies, but never in real life. "Well," he said, "another problem solved on time and under budget. Shame it's not the problem we were trying to fix."

"We could have just left him there," Gina said mournfully. "Ah well, never mind. He ought to be grateful but I bet you anything you like he won't be. Sorry, where were we?"

Jenny was stowing the steel box away under the desk. "Excuse me," she said, "but would it be all right if you all went away and discussed things somewhere else? No offence, but it's not exactly the Albert Hall in here, and I do have work to do."

"Sorry," Gina said. "Come on, Brian. And you," she added, giving Tony a frosty look. "I'm not sure I've finished with you quite yet. Of all the—"

All the lights went out. The blinds skittered down over the windows. A week's work disappeared from Jenny's computer screen and was replaced by a single lidless red eye against a black background. The temperature dropped to zero, freezing the dregs of Jenny's caramel latte. A shadow in the corner of the office took a step forward and turned into Mr Ahriman, and the pale green glow from his eyes was the only light in the room.

"Hi, everyone," Mr Ahriman said. "Don't mind me, I'm not stopping."

"Good," Gina said loudly.

Mr Ahriman favoured her with a mild scowl. "I just dropped by to collect my share of the partnership. I'm leaving."

Under Jenny's desk, inside the steel box, there was a frantic scrabbling. "Best news I've heard all week," Gina said. "But I don't know what you mean about your share of the partnership. You can't just breeze in here and—"

"Actually," Mr Ahriman said, producing a sheet of paper, "I can. It's all here in the partnership agreement. I'm entitled to be paid in full on giving three seconds notice in writing. Now I appreciate that you don't have that much cash money lying about, so I'm happy to take my slice in diamonds." He turned to Gina. "To be precise, the Queen of the Night tiara. There's not much on this godawful planet that's worth anything offworld, but I reckon I might get something for it in the flea market on Sigma Orionis Four." He paused for a moment, then added, "Come on, Gina, hand it over. I haven't got all day."

"Get stuffed," Gina said. "Besides, it's not partnership property, it's mine."

Mr Ahriman shrugged. "I'm sure your colleagues will settle up with you in due course. Otherwise I'm going to have to take a third of everything, which would, of course, include this building. In which case, I think I'll have the first two floors. That wouldn't leave anything holding the rest of it up, but that wouldn't be my problem. Well?"

Gina hesitated. The stones set in the tiara weren't technically diamonds; rather, they were nine neutron stars, compressed in the event horizon of a black hole and set in platinum by Fabergé. She had a shrewd idea of the uses Mr Ahriman might find for that much neutronium, out there far beyond the stars. On the other hand, she thought, it's a big galaxy, and if he goes away, we won't have to be bothered with him any more. Assuming we aren't all smashed to bits by an asteroid, of course, but we'll cross that bridge when we come to it. "Bastard," she said succinctly. "All right, but I'll want a receipt. Plus your formal resignation from the partnership, settled in full."

Mr Ahriman shrugged. "Of course," he said. "Everything strictly by the book, you know me. In fact, it just so happens I have precisely the right documents with me, drawn up by my in-house lawyers." He smiled. "All lawyers end up in my house eventually," he added, "which is handy, isn't it?"

"Just a moment," said Mr Teasdale. "Why the rush?"

Mr Ahriman ignored him and held out a shadowy hand. Reluctantly, Gina put a hand to her head and pulled out a hairpin. It turned into a simple but breathtakingly lovely tiara, studded with nine jet-black diamonds. Mr Ahriman took it. It slipped through his fingers and fell on his toe. "Fuck!" he yelled and hopped round the room, bumping into the furniture.

"Heavier than it looks," Gina said. "Sorry, I should've mentioned that."

Mr Ahriman limped across to where the tiara lay and picked it up. He gave Gina a baleful stare. "Not a problem," he said. "Just give me two seconds while I adjust the gravity." He dropped the tiara in his pocket, then turned to Mr Teasdale. "You wanted to know why the rush," he said, "I'll tell you. That asteroid's going to be here any minute now, and you're all going to be smashed into atoms. I won't be here, of course. I'm a god, so I'm leaving."

"Like hell you're a god," Gina said, rather more accurately than she'd intended. "Since when did you have any worshippers?"

"Since about ten minutes ago, since you ask," Mr Ahriman said pleasantly. "Just the one," he added, "in a remote area of the Himalayas. But one's all it takes, I'm delighted to say. Sayonara, creatures of a day. If any of your component atoms ever happen to drift over into the Doghead Nebula, be sure to drop in and say hello."

"Hang on a second," Mr Teasdale said. "You're a god? Seriously?"

"Yes. I'm also a god in a hurry, so if you'll excuse me—"

Gina started to say something, but Mr Teasdale spoke over her. "If you're a god," he said, "you can save the planet. You've got the power."

Mr Ahriman shrugged. "Presumably," he said. "Yes, now you mention it, I probably have. There's not much I can't do, now I come to think of it, though making a rock too heavy for me to lift might be a bit of a challenge, I just don't know. Nor," he added, "do I care particularly. This planet's always been so damned provincial. I'm looking forward to spreading my wings."

"All right, then," Mr Teasdale said. "Save the planet. Please. We'll make it worth your while."

Mr Ahriman looked at him and laughed. "Really?" he said. "I don't think so. No offence, but my while takes a lot of making. I don't think you can afford it."

"Try me," Mr Teasdale said. Then he looked at Gina. She pulled a horrible face, then nodded. "Try us," Mr Teasdale amended. "Name your price."

Mr Ahriman beamed at him. "That's so sweet," he said. "I love melodrama. You know the one thing I'm going to miss about this useless ball of rock when it's gone? Daytime soaps. They get me," he added, knuckling his chest, "right here." Then he frowned. "You're serious, aren't you?"

Mr Teasdale made a gulping noise, like a frog swallowing a screwdriver. "Yes," he said. "How about you? Are you serious? Or are you just some two-bit bogeyman who cuts and runs the moment things start to get heavy?"

"Are you questioning my commitment?" Suddenly Mr Ahriman was different. "Are you saying I'm not—?"

"Evil?" Mr Teasdale grinned at him. "No, I don't think you are. I think you're a nasty piece of work and more full of shit than an effluent digester, but evil? Nah. You don't have the moral fibre."

Mr Ahriman had started to glow red. "How dare you?" he said.

Mr Teasdale shook his head. "You," he said, "evil? Don't make me laugh. If you truly gave a stuff about the greatest harm to the greatest number, you wouldn't be taking the money and running. You'd stick it out like a man. An evil man, naturally. You'd want to be here when everything turns to steam and gravel. Nothing could be more important to you, not if you were what you say you are. No, you're just enlightened self-interest with a thin veneer of unpleasantness."

"You take that back. Right now."

"In fact," Mr Teasdale went on, "if you were really evil, you'd be out there saving the planet this minute. Think about it. No planet, no people. No people, no sinners. Right now there's nearly eight billion people in the world, and you know what? Very few of them are Boy Scouts. They're all out there doing all sorts of really bad things, churning out greed and malice and hate and all sorts of murky stuff. But if the asteroid hits, then boop! No more people, no more wickedness, just a cloud of space dust peacefully minding its own business. All that lost productivity. The thought of that ought to be burning you up. But, no, all you're concerned about is saving your own tail. And horns," he added. "You, evil? It surprises me you haven't got a halo."

For a moment, Gina thought Mr Ahriman was going to hit Brian; also, she couldn't help wondering, why boop? But instead he took a deep breath, took the tiara out of his pocket, dropped it on the desk (which collapsed) and smiled. "I'm going to make you regret saying that," he said, "for a very long time. Which implies," he went on, "you being around for a long time to do the regretting. So fine, you've got a deal. All of you," he added. "No exceptions."

Jenny went as white as a sheet. "That's not what I had in mind," Mr Teasdale said. "That's not fair. And what harm did Jenny ever do you?"

"None whatsoever," Mr Ahriman said. "That's the point, surely. Enlightened self-interest, huh? Wash your mouth out with brimstone and water."

"It's all right," Jenny said in a small, quiet voice, as she tore the receipt Mr Ahriman had given her into small pieces. "I don't want to be smashed to bits, if it's all the same to you lot."

"Clever girl," Mr Ahriman said. "Well, it's pretty straightforward. I save your planet for you, and in return I get your souls. Yours," he added, nodding at Gina, "and yours, and the fat girl's. Not yours," he said, glancing at Tony, "I don't know where it's been. Same deal as I had with Tom Dawson. All you have to do is fall down and worship me. Now that's not a lot to ask, is it?"

"Gina?" said Mr Teasdale. "Are you OK?"

"Sure," Gina said. "Not a problem. If this tosser wants to be the Supreme Being, why ever not? I don't suppose he'll make a particularly worse job of it than the previous administration. You know what they say, doesn't matter who you vote for, the government always gets elected. Oh, he may set out with his head full of starry-eyed idealism about Make Evil Great Again, but once he's been in charge for a month or so – Yes, why not? All hail, glory be and three hearty cheers. You arsehole," she added.

"I'll take that," said Mr Ahriman, "as a hallelujah. That's settled, then. So glad I could be of service."

There was a short, awful silence. Then Gina said, "Well, get on with it, then."

"Excuse me?"

"Saving the world, dickhead. You promised. Now do something."

"Ah, yes." Mr Ahriman wagged a reproving finger. "But please bear in mind, thou shalt not call the Lord thy God a dickhead. I'll overlook it just this once, because you're only a woman and can't be expected to know any better, but if you do it again, I warn you, there will be consequences. Right then, give me that key."

Mr Teasdale looked blank. "Key?"

"The key to the asteroid. I know you've got it, I can smell it from here. Thank you. Now, then. I take it all I have to do is use this key to unlock the asteroid, and then we can get down to the serious business of rationalising this planet. I think I'm going to enjoy doing that."

Another drawer of Jenny's desk flew open, and out of it crawled Mr Dawson. He was covered in dust, and there was a yellow Post-it Note stuck in his hair. The drawer slammed shut. "Oh look," Mr Ahriman said. "Come, all ye faithful. Guess what we've been up to while you were away."

Mr Dawson stared at him. "Oh God," he said.

"Precisely. Many a true word, and all that. You thought you could be rid of me by sneakily dying." He grinned. "You wish."

"He's going to save the planet," Mr Teasdale said sheepishly. "In return—"

Mr Dawson looked at them in turn, then made a sort of keening noise. "You idiots," he said.

"Quiet," Mr Ahriman snapped. "When I want your opinion, I'll ask for it. Right then, that's you and you and you. Where's that old fool Ted Sunshine? We only need him to make up the complete set."

"He's dead," Gina said.

"I don't think so," Mr Ahriman said. "He's a god. Well," he added, "was a god, anyhow. No worshippers, of course, unlike some of us I could mention, so he got struck off the roll. Even so, he can't be dead, that's not possible. Where is he?"

"Dead," Gina repeated. "He got sucked into a black hole."

"Ah." Mr Ahriman nodded. "In that case, he probably is. A black hole, for crying out loud. You've got to hand it to him, he always did have a touch of class. Nothing in his life became him like the leaving of it, or words to that effect. Don't pull faces, Tom, you'll stick like it. Besides, you never liked him much, did you?"

"Fuck you," Mr Dawson said. "He was . . . Fuck you sideways with a barbed-wire banana."

"I'll pretend I didn't hear that," Mr Ahriman said. "Good heavens, Tom, what's that I see? A teardrop? Who'd have thought it? I always assumed you hated and despised him. Considering the way you treated him, I'd have said that was a logical assumption." He smiled. "Maybe I could learn a thing or two from you about being evil, at that. Anyway, this won't do. Time's a-wasting. We need to be getting along if we're going to stop that asteroid. Let's see, we've got the key. Now all we need is transport." He shifted round slightly to face the wall, and pointed. "Appear!" he said. Then he grinned. "I enjoyed that," he said. "It's nice being God."

The wall glowed blue, and a fireplace appeared. Some soot fell down it, and then a chubby man in a red dressing gown. The chubby man looked at Mr Ahriman. "Oh for crying out loud," he said.

"Meet the new boss," Mr Ahriman said. "Not quite the same as the old boss, but close enough for jazz. Bring the sleigh round the back, there's a good chap. I need it to do a spot of interstellar travel, and it's the only faster-than-light vehicle on the—"

He stopped. Something else was coming down the chimney.

BLITZEN

Erica looked at her. "Oh," she said, "it's you."

"Erica?"

"Yes," Erica replied, "me."

One of the first things they teach you at wizard school is, expect everything. It had impressed Consuela so much that she'd printed it out on a bit of card and put it on her desk; good advice, she'd always felt, and she'd tried to live up to it. But everything, when all is said and done, is a bit of an ask, and over the years she'd resigned herself to expecting nearly everything instead. Erica, as the sole contents of a vault designed to protect the most valuable thing on the planet, was a bit more than she could handle. "What the hell are you doing here?" she asked.

Erica shrugged. "Standing by," she said. "I do a lot of that."

"Yes, but—"

"I'm doing what I do," Erica went on, ignoring her in a

way she'd never done before, "when I'm not being useful. Ironic, isn't it?"

"Anyway," Consuela said, "you're here now. I need to find out—"

"It's one of those really stupid things you get wherever there are people," Erica continued, "like where there's chickens there's always rats. On the one hand there's clever, capable people who can be relied on to know things and get things done and know where things are kept, and on the other there's all the other people who couldn't even boil a kettle or change a light bulb, and even if they could they're too disorganised and preoccupied with their own stupid little concerns to do anything useful; and which section of Society do you think is in charge? Well?"

"Erica," Consuela said, "this isn't helping. What I need you to do—"

"Be quiet," Erica said. "You're in my space now, so shut up and listen, you might learn something. There are two sorts of people in this world, those who know what to do and do it, and management. Guess what the second-lowest rank in the US Army is. Go on, guess."

"Erica—"

"Specialist," Erica said. "The implication being, if you have the faintest inkling that there's any material difference between your arse and your elbow, then what you and Society need most of all is some shit-for-brains extrovert to tell you what to do and then shout at you after you've done it. But that's all right," Erica added, "it's fine, don't worry about it. What can I do for you this time?"

"Erica," Consuela said, "what are you doing here?"

"Me? I live here."

Consuela looked round, just in case she'd missed something. "But it's a vault, Erica. It's just an empty—"

"It's to keep me safe," Erica said. "Because I'm valuable."

"Yes, but it's a bit bleak, isn't it?"

"I'm the most valuable thing in this building," Erica said. "And this is a building where they keep particularly valuable things. You might like to think about that, when you've got five minutes. Was that all? Because if it is, I'd like you to go away now."

"No," Consuela said quickly. "Look, I had to go to a lot of trouble to get here, and—"

"Actually, the little gold monkey did it all. He's one of us, by the way."

"You what?"

"A specialist. Only Hanuman's a specialist third-class. Third-class junior-grade, actually."

"You're a—"

"And Harmondsworth – did you ever come across him? He works for Mr Sunshine at Dawsons. Actually, he's my kid brother. Anyway, Harmondsworth's a specialist second-class. And I'm a specialist first-class. The only one there is, actually."

"You're a familiar."

Erica nodded. "Hence the expression, familiarity breeds contempt. Which is what you've always treated me with, Mzz Teasdale, not that I harbour a grudge, because I don't do that sort of thing, in more or less the same way raindrops don't drink. It really isn't worth bothering yourself over. After all, it's only me."

"You're really a—" Erica rolled her eyes, which Consuela took for a Yes. "Whose?"

Erica sighed. "Would you believe, mine? No, of course you wouldn't. All right, I used to belong to the Boss. But he was really nasty, mean and patronising and unappreciative, even worse than you were, so I quit and came here, to JWW. I claimed thaumaturgical asylum, and they built this vault for me, so He'd never be able to find me and get at me. And in return I help out around the place, running errands and doing little jobs for people." She sighed. "It's incredibly demeaning, considering what I am and what I can do, a bit like all those Polish dukes and counts who ended up driving Tube trains in London after the war, but it's better than working for Him, that's for sure."

"Erica," Consuela said, "Who is He?"

Erica looked at her. "God, you're ignorant. Don't you know anything?"

"Apparently not," Consuela said quietly. "I thought I did, but maybe I was wrong." The admission seemed to unlock something deep inside her, or let slip something that had been chained up for a long time, and that served to remind her of what she was doing there in the first place. "Look," she said, "it doesn't matter. All that matters is, there's a huge great big asteroid headed for this planet with an incredibly vindictive woman driving it, and unless somebody does something about it pretty damn quick, the Earth's going to be destroyed and we're all going to die. And what I need to know is, can you help?"

As she spoke, she remembered the vision of herself working in the call centre. Was that some sort of price she'd have to pay, or a punishment or something like that? She decided it didn't really matter. There'd be a way out or a way round or someone she could charm or sleep with, or if all else failed she might even consider regaining her status in the world by sheer hard work and ability. Time for that later. What mattered now was—

"Mr Ahriman," Erica said, "at Dawsons. I used to

work for him. Sorry, you asked me to do something and I wasn't paying attention."

"Save the planet, Erica," Consuela said. "Please?"

Erica sighed. "Oh, all right," she said.

"Look," Jenny said, after six seconds of total stunned silence, "I really don't want to make a fuss about anything, but if you wouldn't mind all going somewhere else I think that'd be much better, because there simply isn't room—"

She had a point. It's an inflexible rule of office design that the space/energy ratio is an inverse curve; the more work there is to be done and the more people that are needed to do it, the smaller the area provided. "Good idea," said Mr Sunshine. "Brian, you're standing on my foot. Let's all go next door, where we can breathe."

"Ted," Gina said, "what the hell are you doing here? You're dead."

Mr Sunshine rubbed soot off the sides of his nose. "Gina," he said, "I'm surprised at you. I thought we'd got past all those outmoded stereotypes years ago. Next door," he said firmly, "now. Oh, and bring the box."

"What box?"

Mr Sunshine pointed at the steel cube containing Jerry Dawson. "I think it's high time we had a partnership meeting." He looked at Tom Dawson. "A proper one."

So they went next door and sat round the table, except for Jenny and Tony Bateman, who sort of hovered by the door. The fat man in the red dressing gown sat at the head of the table, as of right, and nobody seemed inclined to argue about it.

"Right," said the fat man, "first things first. Tom, is that job still going?"

Mr Dawson was still wearing the rather dazed expression he'd had on when he was shot out of the drawer of Jenny's desk. "What job? Oh, that, the god thing. Yes. Why?"

"And you're going to give it to me, aren't you?"

Mr Dawson gazed at him. "Look, Nick," he said, "this is neither the time nor the place—"

"Because if you do," said the fat man, "that'll mean I'm a registered god in good standing and I'll be able to escape the destruction of Earth, taking," he added, "others with me, if I deem it necessary to do so. I'm hoping it won't come to that, but it's always good to have a backup plan, don't you think?"

Everyone's eyes were suddenly on Mr Dawson. "What? Oh, yes, absolutely," he said. "Consider yourself hired."

"Thanks, Tom," said the fat man. "We'll hammer out the details of the remuneration package later, when we aren't so preoccupied with other things. Next on the agenda, what are we going to do about Dolly?"

"His ex-wife," Mr Sunshine pointed out.

"Just a minute." Gina held up her hand, then lowered it. "Nobody's explained how the hell Ted got out of being dead. I for one—"

The fat man sighed. "Suffice it to say," he said, "that for a very short time, the Hereafter had a chimney. Oh, don't all look at me like that. Ted's my brother-in-law, we're mates, we go way back. Soon as Harmondsworth told me what had happened, I got out the sleigh, nipped down and rescued him. So what?"

"Is that possible?" asked Brian Teasdale.

The fat man shrugged. "Presumably," he said, "or I couldn't have done it, could I? You people worry too much about technicalities, that's your problem. Me, I just get stuck in. I'll probably get a snotty letter about it at some point, and maybe they'll have me up before the disciplinary committee, but fuck them, I say. Especially now I'm a god," he added, with just the slightest hint of smugness. "That's what I like about divinity. It's not so much the lording it over others, it's the not having others lording it over you. I could get used to that, I really could."

"Even so," said Mr Sunshine, "thanks, Nick."

"Think nothing of it," said the fat man. "Now then, about Dolly. Somebody said something about a key."

"That's right," Mr Sunshine said. "It turns out we had it all along, only we didn't know what it was."

Gina looked at him. "We?"

"All right, I didn't know. And neither did you, because you looked at it for me. Anyway, the bloody thing was burning holes in the furniture, so I thought I'd put it somewhere safe. Nothing wrong with that."

Gina wasn't so sure that was the whole story, but it didn't really matter for now. "Anyway," she said. "We've got the key, we've got Nick's sleigh, so what are we waiting for?"

Mr Ahriman cleared his throat. "Aren't we forgetting something?" he said.

"I don't think so," Gina replied. "What?"

"The fact that your soul belongs to me," Mr Ahriman said. "And his, and his. You seem to be under the impression that you're at liberty to go charging off doing what the hell you like, without clearing it with me first. That, I ought to point out, is no longer the case."

The fat man looked at Mr Sunshine. "Who exactly is this tosser?" he asked.

"After your time," Mr Sunshine replied sadly. "Let's

just say, if ever you need to visit him in your professional capacity, bring plenty of coal."

"I," Mr Ahriman said, his eyes glowing ominously, "am a god. You're just a delivery driver. Oh, and while you're at it, get your arse out of my seat."

The fat man spread himself in his chair and leaned back. "Not so fast, whoever you are," he said. "I'm a god, too, or haven't you been listening? How about it? Thunderbolts at twenty paces?"

"Really," Mr Ahriman said. "I have five certified worshippers. How many have you got?"

"Oh, I don't know. Billions? Tell him, Tom."

"Nine billion, four hundred and sixty-eight million, seventeen thousand, four hundred and ninety-six," said Mr Dawson, "on the planet Snoobis Prime. Not counting the artificial intelligences and the sentient water coolers."

"On this planet?"

"None," admitted the fat man, "but that's neither here nor there. Rules is rules." (Mr Sunshine winced when he said that.) "Nine billion worshippers, sunshine. I reckon that gives me seniority, don't you?"

"But that's silly," said Mr Ahriman. "You've only just got the job. Those nine billion people – No, let's be shamelessly anthropocentric for a moment. Those nine billion things don't even know who you are. You've never been to their stupid planet. You've done nothing for them. They've never even seen you."

"Blessed are those who have not seen and yet have believed, fish-face," said the fat man. "That's what faith is all about, if you ask me. Look, we can sit here splitting hairs and quoting regulations until Dolly comes along and smashes this place into sub-atomic particles, or we can get off our collective duff and do something about it.

Up to you, really, it's none of my beeswax now that I've got a strange new world to look after. But if you want a lift on my sleigh, say so. If not, so long and thanks for all the mince pies. Well? How about it?"

Mr Ahriman looked at him steadily. "That's fine," he said. "You're leaving, which saves me the trouble of dealing with you when this is over. Meanwhile, yes, I agree. Let's do it."

A ripple of relief went round the table. "I'm so glad we've got that sorted out," Mr Teasdale said. "Do what, exactly?"

Lilith McGregor felt uneasy. It had been some time since she'd stormed out of the unsatisfactory meeting with her mother, but nobody had been in touch with her or told her what was going on. She'd tried ringing the United Nations, but there were so many for-world-peace-press-six options that she gave up. She'd tried ringing JWW, but you had to give them your credit card details before they'd even take a message. It was almost as though – impossible as it might seem – everybody had forgotten about her. It simply didn't make sense.

My mother, she thought, as she Photoshopped an unruly wedding guest into oblivion. Parents can be so embarrassing.

Presumably it had all been sorted out, because she'd scanned the news headlines every day and there didn't seem to be anything about an asteroid, but it would've been nice to have been in the loop, given that she'd been the one who'd drawn everyone's attention to the impending disaster in the first place. If it hadn't been for her, Mummy would've demolished the planet before anybody knew anything about it, and that wouldn't have been so great, would it? She reckoned she deserved something for that; a statue, maybe, or a holiday named after her, or maybe a considerable sum of money. And when you came to think of it, that Teasdale woman had only been able to get involved because of having her as a client, which meant she could call in the UN, so, properly speaking, that made her a sort of UN envoy, like all those film stars who go to Africa for photo opportunities with skinny kids. Surely that meant she ought to get something, even if it was only a flag to fly on her car and possibly a motorcade. It'd have been different if I was a man, she said to herself. It's just not fair.

She called up the next photo, and there was Mummy, standing next to the father of the bride, wearing a ludicrous hat. Oh for crying out loud, she thought.

The screen shimmered, and the people in the picture started to move. "Go away," Mummy said to the bride's father, "I want to talk to my daughter."

Mummy's face got bigger and bigger until it filled the screen. "Hello?" Mummy said. "Are you there?"

"Yes. What do you want?"

"Oh, there you are. I don't know why I'm doing this, but I thought I'd give you one last chance. Not that you deserve it, but you are my daughter, when all's said and done. Here's the deal. I am about to destroy this stupid planet."

"But I thought—"

"Would you please not interrupt when I'm talking to you? I am about to destroy this ridiculous little planet, and I'm giving you one last chance to save yourself, not that you deserve it. Well?"

Lilith went cold all over. "Really?"

"Really."

"Oh."

"Oh," said her mother, "is right." Her eyes blazed red. "Come on, poppet, it's decision time. Are you coming with me, or would you rather die?"

Lilith's eyes were red, too, but a different sort of red. "All right," she said. "If I've got to. But I think you're being really mean and nasty and I hope you're satisfied."

"Splendid." The woman nodded. "I'm so glad we've got that sorted out. Now, are you ready?"

"Ready for what?"

The woman sighed. "This," she said, and hanging in the air a few inches from Lilith's nose was a planet. Smaller than most planets, maybe, or perhaps that was just the effect of perspective; but it had silvery-grey oceans and lavender continents and the cutest little pink icecaps. "Hang on a tick while they have their industrial revolution," the woman said, and Lilith's sensitive nose could just make out a faint scent of burning. "Right, all ready," she went on, as a dark grey mist obscured the sharpness of the outlines. "I've even turned up the temperature two degrees above planetary equilibrium, so unless you get down there and save them right this minute, they're doomed."

Lilith looked at the planet. It would be hopelessly misleading to say the planet looked at her, but not entirely inaccurate, either. "Really?"

"Really. It's all up to you. You can make a difference, if only you decide you want to."

Such a pretty planet; it'd be such a shame if anything happened to it. "All right," she said. "If it'd mean saving the baby seals. And the people," she added.

"Good girl," said the woman. "You can tell them how stupid they've been," she added. "You'll like doing that."

Lilith gazed at the little spinning globe, then reached

out and gave it a gentle pat, sending equatorial storms scudding across its surface. Then it slowly drifted through the air and began to orbit her. "There you go," the woman said approvingly, "now you really are the centre of the universe. What more could someone your age possibly ask for?"

Lilith opened her mouth to say something, but those particular words never came out. On the one hand, she thought, this is all so stupid and typical. On the other hand – She moved slightly and her irresistible gravitational pull drew the planet to her, and then it resumed its lazy, obedient course, basking in the glory of her presence. Actually, Lilith admitted to herself, this does sort of feel right, somehow. This is how it ought to be.

"What are you going to call it?" the woman asked her.

Silly question. "Lilith," said Lilith.

Just for fun, she twitched her head sideways. The planet skidded on its orbit and followed her, then resumed its placid, adoring course, basking in the sheer fact that she existed. The woman nodded her approval. "That's the ticket," the woman said. "Start how you mean to go on."

Lilith wasn't listening. If she concentrated very hard, to the exclusion of everything else, she thought she could just about make out her own face, reflected in the planet's quicksilver southern ocean.

"Ready?" the woman asked. Lilith nodded. "Right, then," the woman said. "Give 'em hell." She clicked her fingers, and Lilith and the planet vanished in a shower of golden twinkles.

Oh what fun it isn't to ride on a nine-reindeer, open-topped, dangerously overcrowded faster-than-light sleigh. Stars slashed past like plutonium-enriched snowballs as the reindeer struggled to maintain a coherent hyperspace field on the outskirts of an inconvenient Oort cloud. Mr Ahriman, Gina noticed, had turned an unusual shade of green, and Tony Bateman's breakfast, from which he'd parted company some time ago, was sloshing about inside their warp bubble like a plastic bag caught by a violent breeze. She leaned forward and shouted in the fat man's ear, "Are we nearly there yet?"

"Shut up and sit down," the fat man shouted back. "I'm trying to do quadratic equations in my head."

Fair enough, Gina thought. Their environment didn't bother her the way it clearly bothered the others. It was, after all, endless night, though where she came from the stars weren't quite so frisky, so it was natural she felt at home here; quite like old times, in fact, except back then the fastest thing in the universe was a trotting camel.

The dominant sound inside the bubble was the frantic wheezing of the reindeer, almost drowning out Jenny's soft whimpering and Brian's mumbled Hail Marys. Ted was sitting at the rear of the sleigh, with his back to the direction of travel; he looked moody and preoccupied, which wasn't like him at all. She speculated about what was passing through his mind at that moment, then decided it was none of her business. Ho-hum, she thought, and wished she'd brought something to read.

"This is fun," said Tom Dawson, who'd climbed out from under his seat and was looking about him. "It's nice to get out of the office occasionally."

"We should make it a regular thing," Gina said. "Office outing to the Perseus Arm, dinner optional." She ducked as Tony Bateman's breakfast sailed past her head and splattered itself against a verteron field. "Oh, I forgot. I'm not talking to you."

"Yes you are," Mr Dawson pointed out.

"Not officially." She gave him a stern look. "When this is all over, you're going to keep your word and let Ted back into the partnership, aren't you? And no more selling your soul to anyone. Agreed?"

Mr Dawson shrugged. "A bit academic, surely. If this is ever over and we're all still alive, we'll have Him to deal with. I think making any plans would be premature."

He nodded towards Mr Ahriman, who was sitting with his eyes tight shut and his hands locked around his kneecaps. Somehow he didn't seem quite as scary as he'd been back in the office. Even so.

"Well, at least there'll still be a planet for him to bully us on," Gina said. "That's something, surely."

"A lot of things are something," Mr Dawson replied. "It doesn't mean I'm going to like them."

"Worrywart," Gina said. "Anyway, I don't see how he can hold Brian and me to anything. The deal was conditional on him saving the Earth, and now Ted and his brother-in-law have taken over doing that, so the agreement's null and void, surely."

"I wish you wouldn't use words like void, bearing in mind where we are," Mr Dawson said. "It's fun, but not as much fun as all that. And maybe you're right about you and Brian, but that doesn't help me much, does it?" He let go a bitter sigh, which froze, fell to the floor and shattered. "For two pins I'd try pushing Him out of the sleigh, except I don't think it'd work."

"There's a normalised graviton wall surrounding the sleigh," Gina pointed out, "that's why we haven't all fallen out. If you tried, you'd only irritate him."

"That's what I figured," Mr Dawson said. "No, like it or lump it, I'm stuck with the bastard. I'm beginning to wish I'd stayed on that mountaintop. If I had, it'd all be over by now."

Gina looked at him. "Don't be like that," she said. "It'll all come right in the end, you'll see."

Mr Dawson looked right back at her. "Oh for crying out loud," he said.

The stars changed abruptly from lines to dots. "We've stopped," Gina said. "What's wrong?"

"We're here," the fat man said. "Thar she blows, look. No, not that one, the other one, looks a bit like a potato."

The asteroid did, at that. They all sat and gazed at it for a moment. Then Brian said, "You sure that's the right one?"

"Yup," said Mr Sunshine. "This is about as close as I got the last time. Watch out. Dolly has a nasty tendency to shoot torpedoes at visitors."

Tony Bateman squealed like a pig. "That's Dolly all right," the fat man said. "When we were married it was mostly crockery, but only because torpedoes hadn't been invented then. But that's all right. What's the time, anyone?"

They all gazed at him. "Local time," he amended. "Oh, you're all hopeless." He felt in his pocket and pulled out a watch. It was a special watch, the last one Salvador Dalí ever made. "Three-fifteen p.m.," he said. "That's all right," he said. "She'll be watching *General Hospital*. If we look smart about it there shouldn't be any trouble. Now, if memory serves, the keyhole should be somewhere around about—" He pointed. "There. See it?" The fat man looked round at the blank faces gazing at him. "Fine," he said. "There's a keyhole, trust me. Right, hold on tight, this may be a trifle rough. Come, Prancer, come, Vixen, Vixen, if you don't pack that in right now I shall be seriously annoyed . . . "

Later, Gina remembered the experience as being something like falling from a great height and hitting the ground on her back, only in reverse. At the time, her mind was occupied with images of flies and windscreens, as the misshapen pink asteroid suddenly became impossibly huge and in her face, and the sleigh spun round and round like a drill bit. "Maybe not so much fun after all," she heard Tom Dawson moan in her ear, and then they landed.

"There now," said the fat man, "that wasn't so bad. I'm guessing Dolly didn't notice us arrive, hence the absence of warheads. Ted, where's that key? Thank you. Well, don't just sit there, you lot."

The fat man was right: there was a keyhole, in a door. The key slid into it. The door opened.

"I'm not looking forward to this, if truth be told," the fat man said. "Ah well, not to worry. Hello?" he called out. "Anybody home?"

No reply. Through the door streamed blinding blue light. "Dolly?" said the fat man. Then he shrugged and went inside, and the rest of them followed.

Brian Teasdale had never been inside an asteroid before, oddly enough, and he wasn't quite sure what to expect. "Dear God," he whispered, in a low, awed voice. "This is just like my cousin Bridget's house in Walton-on-Thames."

You can't live somewhere for a long time and not impress your personality on your surroundings. Dolly had done exactly that. The carpet was deep and violently patterned, the walls were pastel stripes, the sofa was voluptuous and there were cushions everywhere. In the corner of the room the biggest TV screen Mr Teasdale had ever seen was filling all the available space with the very latest medical crisis from Upstate New York. Not far from it, with her back to them, was a woman sitting in an armchair. There was a bottle at her elbow and a box of candy. Chocolate-coated rubies; Dolly liked hard centres.

"Dolly?" said the fat man.

The woman looked round, and Brian recognised the face from Lilith McGregor's photographs. "Piss off, Nick," she said.

"Don't be like that," the fat man said. "I've come to let you out."

The woman made a noise like a high-speed train hurtling through a station, muted the TV, stood up and faced him. "Arsehole," she said.

"Yes," said the fat man, "quite probably, but that's not the point." He laid the key down ostentatiously on a coffee table. "It's all right," he said. "You're free. You can come out now."

The woman threw a glass at him. He ducked, but she'd allowed for that. "You pig," she screamed. "How dare you come waltzing in here after all this time and tell me I'm sodding free, like you're doing me a favour or something? You complete, utter—"

She picked up the bottle and the fat man nipped smartly behind a standard lamp. It provided a degree of cover, but not enough. "Dolly," he said, "be reasonable. Yes, all right, I may have been a bit high-handed—"

This time he dodged the other way, but she'd anticipated that, too. The TV remote hit him on the shoulder, and he yelped. "It's absolutely fine you being upset with me," he said, "but there's no need for you to take it out on anybody else. I'd have let you out sooner, only stupidly I lost the key. But I've found it again now, so if you'll just stop throwing things and come with me to the sleigh, I'll give you a lift to wherever you want to—"

A footstool caught him on the kneecap. He made a dive for the sofa, but fell short, giving the woman a clear shot at him with a glass ashtray. He scrambled to his knees and made it to the sofa just in time to avoid the key, which whizzed past the arm of the sofa and embedded itself in the wall. "Watch it, you stupid cow," he protested. "You could put someone's eye out doing that."

Mr Sunshine advanced across the room and stood between the woman and the fat man. "Dolly," he said, "pack it in."

"Get lost, Ted," the woman said. "You're on his side, you always have been. When I think of all the times—"

"Pack it in," Mr Sunshine repeated. The woman glared at him, then lowered the onyx drinks mat (one of a matching set of six) and put her hands on her hips. "Ted," she said, "get out."

"Not till you promise to stop throwing things."

"Get stuffed. They're my things and this is my asteroid, and if I want to throw things I'll bloody well throw them. And if I want to leave, I will. But I don't. Got that?"

"Come on, Dolly, be reasonable. Of course you want to leave. You can't stay in here for the rest of your life. That'd be silly."

"Don't you dare tell me to be reasonable, you pompous arse. And I have no intention of staying here. I'm going to crash this thing into the Earth and then I'm booked into a spa resort on Gamma Coriolis Three. And the rest of you can bloody well lump it, because I simply don't care."

"There's no need for all that, Dolly, you've made your point. Nick's really sorry for what he's done, so you just turn this thing around and we can all be friends. No, Dolly—"

Too late. She'd already thrown the drinks mat. It

whistled across the room and hit Mr Sunshine in the chest, forcing him back two paces. With the impact, a change seemed to come over Mr Sunshine. His eyes burnt, and he reached for the nearest throwable object, which proved to be a terracotta ornament in the shape of a pumpkin. Dolly swerved, showing remarkable agility for a woman her size, and the ornament shattered against the wall.

"Right," she said, "that does it." She snapped her fingers and a thunderbolt sprang into existence, jagged and pointed and glowing an ominous blue. "I'm going to count to three and if you lot aren't out of here by then I'm going to nuke you into cinders. One."

"Dolly, no. Think of the baby penguins in Antarctica."

"Two."

Mr Sunshine knew when he was beaten. He was also dimly aware that he might have phrased his appeals better, but it was too late to do anything about that now. "Dolly," he said, "for the last time. I absolutely forbid you to destroy the Earth. Put that thing down and come with us, and we'll say no more about it."

"Three."

How they all made it back out of the door before the thunderbolt launched is one of those unfathomable mysteries. But they did, and the fat man launched himself into the driver's seat, grabbed the reins and bellowed, "Now, Dasher, you stupid bloody animal", just before a disruptor beam shot out from a nearby emitter. It struck the place where the sleigh had been and turned it into molten glass, but by then the sleigh was a long way off and moving well.

For a while, nobody on board the sleigh spoke. Then Mr Sunshine said, "That didn't go as well as I'd hoped."

"You clown," said Mr Ahriman. "You simply haven't got a clue, have you? All that be-reasonable and I-forbid-you stuff, no wonder the stupid woman lost her rag. It's like young Tom's been saying for a long time, Sunshine. You're past it. You've lost your grip. No wonder he booted you out of the partnership, you're a liability."

Mr Dawson shut his eyes tight. "I did say that," he muttered. "I'm sorry."

"Not that it matters any more," Mr Ahriman went on. "Driver, if you'll just drop me off at the nearest M-class planet I'll make my own way from there."

"Sod that," said the fat man. "What do you think this is, a taxi?"

"It's a thought, though," Gina said quietly. "Where are we going to go?"

"How do you mean?" asked the fat man.

"Well, obviously we can't go back to Earth," Gina said. "You heard her."

"Sorry, but it's not as simple as that," the fat man said. "It's all about registries."

"You what?"

"This is an Earth-registered sleigh," the fat man said. "There's rules about that sort of thing. I can't just go plonking it down on alien worlds, not without visas and clearances and customs declarations. You've got to apply in advance, and they'll only look at your application if it's filed from where you're registered. And since Earth doesn't even know there's other planets out there, they haven't got a duly accredited transit bureau or anything like that. Long and the short of it is, we can't land anywhere except Earth. Sorry, everyone, but there it is. Rules is—"

"Made to be broken," said Mr Sunshine, rather loudly.

"Nick, stop talking rubbish and head for a planet some-where. I've had about enough of today."

"Sorry," the fat man said, "no can do. The nearest habitable planet from here is Earth. Space is big, if you hadn't noticed. There's just enough rolled oats left in the reindeer to get us there, and then that's it. This thing simply wasn't designed for long-haul travel."

A terrible silence fell over the interior of the sleigh's space/time bubble. Eventually it was broken by Mr Ahriman screaming and trying to jump off the sleigh. He hit a force field, bounced and ended up in Gina's lap, whereupon she hit him. "I'm not going back there," he screamed. "It's going to get blown up. I'm a god, I can go anywhere I like."

"Go on, then," said Mr Sunshine.

"But I can't, you stupid old fart. This shiny invisible thing won't let me."

"Then you can't be much of a god, can you?" Mr Sunshine gave him a look that even he probably didn't deserve. "You're not the sharpest knife in the theological drawer, are you?" Mr Sunshine went on. "And clearly you don't know the rules. As a god you're allowed to leave the planet. That doesn't mean the universe is obliged to send a limo every time you fancy a breath of fresh vacuum." He grinned unpleasantly. "Up to you to make your own travel arrangements," he said. "I think it's sort of assumed that if you're truly a god, you can probably manage to buy a ticket."

"The hell with all this," Mr Teasdale said. "Let's go home."

"Since it's our only option," the fat man said, "I'll second that. I reckon I'll just about have time to refuel and set a course for my new planet before Dolly gets there. Sorry, people, but that's how it goes."

"Your new planet?" said Tom Dawson. "What planet would that be?"

"Snoobis Prime," the fat man said. "My planet. The one that goes with the job."

"The job I gave you?"

"Well, yes."

"You can forget that," Mr Dawson snapped.

"You what?"

Mr Dawson glared at him. "Changed my mind," he said. "Clearly I'd be failing in my duty if I recommended my clients to choose a cowardly, treacherous, utterly unreliable flake like you to be a traffic warden, let alone their supreme being. Sorry, chum, but if we're not going anywhere, neither are you. Shut up, Ted," he added, as Mr Sunshine opened his mouth to object. "The way I see it, we're all in the same sleigh, one way or another. So unless someone can think of something clever, right now, we can all go back to Earth and get vaporised together. And won't that be nice."

Tony Bateman burst into tears. "This is so unfair," Jenny Swordfish protested. "It's not our fault, we didn't do anything."

"Don't blame me," the fat man said. "I can't help it if Dolly—"

"Oh shut up," Jenny snapped at him. "If you hadn't been so rude and horrible—"

"Quiet," Gina commanded, and everyone stopped talking and looked at her. "This isn't helping. All right," she went on, "it does look terrifyingly like we've run out of options. That's tough, but there it is. Let's at least try and face the inevitable with a certain degree of dignity, instead of sniping and squabbling like a load of cabinet ministers. Look," she went on, "I've heard a lot of guff lately from the people on this sleigh about gods, but it strikes me that all of us are going to have to do about a billion years' worth of evolution before any of us deserve to be plankton, let alone aspects of the Divine. And since we haven't got time for that, let's all just pipe down and face it. We're going to die. Big deal. Millions of sentient creatures do it every day."

"Piss off, Gina," Mr Sunshine said with feeling. "You don't know what you're talking about. I've been there. I really don't want to go back."

"Tough," Gina said. "It comes to us all, Ted, even you. A man's gotterdammerung what a man's gotterdammerung. So just quit snivelling and try and act like a grown-up. The same goes for you, Tony. Please stop making that ridiculous noise."

"Go to hell," said Tony Bateman. "I'm a mortal, it's what we do."

Mr Dawson sighed. "You're pathetic," he said, "the lot of you. Well," he added, "you are. Look at you. Three demigods, the Queen of the Night, two state-registered sorcerors and a qualified accountant, and you all go to pieces at the slightest little thing. You know what? You don't know you're born. Compared to having him kicking you around—" He pointed at Mr Ahriman. "All this is just a walk in the park. If we go back to Earth and it gets wasted, so bloody what? At least I won't have to go to work in the morning and put up with him." He took a deep breath. "But it won't come to that," he went on. "There's still time. And that bloody woman may be a raving nutcase, but so are most people, and you know what? Life goes on. We'll make a deal. I'll make a deal, I always do. There's always a deal, people, that's all you know and all you need to know. And I don't believe in any of you tossers, but I believe in that."

They gazed at him in silence. Then Mr Ahriman said, "Fair enough, Tom. Here you go; if you can save the Earth and get that dreadful woman off our backs, I'll let you go. You can have your soul back, with whipped cream and sprinkles. Now I can't say fairer than that."

"You heard him," Mr Dawson said. "You're all witnesses."

"Forget it, Tom," Mr Sunshine said wearily. "She's my sister. You don't know her like I do."

"No," Mr Dawson said, "but I know you, and you know what? You're alike as two peas in a pod. And don't make that ridiculous snorting noise; you know it's true. It's true of the lot of you, gods and demiurges and Queens of the bloody Night. You think you're all so entitled."

"But we are," the fat man pointed out. "Well, I am, anyway."

"Yes," said Mr Dawson, "and you're also useless. You're like a bunch of chimpanzees with a tank. You go charging around flattening people and blowing stuff up, but when you run out of gas you haven't got a clue what to do. You don't even know what a filler cap is, let alone how to open it. Well, I'm not like you. I may not be able to grant prayers or chuck thunderbolts, but I'm the master of my fate and the captain of my soul, and I'm going to make a deal or die trying. And the rest of you—" He stopped and looked at them. "The rest of you can do what you damn well like. I'm not interested any more."

Mr Sunshine was shaking with anger. "How dare you?" he said. "Where were you when I laid the foundations of the Earth? Where were you—?"

"Oh shut up," said Mr Dawson.

*

Erica sighed, tucked a stray wisp of hair behind her ear and produced a small grey plastic box, with a lead hanging out of it. She plugged the lead into a socket, then clicked her fingers. A console materialised, almost filling the room. "What's that?" Consuela gasped.

"Tech stuff," Erica replied, typing at a keyboard. "You wouldn't be interested."

Holographic displays soared into the air like fireworks. Erica spared them a quick glance, then went back to what she was doing. Her fingers moved across the keys like soldier ants. More and more virtual read-outs blossomed out of the air, and a dozen viewscreens, each showing a different starscape. "What are you doing?" Consuela asked.

"Please be quiet," Erica said. "I can't think if you're talking."

On one of the viewscreens a tiny image appeared. Enlarge, and enlarge again; it was a tiny sleigh, drawn by reindeer. Another viewscreen showed a small pink dot, which grew into a chunk of rock, shaped like a potato. "Oh my God," Consuela said. "Is that it?"

"Yes," Erica said. "And if you interrupt me again, I'm going to have to ask you to leave."

Consuela gazed at the screen with the reindeer and the sleigh. It was surrounded by a pearl-coloured bubble, but inside the bubble she could just about make out tiny people. She had no idea who they were or what they had to do with anything, but decided it'd be better if she didn't ask. On the other screen, the potato was getting bigger and bigger. "Time to impact," said a mechanical voice, "one minute seventeen seconds."

"Erica," she wailed, "do something."

Erica took no notice. She was tapping keys, her face blank. The potato loomed, until Consuela could clearly see the details of its surface: jagged rocks, dried-up mercury lakes, deep scars gouged by long-distintegrated meteorites, empty pizza trays and prosecco bottles. The rate at which its size increased made her feel dizzy and sick, and she looked away. "Time to impact," said the computer voice, "nineteen seconds."

Erica tapped a couple of keys, then sat back and folded her hands in her lap. The potato completely filled the screen, then went out of focus. "Time to impact three seconds," said the computer, "two, one. Impact."

Nothing happened. The potato screen had gone blank. On the other screen, the tiny sleigh continued its snail's-pace journey.

"Erica."

"Yes, Ms Teasdale?"

"What happened?"

Erica pressed a key, and one of the viewscreens displayed a vision of tumbling rocks and planetary shrapnel. On one rock, as it cartwheeled across the screen and out of sight, Consuela plainly saw the Statue of Liberty. "The asteroid hit the Earth?"

"Yes."

"But we're still—"

"Yes," Erica said. "Will there be anything else or can I go now?"

"Just a minute." Consuela wanted to scream. "It doesn't make sense. That thing was about to hit us, and you're saying it did, and—" She screwed her hands into fists. "Does that mean we're in some sort of bubble or something, and there's nothing left outside, and I'm stuck in here for ever, with you?"

Erica shuddered, very slightly. "No," she said. "You can leave any time you want. Actually, I'd quite like it if you did."

"So what's out there?"

Erica shrugged. "Pretty much everything, really." She snapped her fingers. The displays, the viewscreens and the console vanished. "There may be a few slight changes, but you won't be able to tell the difference."

Consuela looked at her. "What have you done?" she said.

"Oh, I rerouted us into another reality." Erica stooped down and unplugged the small grey plastic box from the wall. "Look, I don't want to be rude but I've got a lot of work to do, so if you wouldn't mind—"

"You did what?"

Erica sighed. "As you know," she said, "we live in a multiverse of innumerable alternative possibilities, and every time a choice is made, causality bifurcates and a new reality springs into being to accommodate the road not travelled by. So it stands to reason that just before the asteroid hit the planet, there was a very slight possibility that the crazy woman flying it would aim it at the Earth amd miss ... Well, that created an alternative reality, so all I had to do was shunt everybody across into it and make it our real reality, and now everything's fine. Look," she added.

She snapped her fingers, and a screen appeared briefly in the air. Do you want to make this your default universe? and a little box with a tick in it. "It's all there in the instructions," Erica said. "It's a pity nobody ever bothers to read them."

"But that's—"

"Magic?" Erica gave her a look. "Yes," she said, "that's how it works. You've got all those degrees and qualifications, I'd have thought you'd have known that."

Consuela's head was starting to swim. "So everything's all right now?"

"Yes," Erica said, "everything's fine. Crisis over. And I'd make you a coffee, only I'm too busy right now."

"Don't—" Consuela bit her tongue. "So, all right, then. If you can do all that, what the hell were you doing gophering for me?"

Erica shrugged. "I live to serve," she said. "Like I told you. I used to serve Ahriman, but he's a pig, so I left, and then I came here. They built me this room where I'd be safe from him, and in return I help out. I help anyone who needs it, unless they turn out to be pigs, too. And you obviously needed help more than anyone else in the building, so—" She gave Consuela a thin smile. "You're not such a pig as Ahriman," she said, "but you're still a pig. Now if you'll excuse me I'd better put this away before anything happens to it. It's a Kawaguchiya XDX9000DTLPro," she added, with the closest thing Consuela had ever known her come to respect. "It's the only one in the galaxy and it's quite fragile."

"That little box," Consuela asked. "It did all that?"

"No," Erica said. "I did all that, using the box. Now, please leave me alone, you're in my way."

She walked towards the back of the room. Consuela felt something tug under her foot, and realised she was standing on the little grey box's lead, just as it pulled out of Erica's hands and fell on the floor with a crash.

"Oh my God," Consuela said. "I'm so sorry—"

Erica knelt down, examined the box, held it to her ear and shook it. "It's ruined," she said.

Consuela felt like she was burning up. "I'm sorry," she repeated helplessly. "Look, I'll get you a new one, I promise."

"They're only available from a single supplier seventy million years ago at the far end of the Andromeda galaxy," Erica said. "But it's all right. I'll go and fetch a replacement, as soon as I've got a minute."

Consuela gazed at her for what felt like a very long time. "I'm sorry," she said.

"No," Erica replied, "you aren't. But that's all right. You don't actually matter very much, after all. Now, please leave, before I turn you into a beetroot."

The sleigh landed on the roof of the Dawsons office. They all sat in their seats for a moment, looking up. The night was still and cloudless, and in spite of the light pollution there seemed to be ever so many stars in the sky.

"It's still here, then," said Mr Teasdale.

Gina climbed out of the sleigh and stood on the roof. "Apparently," she said.

"Only I could've sworn I saw that asteroid go rushing past us about twenty minutes ago," Mr Teasdale said. "And I thought, that's done it, we're going to get there and it'll be too late. But I guess not."

"Something's wrong," Mr Sunshine said. Then he thought about it and added, "No, scratch that. Something's different." He shrugged. "Whatever it is, it doesn't seem to matter very much. This is close enough for jazz." He frowned. "I wonder what happened?"

"It's what didn't happen," Mr Ahriman said, coming out from under the seat where he'd been hiding. "The planet didn't get destroyed. So that's all right." He climbed out of the sleigh and looked around. Not quite all the kingdoms of the Earth, but quite an impressive view nevertheless. "Well," he said, "I'm back."

Gina noticed Mr Dawson looking at him in rather an odd way, a fraction of a second before he yelled something she didn't quite catch, vaulted out of the sleigh, broke into a run and charged at Mr Ahriman. There was a yell; Mr Ahriman disappeared over the edge of the roof and Mr Dawson would've followed him if Ted Sunshine hadn't grabbed him by the arm and hauled him back.

Mr Dawson blinked, like someone waking up out of a dream. "Thanks, Ted," he said.

"Think nothing of it," Mr Sunshine said. "Won't do a blind bit of good, of course."

"I know," Mr Dawson said. "But it was fun."

"That's twice you've used that word recently," Mr Sunshine said. "Don't say you're actually starting to lighten up a little."

"Probably not for long." Mr Dawson went to the edge and peered down. They were a long way off the ground, but not nearly far enough. "I don't even know if he's got bones to break. I doubt it, somehow."

"I've had an idea," Mr Sunshine said. "Harmondsworth."

A drawer materialised in the side of the sleigh and opened an inch or so. "What?"

"Nip down to Jenny's office and fetch that old tin box."

"What did your last butler die of? Fetching."

The drawer slammed, waking Tony Bateman. He'd fallen asleep as they whizzed through the outskirts of Rigel. "Are we there yet?" he mumbled.

"Yes," Gina said. "Get up."

He looked round. "Hey, we're back," he said. "And it's still—"

"Shut up, Tony."

Tony Bateman nodded, and turned himself into an oak tree. Gina and Mr Teasdale stared at it for a moment, then Gina shrugged. "People tend to react to stress in different ways," Gina said, with a shrug. "He'll be fine."

"Excuse me," Jenny said, from inside the sleigh. "But do you think we could get down off the roof now? It's a bit nippy out here."

"What? Oh, sure." Gina looked round for a door of some kind, decided she couldn't be bothered and conjured one up. As an afterthought, she added a staircase under it. "You might as well get off home," she said. "See you in the morning."

Jenny looked at her. "Is everything all right now?" she asked.

Gina thought about that. "No," she said. "But it's a damn sight better than it was twenty-four hours ago. I'd say it's about normal."

"Ah. What's normal?"

"Go home, Jenny," Gina said. "Everything's fine."

Jenny gazed at her for a moment, then opened the door and went down the staircase, which for some reason or other came out in the ladies' lavatory of a pub six hundred yards away. Jenny, who was always a great one for playing the cards she was dealt, had a couple of mojitos and a packet of cheese and onion crisps, then caught the Tube home and went straight to bed.

"Well," said the fat man, "that seems to be that, then. Look, about that planet."

Mr Dawson swung round and scowled at him. "You and your bloody planet," he said. "It seems to me, you haven't exactly covered yourself in glory over this business. Well, have you?"

The fat man shrugged. "I did my best," he said. "I got you to the asteroid in one piece. I tried to reason with Dolly. Not my fault if she wouldn't listen."

Mr Dawson sighed. "It seems to be a sort of universal rule," he said, "that people tend to get the gods they deserve. Just now, when we were in the sleigh, it occurred to me to wonder what sort of life forms get their supreme being from an agency."

"I dunno," the fat man said. "Busy ones, presumably."

"Quite," Mr Dawson said. "So on balance I incline to the view that you and the people of Snoobis Prime were probably made for each other. Also, to be fair, all the other applicants were even more useless than you. Have your rotten planet, and I hope it chokes you."

The fat man grinned. "Good call," he said. "You won't regret it. The people of Snoobis Prime maybe, but not you personally. Well, goodnight to all and to all a good night. Cheerio, Ted. Don't be a stranger." He grabbed the reins, bellowed, "Prancer, you useless sack of camel shit", and vanished in a whirlwind of twinkly sparkles.

Gina gazed at the vector of his departure, shrugged and sat down under the oak tree. "Nobody's explained how come the world didn't end," she said. "Still, it didn't, and that's the main thing." She looked across at Brian Teasdale. "I wouldn't sit on that if I were you."

"Oh." Mr Teasdale got up off the box he'd been perched on. "Why not?"

By way of a reply, Gina nodded towards the edge of the building, off which Mr Ahriman had recently fallen—

He came in fire, his native element, and his flames lit up the city below. Mr Teasdale had to shade his eyes and look away. Gina, who wasn't crazy about light at the best of times, ducked behind the tree. Only Mr Sunshine could endure the ferocity of his glare. He stepped in front of Mr Dawson, folded his arms and stood perfectly still. "You shall not pass," he said.

"Fuck off, Ted," said the flame, soaring up into the sky and billowing like a curtain caught by a breeze. "He's done it this time. Nobody pushes me off buildings and gets away with it."

Ted thought for a moment. "Fair enough," he said. "I never liked him much anyway."

He stepped aside, revealing a crouched figure cowering behind him. "All right, Dawson," said the flame, "it's Judgement Day. I'm foreclosing."

The cowering figure screamed. The flame reared up and curved like a wave about to break. "Full and final settlement, you loser," it hissed; and then it swooped, and there was a sizzle, and that was that. The flame gradually subsided into human form: Mr Ahriman, mopping his forehead with a black silk handkerchief.

"Sorry you had to see that," Mr Ahriman said. "Still, he asked for it. Nobody pushes me around and gets away with it."

"Quite," Mr Sunshine said. "But you meant what you said, didn't you? Full and final settlement."

Mr Ahriman grinned and prodded the scorched patch of concrete with his toe. "I don't think you can get more full and final than that," he said. "Right, let's get down to business. I claim the partnership share of the late Thomas de Quincey Dawson, which makes me the boss of you, and you're out. Pack up your rubbish in a cardboard box and be off the premises in ten minutes, or I'll call security and have you thrown out. The rest of you—"

"Not so fast," said Mr Dawson.

Mr Ahriman spun round, slipped on the greasy burnt patch and fell on his bottom. "What the hell—?"

Mr Dawson smiled. "Ted's idea," he said. "What you just incinerated was my poor, deranged twin brother Jerry. Since you just agreed that that was full and final settlement, I don't think there's any more to be said." He took a sheet of paper from his pocket and slowly tore it into pieces. "You're still a partner, obviously," he said, "and, yes, you get Jerry's share of the business, which means you get a double vote at partnership meetings, which is a bummer but never mind, it'll still be four against two. But as far as you and I are concerned—" He smiled. It was a sad smile, but very happy at the same time. "I'm still senior partner, and I'm telling you to get your incandescent arse off my roof. See you around, plasma-for-brains."

Mr Ahriman gave him a stare so blank that, if it'd stayed there a moment longer, Banksy would've shown up and painted something on it. Then he grinned. "See you around, Tom. On that you can rely." Then he stepped back into the shadows and disappeared.

"Has he gone?" Mr Teasdale asked.

"Yup," said Mr Dawson. "For now."

"Oh good," said Mr Teasdale, getting up off the steel box. His legs had hidden it neatly from view. "I thought all that went rather well. What did happen about the Earth getting blown up, does anyone know?"

Mr Sunshine shrugged. "Presumably Christopher Robin turned up and sorted it all out," he said. "That's what usually happens. I imagine there'll be something about it in the trade papers in a week or so." He brushed a speck of soot off his nose. "I'm just glad there was someone more competent than us out there. It's a great relief to know I'm not the smartest entity in the universe. It gives me hope for the future." He turned his head and gave Mr Dawson a warm smile. "We'll be needing new stationery," he said.

Mr Dawson pursed his lips. "No great rush," he said. "That stuff costs money. Let's use up what we've got before we go changing anything."

"New stationery," Mr Sunshine repeated. "Dawson, Ahriman and Sunshine."

"You think?" Mr Dawson said. "Only, it's really important in this business to stress the continuity aspect – You know, the old firm, solid and reliable, we'll always be there for you, *semper fi*. And there's the catchy acronym, DAD. You can rely on DAD, it's a great slogan."

"Dawson," said Mr Sunshine, "Ahriman and Sunshine. Or I boot you off this building."

"Deal," said Mr Dawson.

Consuela ran into Erica in the corridor. She was carrying six cups of coffee on a tray, and nothing spilt in the saucers. "Oh, hello," Consuela said. "You're back helping out again, then."

"I live to serve," Erica said. "Now if you'll excuse me, Mr Wells wants these in the big interview room."

"Just a moment," Consuela said. "It was pretty neat, you know, what you did."

"Yes," Erica said.

"I hope you don't mind that I didn't actually mention you by name in my report to the UN. Only, it's sort of company policy, we don't mention junior staff by name, even if they were the ones who, you know, did all the work. Basically it's an image thing. And if it had been the other way round, obviously, one of us would've had to carry the can."

"I understand," Erica said. "I expect they were pleased. The UN," she clarified. "About the world not getting blown up."

"Thrilled to bits," Consuela said. "And we were able to bill them till the pips squeaked and they didn't mind a bit, so obviously the partners are happy. A good result all round, I think you could say."

"That's nice."

"Yes, they're all quite pleased. And I'm getting a bonus, of course. Quite a good one, actually."

"That's all right, then."

"I asked if you could have one, too, but they didn't think it would be appropriate, what with you being junior staff. They said it might set a precedent."

"I see."

"And," Consuela went on, "I've been offered the Kawaguchiya Integrated Circuits chair of pure metaphysics at Uppsala, and I think I'll take it, because they've got a very strong department there and it's generally considered to be one of the main stepping stones to Yale, and Hindemann can't go on for ever, he must be nearly eighty, so career-wise it'd be a pretty sound move, so—"

"But you don't know the first thing about metaphysics," Erica said. "You proved that, the other day. All you know are a few conjuring tricks."

Consuela looked at her. "Well, yes," she said. "So I was thinking, how would you fancy coming along with me as my research assistant? I can guarantee you double what you're getting here, plus a pension and a car and a really great health plan, and the skiing out there in Uppsala is unbelievable. Please?"

"No, thank you," Erica said.

"But it'd be great to have you with me," Consuela said, "and I promise you'd never have to make the coffee, they've got a machine, and it'd be the cutting edge of thaumaturgical research, you'd like that."

"Yes," Erica said, "and it'd be better than here, and I'd be safe. But it would mean seeing a lot of you. So, no thank you."

Consuela fought down the surge of rage so it didn't show. At least, she hoped it didn't. "Ah well," she said, "no hard feelings. Did you manage to get your thingama-jig fixed, by the way?"

"Yes," Erica said. "Thank you for asking."

"That's all right," Consuela said. "Well, so long. If you change your mind about the job—"

"I won't," Erica said. "Goodbye."

It was a dark and stormy night, and Alice's car had just died. She tried the engine: nothing. Then everything around her was bathed in unbearably bright light.

"Oh come on," Alice yelled, thumping the steering wheel with the heels of her hands. "Seriously?"

She felt the car float upwards, and then stop; then she heard a clunk, followed by a tapping at her window. She wound it down and heard the voice inside her head. *Excuse me, this is Earth, yes?*

"Yes. Now look, this is starting to get on my nerves. Next time, try the Moon, OK? I've got better things to do than run around delivering parcels all day long."

Sign, please. There, and there, and there. Thank you.

A hideous bony arm slid through her window and inserted a disc into her car's CD player. Then the lights went out, she felt the car touch down and the engine started. She was all alone in the night once more. "For crying out loud," she muttered, and tried to edge the stick into first. It was stuck.

"Bastards," she said; and then a beam of light shot out of her CD player and stopped in mid-air, the way light tends not to do. It flickered, and turned into a hologram.

It was a harrassed looking young woman in a white dress and a most unbecoming hairstyle. She stooped, put something into something and turned to face an invisible camera.

"Help me, Mr Sunshine," she said, "you're my only hope. Years ago you served my father in the Custard Pie wars, and now—"

Alice sighed and switched the CD player off. The projection faded. She closed her eyes, drummed her fingers on the steering wheel and counted to ten.

Screw it, she said to herself, I can't be bothered. She ejected the CD, threw it out of the window and drove off. The CD crunched under her car wheels, but she didn't hear it.

extras

orbit

meet the author

Tom Holt was born in London in 1961. At Oxford he studied bar billiards, ancient Greek agriculture and the care and feeding of small, temperamental Japanese motorcycle engines. These interests led him, perhaps inevitably, to qualify as a solicitor and immigrate to Somerset, where he specialised in death and taxes for seven years before going straight in 1995. He lives in Chard, Somerset, with his wife and daughter.

Find out more about Tom Holt and other Orbit authors by registering for the free monthly newsletter at orbitbooks.net.

if you enjoyed
THE EIGHT REINDEER OF THE APOCALYPSE

look out for

SAEVUS CORAX DEALS WITH THE DEAD

The Corax Trilogy: Book One

by

K. J. Parker

From one of the most original voices in fantasy comes a twisted tale of murder, betrayal, and battlefield salvage.

There's no formal training for battlefield salvage. You just have to pick things up as you go along. Swords, armor, arrows—and the bodies, of course.

extras

Over the years, Saevus Corax has picked up a lot of things. Some of them have made him decent money, others have brought nothing but trouble. But it's a living, and somebody has to deal with the dead.

Something else that Saevus once buried is his past. Unfortunately, he didn't quite succeed.

1

Lying is like farming, or draining marshland, or terracing a hillside or planting a grove of peach trees. It's an attempt to control your environment and make it better. A convincing lie improves on bleak, bare fact, in the same way human beings improve a wilderness so they can bear to live there. In comparison, truth is a desert. You need to plant it with your imagination and water it with narrative skill until it blossoms and bears nourishing fruit. In the sand and gravel of what actually happened I grow truths of my own; not just different truths, better ones. Practically every time I open my mouth I improve the world, making it not how it is but how it should be.

In order to grow strong, healthy plants you also need plenty of manure, but that's not a problem. According to most of the people I do business with, I'm full of it. I accept the compliment gracefully, and move on.

Rest assured, however, that everything I tell you in the pages that follow is the truth, the whole truth and nothing but the truth. This is a true and accurate history of the Great Sirupat War, told by someone who was there.

A big mob of crows got up as we—

No, hang on a moment. I was going to leave it at that, but I did say I'd be honest with you, and now is as good a time as any.

People tend not to like me very much, and I can see why. They say I'm arrogant, callous, selfish and utterly devoid of any redeeming qualities; all, I'm sorry to say, perfectly true. I'm leaving out devious, because I happen to believe it's a virtue.

Arrogant, yes; I was born to it, like brown eyes or a weak chin, and the fact that I'm still alive after everything I've done, with luck not usually in my favour, suggests to me that I've got something to be arrogant about, even if it's only my deviousness, see above. I'm callous because I'm selfish, not because I want to be, and I'm selfish because I like staying alive, though God only knows why. People say the world would be a better place without me and I think on balance they're right, but it's stuck with me for a little while, as are you if you want to hear the truly thrilling story. And you do, I promise you, but unfortunately I come with it, like your spouse's relatives.

When I started writing this, I edited myself, naturally. I neglected to record some of my more objectionable remarks and barbarous actions, because I wanted you to like me. If you don't like me, you won't want to read my story, and I'll be wasting my time and a lot of forty-gulden-a-roll reed-fibre paper telling it, and the truth about the war (which actually matters) will never be known. It even crossed my mind to stick in a few not-strictly-true incidents designed to show me in a better light, because nobody would ever know, and then I'd be a lovable rogue instead of a total shit. Then I thought: stuff it. The truth, and nothing but the horrible, inconvenient truth. All those facts have got to go somewhere. You might as well have them, if they're any use to you. I certainly don't want them any more.

A big mob of crows got up as we walked down the hill onto the open ground where the main action had been. Crows hate me, and I don't blame them. They rose like smoke from a fire with no flames, screaming abuse at us as they swirled round in circles before reluctantly pulling out and going wherever it is that crows go. I got the impression that they had a good mind to lodge an official complaint, or sue me for restraint of trade. All my years in the business, and they still make me shudder. Probably they remind me of me.

You don't usually find crows in the desert; in fact, I think that particular colony is the only one. They used to live off the trash and dunghills of a large town, which was razed to the ground in some war or other thirty years ago. But the crows stayed. There are enough wars in those parts to afford them a moderate living without the need to prod and worry about in shitheaps, and for water they go to the smashed-up aqueduct, which still trickles away into the sand, now entirely for their benefit. I guess the crows figure the austerity of their lifestyle is worth it for the peace and quiet, which I'd just come along and spoiled.

I hadn't watched the battle but I could figure out what happened from the spacing and density of the bodies. Over there, a shield wall had held off the lancers but couldn't handle massed archers at close range; they'd broken and charged, and the hussars hidden in that patch of dead ground over there had darted in to take them in flank and rear. That was the end of them, but no big deal; they were just a diversion to bring the other lot's cavalry assets over to the left side of the action, nicely out of the way so that the dragoons could burst out of those trees over there and roll up the heavy infantry like a carpet. After that, it was simply a matter of the losers salvaging as much as they could from the mess; not much, by the look of it. The hell with it. All the more for me.

I glanced up at the sky, which was pure blue from one side to the other. I have strong views on hot, sunny weather. I'm against it. Nobody wants to work in driving rain, naturally, but I'd rather be drenched in rainwater than sweat any time. Heavy manual labour in searing heat isn't my idea of the good life, not to mention the flies, the seepage and the smell, and hauling dead bodies around when they've been cooking up in the heat isn't good for you. This was going to be a four-day job, quite possibly five unless we could face working double shifts by torchlight. We're used to that sort of thing, but even so. It was one of those times when I wished I'd stayed at home, or got into some other line of work.

Gombryas had been going round picking up arrows. He had a sad look on his face. "They were wearing Type Sixes," he said, showing me a half-dozen bodkin heads, their needle points blunted or bent U-shaped by impact on steel. Poor arrows; I felt sorry for them, in a way I find it hard to feel sorry for flesh and blood. Not their fault that they'd been wasted by an idiot in a futile attempt to pierce armour. Theirs not to reason why, and we'd see them right, so that was fine.

"It's only taxpayers' money," I said. He grinned. He grumbles, but he knows the score. It would be the job of his division to straighten out and repoint all those cruelly maimed arrowheads; then he'd winkle the broken shafts out of the sockets, fit new ones, replace the crushed and torn fletchings, all to the high standard our customers have come to expect from us. What Gombryas doesn't know about arrows isn't worth knowing.

He swears blind he can recognise an arrowhead his boys have worked on when he pulls it out of some poor dead bugger in a place like this. Some of them, he says, are old friends, he's seen them and straightened them out so many times.

The Type Sixes that had annoyed Gombryas so much were mostly in a small dip, where the hussars had rounded them up and despatched them. Personally, I like the Type Six infantry cuirass. It's built from small, rectangular plates laced together, so all you have to do is cut the laces, fish out the damaged plates, replace them and sew the thing up again, and there you are, good as new. Buyers go mad for the stuff, though it's a shame the various governments can't get together and agree on a standard size for the plates. We have to carry a dozen different sizes, with variations in lace-hole placement, and occasionally you get really weird custom jobs where you have to fabricate the new plates from scratch.

Armour is Polycrates' department, and his boys were straight on to it as usual. They've had a lot of practice, and it's a treat to watch them when they get into the swing of it. One man rolls the body over onto its back, kneels down, gets his arms under the armpits and stands up, lifting the body so his mate can dive in underneath, undo the buckles and shuck the armour off in one nice easy movement, like opening shellfish except that the bit we want is the shell, not the meat. Then on to the next one, leaving the body for Olybrius' clothes pickers and Rutilian's boot boys. Rings, earrings, gold teeth and bracelets we leave for Carrhasio and his crew, the old timers who've been with the outfit for years but who can't manage the heavy lifting like they used to. Then all that remains is for me to come round with the meat wagons. By this point, of course, heat, wildlife and the passage of time have all started to work their subtle alchemy, which is why I handle the final stage of the process myself. I wouldn't feel right asking one of my friends to do a job like that. They may be tough, but they have feelings.

The Asvogel brothers – the competition; I don't like them very much – have recently taken to dunking the bodies in pits of quicklime, to burn off the flesh and leave the bones, which they cart home and grind up for bonemeal. I guess it's worth their while, though I can't see it myself. For a start, it takes time, which is proverbially money, not to mention the cost of the lime, and then you've got the extra transport, fodder for the horses there and back, drivers, all that, in return for a low-value bulk product. Waste not, want not, the Asvogel boys say. It's a point of view, but I'm in no hurry to get into the bonemeal business. I burn all ours, unless it's so damp you can't get a decent fire going. Chusro Asvogel thinks I'm stupid, pointing out the cost of the charcoal and brushwood. But we cut and burn it ourselves between jobs, so it doesn't actually cost us anything, and we take it there in the carts we use for the job, which would otherwise be empty. Burning gives you a clean, tidy battlefield, and the ash does wonders for the soil, or so they tell me. That's nice. I think it's our moral duty to give something back if we possibly can.

No rain in the night, but a heavy dew. The next day's the best time to handle them, in my opinion. The stiffness has mostly worn off, so you haven't got arms and legs sticking out at awkward angles, which makes them a pain to stack, and with any luck they haven't begun to swell. This point in the operation usually turns into a battle of bad tempers between me and Olybrius. I want to get the meat shifted and burned before it starts to get loathsome. Olybrius wants to do a thorough job with minimum damage to the stock in trade, which means carefully peeling off the clothes rather than yanking them about and cutting off buttons. Ideally, therefore, he doesn't want to start until the stiffness goes. He's quite right, of course. It's much easier to get a shirt off a dead man when he isn't stiff as a board, and sewing buttons back on costs a lot of money, which comes out of his share of the take. But he works for me, so he has to do what I tell him, or at least that's the theory. By now our tantrums are almost as ritualised as High Mass at the Golden Spire temple. We know we're getting fairly close to the end of the arguing process when he points out that in the long run rushing the job and ruining the clothes costs me money, not him, and I come back at him with something like, it's my money and I'd rather lose out on a few trachy than catch something nasty and die. When we reach this point we both know there's nothing more to be shouted; we then have a staring match lasting between two and five seconds, and one of us backs down. It would probably be easier and quicker if we flipped a coin instead, but I guess the yelling is more satisfying, emotionally and spiritually. Anyway, that's how we do it, and it seems to work all right.

On that particular occasion, I won the battle of the basilisk glares, so we got a move on and had the pyres burning nicely barely seventy-two hours after the last arrow was loosed. In the greater scheme of things, General Theudahad and the Aelian League had taken a real shellacking, losing 5,381 men and 3,107 horses to Prince Erysichthon's 1,207 men and 338 horses. It was a setback, but it didn't really make a difference. Theudahad's relief column was only thirty miles from Erysichthon's main supply depot, less than a day's brisk ride for the Aelian heavy dragoons, and without supplies for his men Erysichthon would be forced to risk everything on one big pitched battle somewhere between the river and the sea. He'd still be outnumbered three to one, his allies had had enough and wanted to go home, and he'd made Theudahad look a complete idiot, which meant the Great Man had a score to settle, so all the young prince had actually achieved with this technically brilliant victory was to get a superior opponent really angry. Another reason for us not to hang about. I'd paid a lot of money for the rights to this campaign, and the last thing I wanted was to turn up late for the grand finale and find the battlefield had already been picked over by the local freelancers.

"My money," Gombryas said to me as we stood back from the newly lit pyre, "is on the prince. He's smart."

"You're an incurable romantic, is what you are," I told him through the scarf over my face. "You always root for the little guy."

He glared at me. "Fine," he said. "I've got twelve tremisses says that Erysichthon'll squeeze past the allies and make it back to the city before Theudahad can close the box. Deal?"

The oil-soaked brushwood caught with a roar and the wave of heat hit me like a smack on the face. "In your dreams," I said. "I don't bet on outcomes, you know that. Besides," I added, a little bit spitefully, "surely you want Theudahad to win so you can make up the set."

Gombryas collects bits of famous military and political leaders – bones, scalps, fingers and toes and scraps of innards carefully preserved in vinegar or honey – and why not? After all, their previous owners don't need them any more, and it presumably gives him some sort of quiet satisfaction. He has quite possibly the best collection in the south-west, though Sapor Asvogel might dispute that, and one of his prize exhibits is the skull of Erysichthon's father, which he acquired six years earlier, when we cleaned up after the last war in those parts. He's also got Erysichthon's grandfather's ears and his uncle's dick – he swapped two royal livers and a minor Imperial shoulder blade for it with Ormaz Asvogel – and various other family bits and bobs, so it'd be only natural for him to want a piece of the prince, too. Given that Erysichthon had no children and all his male relatives had contributed freely to Gombryas' collection, it'd mean that getting the prince would complete the series (I think that's the technical term in collectors' circles) and a complete series is worth far more than just a dozen or so isolated pieces. Not that Gombryas would ever think of selling. He loves his collection like family.

Anyway, he decided to take offence at my tasteless remark and stomped off in a huff. I gave the pyres a last once-over to make sure they weren't going to collapse or fall sideways, then turned my back on the glorious battle of wherever-the-hell-it-was and trudged back to the column. One more thing to do and then I could give the order to move out. Fingers crossed.

if you enjoyed
THE EIGHT REINDEER OF THE APOCALYPSE

look out for

THE HEXOLOGISTS

by

Josiah Bancroft

The first book in a wildly inventive and mesmerizing new fantasy series from acclaimed author Josiah Bancroft, where magical mysteries abound and only one team can solve them: the Hexologists.

The Hexologists, Isolde and Warren Wilby, are quite accustomed to helping desperate clients with the bugbears of city life. Aided by hexes and a bag of charmed relics, the Wilbies have recovered children abducted by chimney wraiths, removed infestations of barb-nosed incubi, and ventured into the Gray Plains of the Unmade to soothe a troubled ghost. Well acquainted with the weird, they never shy away from a challenging case.

But when they are approached by the royal secretary and told the king pleads to be baked into a cake—going so far as to wedge himself inside a lit oven—the Wilbies soon find themselves embroiled in a mystery that could very well see the nation turned on its head. Their effort to expose a royal secret buried under forty years of lies brings them nose-to-nose with a violent anti-royalist gang, avaricious ghouls, alchemists who draw their power from a hell-like dimension, and a bookish dragon who only occasionally eats people.

Armed with a love toughened by adversity and a stick of chalk that can conjure light from the darkness, hope from the hopeless, Iz and Warren Wilby are ready for whatever springs from the alleys, graves, and shadows next.

1

THE KING IN THE CAKE

"The king wishes to be cooked alive," the royal secretary said, accepting the proffered saucer and cup and immediately setting both aside. At his back, the freshly stoked fire added a touch of theater to his announcement, though neither seemed to suit what, until recently, had been a pleasant Sunday morning.

"Does he?" Isolde Wilby gazed at the royal secretary with all the warmth of a hypnotist.

"Um, yes. He's quite insistent." The questionable impression of the royal secretary's negligible chin and cumbersome nose was considerably improved by his well-tailored suit, fastidiously combed hair, and blond mustache, waxed into upturned barbs. Those modest whiskers struck Isolde as a dubious effort to impart gravity to a youthful face. Though Mr. Horace Alman seemed a man of perfect manners, he sat with his hat capping his knee. "More precisely, the king wishes to be baked into a cake."

Looming at the tea cart like a bear over a blackberry bush, Mr. Warren Wilby quietly swapped the plate of cakes with a dish of watercress sandwiches. "Care for a nibble, sir?"

"No. No, thank you," Mr. Alman murmured, flummoxed by the offer. The secretary watched as Mr. Wilby positioned a triangle of white bread under his copious mustache, then vanished it like a letter into a mail slot.

The Wilbies' parlor was unabashedly old-fashioned. While their neighbors pursued the bare walls, voluptuous lines, and skeletal furniture that defined contemporary tastes, the Wilbies' townhouse decor fell somewhere between a gallery of oddities and a country bed-and-breakfast. Every rug was ancient, ever doily yellow, every table surface adorned by some curio or relic. The picture frames that crowded the walls were full of adventuresome scenes of tall ships, dogsleds, and eroded pyramids. The style of their furniture was as motley as a rummage sale and similarly haggard. But as antiquated as the room's contents were, the environment was remarkably clean. Warren Wilby could abide clutter, but never filth.

Isolde recrossed her legs and bounced the topmost with a metronome's precision. She hadn't had time to comb her hair since rising, or rather, she had had the time but not the will during her morning reading hours, which the king's secretary had so brazenly interrupted, necessitating the swapping of her silk robe for breeches and a blouse. Wearing a belt and shoes seemed an absolute waste of a Sunday morning.

Isolde Wilby was often described as *imposing*, not because she possessed a looming stature or a ringing voice, but because she had a way of imposing her will upon others. Physically, she was a slight woman in the plateau of her thirties with striking, almost vulpine features. She parted her short hair on the side, though her dark curls resisted any further intervention. Her long-suffering stylist had once described her hair as resembling a porcupine with a perm, a characterization Isolde had not minded in the slightest. She was almost entirely insensible to pleasantries, especially the parentheses of polite conversation, preferring to let the drumroll of her heels convey her hellos and her coattails say her goodbyes.

Her husband, Warren, was a big, squarish man with a tree stump of a neck and a lion's mane of receded tawny hair. He wore unfashionable tweed suits that he hoped had a softening effect on his bearing, but which in fact made him look like a garden wall. Though he was a year younger than Isolde, Warren did not look it, and had been, since adolescence, mistaken for a man laboring toward the promise of retirement. He had a mustache like a boot brush and limpid hazel eyes whose beauty was squandered on a beetled and bushy brow, an obstruction that often rendered his expressions unfathomable, leading some strangers to assume he was gruffer than he was. In fact, Warren was a man of tender conscience and emotional depth, traits that came in handy when Isolde's brusque manner necessitated a measure of diplomacy. He was considerably better groomed that morning only because he had risen early to greet the veg man, who unfailingly delivered the freshest greens and gossip in all of Berbiton at the unholy hour of six.

Seeming to wither in the silence, Mr. Alman repeated, "I said, the king wishes to be baked into a ca—"

"Intriguing," Isolde interrupted in a tone that plainly suggested it was not.

Iz did not particularly care for the nobility. She had accepted Mr. Horace Alman into her home purely because War had insisted one could not refuse a royal visitor, nor indeed, turn off the lights and pretend to be abroad.

While War had made tea, Iz had endured the secretary's boorish attempts at small talk, made worse by an unprompted confession that he was something of a fan, a Hexologist enthusiast. He followed the Wilbies' exploits as frequently documented in the *Berbiton Times*. Mr. Horace Alman was interested to know how she felt about the recent court proceedings. Iz had rejoined she was curious how he felt about his conspicuous case of piles.

The royal secretary had gone on to irk her further by asking whether her name really was "Iz Ann Always Wilby" or if it were some sort of theatrical appellation, a stage name. Iz patiently explained that her father, the famous Professor Silas Wilby, had had many weaknesses—including an insatiable wanderlust and an allergy to obligations—but none worse than his fondness for puns, which she personally reviled as charmless linguistic coincidences that could only be conflated with humor by a gormless twit. Only the sort of vacuous cretin who went around asking people if their names were made-up could possibly enjoy the lumbering comedy that was the godless pun.

Though, in all fairness, she was not the only one to be badgered over her name. Her husband had taken the rather unusual step of adopting her last name upon the occasion of their marriage. He'd changed his name not because he was estranged from his family, but rather because he'd never liked the name Offalman.

Iz had been about to throw the royal secretary out on his

inflamed fundament when War had emerged from the kitchen pushing a tea cart loaded with chattering porcelain and Mr. Horace Alman had announced that King Elbert III harbored aspirations of becoming a gâteau.

His gaunt cheeks blushing with the ever-expanding quiet, Mr. Alman pressed on: "His Majesty has gone so far as to crawl into a lit oven when no one was looking." The secretary paused to make room for their astonishment, giving Warren sufficient time to post another sandwich. "And while he escaped with minor burns, the experience does not appear to have dissuaded him of the ambition. He wants to be roasted on the bone."

"So, it's madness, then." Iz shook her head at War when he inquired whether she would like some of either the lemon sponge or the spice cake, an inquiry that was conducted with a delicate rounding of his plentiful brows.

"I don't believe so." Mr. Alman touched his teacup as if he might raise it, then the fire behind him snapped like a whip, and his fingers bid a fluttering retreat. "He has long moments of lucidity, almost perfect coherence. But he also suffers from fugues of profound confusion. He's been discovered in the middle of the night roaming the royal grounds without any sense of himself or his surroundings. The king's sister, Princess Constance, has had to take the rather extreme precaution of confining him to his suite. And I must say, you both seem to be taking all of this rather in stride! I tell you the king believes he's a waste of cake batter, you stifle a yawn!"

Iz tightened the knot of her crossed arms. "I didn't realize you were looking for a performance. I could have the neighbor's children pop by if you'd like a little more shrieking."

War hurried to intervene: "Mr. Alman, please forgive us. We do not mean to appear apathetic. We are just a bit more accustomed to unusual interviews and extraordinary confessions than most. But, rest assured, we are not indifferent to horror; we are merely better acquainted."

"Indeed," Iz said with a muted smile. "How have the staff taken the king's altered state of mind?"

Appearing somewhat appeased, the secretary twisted and shaped the points of his mustache. "They're discreet, of course, but there are limits. Princess Constance knows it's a secret she cannot keep forever, devoted as she is to her brother."

"Surely, you want physicians, psychologists. We are neither," Iz said.

The secretary absorbed her comments with an expression of pinched indulgence. "We've consulted with the nation's greatest medical minds. They were all stumped, or rather, they were perfectly confident in their varying diagnoses and prescriptions, and none of them were at all capable of producing any results. His condition only worsens."

"Even so, I'm not sure what help we can be." Iz picked at a thread that protruded, wormlike, from the armrest of the sofa.

The secretary turned the brim of his hat upon his knee, ducking her gaze when he said, "There's more, Ms. Wilby. There was a letter."

"A letter?"

"In retrospect, it seems to have touched off His Majesty's malaise." The royal secretary reached into his jacket breast pocket. The stiff envelope trembled when he withdrew it. The broken wax seal was as sanguine as a wound. "It is not signed, but the sender asserts that he is the king's unrecognized son."

Warren moved to stand behind his wife's chair. He clutched the back of it as if it were the rail of a sleigh poised atop a great hill. Iz reached back and, without looking, patted the tops of his knuckles. "I imagine the Crown receives numerous such claims. No doubt there are scores of charlatans who're foolish enough to hazard the gallows for a chance to shake down the king."

"Indeed, but there are two things that distinguish this particular instance of blackmail. First, the seal." Mr. Alman stroked the edge of the wax medallion, indicating each element as he described it: "An *S* emblazoned over a turret; note the five merlons, one for each of Luthland's counties. Beneath the *S*, a banner bearing the name Yeardley. This is the seal of Sebastian, Prince of Yeardley. This is the stamp of the king's adolescent ring."

"He identified it as such?" Iz asked.

"I did, at least initially. Of course, I like to believe I'm familiar with all the royal seals, but I admit I had to check the records on this occasion. Naturally, there is much of his correspondence that His Majesty leaves me to open and deal with, but when something like this comes through, I deliver it to him unbroken."

"The signet was no longer in the king's possession, then?"

"No, the royal record identified the ring as lost about twenty-five years ago, around the conclusion of his military service, I believe."

"That's quite a length of time to sit on such a claim." Iz reached for the letter, but the secretary pulled it back. She looked into his eyes; they glistened with uncertainty as sweat dripped from his nose like rain from a grotesque. "What is the second thing that distinguishes the letter?"

"The king's response to the correspondence was...pronounced. He has thus far refused to discuss his impressions of the contents with myself, his sister, or any of his advisors. He insists that it is a hoax, that we should destroy it, though Princess Constance won't hear of it. She maintains that one doesn't destroy the evidence of extortion: One saves it for the inquiry.

But of course, there hasn't been an inquiry. How could there be, given the nature of the claim? To say nothing of the fact that the primary witness to the events in question is currently raving in the royal tower."

"The princess wishes for us to investigate?" she asked. Though Isolde held little affection for the gentry, she liked the princess well enough. Constance had established herself as one of very few public figures who continued to promote the study of hexegy, touting the utility of the practice, even amid the blossoming of scientific discovery and electrical convenience. Still, Isolde's vague respect for the princess was hardly sufficient to make her leap to her brother's aid.

Mr. Alman coughed—a brittle, aborted laugh. "Strictly speaking, Her Royal Highness does not know I am here. I have taken it upon myself to investigate the identity of the bastard, or rather, to engage more capable persons in that pursuit."

"I'm sorry, Mr. Alman, but what I said when we first sat down still holds. I am a private citizen. I serve the public, some of whom come to me with complaints about royal overreach, the criminal exploitations of the nobility, or the courts' bungling of one case or another. I don't work for the police—not anymore. Surely you have enough resources at your disposal to forgo the interference of one unaffiliated investigator."

"I do understand your preference, ma'am." The royal secretary rucked his soft features into an authoritative scowl. "But these are extraordinary circumstances, and not without consequence. The uncertainty of rule only emboldens the antiroyalists, the populists, and our enemies overseas. You must—"

Isolde pounced like a tutor upon a mistake: "I *must* pay my taxes. I *may* help you. Show me the letter."

Mr. Alman tightened like a twisted rag. "I cannot share such sensitive information until you have agreed to assist in the case."

"There is another way to look at this, Iz," Warren said, returning to the tea cart. He poured water from a sweating pitcher into a juice glass and presented it to the dampened secretary, who readily accepted it. "You wouldn't just be working for the Crown; you would be serving the interests of the private citizen who has come forward with the claim... perhaps a *legitimate* one." The final phrase made Mr. Alman nearly choke upon his thimble swallow of water. "If the writer of this letter shares the king's blood, and we were to prove it, I don't think anyone would accuse you of being too friendly with the royals."

Isolde bobbed her head in consideration, an easy rhythm that quickly broke. "But if I help to prove that he is a prince, I'd just be serving at the pleasure of a different sovereign."

"True." Warren moved to the mantel to stir the coals, not to invigorate them, but to shuffle the loose embers toward the corners of the firebox. "But if you don't intervene, our possible prince will remain a fugitive."

"You think we should take the case?"

"You know how I feel about lords and lawmen. But it seems to me Mr. Alman is right: If there's a vacuum in the palace and a scramble for the throne, there will be strife in the streets. We know who suffers when heaven squabbles—the vulnerable. Someone up on high only has to whisper the word 'unrest' and the prisons fill up, the workhouses shake out, the missions bar their doors, and the orphanages repopulate. And when the dust settles, perhaps there'll be a new face printed on the gallet bill or a fresh set of bullies on the bench, but the only thing of real consequence that will have changed is the number of bones in the potter's field. Revolution may chasten the rich, but uncertainty torments the poor."

orbit

Follow us:

f **/orbitbooksUS**

𝕏 **/orbitbooks**

▶ **/orbitbooks**

Join our mailing list
to receive alerts on our
latest releases and deals.

orbitbooks.net

Enter our monthly
giveaway for the chance
to win some epic prizes.

orbitloot.com